A Girl Undone

ALSO BY CATHERINE LINKA

A GIRL CALLED FEARLESS

A Girl Undone

CATHERINE LINKA

ST. MARTIN'S GRIFFIN ⚓ NEW YORK

A GIRL UNDONE. Copyright © 2015 by Catherine Linka.
All rights reserved. Printed in the United States of America. For information,
address St. Martin's Press, 175 Fifth Avenue, New York, N.Y. 10010.

www.stmartins.com

Designed by Anna Gorovoy

The Library of Congress Cataloging-in-Publication Data is available
upon request.

ISBN 978-1-250-06867-5 (hardcover)
ISBN 978-1-250-03932-3 (e-book)

St. Martin's Griffin books may be purchased for educational,
business, or promotional use. For information on bulk purchases, please contact
the Macmillan Corporate and Premium Sales Department at 1-800-221-7945,
extension 5442, or write to specialmarkets@macmillan.com.

First Edition: June 2015

10 9 8 7 6 5 4 3 2 1

TO MRL AND HAL

ACKNOWLEDGMENTS

Launching a book is an epic journey, perhaps not as terrifying as trekking to Mordor, but still it's one where you are really grateful for the loyal friends and allies by your side. And as *A Girl Undone* follows *A Girl Called Fearless*, I marvel at who has joined the quest.

Thank you to:

The brave team at St. Martin's Press, including Sara Goodman, my wise, unflappable editor who asked for more, and gave me the time and space to do it, Talia Sherer and Anne Spieth, who championed the story among our noble compatriots—the librarians, and unsung heroes, Anna Gorovoy, Bridget Hartzler, Michelle Cashman, and Alicia Adkins-Clancy.

Sarah Davies and Pete Donaldson for their wisdom, valor, and persistence in finding the right partners for my story.

Amy Baer, Brad Luff, RD Robb, Aimee Carlson, and Jes Bickhart for believing in *Fearless* and investing their time, creativity, and passion in the project.

The LAFourteeners for providing critical support and perspective, with special thanks to Tracy Holczer, Mary McCoy, Jessica Love, Rachel Searles, Nicole Maggi, Livia Blackburne, and Edith Cohn.

Mollie Traver, Lupe Fernandez, Barbara Fisch, Sarah Shealy, Roz Hilden, Kendell Shaffer, Amber Sweeney, Alethea Allarey, Cori McCarthy, Amanda Thorpe, Cecil Castelucci, Nutschell Windsor, Cynthia Bracken-Levin, Mary Ann Fraser, Beth Navarro, Rebecca Langston-George, Kathryn Fitzmaurice, Tamara Smith, Sharry Wright, Ann Jacobus, Adriana Leavens, Deborah Gonzales, and Annmarie O'Brien for bestowing advice, friendship, and opportunities I never anticipated.

And to Bob, Max, and Haven. I love you more than I could ever have imagined.

Southern Idaho
December

1

Yates moaned, and I checked the readouts from the machines surrounding the hospital bed. His fever was holding at 105.

Bags of fluids and drugs hung over him, the tubes snaking into his veins. His beautiful face was almost unrecognizable. One eyelid was purple and swollen shut and a strip of white tape bridged his broken nose. Black stitches crisscrossed the shaved strip on his scalp.

Yates' hand was hot in mine, but every time I set it down, I reached for it a moment later.

His good eye fluttered open, and I stretched for the cup of ice chips. "You thirsty?"

"Yeah."

His iris was a dull blue, not the cobalt I was used to. It's the fluorescent light, I told myself. It makes everyone look sick.

I tipped the cup to his lips, but before the ice reached them, he'd lost consciousness again.

In the hall, I heard footsteps. Not the night nurse's muffled squeak, but a cautious step like someone in leather shoes trying not to be heard.

I pulled my feet onto the bed, and sat stone-still behind the privacy curtain.

It was one A.M. No one else should be on the hospital ward except the patients and Ed, the one nurse.

The footsteps came closer. Whoever it was had entered Yates' room. I held the cup of ice, afraid of the noise it would make if I set it down.

I glanced at the floor below the curtain and spied a battered pair of boots, then steeled myself as the curtain rolled back.

"Luke!" I whispered.

Luke stood there in his sheepskin coat, his black cowboy hat dusted with snow. He swept his brown eyes over me and then Yates. "You should have been out of here two days ago, Avie," he said, his voice low.

My cheeks went scarlet. "I can't leave him."

"They're looking for you and Yates, and you're putting him in danger by being here."

Ed, the nurse, appeared at the door. "The front desk just called. A couple cops are on their way up."

I smacked the cup down on the table and scrambled off the bed.

"That's it," Luke said. "Where's your stuff, Avie?"

"In the closet." I bent over Yates, who was still unconscious. "I have to go," I said, "but I promise I'll be back." Then I leaned in and kissed him lightly on the lips.

Luke tossed me my boots and grabbed my pack. Ed snatched the remains of my sandwich off the bedside table.

Luke and I hurried toward the stairs at the end of the hall. The huge plate-glass window ahead of us reflected Ed wheeling a linen cart to block the hall.

The elevator pinged, and Luke pushed me through the stairwell door, then caught it as it closed and peered through the crack while I pulled on my boots.

"I can't get a clear view around the cart," Luke whispered, "but they look like state troopers, not feds. Still, they're armed."

The troopers didn't bother to keep their voices down. "We're looking for a young man about nineteen. Medium height. Dark hair. Accident victim. We got a tip he might be here."

I held my breath. Two days before, a photo of Yates had been broadcast on the national news along with mine. "Suspected Terrorists in Salvation, Idaho, Shootout."

Ed took his time walking toward them. "Between idiots playing with chain saws and drunken snowmobilers, we've got a lot of patients to choose from. You have a name?"

"Yates Sandell."

"Nope, nobody by that name."

"Still, we'd like to take a look."

"No problem, Officers. But I need to ask you to put on masks and booties before you enter any rooms on this floor. Some of these patients have compromised immune systems—"

Luke let the door close. "Let's go. I've got a car outside."

I blocked Luke as he moved for the stairs. "No, wait. Maybe they won't recognize him. By tomorrow, Yates might be better and we can take him with us."

A look flashed across Luke's face. I was acting like a fool.

"How long do you think your luck's going to hold?" he said.

I dropped my gaze to the carved-bone buttons on his coat. "I don't know."

"How long before someone here figures out that a girl's hiding in one of the unused rooms? And not just any girl, but one the feds are hunting." Luke tipped up my face so I'd look him in the eyes. "I know you love him, but the safest place for Yates right now is in that bed."

The infection in Yates' blood could kill him. He needed those antibiotics dripping into his veins.

"Even if they arrest him," Luke said, seeming to read my thoughts, "the docs will keep Yates here until he's well enough to move. You can't help him now."

I glanced down the stairs. I knew I couldn't hide out here forever with Yates—not with my face and the word "Wanted" all over the news. "All right, I'm going. For now."

"You've got the thumb drive Maggie gave you?"

"Yeah." It dangled between my breasts on a steel chain. I breathed in, double-checking that the piece of silk she'd given me was still pinned around my waist, then felt for the phone in my pocket. All three together provided enough evidence to imprison or impeach at least a dozen of the most important political leaders in the country.

When federal agents had trapped the entire town of Salvation in the church, Yates and I had promised Maggie we'd get this evidence to a friend of hers in D.C., and start the wheels of justice turning. I'd barely taken it off my body since.

Luke and I crept down three floors, and through a door that released us just above the parking lot. Snow coated the roofs and hoods of the cars and pickup trucks. The cold slapped my face, and my limbs moved stiffly like I'd been cut out of a cocoon.

"Down that row," Luke said.

I pulled my hat out of my pocket, then stuffed it back in. The shots of me that the newscasters used from the video broadcast of my distress call had zoomed in on the llama design. Put this hat on, and I might as well wear a name tag.

I flipped the hood of my down coat over my hair and followed Luke. My black coat was anonymous, but the red scarf was a giveaway. I needed to change my appearance if I wanted to stay alive.

The lot was quiet, but I kept my head down so security cameras couldn't see my face. We didn't talk.

Luke stopped by a car so beat-up I couldn't believe it ran. The front was torn up and the panel was missing over the right front wheel. Luke climbed in and unlocked the door from the inside.

"Keep your gloves on," he said as he wiped the windshield with his sleeve. "Defrost should kick on in a few minutes."

"Where'd you get the car?" I said.

"It's a beauty, isn't it? Just goes to show what you can get for five hundred dollars cash, no questions asked."

Luke pulled out of the space, drove through the lot, and turned onto the road. He sped up, and as the hospital shrank behind us, my heart tugged like it was still tied to Yates. Take care of him, I begged the powers above. Protect him.

I saw us back in Salvation in the unfinished cabin we'd borrowed for our one night together, our bodies entwined, the fire in the potbellied stove giving his face a golden glow, his eyes dark blue as a night ocean.

What if I never see you again?

"I shouldn't have left Yates," I murmured.

"He'll forgive you," Luke said. "He knows what's at stake."

I buried my nose in my scarf. The truth was Yates would have thrown me out if he'd been halfway coherent. After he'd been injured in a fall back up on the mountain, he'd told me to leave him, to finish the mission we'd started.

But that was before we were rescued, and I'd wrongly thought we were safe. Government agents were caught threatening American citizens, but Yates and I had somehow become the terrorists in the media's eyes.

Luke turned onto a broad avenue and street lamps lit the car like spotlights. He handed me a torn scrap of paper with penciled directions. "Help me read this."

Cars approached and I ducked my head as I guided him toward the highway. We couldn't get off this road fast enough, but we had another three miles to go.

A part of me wanted back in that bare, unused hospital room Ed had locked me into the last two days, where all I had to do was sleep and wait for his shift to begin.

When I came down from the mountains with Yates, I thought I was fearless, but lying there on the hospital linoleum, watching the news reports, and reliving the siege, I realized I wasn't as fearless as I thought.

I was scared for good reason, carrying secrets that could get me killed.

"I hate this," I said.

"We'll be on the highway soon."

"What if there are roadblocks?"

"Better pray there aren't, because I don't have a license."

Of course, why would he? When you live in a community that's left the rest of the world behind.

The shock of having Luke pull me out of the hospital was wearing off, and I shivered as the heater kicked out cool air. "How'd you find me?"

"Followed your tracks out of Salvation until I got to the tree where Yates had his accident. When I saw the cuts the dogsled left, I guessed Spoke Coleman picked you up and brought you here."

Luke unbuttoned his sheepskin coat with his free hand and loosened the scarf around his neck. A faint light from the dash carved his profile out of the darkness. Gone was the easygoing calm he'd shown me in the woods around Salvation.

We all had had the crap kicked out of us up there.

Images flashed through my head. Maggie exiting the church, holding up the banner. I SURRENDER. Gunshots. Her body sailing backward like she'd been punched.

I knew I should say something to Luke about his birth mom and dad dying in the firefight. "I'm sorry about Maggie and Barnabas—"

Luke clenched the wheel. "You heard what happened?"

"Spoke told me when he found Yates and me back on the mountain."

"The minute those agents opened fire on Maggie, Barnabas was out the door. He got two of them before they took him out."

During the last forty-eight hours, I'd watched hours of television with the sound off, but no one, not one news crew, reported that story.

"Strange, isn't it?" Luke said. "I spent my whole life angry at my mother for leaving me, and then I have to watch her die, trying to save my life."

I shook my head, unable to speak.

"They've got Salvation surrounded." Luke looked to see if I'd heard him. "The governor sent state troopers to 'assist' the federal agents while they interview everyone."

Hunting for clues for where to find Yates and me, I bet. "How did you get out?"

"Beattie shoved me in the tunnel after Barnabas and Maggie got shot. I hid there until the next night, then came down the mountain."

Sealed for hours in the pitch-black, in a narrow tunnel that smelled like a grave after seeing your birth parents gunned down? Then tromping through miles of snow, the temperature below freezing? How did Luke have the strength to do it?

I wanted to reach over and touch him, let him know I understood what he'd been through, but something stopped me.

"How would the feds even know about you?" I said gently. "You've been off the grid your whole life."

"Yeah, I'm luckier than you are. I'm not in their system, and there aren't any photos of me they can throw up on the news."

Luke slowed and pulled into a parking lot outside a grocery store, stopping alongside a big metal donation box. He got out, letting the engine run, and slid a pair of snowshoes from under a blanket on the back seat, before he walked over and dropped them in the donation box.

Time to toss the hat, I thought. I pulled it out of my pocket, leaving my phone on the dash. Luke held the metal bin door open, and I shoved the hat in. Then we climbed back in the car, and a few minutes later, Luke drove up the ramp onto the freeway, leaving the lights of Boise behind.

"So where are we going?" I said.

"Right now we're headed east."

"And how long before we come back? A week or two?"

He reached down and fiddled with the radio controls. "How about we play that by ear?"

I blinked into the darkness as the radio came to life. "Authorities continue their search for suspected terrorist Aveline Reveare last seen in the survivalist community known as Salvation—"

"Sorry about that." He switched to a country-western station.

"It's not your fault I'm all over the news." I hugged my crossed arms to my chest. "I can't believe I was so naïve. I thought when I got to Boise, I'd turn over Maggie's evidence to the police and be free to go. I was so sure after the video of the feds firing on Salvation was blasted all over the national news that Vice President Jouvert would have to answer for what the feds did."

"The vice president's got powerful allies. The leaders of the Paternalist Party are gonna cover up his crimes so theirs don't get exposed."

"Do you know they said I'm guilty of 'associating with a terrorist'?"

"Yeah, I heard. Pack of liars, saying that about you and Maggie, and calling Salvation a bunch of 'armed extremists passing themselves off as a religious community'! Makes me want to line them all up and shoot them."

Something in his voice made me do a double take. Luke had every right to be angry, but—

He lifted my phone off the dash. "You listen to the message from your friend, yet?"

"No, Sparrow's message was for Maggie, not me." I wasn't exactly lying. I'd only listened to a few seconds before I'd pulled out my earphones after the little I'd heard made me sick.

"Maggie's dead. Don't you want to know what you're carrying?"

I shook my head. "No."

"Why not?"

"It's—" Too dangerous. "I'm not ready."

Luke ran his fingers over the lit screen. "We should listen to it now. Maybe it could protect us if we get caught."

"No," I said, shaking my head even harder. "Maybe later. Not now."

"All right," he said, handing it back to me. "Later."

I pushed the phone deep into my pack, hearing again the breathy murmurs of my friend Sparrow and the powerful man she was with, Vice President Jouvert. Her voice echoed in my ears. This recording was trouble magnified by a hundred.

I hadn't asked for any of this. I hadn't intended to become a revolutionary. All I'd ever wanted was to be free to choose what I wanted to do with my life.

Now Luke had shown up, and I couldn't pretend that this whole huge mess would disappear.

2

The sun was coming up over the mountains when we got to the outskirts of Pocatello, and we followed a school bus into town. Pickups were gathered outside a brightly lit doughnut shop, and the smell of hot sugar made my empty stomach tighten.

A black truck with police lights approached, and I slid below the dash and out of sight. I crouched there, ticked at myself for not checking if Luke's brake lights were working, because he probably had no idea that cops liked to have any little excuse to stop strange cars.

"All clear," Luke said.

I climbed back into my seat.

He drove slowly, his gaze panning left, then right, like he was reading an unfamiliar landscape.

"Have you ever been here before?" I said.

"Once. A few years ago. Barnabas used to take me with him when he had to deliver the guitars he'd built. He sold to a store here, a few up around Casper, and Jackson Hole, and a couple in Spokane. So I'm not completely ignorant of the world outside Salvation."

I saw Luke's face relax like he'd spied what he was searching for. A block later, he pulled into a lot beside a lawyer's office and parked in a spot with a name painted on it.

"Luke, they'll tow the car if we leave it here."

"That's my plan. Take your things."

"What are we doing?"

"We're walking from here."

I glanced at Luke's face to see if he was joking, but he wasn't. He reached in the glove compartment and took out a pistol, then stuck it in his pants under his coat. "You still have your gun?"

"It's in my pack," I said. Stuffed in the bottom with the clip removed. "You want me to get it out?"

"Nah, it's still early. I think we'll be fine."

I wrapped my scarf over my hair. Spiky wasn't a popular hairstyle in Idaho and I didn't want to be memorable.

We were alone on the street, but I felt like I had "fugitive" painted on my back. We walked beside each other with our arms bumping before Luke felt for my hand. "We should look like a couple."

I wove my fingers into his, surprised at how lightly he held mine, despite how strong he was. His hand felt hot through my glove, making me think Luke was as nervous as I was.

I tensed as cars drove by, letting out my breath after they passed. It had been years since I'd walked in the open without a bodyguard, and my neighborhood in L.A. didn't count. There was a guardhouse and cameras on every street.

The street ended at the train tracks, and Luke turned left. Gravel crunched under our boots as we walked along the tracks, sometimes shielded from the road by industrial buildings, only to be exposed by the empty parking lots between them. The nearest trees were on the other side of the tracks, and I wished we were over there.

Cold burned my cheeks and the tip of my nose. The scent of bacon wafted from somewhere nearby. "That sure smells good," Luke said.

"Yeah, I'm starving."

"Maybe we can get some breakfast later."

Yeah, I thought. We could order the Fugitive Special. *Make it to go,* I could tell the waitress. *We have to run.*

"Here's the street," Luke said, and we turned onto it, ducking our heads as a car went by.

A chipped and faded sign for HISTORIC OLD TOWN pointed us to buildings with brick fronts and skinny, old windows that looked like they'd been there forever. Signs for department and jewelry stores, a coffee shop and a hotel hung outside abandoned businesses.

I gripped Luke's hand as we walked. Scarpanol had hit Pocatello hard. The planters outside the florist were empty, and the inside was a shell. The beauty salon windows were thick with dust, and the dress store had nothing in it but a few empty clothes racks. The only signs of life were the three bars and two burger joints.

I wondered how many women had lost their lives, eating meat they thought was safe.

Up ahead, I spied a brand-new sign outside the bank: TURN YOUR HOUSE INTO A HOME WITH A BRIDE MORTGAGE. A smiling cartoon house pointed to a bashful cartoon bride.

I stopped in my tracks. "That's disgusting."

Luke looked from me to the sign and tugged me along. "We need to keep moving."

"Why am I surprised that men buy brides up here? Salvation's the only place I've ever seen where every girl can choose who she marries."

"You can help fix that, you know."

"I know." I avoided his gaze. I couldn't kill Signings and forced marriages, but the evidence I carried could wound the Paternalists badly.

A sheriff's car pulled onto the street and headed toward us. Luke quickened his pace. "Act like I said something funny."

As the black car came closer, I threw off Luke's hand, crying "I can't believe you said that!" and gave him a shove that made him stumble back against the brick storefront. Luke laughed and caught my hands, then held on tight, bugging out his eyes and wagging his lips like a goofy-looking fish. I pretended to laugh at his teasing while the patrol car rolled past. Then I heard it drive off, and Luke dropped my hands. "Sheriff's gone. You can relax."

A steady stream of cars crisscrossed the intersection up ahead. We started walking again, our pace even faster than before. "We need to get off the street. How much farther?" I asked.

"Not too much longer, I'm guessing."

I kept waiting for the patrol car to circle back for another look. It was another ten blocks before we stood outside a church. "This is it?"

A plain cross topped a white-painted brick building the size of a basketball court. The windowpanes were simple gold and purple squares, but they were shiny clean.

"Beattie told me they'll help us," Luke said.

Spying the cross gave me hope that was true. "Are they part of Exodus? Maybe we should talk to them about going to Canada."

"You still hung up on getting to Canada? I thought you had a promise to keep."

My neck turned hot and I loosened my scarf. "I do—I intend to keep my promise—I'm just not sure of the safest way to do that right now."

Luke twisted up his mouth, and I half expected an argument, but then he waved his hand at the church and said, "How about we try going inside?"

"All right."

We followed a sign with a red arrow pointing to the side of the church, where a set of steps led to a door marked OFFICE. The door was unlocked, and the smell of hot coffee greeted us. An older man wearing suspenders over his sweater stood behind a silver-haired woman as she typed on an ancient computer.

A TV screen flickered in the corner. The sound was off, but I recognized the aerial shot of Salvation, the cabins scattered over the snow and the church covered in ripped strips of black solarskin that flapped in the breeze.

"Luke," I whispered. "We should leave."

"No, it'll be fine."

The man peered at us over his wire-rimmed glasses. "Can I help you?"

Luke stepped forward. "Mr. Beaufort?"

"Yes?"

"Beattie sent us."

The woman's mouth fell open. She glanced from us to the TV. "When did you talk to her last?" she asked, her voice trembling. "Is she alive?"

"She was when I left."

She dropped her head. "Ah, my baby!"

The man squeezed her shoulder. "Vera and I've been so worried. We keep waiting to hear."

Beattie was older than my mom so it was hard for me to imagine her being Vera's baby.

"The church walls are real thick," Luke explained. "And the windows are bulletproof. There's a bunker under the church where everyone can take refuge if the church is breached."

"And the rest of the family?" the man said.

"Keisha was safe in the bunker, and Cecilia was away. I wish I could tell you more."

The man came over and shook Luke's hand. "Thank you."

Vera stumbled around the desk, walking as if one leg was shorter than the other. "It's a shameful thing the government did—attacking its own people. Children. Innocents!"

She took me in from the scarf over my hair down to my boots. "You were there. You're the girl that sent out the distress call."

I looked to Luke, and he nodded.

"Yes, that was me."

The man's face went pale.

"Harris," Vera said. "We've got to help them."

Harris wiped a hand over his face, and I grabbed Luke's sleeve. "We should leave, and get the car before it's towed."

"No!" Vera said. "Harris Beaufort—we've waited days to find out about our daughter. We have to help them."

"Vera. Settle down, my flower. Of course we're going to help them. I'm merely trying to think through how we're going to do it."

"They need to get someplace safe."

"I know. I know."

Luke nodded at a construction-paper sign saying BARGAIN SHOP, taped to a nearby door. "Could we buy some new clothes from you?" I asked Vera.

Her eyes formed a question that she didn't ask. She fumbled in her sweater pocket and came up with a set of keys. "Come with me, the both of you."

We clambered after her down some narrow stairs, closing the door behind us. Luke leaned over my shoulder. "See, what did I tell you?"

"I hope you're right about this."

The stairs ended in a basement room filled with circular racks of used clothing and smelling of old carpet. "Men's sizes on that wall. Girls' in the middle. Don't even think of paying," Vera told us. "Just hang your old coats on the rack and we'll call it even."

We heard the basement door open. "Vera," Harris called down. "June from the ladies' league is here."

She lifted her eyes to the ceiling. "Now of all times. You stay here till I come get you."

Vera walked up the stairs and flicked off the light. The key turned in the lock, and light filtered in through three small windows near the ceiling.

"Did you hear that?" I said, scurrying over to the stairs. "She locked us in."

"Locked us in or locked somebody else out?" Luke unzipped his jacket as he strode over to a rack of parkas.

I could hear muffled voices through the floor. "Not sure." I climbed up on a rickety table and tried the latch on one of the windows. "Okay, we're fine," I said, feeling it give.

Luke was going through the men's coats, but there weren't many to choose from, not like the racks of girls' and women's clothing that filled the room. Prom and wedding dresses lined the far wall, while more everyday things filled the center racks.

Lots of the clothes looked barely worn and some still had price tags attached. I pictured hundreds of fathers emptying out their wives' and daughters' closets after Scarpanol ripped their families apart.

And that thought carried me back to the line of Dumpsters outside the Rose Bowl back home buried under mountains of clothes that families couldn't bear to keep.

My throat tightened. *You can't go there now. You need to focus on changing your appearance.*

I found a powder-blue ski jacket, but before I hung my black one in its place, I retrieved the Canadian passport that Maggie's assistant, Helen, gave me in Vegas.

I peeked inside the cover, thinking I should toss it. I didn't look anything like the photo. The customs agent who saw this would have to be a fool to believe it was me.

It's a long shot, but it's the only one I've got, I thought, and zipped it into my new jacket.

From a shelf piled with knit scarves, I picked a fuzzy white one with a matching hat and mittens. Snowflakes embellished with silver sequins were embroidered on the creamy wool.

I pulled the hat over my hair and pouted in a nearby mirror. I looked like a soft, sweet kitten, not the dangerous revolutionary the media was spinning.

Behind me, I saw Luke take off his cowboy hat. His blond-brown hair was tied into a short curly tail at the base of his neck. He stared down at his hat, holding it in both hands almost as if he was saying good-bye.

I threaded through the racks until I stood beside him. "That hat must be special."

"Yup. My dad bought me this hat."

Dad or adopted dad, I didn't ask. All I had left of home was the silver dolphin hanging around my neck that Becca, Yates' sister, gave me. "Then you have to keep it," I said and plucked a hat band with a big, flashy spray of brown feathers off a Stetson. "This look like something you'd wear?"

"Never in a million years."

"Perfect." I fastened it to his hat. "People will be so mesmerized by this stupid thing, they won't bother to look at your face."

He smiled at me with gratitude and something else I couldn't put my finger on. The back of my neck prickled. "I need to go pick out a shirt," I said.

Luke sorted through a case of used paperbacks while I found a shirt I'd never wear in real life. Lilac gingham check to go with a pale pink sweater. I made sure Luke's back was turned, then peeled off my old shirt and put on the new one.

A few minutes later, a car pulled away and Vera cracked the door. "You can come out now." She locked the basement behind us.

"Where's Harris?" I said, seeing that he'd gone.

"He'll be back in a minute."

Then I realized both Luke's and my packs were missing, too. "Wait, where are our packs?" I demanded.

Vera started, and pointed under the desk. "Harris tucked them out of sight when June drove up."

"Sorry," I said. "I'm a little jumpy."

"It's all right. No harm done."

Luke held up a yellowing copy of *Killing Lincoln.* "How much for this?" he asked Vera.

She waved him off. "That? It's on the house. Sorry to say, we don't get many readers here anymore."

"Holy—" Luke crossed the room in two steps and squatted in front of the TV. Vera gasped, and I wheeled around and saw what they saw: an aerial shot of a line of men, women, and children marching out of Salvation's church, hands over their heads.

State troopers flanked both sides of the road. "Looks like they're letting them go back to their houses," Vera said.

I crouched down beside Luke. "Do you recognize anyone?"

He followed the line of people on the screen with his finger. "That's Jemima's family but I don't see her. There's Ramos and his wife and kids—"

Vera wrapped her hands together and began to pray.

I couldn't tell who the people were. The shot was from far away and even Luke was guessing, counting how many adults and children went into each house.

Come on, where's Beattie and Keisha? I thought. Where's Sarah and Jonas, Luke's little brother and sister, and Nellie and Rogan, the mom and dad who raised him?

We watched over a hundred people come out of that church, before the doors closed. Luke bowed his head. I twisted my fingers, wishing I had answers.

"Where's my daughter!" Vera cried. "Where's my grandbaby?"

"There's forty people missing," Luke said.

I went through everyone I could remember before it clicked and I stood up. "The Council. The Council members and their families are all still in the church."

Vera looked at me, panicked.

"I think it's a good sign," I said, wrapping my hand around hers. "I think it means they're probably alive."

"Oh Lord, oh Lord, oh Lord."

Luke got to his feet. "I think Avie's right. We should assume the people still inside are being questioned."

He sounded like Barnabas, the same calm under fire, but his jaw was clenched. He was trying not to freak Vera, but he didn't believe his family was safe.

The door swung open, and the smell of hot eggs and onions blew in. "Who's hungry?" Harris called.

"I know I am." Luke walked toward him, faking a smile. "Whatever that is smells good."

Harris handed Luke a burrito. "What about you?" Harris asked me.

"Yeah, thank you." I tore back the foil and bit into the first hot food I'd had in four days. The cheesy eggs melted in my mouth as I watched Luke wolf down his, grateful he had something to take his mind off Salvation.

Harris sipped his coffee. "You know your way around livestock, son?"

"Yes, sir. Horses, and goats, mostly. I don't know much about cattle."

"That's all right. I thought we might hitch you two a ride with a rancher needing to haul some stock."

"Sounds good."

"You know where you're headed?"

"Laramie," Luke said.

"Laramie? We're not going back to—" *Boise.*

Luke silenced me with a look. *No Boise. Don't even ask.*

"What about Canada?"

Three sets of eyes landed on me. "Canada would be safer," Vera murmured.

"That's not the direction we should be headed," Luke said.

I stared right back at him. Luke hadn't been on the run for as long as I had. If he had, he'd think twice about dodging the feds for two thousand miles so we could hand over the evidence personally, and instead come up with a way to get it there without getting us killed.

The room went silent while Luke and I pretended to be absorbed in what we were eating. Meanwhile, Vera rifled through a shoe box on a shelf.

A moment later, she handed me a gold ring with a dusty chip that looked like a diamond. "Since you two are traveling together, you better look like man and wife."

The gold was scratched like someone had worn it a long time. I slid it on my ring finger and held up my hand so Vera could see it fit.

"A little toothpaste will shine that right up," she said.

Luke frowned into his coffee. Maybe it was me disagreeing with what he wanted or maybe it was his family still trapped in Salvation, but he wasn't happy.

3

Vera packed me into the car as soon as we were done with breakfast. "We're going to Selena's Dream," she said. "Do a little something with your hair."

Vera wasn't criticizing. She was trying to keep me alive.

I smoothed the hat over my hair, surprised that Vera was driving me herself. I scanned the street for people who might be watching. *Two women riding in a car alone?* I was about to say something when Vera laid her purse between us on the front seat. A gun peeked out from a holster sewn right onto her shoulder bag. Vera was packing?

"Wow. That's handy," I said.

"One of the ladies in the hospital assistance league makes and sells them." Vera gave the bag a pat. "A man better think twice before he messes with a woman in this town."

"You know, back in California, girls aren't allowed to have guns."

"Well, why not?"

I shrugged. "I was told it was too dangerous."

"And it's better to leave you unarmed and completely helpless? Where's the sense in that?"

"Crazy, right?"

Vera spent the rest of the drive chuckling to herself about Californians and their strange notion about keeping women safe from guns. Selena's beauty salon was tacked onto the side of a one-story house. We opened the sliding door, and four Chihuahuas raced to greet me, tapping their tiny paws on my shins.

I bent down and rubbed their squirmy bodies.

"Ricky. Lopez. Chico. Jesus! Go to your stations!" The little dogs ran for four doggie beds covered in animal prints. There they sat at attention, wiggling to be let free.

Selena, the stylist, wore a big, yellow rhinestone flower in the black hair that curled down her back. Her jeans looked like they'd been air-brushed on. I didn't know how old Selena was, but she wasn't afraid to flaunt it.

Vera introduced me. "This is Tracy. She's married to my niece's son, Lou."

I was getting used to changing my name. Tracy went with the petal-pink sweater I wore.

"I see you like my dogs!" Selena said. "I rescue Chihuahuas." She pointed at a map of Canada plastered with dozens of little Chihuahua stickers. "Seventy-three dogs I take to new homes across the border. They love them there."

"Do you have another run planned?" Vera said. She checked to see I was paying attention.

"Ay, no. And I have twelve dogs, but the border crossings are closed. Chief Mountain, Whitlash, Del Bonito. Can you believe it? Today only Detroit is open. I'm gonna have to take the *perritos* to a shelter in Denver maybe."

I'm screwed, I thought. If a little *perrito* can't get across the border, no way I can.

I heard only snatches of what Vera was telling Selena about giving me a new look, because I kept thinking about how Luke would push even harder for us to follow his plan if he heard about the border closing. Still, there was a chance we could cross in Detroit. I started when Selena peeled off my hat. "Sorry," I said.

"Is okay." She combed her fingers through my hair. "How do you want to look?"

"I have no idea."

"You think of a word to tell me what you want. Dra-ma-tic? Ro-man-tic? Sex-y?"

"Innocent." I needed to look innocent.

Selena smiled. "This is your lucky day. You're going to be blond."

"Blond?"

She plucked a color chart off the wall and held it up to my face.

She and Vera peered at me. "I think Topaz," Selena said, fingering the fake-hair samples.

Whoa. Suddenly, I'm Norwegian. "But my eyebrows—they're brown."

"I'm gonna do a tip-top job. Do the eyebrows, too."

Selena painted on the chemicals while I sat in the chair, one eye trained on the front door, praying she wouldn't have any other walk-ins.

Then she and Vera visited while I processed under a hair dryer with Lopez in my lap. That's when I spied this week's *People* on the table.

I'd made the cover again, only this time there were two shots: one cropped from the picture of Jessop Hawkins locking the Love bracelet on my wrist, and a fuzzier clip from my broadcast, me—desperate-looking, my spiky brown hair peeking out from the Peruvian knit hat. "Kidnapped Celebrity to Fugitive—What Went Wrong With Avie."

I pulled it over to me. Paparazzi shots of my house and of Dad trying to shield his face. Pics of Hawkins and an aerial of his Malibu compound. And, oh my God, no! Yates' mug shot from his arrest at the anti-Paternalist rally in Sacramento.

All the other pictures I'd seen on the news were so old they didn't even look like him, but this! Selena slid the magazine out of my hand. "Time to wash your hair." As we walked over to the sink, she tossed the magazine in the trash.

I lay back and Selena leaned in with the sprayer. "When I come to the U.S.," she said, "I am illegal. No criminal, but illegal. Every day I wonder if I gonna be caught."

I clutched the chair, not sure where she was going. "That must have been hard."

"I was very lucky. People help me. I meet my husband. We marry. Now I am legal and I help people."

My heartbeat quickened. "Are you—part of Exodus?"

She screwed up her face. "What is that?"

"Nothing," I said, wishing I'd kept my mouth shut.

"Close your eyes. I'm going to spray."

I sat back in the salon chair, and Selena turned me around so I couldn't see the mirror as big clumps of pale blond hair dropped onto my lap.

She blew it dry and then snatched a lipstick off a display and swept it over my lips before she spun me back to face the mirror.

My hair was white blond. I reached up and touched the feathery bangs and the hair that stopped just under my ears. Then I ran my fingers over my icy blond brows.

"Oh." Vera sighed. "She looks like an angel."

I wasn't Hawkins' Letitia lookalike, or Maggie's geisha spy, or the desperate girl broadcasting a distress call. The bright pink lipstick stood out against my pale skin, almost challenging me to be happy in a way I didn't feel.

Selena curled the lipstick tube into my hand. "You keep."

Maybe looking like an angel could keep me safe—at least until my dark roots grew out. If Luke and I could get to Detroit and across the border, we could hide until things cooled down or find someone the feds didn't suspect to take the thumb drive to D.C. for us. Or if that didn't work, we could maybe even reenter the U.S. someplace the feds wouldn't expect, like Vermont. But I had to convince Luke to go to Canada with me, because realistically, it was the best chance we had.

4

Vera drove us back to her house. I sat stiffly in her front seat while she waved and nodded at people in the other cars, acting like it was perfectly normal to have a strange girl with her.

"If anyone asks," Vera said, "we'll say you married my niece's boy and you're up from Salt Lake on your way to visit your daddy in Walla Walla."

She pulled into the drive of a faded blue one-story on a small lot. A pine tree decked out with Christmas lights stood in the center of a yellowed lawn.

The house faced the neighbor's and the two mirrored each other. Both had big, plain windows with rust stains under the frames and a front porch too small to keep you dry in the rain.

An older woman peered at us from a window next door. Vera released her seat belt. "Remember: act like you're visiting."

I leaped out and opened the car door for Vera, and put my arm through hers. I made a big show of asking about a bush with whip-thin red branches, saying I wanted one just like it when my husband and I had our own home.

Vera kept up the improv with me until we got inside. I scanned the wood-paneled living room. The picture window was strung with Christmas lights and a tiny tree stood in the corner. A painting of deer hung over the rust-colored sofa, and a Nativity scene filled the brick fireplace mantel.

The room felt years away from L.A. and Scarpanol and the Paternalists. It felt like someplace from Before.

"You two must have driven all night," Vera said, hanging her purse on a hook.

"Almost."

"How about you give me those clothes you're wearing and I'll throw them in the wash while you lie down for a bit?"

"That sounds really good."

Vera came back from the spare bedroom with a clean towel and a flannel pajama top that had been worn soft. "You can leave your clothes on the bathroom counter. I'll take care of them."

I stripped off my shirt in the bathroom, exposing the strip of red silk wrapped around my chest. As I undid the pins that secured the ends, I caught sight of myself in the mirror. *I look like a suicide bomber.*

I rushed to unwind the hanging from my body and let it fall to the floor. Then I kicked it toward the tub, and pulled in a deep breath. Free.

But as I soaped up my face and arms, I couldn't block out the red silk pooled on the tile floor.

The coded names of dozens of Paternalist politicians and foreign leaders, each one linked to bribes, favors, restrictive new laws, and moneymaking schemes, were embroidered into the crisscrossed branches of a blossoming cherry tree. And on the main branch all the others sprouted from—one name: Vice President Jouvert.

I rinsed off, and dried myself with the towel.

Maggie'd left two sections unfinished. One outlining a pipeline project with the code name "White Gold," the other, the trillion-dollar "loans" Jouvert had taken from a source Maggie hadn't been able to uncover.

There was no one left who could finish what she'd started and get the last pieces of the puzzle. All her girls had scattered around the globe, and her assistant, Helen, couldn't continue Maggie's spying without them.

I picked the hanging up off the floor and reattached the pins. It was my problem now. *But I can't walk around with it like this. It's so red. So obvious.* Soaking it in bleach could lighten it, but I had to be careful not to ruin the coding.

Below the pajama top, ghostly bruises spotted my thighs and broken white lines had replaced the deep scratches I'd gotten when I was attacked on Mom's grave. I ran my finger over the longest one. Was it really only three weeks ago? It felt like months.

Vera had left the door open to the spare room. The bed was turned down, and flannel sheets lay under the faded apricot-colored quilt. It wasn't even noon, but I burrowed under the covers. The soft flannel almost made me cry, it felt so good after two days of sleeping on a cold linoleum floor.

An hour—and I'd get up, I told myself.

I closed my eyes and, for the first time since Luke and I left Boise, let myself think about Yates. I wondered if he was finally awake. If his fever had broken. If the cops recognized him.

I could ask Vera to call the night nurse.

Right, and bring federal agents down on her and Harris? No way. You have to wait until you're someplace safe.

I don't even know where safe is anymore. Is it Canada?

Even if I managed to get over the border, how could Yates? His voice echoed in my head as I relived the night he helped me escape Hawkins, and I left California, thinking I might never see him again. For a moment I was back in the airplane hangar, Yates' face bent over mine, his deeply blue eyes the only things I saw or wanted to see.

I heard him whisper the words of my poem along with me, our lips brushing.

Love wields the scissors. Love is the escape.

I felt his hands on my back, holding me like something too precious to let go.

Love is the rusted fire escape that shouldn't support our weight but does.

I drifted into sleep. *Yates found me once. He could find me again.*

When I woke, the sun was going down, and someone was chopping wood out back. I peeked through the curtains. Luke was working his way through a large stack of wood. I threw on my clothes.

In the kitchen, Vera was peeling potatoes. She nodded at the window. "He's been at that for an hour. Harris got tired of watching him pace the office. Why don't you take him some coffee?"

Cup in hand, I headed outside. A face appeared in a window next door, but I pretended I didn't see it.

Luke had tossed his jacket on the ground, and rolled up his sleeves. His brow was beaded with sweat. He raised the ax over his head and swung it down in a perfect arc and the wood split and flew apart.

"Hey, honey," I said, loud enough for the neighbor to hear. "Thought you'd like some coffee."

He put down the ax and I handed him the cup. "Neighbor's watching," I whispered.

I beamed at him like he was the sun rising over the ocean. The center of my world. The one I loved more than any other.

"I like your hair," he said. Luke smiled, and the look in his eyes made me drop my gaze. It felt real, not like my playacting.

He kept his voice down. "The color reminds me of a snowshoe hare, wears a white coat in winter."

I felt for the soft fringe poking out from under my hat, not quite comfortable with how I was pleased he'd noticed. "Survival of the fittest," I joked.

Luke took a sip of coffee and frowned into the cup. "For the future, Vera's coffee could use a couple tablespoons of sugar."

"That bad?"

"Maybe next time you'd spill a little?"

"Sure."

The sun was dipping down to the west. Mounds of ice lay on the grass like leaf-flecked lace. I nodded at the wood Luke had split. "This was nice of you."

"Least I could do. Them risking arrest for us."

A screen door creaked open behind me, and I heard a woman call, "Here, kitty, kitty, kitty."

Luke caught my eye. "Don't turn around. It's the neighbor. She's come out twice already."

I shivered despite my winter jacket. "Has she tried to talk to you?"

"Nah, she's keeping her distance. Come help me stack."

We filled our arms with wood, then carried it over to the stack, and laid the newly cut pieces on top. The screen creaked again.

"She's gone." Luke picked up his coat, and I saw him stop and look at the mountains brushed with the last light.

They weren't the mountains he'd grown up in. His were a couple hundred miles away. "I miss my home, too," I said.

"I never should have let them put me in that tunnel."

I searched for something to say. "We'll know more about Salvation tomorrow. We shouldn't jump to conclusions."

"You really believe that?"

He took a step toward the house, but I stopped him, wanting a few more minutes alone. "Why Laramie?" I asked.

Luke's gaze darted away from me. "There's a man who can help us."

"Yeah, who?"

"Someone Barnabas knew."

"And he's supposed to help us do what? Because you're insane if you think we should go all the way to D.C. right now."

Luke didn't answer.

"That's what you think, right? The feds didn't stop us on the way to Pocatello so you think it'll be easy. We're risking our lives if we try going across the entire country to find Maggie's contact."

"And you think the solution is to hightail it to Canada," he shot back. "Well, I'm not leaving my country. And you shouldn't, either."

My breath caught at the growl in his voice. I hardly knew Luke, but this didn't feel even remotely like him.

"Okay, so what do you think this man—"

"Not out here," he said. He flicked his eyes at the neighbor's house and reached for my arm to take me inside.

A face peered at us from the neighbor's window and this time I noticed the large lead-colored glasses like a pair of binoculars trained right on us. I hoped Harris found us a ride even if it meant going to Laramie. At least that would take us closer to the border crossing in Detroit.

5

The evening news was on when Luke and I walked in the house. Vera guarded a frying pan on the stove, metal tongs in her hand.

"Anything more about Salvation?" Luke said.

"Not yet. Why don't you wash up? I'll call you if there is."

Luke ducked into the bathroom, and I lingered by the table, where chicken legs were stacked on a plate, ready to be dipped in buttermilk and rolled in corn flakes. "Can I help?"

"That would be nice."

Vera tended the frying pan while I dunked and coated the chicken legs. The lead news story was Congress' new Open Arms policy: an invitation to women from foreign countries who speak fluent English to come to the U.S., surrender their foreign passports, and receive automatic citizenship.

"Open Arms, now that's interesting," Vera said, waving her tongs at the screen. "What do you think about that?"

"I think it sounds like a way to get women to come here and prevent them from ever leaving." I speared a drumstick on a fork. "Sorry, I don't have much faith in politicians anymore."

"You don't need to apologize to me. I bet you're right. I'll be interested to hear what Radio Free America says about it later tonight. Those Canadian reporters always seem to know things about the U.S. that folks here don't."

"Really? Like what?"

A familiar face popped up on the screen. The air emptied from my lungs, and I dropped the leg I was holding. Buttermilk splashed across the table.

Jessop Hawkins sat in an armchair across from an interviewer. Hawkins was bent forward, his hands clasped as if a PR person had briefed him on how to look concerned.

"Do you know him?" Vera said.

"He owns my Contract."

"*That's* the man you were supposed to marry?"

I hadn't seen Hawkins since I'd left L.A. But even if his highly paid PR consultants coached him on how to act caring and distressed, they couldn't change how his eyes were the color of cold, rust-stained cement.

"Aveline is a victim in this tragic story," Hawkins said. "She's like many girls, young and naïve, who put their trust in someone who then takes advantage of them."

"So you contend that Aveline, who is currently wanted for treason—"

A shiver shook my shoulders.

"Aveline is not a traitor! She was kidnapped by a member of Exodus and brainwashed into becoming an active member of the organization."

"You're referring to the young man currently in police custody."

I edged closer to the TV. "No, Yates—"

"Yes," Hawkins answered. "Yates Sandell."

My temples began to throb. I shouldn't have left him.

"But as I understand it, Sandell's not talking," the newscaster said.

"He's critically ill, but the doctors expect him to recover."

"Meanwhile," the newscaster said, "despite evidence that points to your fiancée as a willing participant in the shootout with federal agents, you believe that charges against her should be dropped."

"Aveline is an innocent, and she needs to be found and returned home. I promise you the truth will come out and her name will be cleared."

"And you've offered a $250,000 reward for information leading to her return."

Return? Don't you mean capture? I began to feel floaty, disconnected.

"Yes. Here's the hotline: 1-800-AVE-LINE."

I wrapped my arms across my chest as the number scrolled across the screen. "Oh my God."

Vera guided me onto a chair. "Come on now. Lean over. Head between your knees. Yes, good girl." She rubbed a circle on my back. "You don't look anything like that picture. Not now with your new hairdo."

"Some might say, Mr. Hawkins, that your search for Aveline is actually an attempt to clear your campaign of the scandal associated with your fiancée's actions."

"I understand that people doubt my motives for defending Aveline, but what happened to her could happen to any young woman in

America. This is why Paternalists fight to protect young women, because any girl can become a victim."

"Well, thank you for talking to us this evening, Mr. Hawkins—"

Vera snapped off the TV, and a few seconds later I heard her bang the drapes shut in the living room.

Luke stepped into the kitchen. "What's going on?" When I didn't answer, he bent over until he was looking me in the face. "What happened?"

"They've got Yates," I said, shaking my head. "Why didn't I stay with him?"

"You couldn't have saved him."

"But I left to save myself."

"No. You left because I dragged you out of there."

Vera tapped him on the shoulder. "Avie, why don't you go lie down. Luke can help me in here."

Luke stepped aside to let me by. I was still in the hall when I heard Vera say, "You're pushing that girl—to do what, I don't know—but she needs to get there on her own."

Luke mumbled something.

"Son," she said back, "you've both been through hell. Let her catch her breath."

I collapsed on the bed and pressed my fingers to my head, trying to stop the throbbing. Catch my breath?

In the last two weeks, I'd seen a friend set herself on fire on the steps of the Capitol. I'd seen federal agents threaten an entire town and execute a woman trying to surrender. I'd seen every attempt to expose the vice president's treason turned into proof that I was a terrorist.

The Paternalists had captured the boy I loved and cut off all the exits, and Hawkins had put a price on my head.

And still Luke wanted me to go on what was turning into a suicide mission to deliver evidence that had only a small chance of taking out the bad guys.

How am I supposed to be anything other than scared as hell?

I looked up as Luke walked in. His thumbs were hooked in his belt loops and his head hung down, making him look about fourteen. "Avie, I want you to know, I'm sorry about Yates. If I'd thought there was any way we could have brought him with us—"

I let him sputter for a moment before I sat up. "It's okay, I'm not mad. You were right. If I'd stayed with Yates, the feds would have taken me, too."

Harris tapped on the door. "Vera's about ready to serve dinner."

"We'll be right there," Luke answered. I pushed off the bed and Luke held the door open for me like the gentleman that Nellie and Rogan had raised him to be. We sat down at the table and bowed our heads for grace, then Vera handed me the mashed potatoes, saying, "Help yourself and don't be shy."

Harris picked through the chicken pieces. "I was telling Luke here that even though I haven't found you a ride to Laramie yet, you shouldn't worry. Folks here know me and I expect we'll get some good news tomorrow."

The thigh that Harris had forked hovered over his plate like he was waiting for me to say I was okay.

"I promise I won't worry," I said. "Not yet."

Luke piped up. "Hey, you know your granddaughter's studying to be a midwife?"

Harris jiggled the chicken so it dropped on his plate. "A midwife. Is that right?" He beamed at Vera. "I told you that Keisha was a cracker-jack."

Luke and I could never pay Harris and Vera back for the risks they were taking, but I think Luke came close. Harris and Vera had never visited Salvation, and they hadn't seen Keisha since she was twelve, but they glowed as brightly as the colored lights strung on the tree when Luke told them about Keisha helping the Johnson baby into the world and Beattie teaching the gospel of peace to the children of Salvation.

On the mantel, a chipped ceramic angel spread his wings over the Nativity scene. I stared at his haloed head, hoping there was a real angel up above who'd help Luke and me get out of Pocatello.

6

"We can't risk you sleeping on the couch," Vera told Luke. She pulled blankets from the closet. "Hazel McAllister has a way of seeing right through her neighbors' walls, and if she gets a whiff that something isn't right, well—"

For the first time ever, I saw Luke blush. Vera stuffed a pillow into his arms. "Be a gentleman and leave her the bed."

"Yes, ma'am."

When I came out of the bathroom, Luke had made up a bed for himself on the floor in the narrow space between the bed and the bookshelf. He lay on his side, propped up on one arm, reading the book he'd gotten that morning. His arm muscles bulged even though he was relaxed, and the hair on his forearms was blond in the lamplight.

I crossed to the bed, suddenly conscious of how I wasn't wearing anything under my loose pajama top.

He had undone the leather tie that held back his hair, and now it fell alongside his cheeks, reminding me of when I first saw him and thought he looked like Thor, the god of thunder.

I climbed into bed. "We should listen to your friend's message," Luke said quietly. "The one on your phone."

I flipped the quilt over my legs, pretending I hadn't heard that.

"I know you heard me."

"Not now."

"Vera's busy and Harris is asleep. There's no better time."

"Sparrow said that the message was for Maggie. She specifically told me not to listen to it."

"What would she have said if she knew Maggie would be murdered?"

Listen to it. Get it to the right person. "I don't know."

I eased the chain with the thumb drive over my head, and Luke watched as I let it coil on the nightstand.

"What do you intend to do about that?" he said.

My cheeks stung. What did I intend to do with the video of Maggie describing the Paternalists' secret dealings, the one I promised to get to her friend in Washington? "I'll take care of it."

"How?"

"I don't know. But you'll be happy to hear that most of the border crossings are closed so I can't easily escape to Canada."

"I'm not happy about the border closing," he said.

"I find that hard to believe. You seem set on us going all the way to D.C. to deliver this drive in person."

"If Maggie thought that bringing down Jouvert was as easy as sending that thing through the mail, she'd have told you to do it."

I flipped over and turned my back to him, but Luke kept on talking. "Jouvert needs to pay. He killed Maggie and Barnabas, turned his guns on the rest of my family, and right now he's holding them hostage. If you aren't willing to do what it takes, then I will."

I turned around just in time to see Luke snatch the drive off the table and pull the chain over his head. He jutted his chin like he dared me to try to take it off him.

I felt a flash of relief, seeing it around his neck. *You want it so much you can have it.* Then relief dissolved, and I jerked at the sheets that had twisted around my legs. I couldn't just hand off what I'd promised Maggie I'd do.

"Maggie spent five years collecting this information. I will not let her life be wasted," he said.

She and the girls in her escort service had risked their lives, partying and spying on businessmen, bankers, and Paternalist leaders to collect what was on that drive.

"Fine," I snapped. "You want to go to Laramie? Let's go."

"Good. I'm glad we're in agreement." Luke slapped his book shut and drew the blankets over him.

I flipped off the lamp, heat pouring out of me. I'd go to Laramie, but after that—

Out in the living room, the radio was on low. According to the

Canadians reporting for Radio Free America, Congress' Open Arms policy was a response to sixteen European nations banning their female citizens from traveling to the U.S. after too many went missing. Hundreds of thousands of Australians and east Asian women were expected to apply.

I hugged my pillow, wishing I could stay right here, safe and warm, but knowing I couldn't, not with a quarter-million-dollar bounty on my head. And Luke needed to get out, too. Those government agents back in Salvation were probably assembling dossiers on everyone the Council knew or was related to, and pretty soon they'd know Maggie and Barnabas had a son who got away.

7

I woke in the middle of the night. Luke's pillow and blankets were on the floor, but he wasn't. I got up and eased open the bedroom door. Light from the kitchen shone into the hall, and I crept out until I spied Luke alone at the table.

His back was to me, but his gun was dismantled, and the parts were spread out on Vera's red vinyl tablecloth. Luke picked up a small brass brush and inserted it into the gun barrel.

I stood in the shadows, watching his hands move slowly and deliberately. Then I saw my phone lying beside his left hand.

He looked up as I pulled out a chair. I'd have banged it across the floor if Vera and Harris weren't sleeping. "You listened to it, didn't you?" I said, pointing to the phone.

His brown eyes snapped at me. "Somebody had to."

We glared at each other for a minute.

"This is big, Avie. This could force the vice president out of office."

I could hear Sparrow's giggles in my ears, the rustling sounds of clothing, ice, and glasses clinking, the vice president moaning. I knew it had to be more than a sex tape, even though I wanted to believe that was all it was.

"I know you listened to the beginning," Luke said. "I had to rewind it." He slid the phone toward me.

Vera and Harris were snoring in the front bedroom, a quiet snuffle and a ripper. There wasn't a better time unless it was never.

"Fine, if it means getting you off my back." I put the phone to my ear and closed my eyes. I couldn't bear to see Luke watch me as I listened.

Sparrow laughed seductively, and I squirmed in my seat. I wondered where she'd hidden the recording device. Knowing Sparrow, she'd assembled something small, and tucked it into a necklace or her hair.

"Mr. Vice President," she murmured. She praised Jouvert, telling him how much she loved being with him at the meeting, seeing him wield power and get that Saudi sheik to give the U.S. so much money. One trillion. "Do you know how many pairs of shoes I could buy with that?"

"A whole factory." Jouvert laughed. "You could buy Thailand for a trillion dollars."

"Do I want to buy Thailand?"

"Let me think about it, and I'll get back to you."

"I can't believe all the sheik wants is what we want anyway," Sparrow said. "I want a man to pamper me, and take care of me, and decide for me."

"It's the way things should be, isn't it?"

"Ugh, I can't imagine having to get a job and go out and earn money, not when I can stay home and be a wife. And driving? Too scary."

"You should be cherished and protected just as the women are in his country."

"This was your idea, wasn't it, getting the sheik to help us?"

"Guilty as charged."

"Well." Sparrow's voice turned deep and teasing. "Time to pay for your crimes, Mr. VP."

I heard a sharp intake of breath, a moan, and the recording ended. I opened my eyes, remembering the party in Vegas when Jouvert had boasted to the Paternalist leaders about getting the money. Sparrow was at his side.

"You heard what I heard?" Luke said. "Jouvert admitting he made a secret deal with the Saudis?"

"Yeah. That's exactly what I heard." I saw the uncompleted branch on Maggie's hanging, and my mouth went dry. The sheik's name was the one she'd needed to prove Jouvert was a traitor.

"The Saudis bribed the Paternalists, didn't they?"

I nodded. "They changed the laws for women just like the Saudis wanted." I put the phone facedown on the table. "Jouvert brought Sparrow to the meeting with the sheik. Jouvert knows Sparrow hid proof of what she heard—she basically said that in a message she blasted before she died, but he might not know she recorded the two of them."

I dropped my head into my hands. "Why couldn't she have sent this to one of Maggie's allies or a reporter even? Someone who hated Paternalists as much as she did?"

"Sounds like you're the only person she trusted."

"Like I'm supposed to miraculously save the country?"

Luke started to reassemble his gun. "We should divide the evidence. You carry the phone and the wall hanging. I wear the thumb drive. That way if something happens to you or me, the other still has enough to raise hell on Capitol Hill."

I shoved away from the table. It was late. I was tired. "I'm going to sleep."

I felt his eyes on my back, but I refused to think about one of us getting killed or captured, and the other still going on. I was doing what he wanted, going to Laramie, and I wished Luke would shut up about it and leave me alone.

Vera was cooking breakfast when there was a knock at the door.

Luke and I had gotten up when we heard her rattling around the kitchen. We'd moved awkwardly in the cramped bedroom, saying as little as possible, mumbling sorry when we bumped.

Luke was pretending to sip the coffee Vera'd handed him when we heard the determined tapping on the door.

Vera threw down her hot mitt. "Only person with the nerve to show up this early is our next-door neighbor." She pointed at me, then Luke. "Lovebirds, remember?"

We both nodded, slightly guilty. Clearly, Vera had heard us argue last night.

Luke and I couldn't go on being angry with each other like this. As Vera went to the door, I showed Luke the sugar bowl. "Need this?"

"You know darn well I do," he said, cracking a smile.

I held it up out of reach, taunting him for a second before he snatched it away.

Forgiven, at least for now.

I leaned forward to catch a peek as Vera talked to Hazel through the screen. Hazel was bundled in a blue coat and wore a raggedy striped hat over her white hair. She smiled behind her big, gray-rimmed glasses, straining for a glimpse past Vera.

"Hi, Hazel," Vera said. "You're up early."

"I noticed you have a couple young people visiting."

"Did you?"

Hazel waited a moment, but when Vera didn't say any more, Hazel pulled something out of her pocket. "The Pocatello Princess Fundraiser Dance is tonight. I thought maybe they'd like to buy a couple tickets."

"Well, I don't know, Hazel. Let me discuss it with them and I'll—"

Hazel was a snoop and the only way to deal with a snoop was to let her know there was nothing to snoop about.

"I'd love to go to a dance, Cousin Vera!" I strode right over to the door and unlocked the screen. "Hi, I'm Tracy," I said, giving Hazel a big smile. "How much are the tickets?"

Hazel's gaze focused on me through thick, yellowing lenses. "Twenty-five dollars a couple. It's to raise money for the Bannock County Search and Rescue Team."

"Honey?" I called back to the kitchen, where Luke leaned against the counter. "Can we? It's for a good cause."

I'd caught Luke in mid-swallow, but his eyes told me he didn't like the idea.

"It'll be fun!" I said.

Hazel was standing on tiptoe now, trying to see past me. I beamed at Luke, showing off like a lovesick bride.

He reached for his wallet and acted as if he was counting our money. "I don't know—"

"Please," I whined.

"Well, if it'll make you happy." Luke peeled some bills out of his wallet, and I pecked him on the cheek and snatched the money out of his hands.

Hazel handed me the tickets. "Will we see you at the dance?" I said.

She blinked behind her glasses, and her mouth went flat, before she drew it back into a smile. "Yes, indeed. I'm in charge of the cake table."

I skipped back to the kitchen, waving the tickets. "Look, we're going to the dance!"

Vera lingered at the door, watching Hazel retreat. Then she came back to the kitchen and stood over the half-cooked eggs, dabbing her neck with a paper towel. "Hazel's cousin's the chief of police," she muttered to no one.

Crap.

Luke frowned and jerked his head, pointing to Vera with his eyes. *We need to move on.*

I nodded, wishing he was wrong.

"Now that you bought those tickets," Vera said, "Hazel will be expecting you at that dance, and her tongue will wag if you don't show." She sighed. "I guess this is good. Best place to hide is in plain sight."

I leaned over to Luke. "I screwed up. I'm sorry."

"I hope this doesn't mess up Harris getting us a ride."

Harris came in. He greeted us and sat down at the table at the exact moment Vera set down his plate. "Luke?" he said. "Can you give me a hand at the church after breakfast?"

"Yes, sir."

"Let's see if we can get you on the road."

"That would be much appreciated," Luke told him.

"Yes, that would be wonderful," I said. Even though tomorrow didn't feel nearly soon enough.

Hazel McAllister peered through her blinds as Harris and Luke drove off.

"Darn that woman," Vera said. "We'd best get to the market. Hazel knows I always do my shopping on Fridays, and Lord knows we don't need to give her reason to wonder why I'm not at the Albertson's."

Not when Hazel had two hundred and fifty thousand reasons that were a phone call away. Hawkins' reward could provide her a lot of comfort in her old age.

It was still early, but cars were parked outside the grocery store. Vera inserted her key card to release the door. A sign declared: WOMEN-ONLY SHOPPING UNTIL 3 P.M.

A group of women Vera's age were seated at a couple of folding tables just inside the door. They spied us, and waved us over. All six had their eyes locked on me.

Vera sucked in a breath. I could almost see her thoughts spinning.

My feet turned, ready to walk right out and get back in the car. *You can't. You have to stay.* I unzipped my coat, but left my hat on. "Cousin Vera, why don't you relax with your friends while I do the shopping?"

She smiled and handed me the list. "That's sweet of you, Tracy dear."

I waved at the ladies, and received their approving smiles, then grabbed a cart. *Dodged that bullet.*

Rolling up the dairy aisle, I checked the ceiling, noting where the security cameras were placed, and angling my body so they wouldn't get a good shot.

I wanted to get through the list and get out of there, but I could hear Vera and her pals whooping it up, their laughter echoing down the aisles. I needed to draw this out a little longer.

I passed the pet food aisle, and spied Selena. Bags of dog food overflowed her cart. I did a U-turn, and caught up with her. "Hey, how's it going?"

"Ay, Tracy, I don't know what I'm gonna do. I cannot afford this food."

"Can't the Humane Society help?"

"No, they told me to take the *perritos* to the shelter in Denver. Is no-kill. But my husband, he is in Wyoming working the oil fields. I cannot do it myself."

The map I memorized in fourth grade flashed in my brain. Laramie was due east, the same direction as Detroit. *Don't offer to help. Harris has probably found you a ride.* "Sorry, Selena. That sounds really frustrating."

"This is what happens when you have a big heart for *perritos*."

I slid a ten out of my pocket and pressed it into her hand. "For the food."

"No, I don't want to take—"

"Please. I want to."

"Okay. This time." We smiled at each other like we knew there'd never be a next time. Looking over her shoulder, I spied Vera waving me down. "Excuse me, Vera needs me." I pushed the cart over to her. "What's up?"

"Hazel's here," she whispered. "Let's vamoose."

We headed for the only checkout with a cashier, and as we rolled up, I saw my face. Not just on *People*—but on every gossip magazine in the rack. And who was holding the *Enquirer*? Hazel McAllister.

"Teen Terrorist" screamed the headline over my blurry pic.

"Lord Almighty," Vera muttered.

My eyes darted to the exits. *Don't panic. You can't panic.*

I heard Roik, my old bodyguard, in my head. "The best defense is a good offense. If someone's following you, turn right around and nail them with your eyes."

I plastered on a smile. "Hi, Ms. McAllister!"

"Oh, it's Vera's visitor from Salt Lake."

"Let me help you with your cart." I pulled out some cans of fancy cat food and laid them on the checkout belt. "Are you baking a cake for tonight?"

"No, I leave the baking to the girls. I do a lot of tasting, however." Hazel chuckled, showing me her wide, yellow teeth.

"Well, I always make devil's food with marshmallow frosting for Lou. That's his favorite."

Hazel laid the *Enquirer* on her groceries. "You like to bake?"

"Oh, I love to bake!" I was roasting under my hat.

I kept up the chatter while I emptied Hazel's cart, and somehow managed to slip the *Enquirer* back into the magazine rack without her seeing.

Luke and I had to get out of town ASAP, I thought as I watched her pay.

Back in the car, I ripped off my hat and jacket. My striped shirt was soaked with sweat. "Is Hazel everywhere?"

"No," Vera said, "but it feels that way sometimes."

We dropped the groceries at the house. Luke was mixing cement in a wheelbarrow beside the church when Vera and I drove up.

Please tell me you've got good news, I thought, walking over to him. Tell me Harris found us a ride out of here.

We didn't have much time before Hazel put two and two together and came up with two hundred and fifty thousand.

Luke was working on a broken section of the concrete walk. He stirred the cement with a shovel and jerked his elbow at the hose by his feet. "Put a little more water in that slurry, will you?"

"Sure." I pointed the hose so water trickled into the thick gray mud. "Any luck with Harris finding us a ride?"

"No. He's called over forty people. None are moving stock this time of year."

"Damn."

"That's enough water."

I tossed the hose aside. The wood frame that Luke built to form the step was perfectly measured and cut, with angles that were exactly ninety degrees. He was so careful, always thinking through things.

"So we need to come up with another way," I said.

"Harris offered to drive us."

"No. He can't!"

Luke looked up, as surprised as I was by my reaction. "Yeah, I told him no. We're putting him and Vera in enough danger as it is."

"Hitchhiking would be too dangerous. And the police will be watching the buses."

"Yeah, it doesn't look promising, does it?"

I didn't like asking Selena, but what choice did we have? "The woman who did my hair wants to drive to Denver, but she needs help."

"You saying she might offer us a ride?"

"Maybe. She has to take a dozen dogs to a shelter. We'd be doing her a favor."

"Not much of a favor."

"I could ask. I'm pretty sure she knows who I am."

Luke lifted the wheelbarrow, shaking the handles so the cement slopped into the frame. "All right. Your turn," he said, when the frame was full. "Slide that trowel around in a figure eight and even out the top."

I kneeled down and slid the trowel back and forth. "Yesterday, when I asked you how this guy in Laramie is supposed to help us, you didn't answer."

"I can't. I'm not sure he will."

"Then why the hell are we going?"

Luke glanced at the street. "Would you keep it down?"

"I'd be happy to if you'd give me a good reason to risk my life to get to eastern Wyoming to meet him."

"Because Barnabas told me to find him."

We stood there, letting the moment settle. How could I argue with that? "Okay, I'll call Selena."

I was surprised when Selena hesitated only a moment before saying she'd drive us. "Are you sure?" I said.

"You and Lou come over, and help me pack the RV." She explained how she'd get her sister's son to drive up from Denver and meet her in Laramie. Then he'd go the rest of the way with her.

I had just put down the phone and was still marveling at our luck when Vera came up from the basement carrying a dress. She spread the midnight-blue skirt out over her desk. "I think this will fit you."

"Oh, Vera, it's amazing."

The dress sparkled as if stars were caught in the fabric. I touched the halter. For one night, I would be a normal girl like from Before, wearing a pretty dress and going to a dance with a cute guy. Tonight might be fun.

I held the dress up to my body, and realized that I'd called Luke cute. My cheeks turned pink. *Okay, so I called him cute. So what? I'd have to be blind not to notice how good-looking Luke is. And I'm not. So there.*

10

Packing up the RV with the *perritos'* food and gear was a circus, and I realized why Selena couldn't do it alone. By the time Luke and I got back to Vera's we needed showers to get off the doggie smell and slobber.

But once I zipped the blue dress on, I was Cinderella. Light caught on the tiny sequins in the midnight-colored fabric crisscrossed over my breasts. I swished back and forth in front of the mirror, watching the full skirt float away from my body.

I'd been primped and polished by stylists to please Hawkins, and after that, the Paternalist politicos Maggie had me entertain in Vegas, but tonight I was pretty.

Luke knocked on the door. "You decent?"

"Sure, come on in."

He stood there in a skinny tie and a pressed shirt, his mouth open.

"That bad?" I said.

"No, not bad at all—I mean, good—you look nice." His gaze darted from me to the chair where his hat was perched. "Whenever you're ready—"

His confusion was teasing a smile out of me, but I ducked my head so he wouldn't see it. Butterflies crashed into each other in my stomach as I reached for his hat. "I'm ready," I said, handing it to him.

Harris and Vera loaned us their car and Luke and I drove to the high school, barely talking except to read the street signs or Vera's directions. The parking lot was almost full by the time we got there, and Luke pointed out two squad cars by the doors to the gym, their blue lights slowly revolving.

My toes turned to ice in my silver slingbacks. "Maybe Hazel McAllister tipped off the police."

"I doubt it," Luke answered. "Hazel seems more like someone who'd call 1-800-AVE-LINE to claim the reward."

"Not funny."

"Sorry."

We parked and walked toward the building. I wobbled in my heels over the icy ground. A dozen women, men, and teenage boys milled near the front door, waving signs. AUCTIONS ARE FOR COWS, NOT WOMEN. LOVE YOUR DAUGHTERS, DON'T SELL THEM.

"I don't like this," I said.

"Yeah, but we gotta show our faces." Luke twined his fingers into mine. "Hazel's waiting."

We'd almost reached the door when a sinewy woman in a rancher jacket and jeans pushed out of the crowd. "Shame on you for taking your sister in there!" she snapped at Luke.

She glared at him, her eyes granite hard, and I tightened my grip on his hand. *Let's go.*

Luke didn't even blink. "I promised my wife I'd take her to the dance."

"How much did you pay for her?" the woman demanded.

"Nothing!" I shoved my ring in her face. "We married for love. He saved two years to buy me this ring."

She stepped back but her expression didn't change. "You go in there and you're supporting the subjugation of young women."

"With all due respect, ma'am, I'm here to support Search and Rescue. Good night." Luke tipped his hat, and we left her openmouthed as Luke steered me toward the door.

We passed under a banner hanging over the gymnasium doors: WELCOME TO THE POCATELLO PRINCESS WINTER DANCE. A half-dozen state troopers formed a line by the entry.

"Easy does it," Luke whispered. I squeezed his hand tighter.

Luke went to guide me past them, when one stepped forward. "Your gun."

We froze. I held my breath, knowing a pat-down was next and then arrest.

"Mister," the officer said quietly, but firmly. "No guns or alcohol are allowed inside. You need to check your firearm here."

"I left my weapon at the house, sir," Luke said.

The officer stepped aside. "Thank you and enjoy the dance."

We both drew in a breath, and Luke handed our tickets to the man at the door.

Silver garlands and giant glittery snowflakes hung from the gym ceiling. A fiddler, guitarist, and bass cranked out a country-western tune on the stage up front.

"Well, this doesn't look too bad," Luke said. A smile opened up his face. "Heck, we might even have a little fun tonight."

"I hope so," I said, trying to make my smile match his. I felt my toes wanting to tap to the beat as if my body craved a few hours of cutting loose. A row of booths decorated with crepe paper like at a school carnival were lined up along the basketball court, but no one was manning them yet.

Men of all ages sat on the bleachers on the far side of the room. Some had wives with them, and I realized many of the women were Mom's age or the age she'd be if she was alive. It was the most women I'd seen her age outside of Salvation.

"What are you staring at?" Luke said.

"Those women. How did they survive?" I forced myself to look away.

"Maybe they're ranchers who raised their own cattle."

Luke was probably right. They were cancer-free, because they'd never eaten beef tainted with Scarpanol. If only everyone had known.

"Hey, how about some cake?" Luke said.

"Mmm. Okay."

Twenty girls who looked like freshmen clustered behind long tables of frosted and decorated cakes. A blonde in a white dress with yellow roses at the neck spied Luke, and practically threw herself across the table, waving him over. "Hey, come see my cake. It's applesauce with caramel frosting."

Her girlfriend in hot pink muscled her out of the way with a good-natured shove. "Nah, you don't want that. You want my coconut cake!"

I linked my arm protectively through Luke's. Maybe these girls were only fifteen, but Luke had never seen girls like them in Salvation.

"You mean we bid on these cakes?" he said.

"Every dollar we raise goes to equipment for the Bannock County Search and Rescue," Blondie said.

"Opening bid's thirty-five dollars!" her friend added. "But you can buy a slice for ten."

"What's your favorite type of cake?" Blondie purred at Luke.

I spotted Hazel McAllister making a beeline for us. "Why hey, Ms. McAllister!"

The girls pulled apart like they'd been caught doing something wrong. Hazel loomed over their shoulders. "I'm glad you came," she said. "Are you enjoying the dance?"

I gripped Luke tighter. "Yes, ma'am," he said. He turned his chestnut-brown eyes at her, and I saw Hazel McAllister soak up Luke's smile like a cat soaking up sunshine. My teeth hurt, I was smiling so hard, hoping Luke's charm would protect us from Hazel's suspicions.

We escaped after a few minutes of small talk and crossed the dance floor. The band went quiet as the master of ceremonies took the stage. Single men came down from the bleachers and left the cake table to gather in front of him.

"Welcome, everyone, to the Third Annual Pocatello Princess Winter Ball," the MC said. "Before I bring out the princesses, I want to remind you that all the money we raise tonight goes to buy new equipment for Search and Rescue. Each princess will dance ten dances with winning bidders, so open your wallets, boys!"

The men clapped and the band struck up a song that sounded like it came from a Disney movie. "Our first princess is Melodie Goshawk."

Melodie stepped on the stage with a man who held her arm so proudly, I knew it had to be her dad. She glided along in her long red dress and rhinestone tiara, while her father was country formal in his polished boots, jacket, string tie, and Stetson.

"Melodie has just completed her 4H steer project," the MC said. "She loves trout fishing, and working her hunting dog. She prefers her pizza with pepperoni and sausage."

The clapping continued as Melodie paraded down the center of the gym, beaming like the queen in the Rose Parade. Then she walked to the line of decorated booths and stepped into the first one. Over her head hung a silver-spangled sign that read MELODIE.

My stomach tensed, seeing Melodie in that booth. Stop being so sensitive, I told myself. They're selling dances to raise money for a good cause, that's all.

After four more girls were introduced, the MC waved his program. "Men, if you're looking to get married, the parents of each Pocatello Princess are here tonight to talk Contract terms, and Mr. Tellerman from the bank has a table set up to help with the financing. And be sure to bid on some dances, because this is your chance to get to know these girls."

I turned my back on the stage, and saw the banker sitting at a table with a sign reading TURN YOUR HOUSE INTO A HOME. ASK ME ABOUT A BRIDE MORTGAGE! A line of men waited to talk to him.

I muttered a string of swear words under my breath. No matter where we went it was the same, men buying and selling girls' lives, their happiness.

Luke squeezed my hand. "What's got you so upset?"

"These girls are going to be sold off like 4H projects. Some of their moms are right up there in the bleachers. How can they sit there and let this happen?"

"Tracy, honey, you're drawing attention to yourself, glaring at everybody like that."

I tried to force myself to smile, but I couldn't quite do it.

"How about we get some punch?" Luke said.

"Fine."

Luke guided me over to the punch table, where I sipped my drink and I made myself clap for the princesses as each made her debut. Across the room, men lined up at the booths to bid on a dance.

I kept glancing at the women on the bleachers, especially the one who couldn't take her eyes off Charlene, the princess in booth five, and who had to be Charlene's mom. I nudged Luke. "Look at that woman in the green dress. How can she let her husband sell their daughter? My mom would have fought my dad to the death before she'd let that happen."

"Well, maybe somebody should do something about Contracts," Luke said.

"You think I'm that somebody, don't you?"

Luke shrugged. His faith in me was greater than it should be. How was I supposed to stop Jouvert when I wasn't even sure I could save myself?

Luke eased my empty cup from my hand. "Let me throw this away."

While he did, I watched Charlene. She greeted each bidder with a camera-ready smile, no matter if he was a sunken-eyed grandpa or a beer-bellied cowboy. My heart fell, seeing only two young men about her age in line. *Did they even have a chance?*

Her eyes brightened as one of them came to the front. A dimple creased his smooth face, and Charlene held out her pen as if she'd been saving it just for him. He frowned at the bid sheets, not cracking a smile until the last one. He scribbled his bid, and I crossed my fingers for him.

The MC announced the close of the bidding, and the band started up. Older couples came out on the floor, and the girls stepped out of the booths into the arms of the men who'd won that dance.

"We should dance," Luke said. "All the other married couples are."

"I'm not very good. I'll probably step all over your feet."

"Don't worry about that. If these boots can protect me from Shelby's hooves, they'll keep me safe from a little thing like you."

He reached for my hand, and set the other on my back, leaving several inches of space between our bodies. "You need to look at me," I said. "If you want people to think we're in love."

He dropped his eyes and met mine, and I was suddenly aware of the warmth coming off his body and the muscles under his shirt. Of the warm brown of his eyes. Of the golden stubble along his chin.

My stomach began to feel fluttery, like it was warning me I might do something I shouldn't. Luke and I were just dancing, I told myself, but the fluttery feeling continued to grow, and after a few more turns around the floor, I broke away. "Will you excuse me?"

I was relieved the ladies' room was almost empty. I'd be fine; I just needed a little cool water on my face.

The only other person in there with me was a princess redoing her makeup at the sink. Her hand was shaking as she brushed on more mascara and a faint tear track had bleached through the blush on her cheek.

"Are you okay?" I said.

She met my eyes in the mirror. "I'll be fine," she told me in a voice that said there was no way she was going to be fine. She screwed the top back on her mascara.

I wet a paper towel and dabbed my face. *Don't say anything. It's none of your business.*

"Dammit." A black streak of mascara coated three of her fingers.

"Hold on." I grabbed another towel. "I'll get it off."

Her chest was going up and down and I could feel her trying to keep from losing it. Her parents shouldn't have done this to her. It wasn't fair of them to force her.

I scrubbed the smear on her hand. *You can't say anything.*

A tear trickled from her eye and she swiped at it with her other hand. "I have to stop crying," she said. "I'm up next. I have to look pretty."

Her fingers were clean, but I couldn't let go of her hand. I knew I should just walk out the door and go back to Luke.

"You don't have to do this," I said quietly. "There are people who can help you."

"What?"

"They can take you away and hide you until you turn eighteen. Then your parents can't Contract you."

She wrenched her hand out of mine. "Get away from me."

"I know it sounds scary—"

She snatched up her makeup bag. "You think you're so smart, but you have no idea. My brother broke his back, and we'll lose our ranch if we can't pay the hospital. I'm going out on that stage and I'm going to save my home. Not that it's any business of yours."

I stepped out of her way. "I'm sorry. I was just trying to help."

She pushed past me, leaving my stomach in cinders. Then the lock on one of the stalls clicked open, and Hazel McAllister emerged.

Oh my God.

"Hi, Tracy, are you having fun?"

My hands dove into the folds of my skirt and I sidled toward the door. "Yes, I'm having a wonderful time, but I got so warm while we were dancing I needed to freshen up." I grabbed hold of the doorknob. "I shouldn't leave my husband out there all alone."

And I was out of there.

I spied Luke on the far side of the dance floor and darted through the crowd to get to him. Once I reached him, I threw my arms around his neck. "Act like you love me!"

Luke lifted me onto my tiptoes and brought his face in close to mine. "Any particular reason?"

"Hazel. She was in the bathroom. Is she watching us?"

"Like a snake on a rabbit. We might want to give her a show."

Before I could say yes the band started up, and Luke spun us out on the dance floor. He held me to his chest and my toes hop-skipped across the wood, trying to keep up with him.

"Wait, I don't know how to do this," I cried.

"You've never danced a polka!"

"No, never."

"Then hold on, and leave it to me."

He danced us around the other couples, picking up speed as we circled. My feet flew out from under me, and the faster he danced, the tighter I held him.

The dance floor began to empty, as people made room for us, and the fiddler turned to watch, his bow strokes turning shorter, bolder, faster like he was pushing Luke to break into a gallop.

Luke grinned, his smile so big it blew up my heart like an overfilled balloon, and when he threw back his head and yelled, "Whowee!" I did, too.

One last circle round the floor, and the fiddler struck the final note.

The dancers put their hands together, clapping first for the fiddler and then for Luke and me. He set me down on my feet, but didn't let go while I stood there, catching my breath and waiting for the spinning in my head to stop. Luke's cheeks were bright pink, and when our eyes met, his expression made my breath catch. *I'm so lucky you're mine.*

Heat rose in my cheeks. *Calm down. He's acting.*

Luke nodded over my shoulder and his hand tightened around mine. "Hazel McAllister's still watching us."

"I guess we should keep dancing then."

"You know how to do the two-step?"

"Nope, not a clue."

Luke led me through the two-step, the cowboy cha-cha, and a waltz, before we broke for punch and shared a slice of chocolate cake. I licked the fluffy icing from my fork, and the thought hit me that even though Luke and I were putting on a show, this is how it might feel to be a newlywed, enjoying a last night on the town before heading up to fix my pa's roof in Walla Walla—to be exhausted from dancing my heart out in his arms, but wishing the music would never end.

The band was playing a slow song when we left. Luke held me to his side as I teetered in my silver shoes, navigating around the iced-over puddles in the potholed parking lot, too hot from dancing to zip my parka despite the frosty air.

Back at Vera's, I locked myself in the bathroom and peeled off the dark blue dress, replaying how Luke and I had whirled around the dance floor. His joyful face floated before mine and I blinked, my gut telling me that what I'd sensed from him when I was in his arms wasn't acting. It was real.

I plunked down on the edge of the tub, the dress a dark cloud beside me. Maybe my gut was completely off, but I had to be careful Luke didn't get the wrong idea. Yates might be handcuffed to a hospital bed hundreds of miles away, but that didn't mean my heart wasn't right there with him.

11

We left the house a little before five A.M., so it looked like we were heading out to catch the Greyhound 5:20 pickup downtown. Harris had bought Luke and me bus tickets to Walla Walla to cover our tracks, and he made a point of handing them to us as we got in his car. The light was on in Hazel's kitchen. "We'll call you when we get to Walla Walla, Cousin Vera," I said, loud enough for Hazel to hear.

"I'll be praying for your family," Vera told Luke, embracing him.

She pulled me in for a last hug and I clung to her, wishing this wasn't good-bye. "You be safe," she whispered. "And don't you worry about Harris and me. We're tough old birds."

Pocatello was quiet. Just the doughnut shop was awake.

At Selena's, a dozen little dogs raced around the room like windup toys. Selena caught each one, and Luke and I popped them in crates and loaded them into the RV. We stowed our packs in a cabinet and Selena made us lock our guns into her gun safe. "I hope the police don't stop us, but if they do," she said, "it's better like this."

Ten minutes later, we were gone.

Selena drove, and Luke sat up front in the other captain's chair while I sat farther back, peeking at the still-dark town from behind a half-drawn curtain.

"How long until we get to Laramie?" I said.

"Is over four hundred miles," Selena answered. "This afternoon, I think. Depends. You travel with dogs, you need to stop more."

The first couple of hours were quiet, but I couldn't relax even though there were long stretches on the two-lane highway where the only light was the stars. Every time a beer truck or pickup roared up, its headlights blaring, I gripped the seat until it passed.

The dogs slept in their crates in the cramped bedroom in back. The radio was tuned to country-western, and every few miles, I'd recognize a song from last night, and I'd catch myself looking at Luke. The light from the dash lit his profile and his thumb tapped a beat on the arm of his seat.

Selena must have picked up on something. "You went to the dance last night?" she asked Luke. "How was it?"

"It was real fun," he answered. "Band was all right. We danced up a storm, didn't we?"

I gave him a sleepy smile, careful not to sound flirty. "Yeah, we did."

Selena nodded at me in the rearview mirror, her eyes crinkled at the edges like she was sure something more had happened.

Nothing happened. We were acting, throwing Hazel McAllister off our tracks. That was all.

"Hey," I said, "could you turn up the radio, please?"

Three hours in, dawn was finally breaking, turning the snowy landscape gray white. I began checking the silhouettes of oncoming cars for patrol car lights. The RV wasn't breaking any speed records. Fifty-five made the ancient engine groan.

About twenty miles from the interstate, the DJ announced breaking news.

"The federal manhunt in Colorado, Utah, Montana, Idaho, and Wyoming continues for Aveline Reveare, suspected terrorist connected to the recent shootout in Salvation, Idaho."

Selena and Luke glanced at each other. She knew who she was helping.

"Authorities are also on the lookout for a man they're calling a person of interest, Luke Stanton, the son of two terrorists killed in the shootout. Investigators have not released a description of Stanton as residents of Salvation are resisting the investigators' attempts to question them."

Luke's hands curled into fists. "Son of a—"

"Luke?"

"You get what they're doing? They're holding my family in the church, and forcing them to talk."

I crawled into the gap between his and Selena's seats. "I know. It's awful."

"Jonas is only six and Sarah's ten! The feds are probably telling them that they'll go to hell if they don't tell the truth. Or threatening to hurt Nellie and Rogan."

I wanted to tell Luke he was wrong, but the men who'd attacked us were capable of anything.

Luke tried to swivel his seat, but I was in the way. "Pull over," he told Selena.

She shot me a worried glance.

"Pull over! I've got to go back."

"Keep driving, Selena," I said.

Luke glared at me, his chest heaving. "Get out of my way."

"No."

He went to climb over me and his boot caught me in the ribs.

"Ow! That hurt!"

His mouth fell open, seeing what he'd done. "You should have gotten out of the way!" He jerked his pack out of the cabinet, and grabbed hold of the gun safe. "What's the combination, Selena?"

"Don't tell him!" I scooted across the floor to get to him, one hand holding my bruised rib. "Luke, no you—"

"Give it to me!" He slammed his fist down on the keypad, and the RV swerved onto the shoulder, throwing me against the cabinets.

"Stop it!" I yelled.

Luke righted himself as Selena straightened out the wheels and got us back on the pavement.

I looked up, wanting to take his hand, but knowing he'd only shake it off. "You can't go back. Nellie and Rogan sent you away to keep you safe."

"They shouldn't of done that."

"Maybe not, but if you go back, everything they've gone through will be for nothing."

"It's not right. It's not right for Sarah and Jonas to suffer because of me."

"I know," I said softly. "I know."

Luke stood there, leaning over the gun safe, while I waited, hunched at his feet, praying for a sign that he'd heard me. Then, finally, he slid the black steel box back next to the toaster. "I'm sorry I kicked you."

"It's all right, I know you didn't mean to."

"How bad does it hurt?"

"It stings." I straightened up to show him I'd be fine.

He helped me onto the bench seat, then slid back into his seat. "Selena, I apologize for yelling at you," he said quietly. "I shouldn't have lost my temper."

"Is okay. We all get a little crazy sometimes."

Luke leaned back and stared out the windshield. On the outside he looked like he'd pulled himself together, but his calm felt as unreliable and unsteady as the eye of a hurricane.

He had to be terrified, not knowing if his family was alive or dead. I remembered how I felt watching Mom go through hell, but not being able to help her; Mom crying for more painkillers and the nurse snatching the pills out of my small hand.

I wish you'd tell me what you need from me, Luke. I wish I knew how to help you.

I pictured Sarah's angel face, and Jonas in his cowboy hat. If the feds hurt them, Luke would never forgive himself. And if they hurt Nellie and Rogan, he'd never forgive the feds.

The highway ended at the interstate, and Selena merged into a string of eighteen-wheelers. The big trucks walled us in back and front. The sun was hidden behind thick pewter-colored clouds. Hills of scrub went on for miles, uninterrupted by billboards or houses. Mountains loomed in the distance, but I couldn't tell if they were five miles or twenty miles away.

I stayed tucked behind the curtain and out of sight. Patrol cars passed us, but the sheriffs inside didn't glance our way.

When the dogs started whining, Selena pulled off at a truck stop. We put sweaters on them and leashed them by twos, then Luke walked them around the gas station parking lot before we crated them back up. Even though we hurried, it took thirty minutes with all three of us working together. We ate carnitas sandwiches, standing up, and the pork was spiced with cumin and jalapeño, but I could barely taste it. We still had a hundred and fifty miles to go before we were off this road.

We were only an hour from Laramie when the traffic began to slow up ahead. A few minutes later, both lanes were at a crawl and the left lane was merging into ours. Selena leaned out the driver's window. "*Dios mio*. It's the police."

My heart started to pound. *You can't freak. You have to stay focused.*

"What are they doing?" Luke said.

"I don't know. Maybe there's been an accident." I strained to see. Red and blue lights flashed, reflecting off the steel body of a trailer truck up ahead.

A moment later we were stopped, stuck in the line of traffic with no exit for miles.

"I'm going to take a look," Luke said.

I followed him out. Black highway patrol cars lined the shoulder. "There's more on the other side." Luke pointed through a gap between two trucks.

"I don't see any emergency vehicles."

Our eyes met. "This isn't an accident," I said. "It's a roadblock."

We crept alongside an eighteen-wheeler. A couple hundred feet ahead, troopers surrounded a car. The driver and passengers got out, and the troopers lined them up along the shoulder.

People were reaching into their pockets, and I saw a man offer a trooper his wallet. "They're checking IDs."

Luke frowned.

A trooper pulled a semiautomatic out of the car trunk, and suddenly, all five passengers were standing spread-eagle, being patted down.

Holy crap. I pressed against the side of the truck and scanned the land along the highway. It was flat and open with low scrub and no cover for a quarter mile to the south and more to the north. The snow was deep enough to lead the law right to us.

"Bad spot to try and make a run for it," Luke said.

"Yeah." I swallowed, trying to push down my fear. Luke and I turned toward a *chop-chop* sound. A helicopter was flying up the line of cars.

The troopers finished with the car they were inspecting, and moved on to an SUV. Light bounced off the telescopic mirror a trooper was about to pass under it. The passengers unloaded boxes and suitcases from the rear, and the troopers ordered them to open them.

"We can't hide in Selena's RV," Luke said. "We're going to have to bluff our way out."

"Right."

We turned back toward the RV and had gone just a few steps when Luke said, "I never thanked you for climbing up that ridge and saving my family back in Salvation. Not many people would risk their lives like that—"

A chill blew through me and I yanked his arm hard so he almost tripped. "No. You do not get to say good-bye to me. Not here. Not now. You need to tell me you think we can do this even if you have to lie."

Luke glanced past me to the officers, then took a deep breath and squared his shoulders. "All right. We can do this. We're going to do this."

Back in the RV, Selena had freed the *perritos* from their crates. Twelve tiny dogs were bouncing from the floor to the seats, yapping and begging for treats. A few had sweaters on and dragged leashes behind them.

The coffeemaker was choking out the java and Selena was stacking paper cups beside it. "Immigration comes," she said, "you don't run. You run, and they know: *illegal*. So you smile. You give them coffee."

It was the same lesson Ms. Alexandra had taught me: be audacious when you break a rule, and people will assume you have permission.

The troopers were now two vehicles ahead. If they discovered Luke and me, we could not leave Selena holding the evidence.

I crammed my phone into my back pocket and knotted the wall hanging around my neck like a scarf, glad Vera and I had bleached it to a nondescript off-white. "Do you have the thumb drive?" I asked Luke. He hooked his finger on the chain around his neck. "Right here."

Showtime.

I snapped up three leashes. Bruno, Hernando, and Felix wore their red and blue sweaters. "I'm going to walk some dogs."

"I'll come with you," Luke said.

"No," Selena told him. "You stay. Maybe she can—" Selena batted her eyes, and swept her fingers down her hair.

Flirt for survival.

Vera had pushed me to wear a short skirt and tights, and now I knew why. I walked up the shoulder toward the line of patrol cars, my heart pounding, and a hot-pink-lipstick smile on my face. The dogs tugged at their leashes.

The man in the truck ahead rolled down his window. "Hey, baby, I'm freezing. How about you come warm me up."

Drop dead. I kept going. Up ahead, a young officer wearing body armor, tall, freckles all over his clean-shaven face, guarded an older man and his shivering wife.

I scooped Felix into my arms and sashayed up to the officer, noting the words U.S. MARSHAL on his bulletproof vest. "Hey, Officer, what's going on?"

He smiled at me, before he remembered not to. "Miss, you need to return to your vehicle."

"Is there an accident? Is anybody hurt?" I stepped closer to the marshal and Felix stretched out to sniff him.

"No, miss. We're trying to apprehend some felons. For your safety, we need you to return to your vehicle." He tried not to smile at Felix, but couldn't help it. "What's his name?"

"Felix. And that's Bruno and Hernando. I thought I'd walk them as long as we were stopped."

The marshal petted Felix. "I've got a Lab at home."

"Oh, I love Labs."

"Officer Barton!"

Officer Barton snapped to attention. "Yes, sir."

An older officer glared at him. "Escort that civilian back to her vehicle."

"Yes, sir."

Barton winked at me as soon as his boss wasn't looking. He walked me back, handing me the dogs after I'd climbed into the RV. I gave him a big smile. "Thanks for your help."

Selena had stripped down to a rhinestone tank, and she leaned over Luke, her breasts inches from his face as she scrunched his hair. I threw off my down jacket, and peered at Luke. "Are you wearing eyeliner?"

"So what if I am?"

"No big deal. Just asking."

A knock hammered the door. Selena straightened and put on her game face. Luke moved toward the door. "I'll get it."

He set two dogs on the steps by his feet and opened the door. Whoosh! Cold air poured in and the dogs leaped out and dashed between the legs of the officers gathered outside. The men split apart, letting Luke tear after the escaping dogs. Through the back window, I saw Officer Barton jog after him.

The ten other *perritos* yelped and snarled as four officers climbed into the RV. I read the law enforcement division names silkscreened on their bulletproof vests: Sheriff, ATF, FBI, U.S. Marshal. The government wasn't taking any chances.

Some dogs cowered at the mens' feet, while others leaped on the chairs and table and snapped at them. The officers moved carefully, trying not to get too close. I picked up Nestor and hugged him to my chest. He was trembling even worse than I was.

Two officers began to search the cabinets, the oven, and the drawer under the bench seat, and I knew it was only a matter of time before they frisked us, too. "Ma'am," one said to Selena, his hand on the gun safe. "Would you please open this?" I listened to him call in the serial numbers on the guns, hoping none would link us back to Maggie or Salvation.

The sheriff took Selena into the tiny bedroom, saying, "Where are you headed today?" I inched toward the flimsy door. What was the purpose of our trip? he asked. How was she related to the people with her? We were stylists at her salon, Selena told him.

Sweat trickled down my side. Steady, I kept telling myself. Breathe. Act like you have nothing to hide.

Then I saw the U.S. Marshal checking me out against a flyer he was holding. The top was folded over, but I could read it upside down.

"WANTED BY THE FBI. Suspects in the Salvation Shootout. Aveline Reveare and Luke Stanton."

There was a black silhouette of a man's head under Luke's name, but there were two photos below mine. The blurry, bleached-out one must have come from the video broadcast, while the profile of me with my long, brown hair held back by a Hawkins-approved headband was from the *People* shoot.

The marshal's eyes met mine then traveled to my hair.

I'm not her. I'm not her.

"Could you please step outside, miss?"

My heart stopped. "Sure, Officer."

I picked up Nestor and cradled him in my arms. The marshal followed me out of the RV, our shoes hammering the metal stairs. The door closed, barely muffling the dogs frenzied barking. Outside, four officers made a wall between me and the road.

This is it. This is the end.

"Could I please see your ID?" he said.

Shit. I had no ID. Nothing but a fake Canadian passport zipped into my jacket.

"Miss, your ID?" He looked from me to the wanted poster, and I saw myself handcuffed and shackled in the back of a squad car. Unless they shot me right here. Nestor yelped and clawed at my arm, and I realized I was crushing him. I had to say something.

Don't just stand there. Say something!

"I think it's inside somewhere—in my coat or backpack or something."

"I need you to retrieve it."

My throat closed until I could hardly breathe. "Yeah. Right now? I mean, it's kind of crowded in there."

"Yes, now."

I glanced back at Luke, but he was splayed out on his stomach, reaching under a car with Officer Barton crouched beside him. If I didn't play this right, he and Selena would be on their way to prison.

The men near me snapped to attention, and I saw a tall officer approach. "What the hell's going on in there?" He wrenched open the RV door, and the men inside stopped what they were doing. He looked at ATF and FBI. "Anything?"

"Three handguns," ATF answered. "All locked and legally registered. No sign of explosives."

"You done here?"

"Yessir."

"Go check out the freezer truck five vehicles down."

The officer looked from me to the flyer the marshal was holding. "That's not her."

I got very still. The marshal didn't answer, but the way his mouth hardened told me he didn't like the other officer telling him what to do.

The tall officer walked away and the marshal's eyes followed him. He folded the flyer and put it back in his pocket. "I won't need your identification."

Okay. Okay. I'm okay, I thought, as he walked off. I thanked Selena silently for making me blond and for the bright pink lipstick she had insisted I wear.

Luke was still trying to retrieve the dogs. Three FBI agents stood between us, sizing up the cars and trucks they hadn't yet searched. Scratchy chatter on their two-way radios mentioned roadblocks across five states.

I nuzzled Nestor, and kept my head low, wondering if any of these agents had been instructed to look for a piece of embroidered silk like the one wound around my neck.

It was freezing even with Nestor in my arms. The cold blew through my tights, but I wasn't going back inside the RV without Luke. Finally, he and Officer Barton headed back with both dogs. Barton faced forward. No easy conversation with Luke.

When they reached us, the FBI turned to check out Luke. They glanced at his face and then at each other. One looked away, uncomfortable, while the other raised his eyebrows and faked a cough.

It's the eyeliner, I realized.

Then the sheriff stepped out of the RV, carrying a steaming cup of coffee. "You're free to go." He handed me a flyer. "The people we're looking for are armed and dangerous. If you run into them, give us a call. The number's here."

I don't know how I managed to say thank you, seeing not one, but two direct lines to my capture. Both 1-800-CALL-FBI and 1-800-AVE-LINE. Somehow I climbed back in the RV, where Selena, Luke, and I stripped the sweaters off the dogs. We moved around each other, barely talking, as we stowed the dogs in their crates.

Selena slid behind the wheel. She shifted into gear and drove forward between the squad cars and the black SUVs painted with U.S. Marshal and FBI emblems.

The RV lumbered along until the freeway was wide open, then the engine rumbled and picked up speed. Selena drove until the roadblock was out of sight, and then without warning, pulled over. Then she bent over the wheel, and started to sob.

I got up and draped my arm across her shoulder. "Selena, I'm sorry. I'm so sorry we got you into this."

She shook her head, still crying, and wouldn't look at me.

"Selena, this was wrong. I never should have asked you for help."

Luke handed Selena a glass of water. She gulped it down, then her shoulders dropped and she stared into the empty glass, shaking her head. "I forget what it's like to be afraid of police. Today I remember."

I felt sick to my stomach, hearing that. *I'd asked her to risk her life for me. For me! What makes me think I'm so special, I deserve to ruin other people's lives?* Selena pulled herself together and started up the engine. I got up and went back to my seat.

Selena fiddled with the radio, and then as the RV filled with the sounds of trumpets and a man belting out a song in Spanish, she pulled back onto the road. She bobbed her head to the beat, and began to sing along, quietly at first, but soon stronger and then almost defiant as we hit cruising speed.

I fingered the embroidered silk at my neck. I probably didn't deserve Selena protecting me or Vera or Harris risking prison to hide me—but the evidence Luke and I carried did.

Suddenly, I realized why Maggie had walked out of the church into what she knew would be a firing squad. She didn't believe her life mattered. What was important was Yates and I continuing the fight.

Her cause mattered and I knew it. Exposing the Paternalists could change millions of lives, but I wondered if I had anywhere near the strength or conviction Maggie did, because it would take all that for Luke and me to succeed.

Luke sat down beside me "You okay?"

His legs brushed mine, and I knew if I leaned against him, he'd hold me up like a pillar.

Careful, I told myself, it could just confuse things, and I moved my leg slightly so our legs didn't touch. "I'm trying, but what if I can't do this?"

"Yeah, well, you got to. You got no other choice." The way Luke looked at me, I saw a glint of Maggie in his eyes where before I'd only seen Barnabas. And I wondered if Luke had another side that I was only now beginning to see.

Streicker

12

Selena drove the RV down a country road while Luke watched for landmarks. The houses were far apart, and the land rolled out like a churning, white sea broken by green-gray shrub and dried grass. Barbed-wire fences edged the road. Snow-covered peaks loomed far off in the distance.

Finally, Luke pointed Selena toward a tidy tan house set back from the road. It was boring looking, a house someone would pass by without thinking about it twice.

The RV lumbered up the long, gravel drive, and Selena slowed to a crawl. Behind the house stood a big, beige metal building with a door large enough to drive a truck through. A tall chain-link fence with razor wire surrounded the building and its gravel parking lot, cutting it off from the house.

We drew closer, and my skin began to itch. The house looked perfectly innocent, no peeling paint or broken windows, and the porch was clean and bare. It would have fit in a suburb anywhere if it had

had a lawn out front instead of the stubbly, wild grass that was mowed short.

We were within seventy-five feet of the house when the front door opened, and two Rottweilers barreled out. They hurtled toward the RV, barking and baring their teeth. Selena braked. *"Ayee."*

I crouched behind her seat. "You can say that again."

She put the engine in park, but left it running.

Luke peered out the windshield. "Streicker'll come out. We need to give him a minute."

I saw Luke slip his gun into the back of his jeans under his jacket. "Luke," I said quietly, "what are you doing?"

He turned, and saw that I'd caught him. "I'm not doing anything," he said, showing me his empty hand.

You just lied to me. You don't trust this guy at all.

The Rottweilers leaped against the door of the RV, and the *perritos* yowled and whined in their crates. Selena threw the RV into reverse. "Let's go."

"Hold on," Luke said.

She put the RV in park, and brushed past us to get to the crying dogs in back. I heard her coo in Spanish, trying to calm them.

A tall man with a shaved head stepped onto the porch. He stood, motorcycle jacket open, hands on his hips, looking us over.

The muscles along my spine pulled tight as I spied the big, black tattoo on his neck. "Is that Streicker?"

"I'm guessing it is," Luke said. He squinted, sizing him up, but I'd already sized Streicker up, and I did not believe Barnabas told Luke to find him.

"I'm going out," Luke said.

"Wait. Are you sure about this guy?"

"Yes," Luke shot back. He opened the door, but left the screen closed between him and the snarling dogs. As if that flimsy thing could stop a hundred pounds of attack dog. "Hey, I'm here to see Streicker."

"Yeah, what do you want with him?"

"He knew my father—Barnabas."

Streicker stood for a long minute, letting his dogs' aggressive barking speak for him. I was about to tell Luke to give it up when Streicker shouted, "Glock, Luger, heel!"

The Rottweilers wheeled and raced back to Streicker. At his signal, they dropped, and he walked past them.

Luke stepped out of the RV. Selena and I watched through the screen, riveted, as Luke approached the house, completely exposed and too far from safety if Streicker set the dogs on him.

What the hell are we doing here, Luke?

Streicker stepped down from the porch and met Luke partway. Wind whipped Luke's jacket as they talked. Even from far away, I could see Streicker becoming angry.

We need to get out of here. I wrenched open the screen to call Luke back when Streicker grabbed him. He pulled Luke into a bear hug, and pounded him on the back.

What the hell?

Luke pointed to the RV, and Streicker broke into a grin. They walked toward us, and Selena shoved the dog she was holding at me. She reached for the gun safe and tapped in the combination, took out her gun, and set it on the counter.

Luke climbed in first and shot me a look that said "don't worry." Behind him, Streicker filled the doorway. "This here's Mr. Streicker," Luke said.

Streicker eyed Selena's gun and tossed her a smile. "*Hola.*"

"*Hola,*" she muttered.

The tattoo on Streicker's neck was a dense pattern made up of words, and the few I could pick out made my skin crawl. Words like "Righteous Man" and "Tyranny."

Streicker looked me up and down, his eyes cutting through my clothes like the tip of a knife.

I hugged the dog to my chest and felt her tiny little chicken heart go crazy. "Hi."

"Hi." Streicker nodded at the dog crates lashed together and laughed. "Shit, Luke. When you said you had a bunch of Chihuahuas in here, I thought you were joking."

"So, can you get them over the border?" Luke said.

Streicker reached for the dog in my arms. I forced myself not to pull away as he stroked the silky ears. "Over the border. Under the border. Easy as one-two-three."

Selena shook her head. "No, is okay. I take them to Denver."

"You sure?" Luke said.

"I'm sure," she answered.

Streicker shrugged. "Suit yourself. Grab your stuff," he told Luke, "and come on up to the house."

Streicker left, and Luke gathered our packs and guns.

"How about you, Selena?" Luke said. "You need a break? Want to walk the dogs before your brother gets here?"

"No, *gracias.*" Selena lifted the dog from my arms. Luke stepped outside, and Selena dropped her voice. "I'm not waiting for my brother, I'm leaving now. You should too."

Every cell in my body was saying the same thing, but Luke wasn't about to leave here, and I couldn't leave him.

"I can't."

Selena shook her head sadly and set the pup down before she took my hands and kissed me on both cheeks, leaving smudges of red lipstick I could feel. "Thank you," I said. "I'll never forget how you helped us." Selena watched me climb down the steps and I saw her fingers making the sign of the cross.

I wiped her lipstick off my cheeks as the RV backed down the drive and onto the country road. Selena turned south toward Colorado, and I watched her drive off, already regretting that Luke and I hadn't left, too.

13

I felt like an animal sniffing out danger when I stepped into Streicker's house. The first thing that struck me was that it was eerily immaculate. New paint. No dust on the shiny floor. No dog smell despite the two curled in the corner.

The front room was stripped down to a brown leather couch, chair, table, and a Sportswall. All four screens were tuned to news. Financial. International. Domestic. Not what I expected from a man dressed like a member of a motorcycle gang.

Streicker slapped shut the open laptop on the coffee table. "Closet's behind you."

Luke and I stowed our coats and packs in the empty closet. My shoulders pinched and I began to wonder if the bare walls and absence of anything personal were intentional, as if Streicker wanted to be able to walk out the door and not leave a trace of who he was behind.

"Make yourself at home, Luke."

I waited for my invite, but Streicker kept me standing. He stripped off his jacket, revealing his cut arm muscles and a stomach that was military flat under his gray tee.

The tattoo on his neck was now completely exposed, and I saw that these weren't random words, but a long passage in the shape of a gun with a barrel, handle, and trigger. I made out a phrase before Streicker turned away.

"For I Will Strike With Great Vengeance."

Who is this guy?

Luke was caught up in the headlines scrolling across the Sportswall screens. I glanced at the road, knowing Selena was long gone.

Streicker looked me in the eyes, a slightly amused smile on his face. "How about you go get us a couple beers?"

My mouth dropped open, and I was about to say something, but Luke shot me a look: *Just do it, okay?*

"Beer?" Streicker repeated.

Go to hell. "Sure."

I headed down the hall toward the sound of cooking and saw a glistening tile floor that had to be in the kitchen. The next room was almost empty, too, except for a table and chairs and a steel gun case fixed to the wall.

I took a quick count. Six semiautomatics in the center of the house, only a few steps from any room, secured by a grille and a coded lock.

A shiver ran through me as if the temperature had dropped to freezing. This wasn't like Salvation, where hunting rifles were kept handy but weapons like these were double-locked in the church basement.

Luke's and Streicker's voices were hushed, and for the first time since Luke and I'd started out on this journey, I wondered if I could trust him.

I stepped into the brightly lit kitchen. Everything looked new: countertops, appliances, cabinets, but none of it was expensive.

A girl who seemed to be a few years older than I stood at the stove browning onions. When she saw me, her black eyes widened, and she glanced toward the front of the house.

"Hi, I'm Tracy."

She looked like she had no idea why I was talking to her. "Lola." She said it with an accent like she was Eastern European or maybe Russian.

"I'm supposed to bring the guys some beer?"

Lola kept stirring like she hadn't heard me. She was tall and model skinny in perfectly cut jeans, but her dark hair was badly styled with thick bangs and a pageboy that curled below her ears.

"Um, beer?" I said.

Lola called out to Streicker in a language I swear I'd never heard before. I don't know what he said back, but Lola opened the fridge and shoved two beers into my hands. Her sleeves were pushed up to her elbows, giving me a clear view of the scars that circled both her wrists.

She'd been tied up or chained.

"What the hell—" I stared at her wrists, my brain spinning,

She forced the beers into my hands and jerked the spatula at me, telling me to get going.

I mumbled thanks and headed back to Luke in the front room, fighting the urge to break into a run. A foreign girl with scars on her wrists? There was no way Streicker was a "friend" of Barnabas.

Streicker raised his hand for a beer without looking up. I slapped it into his palm. "Have a seat, Avie."

Once I heard him say my name, I knew Luke and I were trapped. Luke must have spilled his guts, thinking Streicker would take up our cause. I sat down beside him on the couch, terrified and pissed at myself for leaving them alone.

"Luke's been telling me about the attack on Salvation."

I held perfectly still. Always wait for the question, my teacher, Ms. Alexandra, taught us. Answer exactly what is asked.

Streicker's eyes almost sparkled. "Why'd the feds attack, Avie? Why'd they kill Barnabas, and what do they want so badly they've got people looking for you in five states?"

So Luke hadn't told him everything. "Why should I tell you?"

Streicker snorted, and Luke turned and glared at me.

I held my ground.

"You're sitting in my house, little fugitive," Streicker said. "Now I would *like* to honor my friendship with Luke's father, but I'm not going to risk my ass unless I know exactly what I'm dealing with. You come clean or you're out on the road."

"And if I do—then what?"

"Then you've got options."

"Like what?"

Streicker shrugged. "Depends on what you want. I could smuggle you out of the country, for one."

"You could get us over the border?"

Luke shook his head, disgusted.

"Like I told your lady friend with the dogs," Streicker said. "Easy as one-two-three."

Canada. No roadblocks to worry about. No U.S. Marshals or FBI on our trail. It could be a detour; it didn't have to be the end—but only if Streicker wasn't lying.

"Or," Streicker said, "I get you a new life. New identities. Help take out the bastard who's coming after you."

"That's not the help we're looking for," Luke said.

Walk out the door and end up dead or in prison. Or put my life in Streicker's hands? "Luke, can I talk to you?"

Streicker hauled himself out of the chair. "Take all the time you need."

"I don't trust him," I told Luke when we were alone. "He's got six semiautomatics in the next room. Six! And there's a girl in the kitchen with scars around her wrists like she was chained up. Not to mention that tattoo. You can't tell me that he and Barnabas were friends."

"They weren't."

"Then what were they?"

"They worked together."

By not saying more, Luke said it all. Streicker's and Barnabas' pasts in the CIA were covert, classified, and erased from public record. I blew out a breath. "Did Barnabas trust him?"

"He said Streicker owed him. Said Streicker's code of honor would protect me."

"So Barnabas didn't trust him."

"You got a better idea? You know any good, decent people who can smuggle evidence and evade capture, because I don't."

He had me there. "No."

Luke fixed his gaze on the Sportswall. An aerial camera over Salvation zoomed in on state police carrying two children out of the church. The kids struggled to get free, but the men ignored their thrashing arms and legs.

I laid my hand on Luke's arm, half expecting him to shake me off. "Can you tell who they are?"

"Not sure."

· Luke sat transfixed as a gray and black dog leaped down from a porch and bounded through the snow to get to them. It circled the officers, barking and carrying on. Luke cupped his hands over his mouth. "It's Jonas and Sarah."

"Oh thank God." But where were Luke's parents? I gripped his arm, praying they'd come out of the church next. It took far too long before two more figures came down the snow-covered steps. "Luke, look, is that Nellie and Rogan?"

"No."

"Are you sure?"

"Dammit, it's not them."

The men carrying Jonas and Sarah passed through the gate of the house closest to the church, and my voice dissolved in my throat. "Beattie will take good care of Sarah and Jonas. They'll be okay."

"Not if Nellie and Rogan don't make it." Luke's voice was flat.

"The feds won't kill your parents with the cameras watching." Streicker had slipped back in the room without us hearing him. "But the media's attention span is dangerously short. And once they leave—" Streicker looked at me. "You ready to talk now, Avie?"

Streicker had me cornered. Luke would hate me if I didn't cooperate. Either he'd go ahead and tell Streicker everything himself or he'd blame me if anything happened to Nellie and Rogan.

"Fine, you win," I said, not feeling fine at all.

14

Streicker took in everything we said about Jouvert and the tapes, and didn't doubt a word of it. But when Luke told him we needed to get the evidence we had to Congressman Paul, Streicker told us that wasn't happening.

"You must not have heard. He got jumped about a week ago leaving a bar on Capitol Hill. The guy beat him pretty bad, and the docs don't know if he'll live."

"Damn," Luke muttered.

"Maggie talked about a friend at the Department of Justice," I offered.

Streicker looked like he wanted to spit. "You want to bring DOJ in on this? You do realize they're probably orchestrating the hunt for you."

"No, I didn't."

"FBI, ATF, U.S. Marshals—they're all DOJ."

"Stop badgering her," Luke said. "Maggie told us to contact this guy." He gave Streicker a name and title.

"So, he's in the inspector general's office."

"That's what Maggie said."

"Then his job is to find out who's dirty in the government. There's a chance he's clean and knows who else can be trusted."

"How do we find him?" I said.

"I'll find him," Streicker said.

"You will?"

Streicker cocked his head, giving me a clear view of his tattoo. *The path of the righteous man is beset by the tyranny of evil.*

"Nothing would please me more than taking out Jouvert," he said.

I shrank from Streicker, not wanting even his breath to touch me, but Luke leaned forward. If Satan had a recruiter, Streicker was it.

"Interesting," Streicker mused. "The Saudi king demands that Jouvert restrict women in the U.S. But we know that isn't what he's really after."

"No? Why not?" I said.

"Because he's a calculating political strategist who doesn't give a rat's ass about you and your girlfriends. Right now, he's testing Jouvert."

"Testing him? Why?"

"To see how much he can control him."

"So the king's got something bigger in mind," Luke said.

"Absolutely, and Jouvert's playing right into his hands."

I remembered Father Gabriel saying that girls were the pawns in a big game that powerful people were playing. "So what do you think the king wants?"

"Don't know," Streicker said, "but if I had to bet, it involves cutting the legs out from under his archenemy, Iran. Jouvert's meeting with the Saudis in two weeks, so a deal's probably already on the table. And if the king gets what he wants, he'll make damned sure Jouvert gets the money he needs to take the White House in the next election."

"Jouvert can't be the next president! He has to be stopped."

I cringed, hearing the tone in Luke's voice. It was the same one I heard in Sparrow's when she'd talk about Paternalists.

Streicker's phone hummed and he checked the screen then tapped out a message. "How about you do me a favor?"

"What kind?" I muttered right as Luke said, "Sure."

Streicker snapped a set of keys off his belt and tossed them to Luke. "I've got something that needs to be picked up."

Luke was already on his feet before I could protest. "You're sending us back out on the road?" I said to Streicker. "We barely made it through the roadblock."

"Well, I'd have gone myself, but unexpected visitors showed up." Streicker let that sink in for a second. "Relax. There aren't any roadblocks on this stretch. It's back roads, about ten miles each way. Besides, I think this will appeal to your sense of righteousness."

Luke ignored my raised eyebrows as I followed him and Streicker out. Streicker let us into the fenced-in yard around the back building. A white, windowless van was parked outside, and he slapped two magnetic signs to its sides. RED ROCK PLUMBERS.

Luke climbed into the driver's seat and I buckled into a jump seat right behind him. The van was empty except for the nine other seats folded against the stripped-down walls. Streicker waved as we drove off.

"I don't understand why you're so ready to trust Streicker," I said. "You see what kind of person he is, right?"

"The enemy of my enemy is my friend."

"What kind of bullshit answer is that? You trust him because you both hate Jouvert?"

"I don't trust him, but yeah, we both hate Jouvert."

I watched the road over Luke's shoulder. The sun had set and the moon hadn't come up. The sky was washed with stars over the solid black hills.

Luke didn't say a word for a couple of miles, and I couldn't stand the tension. "I'm not trying to be difficult," I said.

He drove another minute or so. "Well, you're mighty talented to be able to do it without trying." His eyes caught mine in the rearview mirror and I smiled back.

"Yeah? Well, what about you? Were you always this stubborn?"

"No, I was worse. Pa used to make me chop wood when I got that way. I think I chopped wood for half of Salvation one summer."

I laughed. "What was going on that summer?"

"That summer? Barnabas."

"What about Barnabas?"

"I was twelve when he moved to Salvation. Nobody'd told me he was my father, but everybody knew."

"That must have sucked."

"I wouldn't look at him, wouldn't answer him, and the harder Pa pushed me, the worse I got."

"But you and Barnabas seemed so close."

"Yeah. He was even more stubborn than I was."

"So how did he conquer you?"

"He didn't. He wasn't about conquering people." Luke's voice caught. "He'd take me off fishing or hunting. He'd talk and show me little tricks with traps or tying flies. But he didn't ask me to talk."

"And Barnabas never got mad?"

"Not that summer. But the next summer Maggie showed up? Nobody would have blamed him if he'd decked me."

I wasn't surprised to hear that Maggie's return had set Luke off. He was a newborn when she gave him to her brother to raise. "What did you do?"

"I smashed a custom guitar he'd been working on all winter. The wood was imported from Honduras. It cost hundreds of dollars."

"You must have chopped a lot of wood that summer."

"Nope, not a single cord. Barnabas told me to pack up, because we were going into the woods. Then he took most everything out of my pack. For three weeks, we survived using a knife, fishing line, and a plastic sheet for a tent."

I could see them disappearing into the mountains. Barnabas might have told himself he was teaching Luke a lesson, but after hearing the song he wrote for Maggie, I knew she'd broken both his heart and Luke's.

I felt Luke sinking into the past, so I tried to lighten things up. "So if you had a knife, a fishing line, and a plastic sheet, you could keep us alive?" I joked.

"I've been thinking about that."

The way he said it, he wasn't joking. "What do you mean?"

"Once we hand off the evidence in D.C., I could take us up the Appalachian Trail into Maine. No one would be looking for us there. We could cross over the border into New Brunswick or Quebec."

Luke was ignoring all the obstacles we faced getting to D.C., but the fact that he had a plan for what we'd do after the handoff made me feel slightly better. "How far is it from D.C. to Maine?"

"Five or six hundred miles."

Hiking in the mountains in the dead of winter? It would take weeks. "Well, we probably wouldn't run into a lot of people."

Luke turned his attention back to the road because we were com-ing up on our destination. In ten miles, we'd seen only two other cars. Now we strained to read names on mailboxes at the edge of the road using our headlights.

Finally, we found the name on the mailbox that matched the one Streicker had given us. The kitchen light was on in the ranch house and a security light beamed over the garage. As we drove in the gate, a large brown-and-black dog leaped up. It ran until it reached the end of its chain by the garage, and then stood on its hind legs, barking and straining to get free.

An older woman came out and snapped, "Lie down," at the dog. It silenced, and she called out, "Mikhaela! He's here."

The woman motioned to us to stay in the van as she came around to Luke's window. "Here's her birth certificate. An official copy just like you asked. And here's the money." She shoved the envelope into Luke's hands. "It's all there. Seven thousand in cash. Nothing bigger than a fifty."

She turned back to the house. "Mikhaela, hurry!"

Damn!

"Did Streicker tell you we're picking up a girl?" I whispered.

"Nope. But he said if I saw a maroon pickup out front to drive on." Luke reached up and felt for a length of copper pipe snapped to the ceiling above his head.

Great, I thought. Streicker sent us out to do his dirty work because he expected trouble.

A girl came out of the house, a backpack slung over her shoulder. Her head was down, and she swiped her cheek with the back of her hand. She stood on the porch, the yellow light from the kitchen tint-ing her face and red ponytail. Even from twenty feet away I could tell she'd been crying.

The older woman marched over and wrapped her arms around her, and my eyes began to fill, remembering the night a couple weeks before in the darkened airplane hangar when I said good-bye to Yates, my heart fighting to believe we would be together again.

The woman raised her voice and I heard her say, "I cannot let your stepfather get his hands on you."

"But, Gran, Canada's so far away. I might never see you again!"

"If that man gets custody, he'll auction you off before you turn fifteen. And if that happens, I don't know where you'll end up. This way, I know you'll be safe."

I watched her stroke her granddaughter's hair. Streicker had demanded seven thousand to get this girl to Canada. He wasn't like Father Gabriel, who risked his neck for the cause but would have never taken money for himself.

"Do you believe Streicker's really going to smuggle her out?" I said to Luke.

"You think he's lying?"

"I don't know. Doesn't it bother you that there's a girl in his house with scars around her wrists? What if Streicker takes this woman's money and does something bad to this girl?"

A truck roared up the drive, catching Mikhaela and her grandma in the headlights, and they broke apart.

"Holy mother, he's speeding up," Luke said.

"Brace yourself!" I said, grabbing hold of his seat.

The truck veered before it hit us, thumping across the dirt to a stop. Then a man hopped out, his coat half on and arms flailing as he landed awkwardly on the ground. "I came to take you home, Mikhaela. Get in the truck."

The chained dog barked wildly, frantic to get at him. "Tell that dog to shut up!" he yelled.

"What should we do?" I whispered to Luke.

"Hold tight. Don't do anything just yet."

The woman stepped in front of her granddaughter. "What are you doing here, Hatch?"

"I came to pick up my daughter."

"She's not your daughter."

"Law says she is."

"Law says you're not allowed within a hundred feet of us."

"I got me a lawyer, and I'm getting custody."

"Over my dead body."

Hatch laughed. "So be it, old woman!" He drew a gun and pointed it at her face.

I gripped Luke's shoulder. "What should we do?"

"This cannot happen." Luke reached for the pipe.

"Wait, what are you doing?" I said, but it was too late. The van door released with a faint click, and Luke was out the door, cat quiet. He crept behind the truck and out of my sight.

I crawled into the front and peered out, praying that the dog would keep barking, and the man wouldn't hear Luke behind him. I fished inside the glove compartment and under the seat, hoping Streicker had another weapon stashed away, but all I found was a crushed soda can and a first-aid kit.

Oh God, Luke, be careful!

The man wobbled ever so slightly. "You've got to the count of three to get in that truck, Mikhaela, before I blow your grandma's head off that skinny body of hers. One."

Mikhaela took a step toward her stepdad, but the old woman threw out her arms to hold her back. "You're drunk, Hatch. Six hours out of jail, and already drunk."

"Two. I'm warning you, Mikhaela. It's your fault if I hurt her!"

I saw Luke behind Hatch, inching forward, the pipe raised over his shoulder like a baseball bat.

"Three!"

Mikhaela screamed, and I slammed my fist down on the horn. The man jerked his head, and our eyes connected as the pipe slammed into his skull. He dropped to the ground, and the gun flew from his hand.

Luke straddled the body, his chest heaving. I scrambled out of the van, and Luke raised the pipe again.

"Luke, stop!" I yelled, hurtling toward him. "Put it down!"

He looked up at me, his face transformed into something so dark and disturbed, I spun to a stop. I locked my eyes on his and stretched my hand out, praying that the Luke I knew was still in there.

"You got him," I said quietly, easing closer. "He can't hurt them now."

Please, please give me the pipe. You're not a killer. You don't want to kill him.

I saw Luke's shoulders drop, and I held my breath as he lowered the pipe. I slid it out of his hands and heard Mikhaela whimper, "Is he dead?"

My heart was pumping like I'd been running flat out, and all my senses were ramped up.

Luke and the grandmother stayed where they were. I dropped the pipe on the snow and crouched by the body. I set two fingers on the man's neck and felt for a pulse, grateful he was facedown. "He's still alive. We should call an ambulance."

The woman reached over and picked up the man's gun. "Go," she told us. "I'll deal with this. You get Mikhaela taken care of."

Luke stood over the man, not moving. I tugged on his arm. "Luke, please. We need to go. We need to get Mikhaela out of here."

The dark presence in Luke's face was gone, but he looked dazed like he'd capsized at sea or crashed in a desert. He blinked, and took a couple steps toward the van. "I'll get the engine started."

"Okay. Good." I was breathing hard and trying to stay focused. I had to get Mikhaela.

She'd backed up almost to the porch, and as I walked toward her, she shook her head at her grandma. "The police will think you hurt him. I have to stay and tell them you're innocent. That it was someone else."

Help me, Mikhaela's grandmother asked me with her eyes.

I put my arm through Mikhaela's. She was shaking so hard, I was afraid I'd have to ask Luke to carry her. "Mikhaela, we need to get in the van so your grandma can call the paramedics."

I wished I knew if I was doing the right thing, taking Mikhaela to Streicker. I wished I could guarantee she'd get safely to Canada, but all I knew for sure was if I left Mikhaela here, she could end up with her stepdad if he lived, or in an orphan ranch if he died.

Her grandmother set the gun down and took Mikhaela's other arm.

"Nobody's going to lock up an old woman," she promised. "Not one who was defending herself."

We walked Mikhaela to the van, and I belted her into the seat beside mine. I held her hand as tears ran down her cheeks. "What's going to happen to us?" she said.

"Everything's going to be okay." I hoped I wasn't leading her into a trap. "We're going to get you over the border."

Luke backed down the drive, and Mikhaela rocked in her seat like she was winding up for full-blown hysterics. I rubbed her back, knowing I had to calm her down.

"Don't be afraid," I said. "You won't be alone. The people at Refugee Assistance in Canada will find you a nice family to live with." I thought back to the promises Yates had made me about them. "They'll get a message to your grandmother so she knows you're okay."

"But I'm never going to see her again!"

I turned so she couldn't see my face. "You'll see her again. The border won't be closed forever. I bet your grandma will be there to see you graduate from high school."

I kept babbling, promising things I couldn't deliver, trying to keep Mikhaela from losing it, even though I was barely holding on myself.

When we drove onto Streicker's property, I was ready to collapse. If Mikhaela's stepdad lived, I could be looking at kidnapping charges on top of all the other charges the feds had against me.

But if he died, Luke had just killed a man.

15

Streicker didn't thank us for the favor. He met the van outside the back building, taking Mikhaela's birth certificate from Luke and then thumbing through the money. "Seven grand. All here."

Then he ordered Mikhaela to go inside and get some food, jerking his head at the metal building. "You want to eat. It's gonna be a long night."

I pulled my hat over my hair, and stepped down from the van. The adrenaline rush from extracting Mikhaela was fading and I wondered if Yates had felt like this when he helped girls escape into Exodus: bruised, but still standing, in a world I'd tried to make a little bit better.

Luke went to follow Mikhaela in, but Streicker held him back. "Something happen out there?"

"Her stepdad showed up," Luke said. "He pulled a gun on her grandmother."

"You okay?"

Luke shrugged.

"You kill him?"

"He was alive when we left."

Streicker narrowed his eyes at me like he'd decided this was my fault. "I'll take care of it," he said. I watched him head back to his house, ticked he'd put this on me.

I didn't push Luke to hit that man, but maybe what Streicker really blamed me for was bringing trouble to Salvation and getting Barnabas killed.

Luke leaned against the side of the van. The darkness and confusion had left his face, but I felt he'd pushed it deeper inside him. "You did good back there," he said.

"Yeah?"

He raised his hand, and my heart skipped, sensing he was about to touch my cheek, and even though I wanted to hold Luke and have him hold me after what we'd just been through, I made myself reach up and adjust my hat, and his hand fell back the way I thought it might.

"You got Mikhaela into the van," he said. "She wouldn't have left if it was just me. And you calmed her down. I couldn't have done that."

"I hope we did the right thing, bringing her here. Are you okay?"

He looked into the dark. "Yeah. Tired. Hungry as a wolf that missed a kill." He shook his head. "Forget I said that."

I followed his gaze. Luke was pretending he was fine, but he wasn't. "Let's get something to eat."

The metal building was a big open space, divided by a partition that rose most of the way to the ceiling. In the front half, cardboard boxes were stacked on pallets, and a long folding table and chairs were set up in the middle.

Sure, I was exhausted, but it took me a second to register the six teenage girls sitting around the table eating stew. They were probably here when Luke and I first arrived, but we never picked up a clue, which I was sure was what Streicker intended. They were all about my age except for Mikhaela, and looked so young and fresh-faced, so unaware of what could happen, I felt years older. I hoped none of them would have to go through anything like what I'd been through.

Clearly, Streicker had a whole operation going. Six girls supposedly headed for Canada. Thousands of dollars in cash. A van tricked out to carry ten girls at a time. God, I hoped he was for real.

The smell of warm beef stew filled the room, turning my stomach. I knew it was Scarpanol-free, and I was starved, but I couldn't eat it.

I cut a couple slices of bread and spread butter on them. Luke sat, hunched over his stew, while the girls talked quietly among themselves. I stood, watching him, wishing we were alone and far away so we could talk about what had just happened.

It was only a week or so ago that he talked Ramos out of aiming his gun at me, but that was before Luke saw Maggie executed. He'd changed.

He wasn't the guy I could trust to keep his head and think things through.

At least he didn't boast to Streicker about almost killing that man. If he had, I don't know what I would have done.

Luke finished eating, then got up and went over to help two men load a dolly with cartons of prescription drugs. Pharmaceuticals had paid my private school tuition, so I knew there was big money in pain-killers people stole and sold on the street, but the drugs in those boxes didn't look like the ones I knew addicts wanted.

Still, there were thousands of dollars in pills, and I couldn't believe Streicker ran a legitimate business out of here. I slid around the partition separating the front half of the building from the back and spied stacked blankets and cots, and the open door of a bathroom, but what really drew my attention was a backdrop surrounded by light stands and the shiny silver umbrellas that photographers use. I peered at the life-sized photo taken inside of a barn or a rodeo ring. Real bales of hay were stacked beside it.

"Hey!"

I jumped, and Streicker gave a laugh. "Like a hound on a scent, aren't you?"

I tried to look casual. His hands were full of navy blue passports, and I was asking myself how he'd gotten real U.S. passports when I saw the lion and unicorn on the covers. Like my fake passport, they were Canadian.

Streicker flipped two open. "Who do you think Mikhaela looks more like?"

Mikhaela didn't look anywhere close to twenty-one, but at least she had the same red hair as the girl on the left. "This one."

"Good choice." Streicker walked over to Mikhaela and held out the passport. She glanced at me, wide-eyed, and I nodded for her to take it. She gulped and shoved it deep in her pocket.

Then Streicker zipped up his parka. "Toss your plates, everyone. Time to go."

Outside, the girls lined up to climb into the van, and I stood back, watching. Mikhaela looked over her shoulder at me, and I gave her a little wave. Then she darted out of the line and flung her arms around my neck. "Thank you for helping me."

I closed my arms around her. "Be brave and make your grandma proud. You can do this," I whispered. She was trembling and scared, but I knew she might be one of the lucky ones who got away. And I'd helped. In my own small way, I'd helped.

Streicker tapped her on the back. "Let's go."

She squeezed into the last jump seat, her knees knocking against the cases of pills that made a wall down the center of the van, and I realized what I was looking at. Heart meds. Cancer meds. Embargoed drugs that Canadians desperately needed, but the U.S. was holding back to force Canada not to take in American refugees.

The van drove off, and I followed the red taillights until they disappeared.

Streicker is a smuggler. He knows how to get past the border patrols. If Luke would only agree to go, Streicker could get us both out.

Streicker came up behind me. "You're jealous of those girls."

I didn't turn around. "No, I'm not."

"You're lying. You wish you were on that van right now, because you don't agree with Luke's plan."

I refused to answer.

Streicker leaned in until I felt his breath on my neck. "Admit it. You're going to try everything in your power to talk him out of going to D.C."

I was trembling, fighting the urge to run for the house, but I shoved my hands deeper into my pockets, and stood my ground. "How can you get the girls over the border when it's closed?"

"There's an airfield a few miles from here."

"You fly them into Canada?"

"No. The plane sets down in Montana near the border. There's a tunnel that comes up in Alberta."

"Aren't you afraid of getting caught?"

Streicker chuckled. "First, the airfield and tunnel are not on U.S.

soil. It's the Blackfeet Nation. Second, no one's going to rat me out, because everybody's making too much money."

"But what about the border patrol?"

"Border patrol's making more than anyone, but don't tell that to the tribal leaders."

Bribes. Corruption. Exploitation.

"But the third and most satisfying reason I will not get arrested for smuggling is that the men who own the tunnel, or what we like to call the White Gold Pipeline, those investors contributed millions of dollars to reelect Fletcher and his Paternalist cronies."

It took a moment for what he said to sink in. "But the Paternalists closed the border."

"Funny, how it all works out."

I felt like I was going to be sick. "So smuggling out a girl helps make money for the Paternalists."

"Every girl, every pill." He started to walk back to the house. "God, I love America."

I waited until I heard the kitchen door close before I turned around. This was one big sick game where the Paternalists won even when they lost. And Streicker didn't care that they made money as long as he was getting his.

16

Lola was drinking coffee in the kitchen when I walked in. Her sweater sleeves were pushed up, exposing the scars on both wrists. Streicker's men were taking the girls to Canada, but then what? What would happen to the girls once they got there?

I took hold of Lola's wrist and flipped it over. "Did he do this?" I said, pointing to the front room, where Streicker sat, then pointing to her scar.

Lola glared at me.

"Did *he* do *this*?" I repeated.

"Don't be an idiot," she said, and ripped her wrist away.

"You speak English?"

She gave me a look that could melt skin. "He found me in a garage chained to a wall. He freed me."

Then she told me about leaving Ukraine for the promise of a nanny job in Montreal, only to find out it was a lie. Two brothers kept her locked in their house, and the harder she fought to get away, the more they beat her.

"How did Streicker get you away from them?"

Lola stirred her coffee. "Is not important."

I got up from the table. I had no doubt that if someone went to that house, they'd find the decomposing remains of two paunchy, middle-aged men.

When I came into the front room, Luke and Streicker were hunched over together, their heads just inches from each other's. They were watching the Sportswall, and Streicker was pointing at two of the screens and flipping the sound back and forth between the broadcasts.

A thousand college students at a protest march in Boston had torched a life-sized image of Senator Fletcher outside the Old South Meeting House. The fire-blackened body sagged in a suit and tie from the top of a flagpole.

"Right there. That's what I'm talking about," Streicker said.

Luke focused hard on the screens and I sat on the edge of the chair, wondering what exactly Streicker wanted him to see. Then Luke shook his head. "Damn, it's just like you said."

Streicker clapped him on the back and my stomach turned. "All you got to do is pay attention," Streicker told him.

"Pay attention to what?" I said.

Luke turned to me, his face all fired up. "To how the reporters talk about the Paternalists. Like what adjectives they use to describe them. The stations the Saudis own talk about the Paternalists like they're the real patriots. Even the photos of the Paternalists they use make them look, I don't know, heroic."

"But I thought all news stations treated Paternalists like heroes."

"The Saudis are way worse. And they're buying up stations left and right. Streicker says they own almost a quarter of all the TV and radio stations in the country."

"Is that right?" I said.

Streicker smirked. "That kind of media support could put a man in the White House. The man the Saudis want to see there."

He watched me to see if his message sank in. "Yeah, I can see how that would be a big help," I said.

Crap. The Saudis had the money and power to get Jouvert elected, and we had only days to get the thumb drive past Homeland Security to D.C. if we wanted to shut Jouvert down.

Streicker was egging Luke on in a way that made me nervous, taking advantage of how angry and lost Luke was right now, and encouraging Luke to ignore the dangers of what was facing us.

"Is there someplace you'd like Luke and me to sleep?" I said.

"There's sheets and a blow-up mattress in the rear bedroom, but maybe you'd like more privacy?" Streicker tapped Luke on the calf. "You can sleep on one of the cots in the back building—"

"Yeah," Luke said, "I'll be fine anywhere. You just—"

"No," I said. Streicker grinned behind his hand, but I was not going to let him separate us. "Luke and I can share. It's no problem."

"Suit yourself."

"Well, I'm going to bed. You coming, Luke?"

"No, not just yet."

The top left screen caught my eye, and I gasped. Yates was handcuffed to a wheelchair pushed by an ATF agent. "Suspect Taken to Prison Hospital." Yates' nose and eye were still purple and swollen, and his head had flopped to the side.

"Looks like someone beat that poor bastard pretty bad," Streicker said.

"He hit a tree coming down the mountain," I shot back. I stood up. "Good night."

If Luke had looked up, he would have seen how much I wanted him to come with me, but I refused to say it in front of Streicker.

I retreated to the back bedroom and set up the bed, but I couldn't sleep. There wasn't any heat coming through the vents, but I would die of hypothermia before I'd ask Streicker to fix it. I curled up under the two blankets on the freezing air mattress and stuck my hands between my knees, trying to stay warm.

Muffled sounds of basketball games and newscasts came through the closed door. Wind whooshed over the roof, and the window blinds sliced the security light outside into sharp shadows on the bare wall and floor.

I didn't know what to think. Luke was changing before my eyes, almost killing that man when he hit him with the pipe. And the way he acted out there just now, it was as if Luke wanted to learn everything he could from Streicker. Like he was Streicker's apprentice.

My knees ached from the cold. I slid my down jacket under the blankets and spread it over me. *I wish I knew what to do.*

If only Yates hadn't gotten hurt. If he and I were on the run together, things would be so different. We might have argued about what to do, but we would have worked things out. We would have decided together.

Luke wasn't asking my opinion or sharing his thoughts with me. He just expected me to do exactly what he thought we should do.

If I stayed with Luke, Streicker could get us both killed. But how could I leave Luke alone with that man? Luke had never known anyone so—untrustworthy.

Luke tiptoed into the room a few minutes later, slipped off his boots, and set them down.

"I'm awake," I said.

"You having trouble sleeping?"

"Yeah, a little."

"I'm sorry about Yates. It's got to be hard to see him like that."

"At least I know he's alive."

Luke eased down next to me on the blow-up mattress, and it swelled, rolling me up against him. He stretched out on top of the blankets. "You mind if I get under the covers? It's freezing in here."

"No, it's fine. Go ahead." Goose bumps ran up my legs, but that was the cold. Luke wouldn't try anything. He knew I loved Yates.

Luke stripped off his belt and slid under the blankets. "Damn. No wonder you can't sleep. Get closer so I can warm you up."

Coming from Luke, that didn't sound sleazy. Heat radiated off his body, and I hesitated for only a second before edging up next to him. He wrapped an arm around me. "Go ahead and lay your head on my chest."

I relaxed into him, aware of how different his body was from Yates'. Yates was long and lean, his muscles toned from swimming, but Luke was broad-chested from years of chopping wood. I felt small, protected, beside him.

"You warming up?" he said.

"Yes, this helps." It was quiet, and we were finally alone after a day that had been brutally long. "Were you watching the news?"

"Yeah."

"Anything about us?"

"Nothing new—except they put out a description of me."

I lifted my head. "No!"

"Relax. They called me a giant, and said I'm six four and two hundred and fifty pounds."

"But you're not—"

"I'm betting they talked to Jonas. I used to chase him around sometimes and pretend I was Goliath from the Bible story."

The sadness in his voice made me ache. "I'm sure Jonas didn't mean to—"

"It's okay. Jonas sent the trackers down the wrong trail."

I laid my head back down. *I'm worried about you. I wish I knew what's going on inside you.* "Luke?"

"Yeah."

"Are you okay after what happened tonight—when we picked up Mikhaela?"

He was completely still.

"I didn't expect you to hit that man so hard."

"He would have killed her."

"I know, but—"

"I'm done with trying to work things out peacefully—at least where killers are concerned."

"But he—"

"Avie. I'm tired. Can we go to sleep?"

"Sure," I whispered. "Good night."

Luke was so vulnerable. In the last few days, I'd realized that in some ways he was really innocent, like a little kid, and even though he was probably ten times as strong as I was, I needed to be alert and watch out for him.

Hours later, I woke at the sound of tires crunching through the snow outside the window. The sky was still black, but I got up to look.

The white van rolled slowly past, and I moved to the other window. Peeking through the blinds, I watched the van pull up to the fence circling the back building, where a man got out and unlocked the gate. He held it while the van drove through.

Exhaust clouded my view of people exiting the van, but from their size and how they walked, I knew they were girls. They must have run into trouble getting over the border and turned around.

I balanced on my toes on the icy floor. I heard the back door open, and a few seconds later, Streicker walked into the pool of light around the building. Glock and Luger trotted at his side.

In the kitchen, the microwave hummed, telling me Lola was up. I waited at the window until Streicker reappeared, and then crept over and cracked open the hall door.

I heard Streicker drop his boots, and Lola ask him something in her indecipherable language. "It's all good," he answered.

It's all good? If it's all good, then why are the girls back?

I strained to hear them, but couldn't make out anything else they said. Finally, they padded back to Streicker's bedroom and I lay back down beside Luke.

He turned toward me in his sleep, and pulled me close, and I wrapped my arm over his. Luke was a good guy. He wouldn't let anything happen to me if he could help it, but he wasn't thinking clearly when it came to Streicker.

I had to get Luke away from him. The sooner the better.

17

When we came into the kitchen the next morning, Streicker let us know that Maggie's contact at the DOJ had disappeared five days ago during his regular evening run in Rock Creek Park.

Lola set a tray of hot rolls on the stove to cool. She acted like she wasn't paying attention, but she closed the oven extra quietly.

"The timing's interesting," Streicker said. "You're pinned down in the church with feds firing at you, and Maggie's key contact at the Department of Justice goes missing."

First, Congressman Paul was mugged outside a bar, then Maggie's secret ally went missing from a D.C. park. "This wasn't random, was it?" I said.

"Not likely."

Luke crossed his arms over his chest. His fists were clenched, and I could almost feel him wanting to hit something.

"Maybe we should rethink—" I offered.

"Rethink?" Luke snapped.

I shrank back.

"You mean quit." He shoved away from the table. "Give up trying to get justice for my family and trying to get rid of Jouvert and Fletcher and the rest of them."

"I'm not saying quit! But we can't just show up in D.C. when we don't have a clue who can help us."

Luke stomped out the door into the snowy field.

Streicker raised an eyebrow, but didn't say anything. He glanced at his phone. "Save me some food," he told Lola, and headed out back.

She passed me a roll and went back to scrambling eggs. The roll was hot and soft, but I could barely choke it down. I had to convince Luke that getting out of the country was the only choice that made sense right now.

Lola piled the rolls into a plastic bin and put a lid on the huge frying pan. She was bringing breakfast to whoever was in the metal building.

I had to see if Mikhaela had returned. "Let me help."

Lola said something that might have been thanks, and cracked a smile for once.

None of the six girls who swarmed the table as Lola and I set down the food were ones I'd met last night. They were all older than me; I guessed early twenties, and they were laughing and joking with each other like they were on a vacation or a school trip, not trying to get to freedom. "So where are you from?" I said as I passed the jam and butter.

"Red Deer in Alberta."

"I'm from Alberta, too. From Peace River."

"I'm not far from you. Grand Prairie."

"You're all from Canada?" I said.

Lola bumped me. "Sorry." She scowled, and I backed away from the table.

They came from Canada? Why? I saw a girl show off her nails, and heard two others describe the outfits they'd brought. A couple talked excitedly about the "auction," and the contracts they'd signed with Streicker to get them husbands.

I circled the table, clearing off the plastic forks and paper plates, and I could barely keep from screaming. *Don't you know what this country is like? Don't you have a clue what you've done?*

I tossed the trash and realized I was standing next to a stack of boxes that weren't there the night before. The labels were in French and English, and I saw they were morning-after drugs the Paternalists had outlawed in the U.S.

My stomach twisted. These drugs, these girls. Luke needed to see this.

"Can I have your attention?" Streicker announced.

The girls quieted down. I bit my lip, fighting the urge to tell them to run.

"We start filming in a couple hours and the auction will go live at six. Once your bids reach the reserve amount we've set for each of you, you are free to choose any bidder who has bid more than the reserve. You can view the profiles of each qualified bidder on our site and you'll have two hours to review those profiles and make your selection. Any questions?"

The girls peppered him with questions, and Streicker became charming, reassuring. I could see their faces light up, and one bounced in her seat when Streicker promised that at the end of the evening they would all have Contracts and be on their way to wedded bliss.

"One last thing," he said. "From now on you will be called by your American names—the ones on the birth certificates you received."

A rush of loathing mixed with admiration swept through me. Streicker had traded Mikhaela a Canadian passport for her birth certificate. His plan was brilliant: American girls out and Canadian girls in. I tossed the last of the trash, pulled on my jacket, and went outside.

The sky was a chalky gray and clouds were building to the west. A few flurries drifted past. I made out Luke about half a mile away, walking the property.

He wanted to right wrongs and bring Jouvert to justice, and, yes, I wanted to make Jouvert answer for his crimes, but we needed the right contact—someone who could get the evidence we were carrying to people who wouldn't bury it.

We'd reached the end of this road and unless we found a new one, we were done.

Streicker came out of the metal building behind Lola, and I marched up to him.

"Luke and I need to go to Canada," I said. "We can't force Jouvert out of power without the right contacts, and we can't risk the feds catching us on the road with the evidence."

"Luke won't leave this country," he said slowly. "You know that."

"I'm trying to save him."

"That's not how to save him."

"You don't care if he gets killed."

"I care, but not the way you do." He pursed his lips into a kiss.

I felt heat rise into my cheeks, and I wheeled around and started for the house. Streicker was full of it; I wasn't in love with Luke.

"There's some interesting chatter in D.C.," Streicker called after me. "A rumor that a couple of reporters are investigating the homeless man who set himself on fire at the Capitol building."

I stopped in my tracks, seeing Sparrow flick the lighter.

Streicker strolled up to me until he was closer than I liked.

"These two reporters don't believe Sparrow's the crazy that the media claims she is. They think she was the protester at the Capitol that day, and they want to find the proof she said she had of Jouvert's crimes."

I followed the black square of Luke's jacket moving through the brush. He wouldn't rest until he handed off the evidence. "But they're just reporters. Won't they end up dead?"

"We're all going to end up dead—someday." Streicker jerked his head at Luke. "Here's the deal. I'll take you to Canada, but you have to tell Luke about the reporters."

"But if I tell Luke about the reporters, he won't go."

Streicker grinned and leaned in until the tattoo on his neck was almost in my face. *Blessed is he who shepherds the weak.*

"Take it or leave it, Avie. That's the deal."

Screw you, I said with my eyes.

Streicker walked away, whistling as he strolled through the brush in Luke's direction.

Bastard. I won't help you get Luke fired up over a rumor and watch him charge off and do something crazy. I won't be your pawn.

Back inside the house, Lola was kneading bread. "Let me do that," I said, needing to push something around so I wouldn't do anything worse. Lola sat and silently sipped her coffee while I pummeled the dough.

Then a stream of gunshots rang out, and I whipped my head up, trying to determine where they were coming from, but Lola merely pointed a finger at the window. I peeked through the curtains at the field outside.

Streicker stood by, arms folded, while Luke fired away at a target with a semiautomatic. Luke blasted round after round, the sound so loud I felt it. I couldn't look away. This wasn't the Luke I once knew who'd stalk a deer and take it down with one clear shot. No, this Luke acted possessed.

He lowered the semiautomatic, and Streicker traded him for a rifle with a long scope. I'd seen guns like this in movies. Snipers used them.

Streicker ran up to the target, and I thought I saw him mark a spot on it before he ran back to Luke's side.

Luke lifted the rifle. He aimed at the target, stilled himself, then took the shot. The gunshot echoed through the house as Streicker whooped and clapped Luke on the back.

I stomped back to the dough and hit it with both fists. I didn't know what that was about out there, but this thing with Streicker and Luke had to stop. When Luke finally came inside, I dragged him into the back bedroom. "What's going on between you and Streicker?"

"Nothing."

"I don't believe you," I said. The door was shut, but I kept my voice down.

"Yeah, well, what about you? Streicker told me you made a deal."

My cheeks flared, and I didn't answer.

"Let me guess," Luke said. "He offered to take you to Canada."

"Not me, us! We've run out of options for now. We don't have anybody we can trust to pass the evidence to."

"I am not out of options." Luke said it so slowly, so defiantly, I almost stopped breathing.

"What are you going to do?"

"You should go to Canada, Avie. Take your phone, and the hanging, and get them out of the country."

My heart skipped a beat. "You're planning something. Tell me."

"It's better if we split up."

"Why? Why is it better?"

His jaw clamped shut and he stared past me.

"Why?" I said. "Because I keep arguing with you about what to do?"

He shook his head. "You got it all wrong."

"Then why? Are you afraid I'll get hurt?"

He blinked, and I realized what was really going on. "You're planning something dangerous. So dangerous you don't want me there." When he didn't answer, I moved in so he couldn't escape me. "Luke, please. You're scaring me. I need you to tell me what you're going to do."

"There's nothing to be scared about."

"Stop it. You're up to something and—" The truth hit me in the gut. "Holy— You *want* to die!"

He pulled away and my eyes filled. "Luke, no—"

"Living, dying, they don't matter so much anymore. Not when the feds are torturing my family."

I squeezed Luke's arm so he'd look at me. "Beattie will keep Jonas and Sarah safe. She won't let anyone hurt them. And Nellie and Rogan are strong. They'll be okay."

"You go to Canada, Avie. You'll be safe there."

"No. I refuse to listen to this." Luke was losing it. I had to stop him from falling off the cliff.

"Hey, Salvation's on the news!" Streicker called out.

Luke tried to shake me off, but I held on. "Wait. You have to promise me something before you go out there."

"What?"

"Promise you won't make any plans with Streicker without talking to me."

"Sure."

"I mean it."

Luke ripped his arm away. "All right. I promise."

The door slammed behind him. *You think this is settled, but I'm not giving up. You are going to tell me what you're up to.*

I refuse to let you throw your life away.

I care about you too much.

My hand slipped off the doorknob. *Yes, I care about him. Luke is my friend and we've been through a lot together. But just because I said that doesn't mean I don't love Yates.*

Out in the front room, Luke was studying the aerial view of Salvation on the Sportswall. "The feds released a whole bunch more people this morning."

"Do we know if they let Nellie and Rogan go?" I scanned the image of snowy rooftops, searching out Luke's cabin. If Nellie and Rogan were free, maybe Luke would let go of his obsession with Jouvert.

Luke shook his head. "There's no smoke coming from our chimney."

Damn. How am I going to stop him now?

18

A little while later, a livestock truck rumbled up the drive. Streicker took off out the back with Luke right after him. I grabbed my coat. I was not going to leave the two of them alone if I could help it.

The truck idled at the gate while Glock and Lugar went nuts, charging the fence around the metal building. Streicker grabbed both dogs and walked them by their collars to a kennel inside the fence, where they barked with their paws on the chain link until Streicker ordered them to lie down.

The truck pulled in, and Luke helped the men lower the ramp. Out came a beef cow with a rough brown coat and white face.

A light snow was falling, and I zipped up my coat. Glock and Lugar eyed me as I passed, and I steeled myself, expecting them to bark.

When I got inside the metal building, the cow was standing in front of the backdrop while a man arranged the lights. Luke was stroking her neck and talking quietly to her.

I couldn't quite put it together: girls and cows?

The girls crowded the makeup mirrors. They all wore jeans and cowboy boots, and Western shirts embroidered with roses and doves around the yokes.

Streicker stood over his laptop, checking the image of the cow on the screen and giving directions to the guy in charge of the lighting. Then Streicker led a girl onto the set and put the cow's lead rope in her hand. He made her put her hand on her hip and tilt her body toward the camera. "Chest out, chin up," he told her. "Now unsnap those top two buttons."

Smile.

I eased over to the laptop and watched over Streicker's shoulder as the image of the girl and the cow came up on the screen. He popped it into position on a page titled "LFOD Livestock Sales."

"LFOD?" I said.

"Live Free or Die."

The caption read "C Alberta Lass. Hereford." Below the photo was a list of statistics, and the words: "A polled heifer we really like. Very pretty fronted and feminine, but still shows lots of body mass and fleshing ability. Scarpanol-free. Minimum bid: $17,500."

My mouth went sour. The cattle auction was the front Streicker was using to sell smuggled Canadian girls.

"Why so cheap?" I asked him.

"Not so cheap. Add a zero and double the price."

Three hundred and fifty thousand was a lot less than I went for.

"Not everyone is part of a fifty-million-dollar package," Streicker said, reading my mind. "This is a good deal for a rancher. He gets a nice girl, saves the seventy percent import tax, and can keep his ranch."

"Yeah, and you make how much?"

"Enough."

Enough? Streicker made money smuggling girls and drugs out of the U.S., and then made even more smuggling other girls and drugs in. It had to add up to a fortune.

A strawberry-blonde walked over. Her face was clean scrubbed, and she didn't have her Western wear on. She played nervously with the gold chain around her neck. "I changed my mind," she said. "I want to go home."

The rest of the girls stopped what they were doing, and shot looks at each other. Streicker raised his head like a snake. "Come outside and let's talk."

The girl reached for her coat, but Streicker said, "Leave it."

"Okay," she said warily.

Don't go, I wanted to tell her. I slipped out after them and hung back behind the cattle truck. Streicker had grabbed her wrist and was dragging her to the dog kennel.

"What are you doing?" She bucked and jerked her arm, trying to wrestle free.

He yanked open the chain-link cage, ordered the dogs out, and then threw her in. She tumbled back as he snapped the lock shut. "You signed a contract," he said, jabbing his finger at her. "There's no 'I changed my mind, I want to go home.' You made a deal."

"I'll pay you back. You'll get your money, I promise. No matter how long it takes."

The temperature was below freezing, and the wind swept loose snow up in the air. She wrapped her arms across her chest and stuck her hands in her armpits.

"I sank twenty thousand into getting you here, not to mention the risk I took bringing you in. I don't believe you can pay that back."

"But I made a mistake," she pleaded. "I didn't realize."

"I don't believe that, Bree. You're a smart girl, and smart girls know what they're getting into."

"I didn't know you'd take my passport. I didn't know you'd make me change my name."

"Bullshit. You knew you were coming here to get married, and married women change their names."

"I didn't know I'd have to pretend I was Bree Greeley from To-pecka."

"That's Topeka, Bree."

"Stop calling me Bree. It's not my name."

"I really don't give a flying—" Streicker turned his back on her and strode toward the gate.

"You're going to leave me out here like this? It's freezing."

"It's up to you, Bree," he called over his shoulder. "Put on the outfit, do the photo shoot, and honor your contract."

I ran after Streicker. "Why don't you let her go? If she doesn't want to be here, she'll just make trouble for you."

"Like you did for Jessop Hawkins?"

Whoa. "I guess I am an example of what can go wrong."

"I can't let Bree change her mind. Not with five other girls watching. It will set a precedent."

I shook my head, frustrated. The girl stood back from the chain link,

her shoulders hunched against the cold as Lugar and Glock paced outside the kennel.

"Of course, you could take her place," Streicker said. "You become
Bree Greeley, and I set this girl free."

"You're joking, right?"

"Not at all. She gets to walk away. You disappear into a safe new
life with a new identity. Forget your fool's errand of trying to save
the world." Streicker laughed when I didn't answer. "No, on second
thought that's too easy. You wouldn't have to tell Luke about the
reporters hankering for the truth about that girl who set herself on
fire."

Streicker had *me* cornered, but for some reason I couldn't walk away
from that girl in the kennel. "You don't have to let the other girls know
you're setting her free. Tell her to fake the photo shoot. Send her back
in a few days."

Streicker's eyes narrowed. "You're full of creative ideas, aren't you?
I will not spend a dime to get Bree over the border. And I will not give
back her passport. It won't come close to covering what it cost to get
her here. You understand?"

"Yeah. Got it." *Prick.*

Streicker walked off, and I looked back at the girl shivering inside
the cage, the snow pelting her. I knew how she felt—lost and desperate to go home.

I couldn't give her the money she needed or get her back her passport. I couldn't do a damned thing—except get her coat.

I tore back to the metal building, and grabbed her red down jacket
and stuck it under my arm. Then I dashed toward the kennel, knowing Lola was probably watching at the kitchen window. "Here," I said,
stuffing the girl's hat and gloves through the chain link. She pulled
them on, and together we worked her jacket under the gate.

Her name was Hanna and her lips were blue. "Thank you. He's not
going to set me free, is he?"

"No. He won't return your passport, and he won't pay the bribes to
get you over the border."

"My dad would pay."

"He would?"

"For sure. He begged me not to leave. I can't believe I was so stupid."

I glanced at the house. No sign of Streicker or Lola. I didn't want to leave Hanna out here by herself. "You must have had a good reason for coming though."

"I thought I did. I couldn't see myself as a miner's wife, living on so little, knowing that one day I could hear those two sharp whistles, telling me I was a widow. So when Mr. Streicker told me he could arrange to marry me to a nice rancher in America, I thought, all right. But I didn't count on it being like this."

"Yeah, it's not what you imagined." I squinted against the blowing snow. It was icy, and felt like tiny nicks on my skin. "Can your father really come up with twenty thousand dollars?"

"It might be hard, but he'd do it. He'd be happy to have me back behind the bar at his tavern."

Maybe Streicker would return her passport, if I told him that Hanna's dad would pay to get her back. I didn't want to get her hopes up, though.

"I'm going inside, but I'll check on you, okay?"

She nodded. "Thank you for the coat."

"It was the least I could do."

The least I could do wasn't nearly enough. I walked back to the house, determined to persuade Streicker to let her go. He had plenty of passports. He could give Hanna hers.

19

Lola looked up from her never-ending baking when I walked in. "Boots," she said, pointing at the row beside the door, and gave her dough a twist. I wrestled off my boots and lined them up with the rest.

The Sportswall was on in the front room, so I knew Streicker was there, too. I padded down the hall in my wool socks, trying not to slide on the slick wood.

Streicker was sitting with his back to me when I heard him say, "D.C.'s covered with cameras and security forces. You'd have a hard time taking out Jouvert. Best place to strike would be an outdoor rally."

What? I hung back, listening hard.

"You want a midsize city with a warm climate like Fresno or Greensboro," Streicker continued. "A city that can't afford a big police force."

Luke mumbled something that I strained to catch.

"Yeah, you'd need access to Jouvert's travel schedule. The timing's good, though. Politicians in every state want him to help with their campaigns. Not hard to guess where he'll show up."

This isn't happening. Oh God. Luke, show me I'm wrong.

"From what I saw earlier, you could use a sniper rifle, but you'd have a better chance of getting the job done if you got closer."

I stepped into the room. "What the hell are you talking about?"

Luke's head snapped up, and the look he gave me was the same as when he took the thumb drive away and hung it around his neck. "We're talking about putting an end to Jouvert."

"You mean, assassinating him."

"It looks like that's the only way to stop him."

"That's murder!"

"What other option does Luke have, Avie?" Streicker nailed me with his eyes. *It's your own fault, girl. You wouldn't tell Luke about the reporters.*

"You put him up to this!" I said. "You hate Jouvert, and you're ma-nipulating Luke into doing your dirty work!"

"No, he isn't, Avie."

I wheeled and faced Luke. *I don't believe you. Say it isn't true.*

"It was my idea. Not his."

I looked back and forth between the two of them, and I didn't know who I hated more, but I had to get away from them. Now!

I wrenched open the door and ran, forgetting I had no shoes on until I hit the third step and my ankle folded under, and I fell, slam-ming my shoulder on the ground. Pain shot up my left side.

I scrambled to my feet, knowing my ankle was sprained, but I had to put distance between me and Luke and that monster he'd sold his soul to. I tore down the drive, snow pelting my face, the gravel ham-mering my feet through my socks. The road was empty. No cars, no houses, no signs of life in either direction. I turned right and ran through the pain.

Luke must have planned this all along. That's why he brought us here.

He lied and led me on. He pretended this was about honoring Mag-gie's sacrifice and continuing her work, but it wasn't.

I trusted him!

"Avie! Avie! Stop!"

Luke was sprinting after me, so I ran harder. "Go away! Leave me alone!"

I was running full out, but he was gaining on me. Rocks littered the drainage ditch on the side of the road, and I swooped down and snatched up one the size of a baseball. Then I stopped, and took a stance, sinking my weight on my good ankle, and drew my arm back. "Stay away from me."

Luke came to a halt, and hunched over, breathing hard. "Avie, we gotta talk."

"You lied to me. You were planning this all along."

"No I wasn't. I swear."

"I don't believe you. You brought us *here*. To Streicker's *house*. You keep saying you want justice, but I think what you really want is revenge."

"Yeah, sure I want revenge." Luke straightened and faced off with me. "I admit it. Jouvert gave those agents the order to attack my family. He gave them permission to kill my parents."

"Killing Jouvert isn't the answer. It's murder. It's a *sin*."

"I don't care if I go to hell."

"Well, I care! I care!"

There was the slightest shift in Luke's face, a flicker in his eyes.

I realized I had to stop him. That I was the only person who *could* stop him. "Killing Jouvert won't bring justice for your family. It will just make him a hero. Is that what you want?"

"No, it's not. But you said yourself, we got no more options right now."

Snow was soaking through my sweater, and I was losing the energy to stand. My foot burned from the ice coating the road. Okay, fine, I give up, I thought, and tossed the rock onto the shoulder.

Luke needed me to help him get Maggie's testimony to the reporters. He wouldn't go to Canada, and I couldn't leave him with Streicker.

I knew what I was about to tell him might get us both killed, but I had to give up believing we could come out of this in one piece. No matter what we did, we'd be lucky to survive.

"We can get Jouvert," I said. "There's another way." I teetered on my good leg, then dropped in a heap on the pavement.

Luke shifted his weight, and I sensed him fighting with himself not to rush over and pick me up.

"Streicker heard about two reporters who are investigating the cover-up of Sparrow's suicide," I told him. "They're looking for the proof of Jouvert's crimes that she claimed she had."

The blowing snow was a screen between us. "I wish you'd told me before now," Luke said.

"I'm sorry. I probably should have."

"So I'll go to D.C. and you'll go to Canada."

"No."

"No?"

"I'm coming with you. Maggie asked me to see this through and I am."

Luke crouched down beside me, and sighed. "I don't need to tell you how dangerous this could be."

"Nope. I already know."

"There's a truck coming. How about you put your arms around my neck and we'll get you off this road?"

I clasped my hands behind his neck, and Luke lifted me into his arms and I saw how Streicker's house was barely visible in the distance. "Ugh," I said. "I didn't realize how far I ran."

"Yeah, it's a good quarter mile. You can sure fly when you get going."

Luke carried me toward the house, and after we'd gone only twenty feet the truck blew by, pelting us with wet snow. Luke stumbled in the truck draft, before he caught himself.

"You should let me walk," I told him. "I'm too heavy to carry that far."

"Nah, you don't weigh more than a day-old foal."

Our faces were so close, his breath warmed my cheeks.

"Why'd you hold off on telling me about the reporters?" Luke said.

"I was afraid it was either a rumor and you'd risk your life to chase it, or if it was true, I was scared those reporters wouldn't have what it takes to not get themselves or you killed."

Luke didn't answer, so I was sure that meant he was mad. But when he started up the porch steps, he said, "Maybe I'd have done the same if it was you."

He lowered me onto the porch, and I stood facing him, my hand lingering on his shoulder. He looked into my eyes, and I knew that if things had been different, we would have kissed.

My heart tumbled with emotion. What Luke and I were going through together was so intense, so extreme, and what we knew and had learned about each other made it feel like we'd packed years into only a few days. But these feelings weren't like the love I had with

Yates—they couldn't be—I'd known Yates my whole life. I tried to steady my heartbeat, slow it down.

"Come on, let's get you patched up," Luke said.

I dreaded facing Streicker, but luckily, he'd ducked out the back. Lola sat me down in the kitchen so she could bandage my ankle, allowing me a clear view of Streicker talking to Hanna. Lola finished wrapping, and pulled out another chair. "Put your foot up. I'll get you ice."

I glanced at the kennel. "I will, but I need to do something first." I got up and wrestled on my boots and coat, and hobbled out to the back.

"What the hell do you want?" Streicker snapped as I approached.

I waited to answer until I got to the kennel, and shoved Sparrow's forged passport through the chain-link fence. "I'm giving Hanna my passport."

Hanna snatched the passport off the ground and hugged it to her chest. "Thank you!"

If looks could kill, the one Streicker gave me wouldn't have left a trace behind.

"Her father will pay to bring her home," I said.

Just you wait, his look told me.

I stared back. *Go ahead.*

"You need to act like you're being auctioned today," I told Hanna.

"I will. I will. Thank you so much. You saved my life."

"Not yet, she hasn't," Streicker said.

The snow stung my face as I limped back to the house, but I had a fire inside me. I wasn't getting out, but Hanna was. I couldn't guarantee Luke and I would be successful in our mission or even survive, but at least now Luke wouldn't destroy himself trying to get revenge. Dad used to say that sometimes there are no good choices, only choices that are less awful.

Now we had to get the hell away from Streicker before anything else happened.

20

A couple hours later, Streicker gave Luke the keys to the white van. Streicker must have been counting on me selling Luke out so I could go to Canada, because one quick call, and the two reporters were on a plane for Denver.

"Leave the van with this guy," Streicker said, handing Luke a scrap of paper with an address. "He'll hide you and get you a ride into the mountains."

"Great," Luke answered.

Streicker thought for a moment before he added, "You might want to ask the reporters what they know about the rumor that the Saudis are pressing Jouvert for nuclear weapons."

"Nukes? That's what this is about?"

"Only two powers in the Middle East have the bomb: Israel and Iran. And they're both enemies of the Saudis. If Jouvert gets nukes for the Saudis, no other candidate will be able to touch the money they'll pour into making him president."

I turned away, sick to my stomach, and went down to the house to say good-bye to Lola. When I returned, the magnetic signs on the van had been changed to ROCKY MOUNTAIN FARRIERS.

As I walked up, I heard Streicker say, "She's dragging you down. I can take her to Canada in my next shipment and free you up to do what you need to do."

"No, thanks," I said.

Streicker wheeled around.

"We're going together," I told him.

"That's right," Luke added.

Streicker shook his head at Luke. "You're making a mistake, but I guess I can't stop you."

Earlier, after he and Hanna's dad negotiated the price for her return, Streicker had turned from cool toward me to arctic. I didn't care, because seeing him release Hanna from that cage made it all worth it.

We went to get in the van, and Streicker pulled Luke into a hug, tossing me a creepy smile over Luke's shoulder that made me shiver. So I was more than happy to strap into the seat behind Luke, and drive off, leaving Streicker behind like something nasty I'd peeled off my skin.

We got on a two-lane highway south of Laramie, headed for Fort Collins, Colorado. It was an hour and a half to Fort Collins, and if we didn't run into problems, another hour or so to Denver.

My swollen ankle throbbed, even though I'd popped more pain-killers. Luke seemed to relax once we hit the road, and I felt lighter, knowing in a few hours we'd have the weight of the evidence off our backs.

I rested my chin on his shoulder. "It feels good, knowing that when the reporters get this story out, Jouvert and the other Paternalists will have to answer for what they did."

"We're going to stop him, Avie, I know it. And just in time." Luke tilted his head so it leaned on mine. "Hey, I want to say I'm sorry. I know I've put you through a lot—"

"Yeah, well, I haven't always been that easy myself." I had enough regrets for both of us. "Let's forget about all that. Deal?"

"Deal." I felt Luke's shoulder relax beneath my chin. "Avie, when this is over, and the feds aren't hunting us anymore, what do you plan on doing?"

"I don't know. I'd say go home, but Jessop Hawkins still owns me. And I'm nervous about trying for Canada if it means having to deal with people like Streicker."

"Maybe you'd consider moving up to the mountains?"

Our eyes met in the rearview mirror and there was the Luke I'd first come to know in the snow-frosted woods. His chestnut-colored eyes invited me to dream, and in that moment, I saw us together. Building a cabin with our own two hands. Riding horses into the hills. Hanging out with Jonas and Sarah and all the other kind people in Salvation.

A life with Luke was idyllic and tempting, but it was a complete fantasy. I wasn't a mountain girl. I couldn't take off with Luke when I still loved Yates.

"Luke, I—" I didn't know how to answer, how to explain my mixed-up feelings. And I didn't want to hurt him.

"I thought I'd ask, what with your situation the way it is—"

Yates in jail. Me Contracted to Hawkins.

I went to speak, but Luke stopped me. "I know your heart's with someone else."

Yes, but—I couldn't let him think he was wrong to ask. "It might have been yours if I'd met you first."

Luke drove for another mile, then he pulled the van onto the shoulder. "Is there a problem?" I said.

"No problem." Luke climbed into the back and kneeled before me. He draped his hand on my shoulder and his eyes searched mine as his other hand moved to my waist. *What are we doing?* Then he eased me closer and kissed me.

His kiss asked if I was sure how I felt about Yates, and my body answered by pressing into his. And the kiss I gave him back told me that I wanted him, too, that love wasn't a simple "either-or." Love could be both.

I want you both.

I know I shouldn't, but I love you both.

After all the drama and fear we'd lived through together, we were connected. We'd saved each other, goaded each other, condemned each other.

I lost track of how long we kissed before Luke pulled away. He held both my hands in his, keeping us at arm's length. Slow down, stop, he seemed to be telling himself.

"I don't know what will happen after we get to Denver," he said, "but I hope you'll come with me."

"Luke—"

"Shush," he whispered. "You don't have to decide now."

He let go of my hands, and I reached up and ran my finger down the gold stubble on his cheek. His smile opened up his face, showing me the Luke who'd share his big, limitless heart.

We gazed at each other for a long moment before Luke climbed back in his seat. I wiped the corners of my eyes. I wished things were simpler. Saving my heart for Yates had seemed like the most obvious thing in the world, but now in this moment, Luke was offering me a future, and my dream of a life with Yates seemed naïve, unrealistic even.

Luke started the engine. "We're low on gas. We'll need to stop in Fort Collins."

I cursed Streicker under my breath for not filling up the tank. Once we hit the outskirts of the city, we started hunting for a station.

Fort Collins looked like it was once a pretty town with gorgeous mountain views, but it hadn't escaped the wrath of Scarpanol. We passed a shuttered preschool. A dead bridal store. Empty nail salons. Cars were parked outside the auto parts store, and the funeral home had fresh Christmas wreaths on the doors. Shiny snowmobiles were lined up outside the dealership, where red and green banners flapped overhead.

Billboards lined the road. "Colorado State Nursing Program for Men. Big $$$ and Guaranteed Job Placement. 100% Government-paid Tuition."

"Mexican Brides! Bring Home a Gorgeous Señorita! Tour Price Includes All Legal Fees and Import Taxes!"

"Granny's Gun Club and Firing Range. Keep Your Independence! Low-cost Classes. Senior and Early Bird Discounts."

We pulled into a gas station with a convenience store, and parked by the pumps. "Looks like I got to go inside to pay," Luke said. "You want anything?"

"No, I'm good." We were the only vehicle pulled up at the station. "I think I'll freshen up, as long as we're here."

I left my pack in the van, not wanting any extra weight on my ankle. The bathrooms were on the side of the building, and I walked gingerly, keeping my head down.

The step into the bathroom was coated with ice. As I reached for the doorknob, my foot slid and I came down hard on my bad ankle. "Aïiee." Colors burst behind my eyelids, and I made myself breathe until the pain subsided.

Inside, I did my business, then tidied up at the mirror. The hanging was twisted around my neck like a scarf and I fingered the stitching. I was so ready to hand it over to the reporters. I'd bleached it off-white at Vera's, but anyone who knew stitch code could help the reporters decipher it.

But what if the reporters aren't reporters?

Luke and I were headed to a meeting, but Streicker didn't know these guys. Sure, he was smart, but even smart guys get fooled.

I slid the phone out of my jeans. This was the crucial piece of evidence, and the hardest to hide. I remembered police in movies frisking criminals under the arms and down the legs and I stuffed it in my boot, thinking I was being ridiculous. If the feds caught me, they'd find the phone in seconds.

Breathe, I told myself. In an hour, this could be past tense.

I opened the door, and a man stood in my way. He had a beard, and a beat-up cowboy hat, and he smelled like Red Hots. "Excuse me," I said.

He tossed the toothpick he was chewing. "Miss Reveare, if you would come with me."

My stomach plunged, and I scanned the pumps for Luke. "He's still inside," the man said. "You can save him a lot of pain if you come quietly."

The man pointed to the open door of the SUV pulled up next to us. Two other men waited inside the idling car.

Apparently, they weren't interested in Luke, only me. "Let me guess," I said. "You work for Jessop Hawkins?"

"Yes, ma'am."

I glanced over my shoulder, knowing I had only a second to decide. I couldn't jump the fence behind me, and I couldn't make a dash for the street, not on this ankle. If I yelled for Luke, these men would hurt him, and who knows what they'd do if they discovered the thumb drive he was carrying.

The choice became crystal-clear. Give up my freedom, and Luke could finish our mission. Go back to Hawkins, and Jouvert would pay for his crimes. I had to surrender so Luke and thousands of girls like me would get justice.

I got into the SUV.

The man climbed in after me, crushing me against his buddy. He peeled off his beard, and chucked his cowboy hat over the seat. "Do we need to handcuff you?"

"No."

The SUV pulled away from the station and I saw Luke exit the store with a bottle of orange soda. I raised my hand to wave, knowing full well he couldn't see me through the nearly black windows.

He strolled over to the van. Luke would probably wait a few minutes before he tried knocking on the bathroom door. When I didn't answer, what would he do? I kept my gaze locked on him.

Go. Go meet the reporters, Luke. Don't wait for me. Go.

The car sped away, and all the fight in me dissolved. A faint memory of a poem surfaced in my head, something about the world ending not with a bang but a whimper.

I'd imagined that when the feds captured me, there'd be guns and noise and blood, that I'd be screaming hysterically, not sitting in a back seat silently giving up.

I had not given up. I had sacrificed myself.

So you have to go, Luke. Go meet the reporters.

I pictured him starting the van, as if by picturing it, I could make it happen. He couldn't save me, and I didn't want him to try. *Go, Luke. Save the Mikhaelas and the Hannas out there.*

And please, for God's sake, don't get hurt.

The Fort Collins airport was only minutes away. We went in a back entrance and drove up to a private jet on the tarmac. "After you," the Retriever said, pointing to the lowered stairs.

I wasn't surprised in the least to see Adam Ho, Hawkins' assistant, in one of the cushy white leather seats. Ho didn't bother to get up or even set down his tablet. "Welcome back, Aveline."

"Yeah. Long time no see."

Seeing him again, I realized why Ho reminded me of a lizard. It wasn't just the taut skin on his face, it was his slender geckolike body.

The Retrievers took the seats behind Ho, leaving me to pick from the three nearest him. I chose the one right across the aisle so I wouldn't have to look him in the face. Ho made a call while I strapped in. "Yes, we have her. We'll wire you the funds immediately," Ho said, slipping his phone back in his pocket.

The person who'd ratted me out was getting her reward money. I imagined Hazel McAllister lounging at a resort in Florida, smacking her toadlike lips.

"Mr. Streicker said to tell you that you did the right thing, going quietly and not getting his man involved."

I shook my head. *Bastard.*

Now the nearly empty gas tank made sense. At least Streicker had kept Luke's name a secret.

A quarter of a million for turning me in. It was pure Streicker, playing both sides of the field. Taking the reward, and turning me over to Hawkins while helping Luke screw the Paternalists—the same guys whose new laws were making Streicker a fortune in the smuggling business.

I unzipped my ski jacket. The plane lined up for takeoff and my eyes began to fill.

I will not cry. I bit the inside of my lip, until I tasted blood, because I'd be damned if I'd let Ho see me lose it. I lifted my chin and sat up straight.

Screw Streicker and Hawkins. Screw them both.

Retrieved

21

During the flight back to L.A., I stared out the window at the smooth white wing, but all I kept seeing was Luke with that bottle of orange soda coming out of the convenience store at the gas station. I prayed he wasn't still there, that he'd realized I was gone and had continued on to Denver.

I hoped he thought I'd bolted. He'd hate me, but at least then he wouldn't torture himself looking for me. The worst was if he believed I'd been taken, because good guy that he was, he'd blame himself for leaving me alone.

The pilot didn't land at LAX, but at a smaller airport in the valley. We taxied up to a waiting helicopter and Ho handed me a big khaki fabric bag. "Put this on."

"What?"

"It goes over your head with the mesh panel in front."

Apparently, the mesh was so I could see out. "You want me to wear this?"

"For a smart girl, you can be quite dense. Mr. Hawkins does not want your face on the news—not before he has ironed out your legal issues. I myself wouldn't mind seeing U.S. Marshals carry you off."

"I bet you'd hand me over to them personally if you thought it would help Jes Hawkins' bid for governor."

"Without hesitation."

As I drew the cotton twill over my head, I saw the label. Chaste Wear. Sparrow had told me she'd seen girls in New York wearing these things, but I didn't believe her.

The small mesh rectangle only let me see what was directly ahead and I couldn't see my feet at all. A hot Santa Ana wind whipped the bag around my legs as I limped down the steps of the plane. I grabbed at the fabric before I found two slits for my hands.

Heat rose off the tarmac, baking me inside the layers of twill, down, and wool. The Retrievers flanked me the short distance to the helicopter and waited until Ho and I were buckled in before they secured the doors and drove off. Mission accomplished.

Ho gave me a thin-lipped smile. "Time to go home."

We flew over the freeway and into the Santa Monica mountains. Tears trickled down my cheeks. *I can't believe I'm going back to Hawkins, and that I went through all that hell for nothing.*

The helicopter pitched in the wind as it approached Hawkins' compound, and I gripped the seat belt across my chest with both hands. Below, the privacy fence cut across the point, severing the compound from the Pacific Coast Highway. The grounds were as welcoming as he was: harsh, rocky, and covered in brush probably riddled with rattlesnake nests.

Once I was inside that fence, chances were I wasn't getting away. And if I did somehow manage to, Hawkins would alert every law enforcement agency and I'd be dead within hours. The feds would make sure I couldn't testify in a trial.

The pilot went to touch down on the landing pad on Hawkins' underground garage, but the wind surged and tossed us out over the ocean. My heart almost stopped, then the pilot maneuvered us back over the house and onto the pad. He shut down the engine, and I rubbed the tear tracks off my cheeks.

Thank God, Hawkins isn't here to greet me. I need time to take this in.

The pilot got out first. I hesitated at the doorway, unsure how to step down without injuring my foot. He raised his wrestler-sized arms. "Let me give you a hand."

"Thanks."

He lifted me down as if I weighed the same as a bag of groceries.

"Deeps is your new bodyguard," Ho said.

"Nice to meet you," I said. Deeps had shaved the sides of his head, but left his bleached-blond hair long on top. It was tied back in a half pony. He was half as old and probably twice as strong as my old body-guard, Roik. Hawkins must have wanted to make sure I couldn't over-power this one.

All the coaching I'd received about bodyguards from my teacher Ms. A came back. Be polite. Get him on your side. Find out what he likes to eat and keep it in the house. Cheer for his sports team, espe-cially if your dad or domestic manager cheers for its rival.

I'd peeled down to my sweater back in the chopper. The wind whipped the ends of the sleeves that were tied around my neck.

The house was out of sight, set into the cliff below us. Ho motioned to the stairs that led down to the entry. "He's waiting."

Hawkins.

My chest filled with broken glass. *This is really happening.* Deeps of-fered me his arm. "Like some help with those steps?"

I looked into his smoky gray eyes, wishing he would read my thoughts, put me in the copter, and fly me away. "Yes, please."

I steeled myself. Hawkins had just dropped a quarter million to get me back, and had to be furious that I'd messed up his bid for governor. That much I knew.

The house was the same. A one-hundred-and-eighty-degree view of the ocean the minute you walked in. The main room a severely bare art gallery with a giant blue acrylic fish struggling on a spear, and a distorted-looking oil painting of slaughtered chickens.

"He's in his office," Ho said.

I followed Ho down the stairs, memories jolting me with every step. Hawkins pinning me to the banister and forcing his tongue into my mouth. Hawkins locking the Love bracelet on my wrist while the camera snapped.

Ho led me down the hall and my heart thudded as we passed the alcove where Hawkins had promised to hurt Yates or even kill him, if we didn't break off our relationship. I wondered if he could get to Yates now that he was in custody. I wouldn't put anything past Hawkins.

The door, a sleek panel of ironwood, opened soundlessly. Hawkins sat in an artistically shaped wood and leather chair, a tablet in his hands, feet propped on a leather cube.

"Thank you, Adam," Hawkins said, dismissing Ho. Hawkins trained his cement-colored eyes on me and said coldly, "Welcome home, Aveline."

I stood, my chin held high, despite the percussion in my chest. "Yes, I'm back."

Hawkins set down his tablet and unfolded from the chair. I took in the unyielding pleats on his pants, the hard charcoal of his golf shirt, and the sharp edges of his belt buckle. He came up until he was only inches away. "I thought I'd lost you," he said, and slapped me hard.

I stumbled back, stifling a cry as pain shot through my ankle. *Screw you.* I lifted a hand to my burning cheek, ready for his next blow.

Hawkins glared at me. "Here is what will transpire. We will attempt to get the government to drop its case against you. If that fails, I, as a concerned and law-abiding citizen, will reluctantly turn you in. Understood?"

I nodded. I knew exactly what would happen if I fell into federal hands.

"However, if the government does drop its case, we will marry in a large, well-publicized ceremony after which you will accompany me as I campaign for governor. Again, is that clear?"

"Yes," I whispered.

"Good. Now get out of my sight."

I limped out of the room. It could have been worse, I thought. All Hawkins had done was slap me. And then it hit me: it would get worse. It was only a matter of time.

Deeps waited a discreet distance down the hall. I angled my face so he'd see the handprint on my cheek. Deeps didn't react, and his eyes didn't betray what he thought. "Come on," he said, "I'll take you up to your room."

The message was clear: Deeps was there to protect Hawkins' interests, not to keep me safe. Getting Deeps on my side wouldn't be easy.

He led me to an elevator and pointed out the buttons. "The gym, pool, theater, and safe room are below us on one. Main rooms on two. Bedrooms on three."

The elevator released us onto the walkway that overlooked the main room. "Mr. Hawkins' room is down the hall," Deeps said, pointing to the right. "Yours is at the opposite end."

Just a few steps away was a smooth wood door that opened at Deeps' touch. I entered a short hall which opened into a room that was glass on three sides. At first, the unlimited view of sky and water made it feel like the room was floating, but then I spied a twin glass box at the far end of the house. Hawkins' bedroom was over a hundred feet away, but he could see right into my room like I was an exhibit in his private zoo.

"No curtains?" I asked Deeps.

"They're recessed. I'll show you how to work them in a minute."

The room was as rigid and spare as the rest of the house. I couldn't have moved the low bed if I'd wanted to, because it was attached to the wall between two narrow shelves that worked as end tables. Two thin pillows lay on bedding the color of fog.

"The bathroom and closet are here." Deeps walked around the bed and pressed the sleek, wood-paneled wall. A hidden door swung open. Then he handed me a remote. "This controls your lights, curtains, and audio."

"Audio?"

"The house system is programmed according to Mr. Hawkins' musical preferences."

Not surprised I could choose what I wanted to listen to as long as it was what Hawkins liked. "Is the room monitored?"

"Yes, both audio and visual."

I sighed, and tossed the remote on the bed. "Your safety is important to us," he added.

That was bull. "Are you going to watch me undress?"

"The bathroom and closet are audio only."

"What about my clothes? Do they have mikes in them?"

Deeps shot me a look of respect. "No mikes, but some have a tracking device that's heat-activated. Execs whose families are vulnerable to kidnapping sometimes use this option over a chip."

I reached for my wrist without thinking, feeling a tiny burst of relief that Hawkins wasn't having me chipped. "Thanks." I didn't have much time to work on Deeps' sympathy before Ho and Hawkins made that impossible. "Did Jessop tell you that there are people who want to kill me?"

"Yes."

"So is the rest of the house safe? Is it monitored?"

"The safest locations are indoors. The terrace has visual, but the audio's not great what with the noise from the waves and the wind."

"All right. Thanks for telling me." Great. The only place I could talk openly was where everyone could see me. Not that I'd ever get the chance to be around anyone I wanted to talk honestly with.

"Anytime. I'll let you get some rest."

Deeps let the door close behind him. I went to lock it, but there was just a sleek chrome pull. I checked the front of the door, expecting to see a lock on the outside, but no. Hawkins, who was obsessed with control, had put me in a room I could walk right out of?

One glance at the door frame above my head answered that question. A remote-controlled, magnetic lock. Not hard to guess who had that remote.

A movement outside drew me over to the far window. Hawkins walked through the brush toward a grove of eucalyptus at the edge of the property. I touched my still-smarting cheek as he disappeared into the circle of trees. The silver-green branches tossed in the wind, allowing me glimpses of him pacing, and sunlight flashing off something metal?

"Observe your captor." I heard Ajax, my kidnapping-survival trainer, in my head, barking out a drill. "Habits, movements, preferences. Knowing these can inform your attempt to get away."

I looked from Hawkins to the ten-foot wall surrounding the compound. The only way out was if Hawkins turned me over to the feds. A sob rose up in my throat, and I threw myself into the bathroom and grabbed a towel from the stack. I shoved it over my mouth and turned the tub on full blast.

I will not let you hear me cry.

I rocked on the hard slate lip of the tub, my chest heaving as I smashed the towel to my face.

If the feds get hold of me, I'll never go home again. Never see Dad. Never say good-bye to Yates. Or Luke.

And they'll never know what happened to me.

I cried into the towel, not even trying to stop. Everything I'd held in since the Retrievers took me—the flight with Ho, Hawkins' slap— came out in a racking mess of tears.

But when they began to slow, I heard Ajax's commando voice again. "At some point you will want to give up. Your captor wants that, because you will make his life easier. But you cannot give up. Not if you want to go home."

I began to catch my breath and set the towel down. I had to get a grip. Hawkins was brilliant. He didn't want to turn me over to the feds. If he did, he wouldn't have brought me here.

The tub was full, so I turned off the water. Steam clouded the air and light filtered through the large glass-block window over the tub, illuminating the cold slate tiles that covered the floor and walls. I undressed and unwrapped my ankle, then lowered myself into the water.

Becca's dolphin still hung around my neck. I leaned back, and ran my finger over its silver fin. "Stay free!" I whispered bitterly, remembering her final message. Years of being Hawkins' captive flashed like clips from movie previews before my eyes. Me as Hawkins' toy. His First Lady. Mother to his children.

I sank down until the water reached my lips. At least Luke got away.

I stared into the steam, but saw him. Kind Luke with the gentle smile, the Luke I watched twirl his sister in the barn, who'd spun me around the dance floor, and who'd kissed me hours ago so we would both know what might have been.

I don't regret letting the Retrievers take me without a fight.

I prayed that Luke met the reporters and gave them the thumb drive. That he disappeared into the Rockies.

But what if he didn't make it?

The wall hanging lay in a heap with my clothes. I had to protect it and the phone, too. Deeps probably wouldn't suspect what the hanging was, so he'd leave it alone, but if he found the phone with Sparrow's audio file of her and Vice President Jouvert, Deeps would take it. I had to hide it, but where?

The bedroom was out.

I scanned the bathroom looking for a nook or cranny, but apparently Hawkins' designer didn't believe in them. Taping it underneath the sink wasn't an option, not when I didn't have duct tape or a way to get it.

I wrapped in a towel and picked up the phone. It was completely dead after two weeks without a charge.

The closet was all smooth, dark wood panels and the same slate floor. I ran my hands over the panels and they opened silently, revealing thirty charcoal gray and white striped garment bags filled with clothes that Hawkins' stylist, Elancio, had selected for my debut as the clone of Letitia Hawkins, Jessop's perfect mother.

I sucked in a breath. Somewhere in this closet was a collection of matching headbands. So what, I told myself. After everything you've survived, wearing a headband to please Hawkins is *nothing.*

The last panel opened to a column of shallow drawers. I tapped each so it rolled open, displaying artfully arranged workout wear, scarves, body skimmers, and not surprisingly, thirty custom headbands. No place to hide a phone, not well at least.

When I got to the sixth drawer, I flinched. I'd forgotten about the expensive bras and panties Hawkins had reserved for me at Sweet Fantasies. Memories from my extract gone wrong came flooding back. Sergio, the owner, showing me what Hawkins selected. Dayla laughing as she dangled the tiny scraps of silk and ribbon. "Mr. Jes, he loves the Naughty Angel collection!" What would I do if he told me to put these on? To come to his bedroom?

I shoved the drawer, but it resisted, and I shoved again, then pounded it as it crawled back into its slot.

Maybe he wouldn't touch me. Maybe he hated me too much to try.

Don't be stupid. You know what he's like. I threw off the towel and pulled on some yoga pants. Hawkins owned me, and now he had me in his clutches.

Dead at the hands of federal agents or Hawkins' prisoner? What kind of choice was that?

Hawkins would dictate what I did, where I went, what I wore, and who I saw.

And he wouldn't stop there. He'd control everything I saw or read or heard.

He'd control my body.

Everything. For the rest of my life.

I slid down, bracing my back against the wall, and stared at the wood door across from me until the pattern of the grain became an island surrounded by reefs.

No. Not everything.

Hawkins couldn't control what I remembered. He'd never be able to take away my memories of Yates or of Luke.

Or how I felt about them. Those memories, those feelings were mine.

And Hawkins couldn't control how I felt about him. He couldn't make me love him or respect him. He'd never have that.

And he couldn't control my thoughts, not as long as I fought his attempts to manipulate me.

I laid my head down on my fists. I sounded like that famous prisoner in the concentration camp who said he survived because he wouldn't let the Nazis own his thoughts. What a joke. That guy was damned lucky they didn't gas him.

I stuck the phone in the band of my yoga pants. I was just as deluded as he was, telling myself that protecting the phone still mattered. Still, I couldn't let Hawkins and Deeps just take it away from me. I had to find a place to hide it or at least try.

22

I took the elevator down to the bottom floor, praying that Hawkins was still up in his office. The phone hugged my hip, barely covered by my cropped hoodie. As I stepped out of the elevator into the dark hall, a soft light came on over my head. Hawkins' designer must have rigged sensors that picked up any movements.

The wine vault was to my left behind a glass wall. Hundreds of bottles lay on their sides in a wire rack that made them look like they were levitating. I tried the door, but it was locked.

Wood lined the back wall of the hall, the pattern of the grain so dramatic it must have cost thousands of dollars a foot. Hawkins had probably denuded an entire rain forest to get it.

I walked toward a sandblasted glass door, expecting it to be locked, too, but it swung open at my touch. Soft lights turned on, illuminating a long, greenish-blue pool. I walked over and dipped my hand into the warm water, feeling as if I'd descended into the depths of an Egyptian pyramid lined in smooth, caramel-colored stone, the lighting subtle and hidden. Like the rest of the house, the room contained minimal furniture, a small glass table and four chairs, but no nooks, no crannies, or clutter where I could stash the phone.

I shook my hand dry and slipped back into the hall. A long glass wall separated Hawkins' gym from the hall, and through the gaps between his cardio and weight machines, I saw the floodlit terrace and outdoor pool.

A faint rumble came from the direction of the elevator. *Dammit, I'm out of time.* I ducked into the gym, scanned the ceiling for the monitor, then turned my back to it. I plucked the phone from my waistband and dropped it on the carpet, then nudged it under the treadmill with my toe.

The treadmill wasn't a great hiding place, but no one was going to move this beast or try to vacuum under it. I pointed the remote at the big screen above it, so I'd look like I was trying to sneak a peek at the news. When the screen turned on, I realized I had access to all the channels. Hawkins hadn't set the Paternal Controls yet.

I flipped through, listening for Deeps and hoping that the reporters Luke met had broadcast their story and exposed Jouvert's treachery. But I didn't hear a single story about Jouvert. Either Luke hadn't made it to the rendezvous or the reporters hadn't filed the story yet.

What I did learn was that the world still thought I was at large. Hawkins was still running ads for 1-800-AVE-LINE while Ho worked their connections to get my charges dropped. According to one news report, I'd been spotted in forty-two states, including Hawaii.

I was about to change the channel when the reporter announced his guests: Dad and Dayla. *You've got to be kidding me.*

I sat down on the carpet, checking over my shoulder to see if anyone was in the hall. Hawkins must have arranged the interview. It couldn't be a coincidence.

I pulled my sleeves over my hands and held on as Dad and Dayla took their seats. Why did Hawkins have to do this to them? Why couldn't he leave them out of this?

Dayla came out fighting. "Listen, I know Avie better than anyone on the planet and I'm telling you, she's completely innocent. And she's not into politics, at all! She got like a B- in American government, because she hates all those boring theories and stuff."

Obviously, I was sucked in by the promise of freedom, Day insisted. I would never, never have run if it wasn't for outside influences. "Help a terrorist? Avie? Get real. She can't even drive and I know she's terri-fied of guns!"

Day blew me away, defending me so fiercely. She really believed every-thing she was saying about me, because those things used to be true.

Oh, Day, you think you know me, but you don't. Not anymore. Poli-tics isn't a bunch of boring theories. It's about girls like us.

I thought about Splendor saving money to buy her sisters' Contracts, and the girl trying to hold on to her family's ranch. And Mikhaela being forced to leave her grandma so her stepdad wouldn't get his hands on her.

Even though Hawkins had made Dayla his pawn, I couldn't hate her. Either she thought she was helping me or Hawkins hadn't given her a choice.

Then Dad spoke and my heart turned inside out. He'd made a huge mistake by Contracting me without asking me first, he said. He blamed himself for everything that had happened, and I felt like a ghost float-ing over my own funeral as he broke down. "Honey, please turn your-self in," he begged. "I'll help you any way I can."

I thought I didn't have any tears left, but my eyes filled. He was only forty miles away, but Dad might as well have been on the other side of the ocean. "That your father?"

Deeps strode toward me.

"Yeah."

He picked up the remote, and activated the Paternal Controls, then clicked off the screen. "Hard to watch, I bet."

I tilted my face toward him before wiping my eyes with my sleeve. I needed Deeps to see the tears I wouldn't show Hawkins, so he'd want to protect me. "So, if I asked to call my dad, I guess the answer would be no, right?"

"Until Mr. Hawkins gets your status amended, it's too dangerous." He ambled around the treadmill, and my heartbeat quickened.

"I gotcha."

Deeps reached under the treadmill and fished out my phone. "You know that the last thing you should do right now is to try an escape."

My thoughts raced. Hawkins could not get his hands on that phone. "I know that. I'm not trying to escape, I mean what's the point?"

"Good."

The phone disappeared into Deeps' pocket, and I got up slowly, making sure he saw me wince as I put weight on my hurt ankle.

"Those men who want to kill me are probably looking for some of the files I've got on that phone. Could you do me a favor and keep it safe?"

Deeps studied my face. "I should turn this in to my boss."

Please don't. "It could put him in danger. Why don't you lock it up where no one can find it? I promise not to even ask where you put it."

In Deeps' eyes, I saw rooms of secrets, sealed away, never to be opened. But somehow his secrets didn't scare me, not the way Streicker's had.

"All right," Deeps said. "For the time being, the phone stays with me."

I nodded. "Thanks."

"No problem."

I turned to go.

"Seminoles are on," he said. "I'm watching the game in the theater. You can join me."

I conjured up a small smile for him. I wasn't a huge football fan, but if cheering for the Seminoles could keep me safe and keep the phone away from Hawkins, I'd be happy to park my butt in Hawkins' cushy lounger for an entire season.

By the time the fourth quarter was over, I'd persuaded Deeps to give me the access code for the Sportswall that opened three, not exactly approved, news channels. I might be caged, but I refused to be ignorant.

When we left the theater, Deeps walked me out. Hawkins was running on the treadmill. His shirt was soaked through, but he was still going strong.

I heard Ajax's voice echo in my head. *Know your captor. Observe him.*

What does it matter? I wanted to snap back. I'm not getting away.

Situations change. Every day you survive is another day you might escape.

"Does Hawkins run every night?" I asked Deeps as we entered the elevator.

"Mr. Hawkins? I couldn't tell you. I just got here two days ago."

"Yeah? Where did you work before?"

"Confidential, Hummingbird."

"Hummingbird?"

"That's your code name since you're small and fast and a flight risk."

"I guess that's better than a lot of other things you could call me."

Deeps grinned. "Yeah, you don't want to know some of the other names I've heard people called."

He saw me to my room. "I'm not going to lock you in. There are sensors in the hall that will alert me if you leave your room. Go get a glass of milk. Fine. Open an outside door. Not fine. Are we good?"

"Yeah, we're good."

The door closed silently behind me. I couldn't lock it and there was nothing like a chair to prop against it. I picked up the remote and drew the curtains closed on the window facing Hawkins' room. It was stupid, but it was the only thing I could do to keep him out.

23

I barely slept. I'd drift almost to sleep, and then my mind would replay the interview with Dad and Dayla. I'd hear Dad begging me to give myself up, and I'd snap awake and kick off the sheets.

And no sooner would I begin to relax than I'd see Dayla acting her heart out, trying to kill the lies the media had spread about me, while her fingers couldn't stop twisting the strand of her hair.

They'd both betrayed me, but seeing their pain made me ache. "I don't blame you, Day," I whispered into the dark, wishing she could hear me. "Hawkins took advantage of you. That's what he does."

Deeps woke me the next morning telling me Ho was waiting downstairs. The skin under my eyes was the color of raisins. I pulled on the same workout clothes I'd worn the day before and didn't bother with a comb. What was the point?

Ho sat at the long, poured-cement table in the glass box of a dining area. I shoved my hands in the pockets of my warm-up jacket and slumped down across from him. He looked up from his ever-present tablet.

You don't scare me anymore. I've met way scarier guys than you. I know the only thing you care about is if I'm useful to your boss.

"The chef left some breakfast for you on the counter," Ho said.

I eyed the yogurt and blueberry parfait the chef had layered so prettily, but I didn't get up. "What are we here for?"

"We are here to reframe your story. Senator Fletcher's on his way from D.C. In order to get the government to drop its case against you, we need to convince him that you were an *innocent victim of circumstances beyond your control.*" Ho sniffed as he said the last part.

"So what do you need from me?"

"Let's start with Father Gabriel, the man who lured you into Exodus."

My stomach twisted, and I shoved my fists deeper in my pockets. "Father Gabriel's a good man."

"Father Gabriel is a lawbreaker awaiting trial on kidnapping charges. There's evidence linking him to over one hundred cases of girls who were Contracted to be married before he pulled them into Exodus."

"I won't testify against him."

Ho pursed his thin lips. "We won't let anyone put you on the stand."

Not because Ho cared what happened to me. "Because it would hurt the campaign, right?"

"Obviously."

"Father Gabriel didn't lure me into Exodus."

Hawkins strode in. "That's unfortunate, because someone did, and that leaves only Yates Sandell. But it's not surprising that your boy-friend enticed you to run."

I raised my face to Hawkins. *Go to hell.*

Yates had pushed me to join Exodus, but I would not give him up. "My friend Sparrow was planning to run, and she convinced me I should do it, too. She introduced me to Father Gabriel."

Ho tapped on his tablet. "Sparrow Currie, your classmate whose video accusing the vice president of federal crimes you broadcast nationwide."

All that was true. "Yes."

"But someone else must have helped you get away, because the day you Tasered your bodyguard, Father Gabriel was in jail and Sparrow had already left Los Angeles."

Yates had picked me up. Dr. Prandip had loaned us her car and Ruby had flown me to Vegas. The only way to protect them was to blame people who'd died.

"Sparrow had arranged a ride for me in the back of a pickup under a camper shell with two guys I'd never met before."

"You're a terrible liar," Hawkins said. "What color was the truck?"

"I don't know. Blue, maybe. It was dark."

Hawkins picked up the yogurt and set it down in front of me. "You need to eat."

"I'm not hungry."

"Starving yourself won't prove anything."

"I'm not trying to prove anything. I'm not hungry."

Ho cocked his head. "So, Sparrow Currie arranged for you to be delivered to Las Vegas, where Margaret Stanton *forced* you to become a hostess in her escort service."

"I wasn't forced. She manipulated me, but she didn't force me to do anything."

"For God's sake," Hawkins said. "Don't you *want* to live?"

My stomach hardened into a rock. I got up and stood by the window. I didn't know if I wanted to live like this, but I didn't want to die. "Yes, I was forced."

Ho and I worked through my story. How I'd briefly entertained clients, playing pool and getting them drinks.

"Margaret Stanton arranged for Sparrow to entertain the vice president during his visit. Is it possible Sparrow asked for that assignment?"

I rested my head on the glass. I had no idea, but I wouldn't have been surprised if she had. "I don't know."

"Ms. Stanton has been accused by the government of stealing defense secrets. She was a spy, wasn't she?"

She called herself a geisha. Maggie wasn't interested in defense secrets, she was only interested in how and why the Paternalists were limiting women's rights.

But if this was the lie I needed to tell to stay alive, then that was what I had to say. "Yes, she was a spy."

"Sparrow Currie manipulated you once more when she got you to forward her video accusing the vice president of wrongdoing. She shocked you into thinking she'd set herself on fire on the Capitol steps."

"She did set herself on fire!"

"The news footage shows a homeless man."

"The news footage is a lie!"

Hawkins shook his head. "Keep this up and you're going to get hurt."

"Really?" I said. "Are you going to hit me again?"

"I am the least of your worries."

I swallowed and looked away, before returning my gaze to Ho. "What else do you need me to tell you?"

"Margaret Stanton forced you to leave Las Vegas with her when the federal agents arrived. What happened to the other girls?"

"They fled the country."

"Do you think they'll come back?"

"I doubt it. They've got a good idea of what will happen to them if they do."

I began to pace along the windows. Through the glass by my feet, I saw waves crashing onto the jagged, black rocks below, and spray shooting high in the air.

"Ms. Stanton took you to Salvation, because she believed her lover, the man who died with her, would help her."

It was time to blame yet another innocent person who wasn't here to defend himself. "Yes, Barnabas."

"The father of her son, Luke?"

My throat tightened hearing Ho say his name. "I don't know anything about that. I barely met him."

"There's a search for the son," Ho said. "It's been on the news."

"I haven't seen the news."

My heart was pounding, and Hawkins must have sensed I wanted to bolt, because he stepped into my path. "How did Yates come to be in Salvation? We know you called him when you and Margaret Stanton left Las Vegas."

"I called him to say good-bye. We were being chased by federal agents. I was completely surprised when he found me."

Hawkins didn't trust me, but he believed me. I saw it in his eyes.

"Did you fire on federal agents?" he said.

"In Salvation? No. And why does that matter? We were trapped in the church under siege. They were trying to kill us!"

"There's a tape of you broadcasting a distress call that was picked up on the national news. It embarrassed the administration."

"Embarrassed the administration? Those men fired on a church full of children!"

Hawkins phone pinged and he slid it out of his pocket and glanced at the screen. "Adam, you can finish with her."

I stared at my bandaged foot, trying to slow my breathing as Hawkins' footsteps faded away.

"Very well," Ho said. "We will explain that your concern for innocent human life prompted your actions, not an attempt to save Margaret Stanton."

"Everyone in that church was innocent," I muttered.

"What did you say?"

"Nothing."

"You will need to explain why you didn't come forward after you fled Salvation."

"I was scared."

"But you got over your fear when you heard your fiancé on TV asking you to come home."

I cocked my head at Ho. *Offering a quarter-million-dollar reward isn't exactly asking me to come home.*

Ho stared back. *Do you have a better story?*

"Fine," I said.

"Good. I think we're done." Ho got up from the table.

"Wait. Do you think the feds will drop the charges?"

"I wouldn't bet on it. Your best chance is if Senator Fletcher can be persuaded."

One glance at Ho's face and I realized: *Ho thinks I'm already dead.*

The air left my lungs, and I shoved through the glass door to outside, and bolted down the steps for the terrace. I needed to get away, away from Hawkins and Ho and this house. On my left, the stairs fell off into oblivion, so I stayed close to the rock wall on my right, pulling in deep breaths of air, trying to fill my lungs.

Oh God, this is the end. I moved faster, seeing my hands shackled behind my back and Ho and Deeps turning me over to agents in SWAT gear.

The stairs curved around toward the terrace, and between the momentum and the urge to flee, I was almost at a run. So when something moved right below me I had to catch hold of the rock to stop myself.

A snake coiled on the step, its head raised to strike.

The air filled with the whirring threat of a rattle, and I must have screamed, because Deeps was suddenly there and, in one move, swung me up to the step behind him. "Go!" He stood over the snake as if they were in a standoff. "Are you hurt? Did it bite you?"

I hugged my arms to my trembling chest. "No. No, it didn't get me."

The snake slowly lowered its head, then slithered into the brush, its fat, diamond-patterned body stretching out to at least six feet.

"Next time, wear boots or let me do a sweep before you go outside. Usually rattlers hibernate about now, but sometimes they like to warm up on a rock."

My chest was heaving as I started back up the steps, the rattle echoing in my ears. Deeps passed me and went inside, and I stopped on the landing, taking in the scrub and the ten-foot-wall that cut the compound off from the world and prevented any chance of escape.

I don't want to die!

I let my head fall back. *But can I survive as Hawkins' prisoner?*

I don't know. I don't know.

A jagged ribbon of cloud floated overhead. *Stop and get a grip. Today. Right now, you're alive. Say it.*

Right now. I'm alive. They haven't beaten me yet.

I'm alive.

My breathing began to slow, and I shook out my arms and legs, and focused on the silvery horizon. *I'm okay. I'm okay.*

24

Senator Fletcher was expected to arrive sometime in the afternoon. Bees swarmed in my stomach. I desperately needed to run, but my swollen ankle had started throbbing again.

I searched the closet, found a racing suit, and snuck down to the indoor pool. Music came on when I entered the room, an annoying tinkling like temple bells as if I'd walked into an exclusive spa. I hobbled over to the control panel and cut the music. *Don't tell me to relax.*

The bees in my belly continued to mass as I dove into the water. I pulled myself along, making my arms do the work my bum ankle couldn't. Back and forth I swam, focusing every thought on the next stroke, the next breath, as the bees quieted and slowly flew off.

When Ho found me, I was catching my breath at the far end. I slowly swam back. He stood at the pool's edge, checking his tablet, the overflow lapping the polished toes of his alligator loafers. I surfaced near his feet with a splash that sprinkled his cuffs.

He glared at the tiny splotches on his pants. "Wear the ensemble in garment bag twenty-three, and be in *His* office by two-thirty." "His" with a capital *H*.

A shiver zipped up my spine. "That's when Senator Fletcher arrives?"

"Yes, and I suggest that if you wish to avoid federal prison that you act naïve and pliable and very, very scared."

"All right," I said quietly.

"Two-thirty."

"Yes, I got it." Ho despised me for all the trouble I caused, but I knew if Ms. Alexandra were here, she'd tell me to stop baiting him and fix that. Ho was almost to the door before I added, "I'll try not to mess this up."

Ho gave me a sidelong stare. "I sincerely hope you don't."

At exactly 2:30, I was at Hawkins' office wearing the assigned outfit: heather gray wool skirt and duckling-colored sweater with the bow at my collarbone. I'd put on the matching headband, figuring I could score a couple points with Hawkins with the tribute to his late, great mother.

I knocked on the door, and Ho came out. He looked me up and down.

"I wore what you told me."

"Yes, I can see that. When Senator Fletcher arrives, keep your hands in your lap and your eyes downcast. This is your role of a lifetime: the frightened little girl duped into betraying her fiancé by her unbalanced girlfriend and a charismatic priest."

"Got it." I took a deep breath and walked in.

Hawkins rose from his chair, and I knew I'd done something horribly wrong from the way he glared, his eyes fixed on my hair. "Don't you dare patronize me."

I froze.

"You think you can ingratiate yourself with me by wearing that thing in your hair? Take it off. Now!"

I slid the headband out of my hair. "I'm sorry—I thought—"

"Put it in the trash." He jerked his head at the leather wastebasket.

I walked over and dropped it in.

"I don't want to see you wear one of those ever again."

"Understood."

We both looked up as we heard the *chop-chop* of a helicopter overhead. "You'd better hope Senator Fletcher likes you," Hawkins warned as he went to greet our guest.

I sat down on the leather cube, my ankles crossed. I pressed down on my thighs, fighting the tremor jiggling my legs.

Then I heard Hawkins' voice in the hall. "I appreciate you coming all this way, Senator."

"Well, I couldn't very well have you come to D.C."

The silver-haired wolf of the Paternalist movement spied me the moment he walked in. I stood, head bowed, as he walked right for me.

"You're the little girl who's causing so much trouble."

"Yes, sir. I'm sorry about that."

I glanced up and saw Fletcher checking me out from my blond hair to my A-line skirt to my lightly mascaraed lashes. I held my breath, hoping he wouldn't recognize me as the smoky-eyed Capitol Hill intern-playing escort he'd met in Vegas.

"As I was telling you, Fletch, this is all a huge mistake," Hawkins said calmly.

"It's not a mistake," Fletcher shot back. "It's a mess. A huge god-damned mess, and it's sucking your candidacy down with it."

"Well, fixing messes is something I excel at. I've got the resources and connections to do it, all I need is your support."

The Fletcher I'd met at the party was charming, jovial—not this steel-eyed, pin-striped politico. "You expect me to believe this is an innocent little girl who didn't know what she was doing when she nailed Jouvert's balls to the wall?"

Fletcher pinched my chin and turned my head from side to side. "Wait. I met you that night in Las Vegas with Jouvert and that girl."

My stomach sank down to my slingbacks and I hung my head. "Yes, we've met."

"Aveline was forced to attend that party and entertain Margaret Stanton's guests," Hawkins said.

Fletcher leaned down until he was breathing in my face. "You sent out that video of your girlfriend accusing the vice president of the United States of being a liar, of committing crimes against this country before she lit herself up like an explosion at a fertilizer plant."

"I didn't know what was on the video," I stammered. "Sparrow told me to send it out. She even gave me the software to use." I was scrambling.

Hawkins tried again. "Aveline was not the mastermind, Fletch. She was the pawn of a girl whose medical records reveal she had serious emotional issues and an obsession with smearing the Paternalist cause."

I hated hearing Hawkins say that about Sparrow even though I'd said worse.

"Av-e-line," Fletcher said, drawing my name out to three tainted syllables, "went on the run with Margaret Stanton, an extremist and accused terrorist. They fled to a radical survivalist community that had stockpiled a cache of weapons and engaged in a shootout with federal agents."

I opened my mouth, but Hawkins shook his head no. "Aveline had no knowledge of Margaret Stanton, her political beliefs, or her crimes before she arrived at Stanton's penthouse. Margaret Stanton demanded Aveline leave with her, giving her no other option."

Fletcher jabbed the air in Hawkins' direction. "Your campaign is over! I will not stump for you, and neither will any of the big boys." He ticked three Paternalist names off on his fingers. "You are done in California!"

I had never seen anyone deny Hawkins what he wanted. Hawkins pulled himself up to his full height, his eyes narrowed and his hands defiantly on his hips.

I took a step back, as Fletcher delivered the final blow. "You have twenty-four hours to get your lawyers up to speed before I notify the authorities. I'll see myself out."

We listened to his shoes smack down the hall. I stood there, afraid to move and afraid not to.

Hawkins turned to me. "We're fucked. You and I are fucked. Do you understand that?"

I didn't nod or even blink.

"Ever since the day I met you, you've been screwing me over. Running around with Yates Sandell behind my back. Humiliating me with your dramatic flight to freedom. Costing me millions to create the fantasy that you were brainwashed by Exodus and Margaret Stanton and costing me even more to get you back. And now you fucking kill my campaign. Everything I worked for—destroyed!"

"I'm sorry. I—"

He grabbed my arms and shook me. "I should call the feds myself. Tell them to come pick you up right now."

I reeled back as Hawkins released me. "Get out of my sight," he said.

I scrambled for the door and took off down the hall.

25

Back in my room, I tore off the skirt, pulled on jeans and a jacket, and wrapped the hanging around my neck. There had to be a way out of the compound. I was not going to just let Hawkins turn me over to the feds.

He was yelling at someone on the phone, loud enough that I heard him in his office as I crept down the hall, hugging my boots to my chest. The double doors were silent as I let myself out.

Hawkins' car collection ringed the subterranean garage, millions of dollars' worth of gleaming performance vehicles in the first row and more lowly luxury SUVs parked behind them along the wall.

I circled the room, looking for unlocked cars, and checking to see if any had keys in them. I knew keys would be a long shot, but I thought that I'd at least find an opener for the gate clipped to a visor. No. Nothing.

I darted up the outside stairs to the parking circle and tugged on the boots, then doubled over and sprinted through the brush for the gate. My ankle was wrapped tight, but it still hurt like hell.

Cameras lined the security wall around the compound, so I prayed no one was looking at them right now. I made it to the wall and crept along, hoping I'd stay out of the cameras' reach. Finally I got to the gate. It was solid steel, the kind that rolled back on a track. I stuck my hand through the two-inch gap between the gate and the wall and felt freedom right outside.

I braced myself, and pushed with both hands, trying to force the gate back, but it wouldn't give. I tried twice more, throwing my whole weight against it. Nothing. I was trying to push a locomotive.

The steel was smooth. Nothing I could step on to pull myself up. I scanned the brush nearby looking for anything that might help.

It wasn't a minute later that I heard someone whistling behind me. My legs started to shake, and I laid my head on the gate as the notes of the Seminoles' war chant came closer.

The song petered out, and I turned around. "That gate's not going anywhere," Deeps said.

"Yeah, I figured that out."

"Come on back to the house, Hummingbird," he said gently. "You've got some time before the federal marshals arrive."

"I don't want to be inside right now."

"We'll hang out on the patio. Play some cards. Wait for the sunset."

I let Deeps take my arm and we started slowly back to the house. I clenched my hands, trying to control the shaking that was taking me over.

"Is there anything you'd like?" Deeps said. "Anything I can get you?"

The feds were going to kill me. I wouldn't make it out of L.A. County alive. Not unless I could get Deeps to help me. I stopped walking and turned to him. "You could let me go."

Deeps groaned.

"Please. Open the gate just enough so I can squeeze through. Give me a ten-minute head start before you tell Hawkins you can't find me."

"Let's not do this, Avie."

"Please. I promise I'll disappear."

"I can't, so stop asking."

"I'm sorry. I don't want to get you in trouble, but this is my life we're talking about."

A car flew by on the other side of the wall, and my eyes followed the beautiful sound.

"You got someone you want to talk to?" Deeps said quietly. "Maybe say good-bye?"

Yates. But Hawkins would die before he'd allow that.

"Can I see my dad?"

"I don't know if Mr. Hawkins will approve that, but I'll ask."

"Thanks."

Deeps reached in his pocket and drew out a black metallic sleeve. CELL SECURE was printed on the cover. He ripped open the Velcro and slid out my dead phone. "Here. You'll need this for your defense."

I turned it over in my hand. "The feds will never let me testify. They'll kill me first."

"What's in those files that scares them so much?"

Really? You don't know? "How about a recording that could get someone very high up impeached?"

"Damn. That would be worth a lot to the right person."

The right person would never get his hands on it. If Luke had succeeded in getting the thumb drive to the reporters, Jouvert's crimes would be all over the news. But either Luke missed his meeting, or the reporters were too scared to run the story, or they'd been permanently silenced.

How could I ever have thought we'd succeed against such impossible odds?

"Yeah, too bad you can't cash that in. I bet the guy on the tape would pay a million bucks to keep his business quiet."

Blackmail. The idea lit my brain like a search flare.

Could I trade this recording for my life? If I couldn't use it to sink Jouvert, maybe I could at least protect myself. "I need to talk to Mr. Ho."

At first, Ho didn't want to talk, but that changed when Deeps played him the first seconds of Sparrow's tape. Ho was suddenly so pleased to get the file, you'd think I'd given Hawkins a ten-point lead in the polls. "You were right to bring this to me," he said. His lips smacked together like he'd eaten a juicy tidbit. "I think we can do something with it."

I fled to my room where I bent over the toilet, and my empty stomach heaved acid up my throat. The cramping brought me to my knees, and I coughed and coughed as my body tried to rid itself of what I'd just done.

When the heaving stopped, I pulled myself up to the sink. The makeup I'd carefully applied was smeared and melted. I washed my face clean, then hung my hands under the water.

I heard Sparrow's breathy whisper teasing Jouvert, the rustle of clothing, his moan. I forced my eyes wide open, trying not to picture what Sparrow had done to get Jouvert to confess to her.

She gave her life to take him down, and I just threw that away.

Oh, Sparrow. I'm sorry. I'm so sorry.

My sweater was soaked and the sleeves sagged over my hands. I peeled it off and dropped it on the floor. Grape-colored bruises dotted my arms where Hawkins had grabbed me.

But desperate people do desperate things, right?

I didn't have another way out. If I hadn't done what I did, I would have been the next of Maggie's contacts to go missing. The Paternalists didn't want a public trial. They wanted silence.

I collapsed on the bed. In the eucalyptus grove at the edge of the property, I spied someone pacing and punching the air, and goose bumps ran up my arms as I saw it was Hawkins.

I hate you, I thought. *I'm glad you're suffering. You don't deserve to win.*

The afternoon crawled by as I waited for Jouvert's response.

Deeps insisted I leave my room and come outside. He carried a couple chairs out on the terrace and tried to teach me Texas hold 'em, but I couldn't focus. He had the chef make me chicken soup, but I threw it up. It was late in the afternoon when I tried asking him if I could call Dad and Yates. "You know I could be dead tomorrow. I just want a chance to say good-bye."

"Mr. Hawkins said no calls until we know your status."

"Please. I won't ask you for anything else."

"You have to be patient."

"How am I supposed to do that?"

Deeps shrugged. "The sun's going down. How about we go inside?"

"No, I want to stay out here. I want to listen to the waves."

Deeps brought me a cashmere throw so I could sit and watch the stars come out over the ocean.

I kept imagining black SUVs barreling down Hawkins' drive. Men in bulletproof vests, rappelling from a helicopter, and dozens of guns trained on me. Maybe there'd be an "accident" and I'd fly, shackled and handcuffed, out of the back seat of a Trailblazer off the Pacific Coast Highway and down the cliff.

The last rays of sunlight left the sky and I realized that Jouvert wasn't afraid of anything on that tape. So what if he'd taken a trillion in bribes from the Saudis? Jouvert knew that as soon as he made a deal with the Saudis for nukes, they'd put him in the Oval Office. He'd be the next president.

The feds would take me, but then at least I'd escape being Hawkins' wife and punching bag. I reached for Becca's dolphin around my neck.

I walked across the still-warm terrace and curled my toes over the stone edge. Black ocean and star-spangled sky spread out before me.

The wind lifted my hair and billowed the blanket around my shoulders into a sail.

For once, I was glad there was no railing between me and the water. I picked a cluster of bright stars way out over the ocean and lost myself in them.

The star twinkle made me wonder if heaven was real, and if Mom was waiting for me. I imagined her watching over me tonight, knowing I'd join her soon. She looked the way she was Before, smiling, her arms open to embrace me.

I didn't have to wait for Jouvert to decide my fate. And I didn't have to do what Hawkins wanted, either. I could decide. I felt my body lean, making a choice.

"Avie?" I recognized Hawkins' voice behind me, but not the careful tone. "I was looking for you."

All I have to do is let go.

"Avie."

I looked over my shoulder. Hawkins hung back about ten feet.

Good-bye.

"Don't you want to hear the good news?" he said.

A wave slammed into the rocks below, sending the force through my bones. "What news?" My voice sounded like it was coming from far away.

"Senator Fletcher has changed his mind about not campaigning for me. Actually, the entire leadership of the Paternalist movement has pledged their support. And do you know why?"

"Why?"

"Because Vice President Jouvert requested their cooperation. Once he heard a few seconds of his pillow talk with Sparrow, Jouvert was eager to help us."

Us? "Is the government dropping its charges against me?"

"That should be settled by morning."

I turned back to the water, dazed like I'd emerged from the wreckage of a tornado. The Paternalists would leave me alone, but now I had to survive Hawkins. I let the blanket drop and the wind threw it over the cliff. It fell in a slow jerky spiral before catching on the rocks below. A second later, a wave tore the blanket off, and it was gone.

"I wouldn't blame you," Hawkins said.

I didn't respond.

"Actually, I might do the same if I were in your position."

I peered at him. Was he *pretending* to understand?

"I shouldn't have hit you. Or shaken you today. That was wrong. I apologize."

I felt the last shreds of Fearless wake up inside me, and I stepped away from the edge. "Don't think your apology makes things right between us, because it doesn't. I don't forgive you. I will never forgive you."

Hawkins didn't move as I skirted around him and retreated across the terrace. On the way back to my room, I replayed what had just happened: Hawkins could have let me jump, but he didn't. He wanted something from me, I was sure of it, but I couldn't figure out exactly what it was.

I'd know soon enough, and I probably wasn't going to like it. But one thing I could guarantee, I would never let him hit me or shake me again. And I'd never let him touch me. Ever.

26

I was dreaming about kissing Luke when I began to awaken. We were back in the van on the side of the snowy highway, our lips breaking apart for a quick breath, before crashing together again. "Avie, come with me," he whispered. "We'll have a good life up in the mountains—we'll be free."

My eyes fluttered open, and I looked out, registering the wall and the grove of eucalyptus trees. I was in Hawkins' compound, but where in the world was Luke?

Had Streicker's contact given Luke a ride to the mountains or had he left Luke to fend for himself on the Denver streets? I felt sick, realizing it had been two days since I'd left him, and I wondered if he'd guessed what happened, or if he was cursing me for running away without a word.

When I turned over, there was a spray of orchids in a glass cylinder beside the bed. They were the palest pink, a flock of butterflies gathered on a stalk. I ran my finger along one waxy petal, chilled that someone had crept into my room and left them while I slept.

Nothing in this house came without a motive or strategy. Every gift had a price, and I knew I'd end up paying somehow.

Minutes later morning fog pressed against the windows, and erased the rest of the world except for the sound of the waves roaring against the rocks below. I pulled the duvet over my shoulders, wondering when Hawkins would demand to see me, and hoping that a campaign speech in San Jose or a crisis in Singapore had called him away.

When someone knocked on the door, I hesitated before I cracked it open. Deeps leaned on the door frame. "Mr. Hawkins has something planned for you. He'd like you to dress in the clothes you arrived in."

If Hawkins insisted I wear those jeans and boots and parka, it could only mean one thing. "Why? Did he change his mind? Is he turning me in?"

"No." Deeps pushed off the frame. "Nothing like that."

"What then?"

"It's good. You'll see."

The fog was lifting when we got into Hawkins' helicopter. Deeps was piloting and Ho was riding shotgun. We flew over the Malibu mountains, and were a few miles inland when the sky cleared. Sun poured through the windshield, and I unzipped my parka and pushed it down around my waist.

We headed east through the valley. The wide open spaces of

Wyoming and Colorado were erased from my mind as we flew over traffic-choked highways, dusty houses, and shopping malls. Where were we headed and why was I wearing this?

Ho and Deeps made small talk up front, acting like I wasn't there. We'd flown about twenty minutes when I realized Deeps was heading north and east. He was taking me home.

The charges against me must have been dropped! I was going to have a fresh start!

"You're taking me home!"

"That's right, Hummingbird."

Maybe Hawkins decided he was tired of dealing with me, that he'd had enough of drama and complications, and was ready to sell me back to Dad.

The hills that hugged my town came into view, covered with oak trees that spread over the winding streets, shading them. I picked out Dayla's house and her swimming pool, and two streets over, the house where Yates grew up.

We buzzed over the public library, my elementary school, and the grocery store. I tugged on my seat belt, ready to leap out.

My house appeared from between the sycamores, and we hovered above the back lawn. The helicopter sent waves across the koi pond and swimming pool, and shot dry leaves off the trees. It felt like I'd been gone for months, but everything looked the same. I was home!

Dad came out onto the terrace. "Dad! Dad!" I waved, crazy excited. Right behind him stood Gerard, our domestic manager, holding Dusty in his arms. She squirmed as if she wanted to snatch the helicopter out of the sky like a giant Frisbee.

Deeps touched down, and I tore off my seat belt and grabbed my parka. I poised at the door, ready to throw it open as soon as the blades stopped.

Ho crawled up behind me. "You don't need your coat."

"Yeah, I know, it's so warm out here."

He peeled it out of my hands. "You're not staying."

"What?" I felt my heart begin to shred.

"Jessop has approved a ninety-minute visit with your father."

I held on to the door latch. Ninety minutes, and then they'd return me to Hawkins to serve out the rest of my sentence.

Deeps caught my eye and winked, and I realized he'd gone to bat for me. "Thank you," I said, forcing my lips into a smile.

"It's safe to open the hatch," he said.

Dad ran toward me, and I leaped into his arms.

"Oh, Avie. Thank God, you're safe." Dad crushed me to him and I held on tight.

"Dad, I missed you so much."

"The news, those pictures of the shootout. I thought I'd never see you again."

"I know. It was awful."

He stroked my hair. "My girl, my precious girl. I'm so sorry."

I was done being angry with him. Hawkins had screwed us both over, and Dad had tried to get me free, but nobody controls Hawkins.

"I'm sorry, too," I said. "Everything turned into such a disaster, and I wanted to let you know I was alive, but I couldn't."

We held each other for another minute while Dusty bounced around our feet. When Dad released me, it seemed as if he couldn't bear to pull away. I lifted Dusty into my arms and rubbed my face against her fur. Dad ruffled my hair.

"You and Dusty are wearing the same haircut."

His eyes were pinched, and I knew he was forcing himself not to ask why. "It'll grow out."

Gerard waited on the terrace, wearing a dress shirt as if I was a special guest. Gerard, who'd guessed I would run, who'd covered for me with my bodyguard, and who'd sneaked me money.

I walked up so we were just an arm's length apart. I could sense Gerard wanting to reach for me, but touching me was forbidden in his employment contract. Then Dad took Dusty from my arms. "It's okay, Gerard. I would never fire you over a hug."

Gerard leaned down and wrapped me awkwardly in his arms. I hugged him back, conscious of how stiffly he held me against his tall, slender body. There was so much we couldn't say aloud, because it would tip Dad off to how he'd helped me, so we just mumbled how glad we were to see each other.

I tried to push back the shakiness, to keep the tears gathering inside me from spilling out. But when Gerard said, "How about some cinnamon toast?" it hit me that home is about small things that the people who love you remember. "Yeah," I said, my lip starting to tremble, "that would be really nice."

Ho shooed us toward the French doors. "We should get inside. We don't want your neighbor to be tempted to send photos of you to the tabloids."

Gerard set up a tray for Dad and me in the library. As he shut the door, I heard him invite Ho and Deeps to help themselves to coffee in the kitchen.

Dusty curled beside me on the couch, her head on my leg. Dad pulled his chair close. His skin was pale, almost ashen, the way he got from spending too much time in the lab. He looked so old. "I tried using my contacts in Washington to find out what's happening in your investigation," he said, "but I've been frozen out."

"It's okay. Hawkins is getting the charges dropped."

"That's great! What a relief!"

"Yeah. It's a big relief."

"But how did he accomplish that? It couldn't have been easy."

I couldn't look Dad in the eyes, couldn't tell him what I'd done. "He pulled some strings."

"Well, he must have some powerful allies. I'm glad to know Jessop's looking after your interests."

"Dad, this is Jessop we're talking about. He's looking after his interests."

Dad hung his head. "I swear I tried to break your Contract, Avie. I even tried to force him out."

"I know," I said quietly.

Dad looked up. His sagging shoulders made my heart ache.

"Yates told me how you tried to buy out my Contract. How you tried to bring in other investors and even offered to leave Biocure. The fact you did that meant a lot to me."

"Is Jessop treating you decently?"

I knew the truth would break Dad's heart. He'd blame himself for failing to get me free. "So far," I lied.

We sat, not speaking for a moment. I got the feeling Dad wanted to believe me, but didn't, and yet he didn't want to force me to tell him what was really going on.

"How's Dayla?" I said. "I saw you in that interview."

"She's fine. Excited about the baby."

"That's good." Dayla'd been through so much, being locked up in Fetal Fed, and losing the guy she really loved. She deserved some happiness.

"Her new husband came with her."

A feeling of sadness washed over me. "What's he like?"

"He seems like a decent young man, hardworking—"

"But I thought—"

"Yes, originally she was Contracted to the father, but for some reason that changed."

"So how's Dayla doing in Montana? I mean, I can't imagine her living on a ranch."

Dad reached for my hand. "Avie, can you tell me what happened in Las Vegas with Sparrow? And who was that woman, Margaret Stanton, you got mixed up with?"

I wanted to tell Dad the truth. I was tired of lying, and Dad would understand why I'd done what I did. And I wanted to share with him what I'd learned—about myself, and the bizarre things going on in the country.

"Dad, I can't tell you everything; I wish I could, so please don't ask me a lot of questions."

He held my hand while I told him about Maggie, and how she was an ex-lawyer, gathering evidence against the Paternalists. I connected the dots the media had publicized, but I didn't fill in the blanks that could put Dad in danger as I revealed the true story of Sparrow's suicide, me broadcasting her suicide video, and the federal agents chasing Maggie and me to Idaho. I'd just started to describe Yates finding me when Dad said, "Yates told me about what happened in Salvation."

"You talked to him?" Dad hadn't had a conversation with Yates in years. "When?"

"A few days ago. I drove up to Atwater Penitentiary to see him. I hoped he could give me a clue as to where you were."

"How is he?"

"He's healing. He told me about the trek up the mountain, and how you pulled him out of that tree. You saved his life—and many others, it sounds like."

Dad wanted to make me into a hero, but I didn't feel like one, not after what I'd just done to save my own life. "Yates saved me as much as I saved him. He's a good person, Dad. I just wish you could see that. I'd never have made it up the mountain if it wasn't for him."

"Hey, calm down. It's okay. I know you think I don't like him and that was why I kept you two apart, but that wasn't it."

"Then why did you keep us apart?"

"When his father Contracted Becca, I finally learned the truth about his gambling problem. I had to put distance between our families. I couldn't be friends with my business partner, if there was a chance he'd do something that could harm the company. Then when Roik warned me that Yates was attracted to you, I felt I had to put a stop to it."

I stroked Dusty's ear, trying to take in what Dad had told me.

"Yates has more than proven himself to me, Avie. I understand what you see in him."

I love him, Dad, I wanted to say, but what good would that do? "Do you think they'll let him go? Since they dropped the charges against me, won't they drop them against Yates, too?"

"I don't know, honey. I suspect Jessop Hawkins likes having Yates right where he is, but I offered to help Yates if I could."

"Thank you."

"Don't thank me yet. I haven't done anything."

Dad tried to get me to tell him where I'd been and who I'd been with since I left Yates. "It's better if I don't," I said.

"Ah, someone you'd like to protect."

I nodded. "Yeah."

The hour and a half went too quickly. Gerard came in before I was ready. "Mr. Ho would like to know if there's anything you'd like to take with you?"

"How about my freedom?"

"Not so loud," Dad murmured.

"Sorry."

"What about Dusty? Do you think Jessop would agree to you having her?"

Hawkins wouldn't tolerate fur on his pristine floor, and he'd freak over her barking. "She couldn't go outside, Dad. She could get bitten by a snake." I got up from the couch. "I'm going to check my room."

"Honey." The tone of Dad's voice stopped me. "They went through your bedroom while you were gone."

"You mean Hawkins' Retrievers?"

"No, the FBI."

I flew up the stairs. Dad wasn't kidding when he said they went through my room. It looked like a psycho had had an episode there.

I walked carefully over the ripped carpet. The agents had torn out sections of wallboard, leaving the wiring and dirty pink insulation exposed.

My bureau and desk were cleared off, and Mom's DVDs were missing from my bookcase. I guessed Roik had my laptop, because he'd traded Yates my photo files for his motorcycle when I disappeared.

My closet was in even worse shape than the room. Every panel of wallboard was cut open. My clothes and shoes were piled on the floor amid the wreckage of hangers and flattened shoe boxes. I dropped to my knees and picked up one of the pumps I wore to Dayla's Sweet Sixteen. The satin-covered heel looked like it had been smashed with a hammer. "What the— Did some jerk think I hid secrets in here?"

I spied a torn scrap of sparkly wrapping paper and carefully slid it out from the wreckage. I smoothed the unicorn's crumpled horn. *Oh no. They didn't.*

I dove into the pile, tossing clothes out of the way, searching for the box where I'd kept Mom's letters, the one covered in glittery pink unicorn paper. My hand closed around the lid, which I tossed aside, and a moment later I found the remains of the bottom.

"Dad! Dad!"

I flung armfuls of clothes out of the way, looking for even a scrap of the lavender-colored paper Mom loved to write on.

I love you. I love you. I love you. Mom had covered two sides of a page, writing it over and over in every color before she died. I love you.

"Avie, what happened? What's going on?" Dad crouched beside me, his eyes scanning the mess.

"They took Mom's letters. I can't believe they took her *letters!* Why would anybody do that?"

Dad squeezed my shoulder. "It will be okay. Our lawyers recorded everything they took. We'll get Mom's letters back, I promise."

I stared at him, thinking how naïve Dad was to believe that. He didn't know what these guys were capable of.

Dad gave me a hand up and I went around my room for the last time. I thought we'd walk downstairs together, but he disappeared, once again leaving me for some work crisis.

At least we had our hour and a half.

But when I got to the bottom of the stairs, Dad came out of the library, holding a small stack of purple envelopes. "Your mother didn't only write letters for your birthday." He pressed them into my hand. "I think she'd want you to have these now."

My eyes filled, seeing my name in Mom's exuberant green scrawl. "Thanks, Dad."

He nodded, and I saw Dad fight to control himself as Ho appeared behind him. "We shouldn't keep Mr. Hawkins waiting."

"Yes, of course," Dad answered.

I slipped the letters inside my shirt, making sure Ho saw. They were mine, and Ho needed to know that he and Hawkins weren't going to get a glimpse of them without a fight.

Deeps waited by the helicopter as Dad walked me out, his arm across my shoulders. "Is there anything you'd like me to tell Yates, if I go back to Atwater?"

"Tell him—" *What?* Nothing I could say would make a difference. Love couldn't save us. It wasn't the escape. Love couldn't always slip free of the knot. "Tell Yates that I love him, and I'm sorry, but I have to marry Jessop Hawkins."

Dad shook his head. "Damn it, Avie, I'm sorry. I wish I knew a way out of this."

"Yeah, well, there isn't any." I felt my throat tighten. Yates had to understand. He had to know that this marriage wasn't my choice.

I climbed into the helicopter, and Dusty leaped up on the metal step, trying to follow. "No. Get down," I told her, nudging her off, but she came right back. I shoved her off again, harder this time, but she circled the step, darting away from Deeps before she tried again. My eyes filled, and she turned into a fuzzy white blur. "You can't come!"

Gerard walked over and scooped her up, and then carried her into the house.

I wiped my eyes on my sleeve and waved to Dad. This was the first time I could remember that he didn't rush off after saying good-bye to me. Today he stayed out on the terrace, and waved until we were out of sight.

27

Deeps flew us back to Hawkins' compound, but this time he followed the Pacific Coast Highway. The fog had lifted over Malibu, revealing the miles-long line of beach houses holding on to the narrow strip of land between the highway and the ocean.

I was on my way to my new life as Mrs. Jessop Hawkins. How was I going to survive him? Moment by moment, I guessed, of me trying to stay on his good side.

Down below, a few surfers were still riding the late-morning waves. Yates used to surf this spot, I remembered, even though Zuma Beach was better. I dug in my pocket for a tissue.

Yates would never be free again to surf here with his friends. Hawkins wouldn't want Yates freed. No, Hawkins would do everything he could to eliminate even the slightest chance that Yates could reappear in my life. And Fletcher? He'd never agree to let Yates go. Not after everything Yates had witnessed.

Tell Yates that I love him, and I'm sorry, but I have to marry Jessop Hawkins.

Yates had to understand. He had to. I had no choice. We were both imprisoned, only in different ways.

We flew past Pepperdine University, and the houses thinned out. "How soon until we arrive at the compound?" Ho asked.

"Six minutes."

"Good, I'll let Mr. Hawkins know."

I stared out at the last few miles of freedom. I would never call Hawkins' compound home. Home wasn't where you were locked up against your will.

We were more than a mile away, when I saw a line of cars and news vans, snaking up the coast. As we got closer, I realized they were parked along the compound fence.

"What's going on?" I said into my headset.

"Your homecoming," Ho answered. "You are returning to your fiancé, grateful and relieved to be back from your ordeal."

Now I got why I had the parka. I had to pretend this was the moment of my big return to civilization and safety, and my reunion with the man of my dreams.

Vans with KTLA-5 and other news station logos clogged the road, equipment sprouting from their roofs like ray guns. *Oh God, look at them.*

Someone must have paid off the electric company, I thought, counting at least thirty Department of Water and Power trucks with big orange buckets on telescopic arms, and men standing in them, huge videocameras on their shoulders. The cameras were trained on Hawkins' landing pad like weapons on a target.

The manhunt for me was over. And now we were going to act like my being called a terrorist was all a big misunderstanding.

My heart pounded, seeing the hundreds of men awaiting my arrival.

A dozen reporters must have made the A List, because they and their crews jostled for space at the edge of the landing pad. Deeps circled closer, and Ho was texting furiously, but Hawkins hadn't emerged from the house.

"What am I supposed to do when we land?"

Ho turned to me and spoke into his headset. "Put your hat on. Oh, and if I were you, I'd make sure everyone saw how happy I was to be reunited with my fiancé."

I tugged the knit hat over my blond hair.

"Pull it down over your eyebrows, too," Deeps added.

I pulled the hat down even more and crammed loose strands up under it. Deeps must have a reason for saying that. "Will I have to answer any questions?"

"No," Ho replied. "Jessop will say a few words, then I will read a prepared statement."

My heartbeat echoed the *chop-chop-chop-chop* of the rotors. Why was I nervous? It wasn't like anyone would try and shoot me. Or—

"Deeps, all these reporters, is this safe?"

"See the yellow jackets? They're security." A squad of men in chrome-yellow jackets walked the walls along the compound, and more guarded the landing pad.

Deeps touched down and the rotors stopped. Ho dragged two fingers down his face.

Cry. I got it.

Hawkins appeared, and the cameramen surged forward. The hired security guys moved down the line, pushing them back. I climbed down on the landing pad into an eruption of voices shouting out my name. "Aveline! Avie! Over here, Avie!"

Hawkins walked toward me, his arms outstretched, relief carefully choreographed on his face. I ran to him, exaggerating my limp, and threw myself into his arms and buried my face in his chest. The musky scent of his cologne and the feel of his body against mine made my stomach heave, and I had to fight the urge to shove him away. *Keep it together. You can't show how you really feel.*

The cameras let loose a machine-gun fire of clicking as Hawkins held me. "Nicely done," he whispered into my hair.

Hawkins cradled me under his arm, and we walked to the podium. I kept my face pressed against his chest, trying to dodge the cameras. "Today I am a happy man," he announced, "owing to the return of my dearest Aveline. I ask that you respect our need for privacy, and I thank you for sharing this joyous occasion."

Hawkins guided me down the stairs until we were out of sight, then he stopped to listen to Ho read his statement.

"After the terrifying shootout with federal agents in Salvation, Idaho, Aveline Reveare feared for her life. Thanks to the help of the media, Aveline was able to reach out to her fiancé, Jessop Hawkins, and request assistance to return home. Aveline is not charged with any crime at this time, and our lawyers anticipate that she will be cleared of any suggestion of wrongdoing. She sustained minor injuries during her ordeal, and after a brief period of recuperation, we anticipate that she will join Candidate Hawkins on the campaign trail. I will take questions."

Reporters shouted out questions as Hawkins and I shut ourselves inside the house. He released his hold on me. "You did well out there. Facing the media can be intimidating, but you handled it like a pro."

I nodded and started toward my room. I didn't care how well I'd done. All I wanted was to be alone with Mom's letters. I'd only gone a few feet when Hawkins said, "Did you enjoy your visit with your father?"

Maybe if I acted grateful, he'd let me see Dad again. I forced myself to turn around. "Yes, thank you."

Hawkins lingered. He wanted something more, but I refused to share how much it meant to me to see Dad.

"I am not evil, Aveline."

Saying that only proves you are. "I never said you were."

"But that is what you think."

I wasn't touching that. Hawkins waited for my reply. I'd saved his campaign, and he gave me what I'd asked for. What more could I get if I cooperated?

"Maybe we could start over," I said. "You can show me what you're really like."

A smile bent his lips and his eyes relaxed. "Yes. We should."

My breath caught as Jessop took a step closer, but then Ho blew through the door. "That went brilliantly." His fingers were doing a happy dance on his cell. "We're on ninety-two stations worldwide, including Al-Jazeera, and barring a terrorist attack on American soil in the next five hours, Aveline's return will be the lead story."

Hawkins clapped him on the back. "Outstanding work. Time to plan our next move."

The two of them headed downstairs, and I retreated to my room and took Mom's letters out from under my shirt.

I pressed the stack to my nose, but the lavender-oil scent Mom used to spritz on my letters was long gone, and the purple envelopes had yellowed around the edges. At least I have them, I thought, seeing "Happy 17th Birthday!!!!" scrawled on the one on top.

I slid a finger under the flap. My birthday was a few weeks away, but I needed Mom now.

"Happy Birthday, my dearest girl."

I bit my lip, reading the first sentences. "What a big year this will be for you. In a few weeks, you'll be visiting colleges. I'm sure your dad would love to have you close in California, but I know you might like to try your wings and go east."

A huge lump formed in my throat. *I tried my wings, Mom. I tried so hard, and they almost took me to freedom before I fell.*

I skimmed the rest of her letter. Mom was so excited, imagining me touring campuses in Boston and Connecticut. "Now don't write off the East just because it's cold and bleak when you and your father visit."

I could barely stand to read her list of hopes and dreams that would never come true, so I skipped to the end, where I knew her "I love you" would be waiting for me.

Down near the bottom of the page, I found it. "I love you more than the stars. Mom." And right below was a P.S.

"People will push you to choose the college they like, but don't let them pressure you into a choice that feels wrong. It's your life and you're the one who has to live with the decision. I would hate for you to know the misery of living with regrets."

I folded the letter gently and tucked it back into the envelope. *I already do, Mom. I already do.*

28

The media hung around for hours. I stayed away from the windows, and my fishbowl of a bedroom, finally ending up in the indoor lap pool, a place I'd figured out that Hawkins rarely used.

I dimmed the recessed lights over the sandstone walls, until the room was black except for the aquamarine water. The glass tiles sparkled like opals in the underwater lights. I dove, imagining myself a thousand miles away in an underground cave.

I must have swum a mile before Deeps came to tell me the coast was clear. He crouched by the edge. "Mr. Hawkins expects you to have dinner with him at seven," he said.

I stood and pushed my dripping hair off my face. This was the first time since I was Retrieved that Hawkins wanted to eat with me. "Does he have guests coming?"

"No, just you two." Deeps flicked some water at me. "You might want to ditch the sweats."

"They're workout clothes, not sweats."

"Whatever, you've worn them nonstop for the last three days."

I stuck out my tongue and Deeps laughed. He pushed his henley up to the elbows, exposing the tattoo on his forearm: *Semper Fidelis.*

"*Semper Fi.* Isn't that the *Navy* motto?"

Deeps smacked the water so it sprayed in my face. "Marines!" I paddled away as he got to his feet. "Be in the dining room at seven!"

"Aye, aye, Captain."

Hawkins' gym was deserted when I came out of the pool. I knew my face was probably still all over the news, but I hoped to find at least one story that would prove that Luke had reached the reporters.

I played with the elliptical controls, and discovered that the access code Deeps gave me worked every channel, as if he got how badly I needed news of the outside world to survive. It was my oxygen.

I muted the audio and clicked through twenty channels running stories on my dramatic return before the screen filled with a close-up of Jouvert. I shivered and wrapped my spa robe tighter over my wet racing suit.

Sunshine poured down on Jouvert's brown, sculpted face. He grinned a big bleached-white smile, and his green eyes crinkled at the edges as if he couldn't be happier.

Acid rose in my throat as I heard his and Sparrow's voices in my head, her murmured questions, and his arrogant, satisfied claim that he'd made the deal with the Saudis. Then I saw Sparrow lift the water bottle over her head and flick her lighter.

My knees went soft and I leaned against the machine. Sparrow should never have trusted me with her secret.

She sacrificed herself to get Jouvert's confession, and I'd traded it away to save my own life.

I reached to shut off the screen, but the camera pulled back, showing the crowd filling the open square that was edged with desert palms. The sky stretched clear and blue above the faded stucco storefronts. Jouvert was in Arizona or New Mexico—just hours from Denver.

My skin prickled as the camera panned the crowd of men in baseball and cowboy hats, and my heart stopped when I saw a black cowboy hat with a big spray of feathers on the band. *No. It can't be.* I paused the controls. The man's head was dipped, his eyes hidden by the hat brim, so I clicked through the frames. *Look up. Show me your face.*

The camera moved on, but I couldn't. What if Luke hadn't met the reporters?

Maybe that was Streicker's plan all along. Get me out of the picture. Send Luke to meet a couple of fictitious reporters, and when they don't show, Luke goes back to his original plan to kill Jouvert.

I tried to visualize the back of the van, anything that could have hidden a rifle, but I couldn't remember what was in it.

But Luke didn't need a rifle. He already had the gun he'd brought with him.

Or maybe Streicker had nothing to do with this, and Luke went rogue. Streicker wouldn't report that the van was stolen if Luke drove off with it. He wouldn't want the law snooping around.

Cold water trickled down my legs as I clicked through the frames, searching for the man in the black hat. He never reappeared, but I did learn the rally was in Phoenix.

The sky was dark outside, so the rally had to be long over, and Jouvert was safe. Otherwise, the story would have been the shooting.

I hoped I was wrong, thinking that Luke was stalking Jouvert, and that he'd met the reporters and was hidden high up in the Colorado Rockies. But I realized I'd never know if Luke was safe. The only way I'd hear about him was if he was arrested or killed or went through with his threat against Jouvert. Then the media would broadcast every gory detail.

The news ended, telling me I was late for dinner. Even if I didn't feel like eating, I had to show up for my first meal alone with Hawkins.

Upstairs, Elancio had labeled all the garment bags in my closet with tags that said "Political Donor Barbecue" and "Kern County Rally," but none said "Post-Retrieval Dinner for Two." I dug through the rack, until I found the least heinous outfit. A simple, dark blue dress that would almost have been cute—if it didn't make me look forty.

When I came down to the dining area, the lights had been dimmed. Hawkins was sitting at the far end of the long, cement table, a line of votive candles leading to him.

He stood up when he saw me. Instead of a steel-colored golf shirt or crisply pressed button-down, tonight he wore a moss-green cashmere V-neck with nothing under it.

I swallowed and my stomach plunged. The candles, the outfit. *He's trying to be romantic.* I tried to smile, but couldn't, as I walked over to the place at his side that was set for me.

The open kitchen had disappeared behind a translucent panel, giving us privacy I didn't want. Hawkins' chef was a blur behind the amber-colored glass.

Soft music muffled the sound of crashing waves, but the room shuddered faintly when a big one hit.

Hawkins drew back my chair. "You look very nice this evening," he said.

I held my arms close to my body, trying not to brush him. "Thank you."

Hawkins gave a short, embarrassed smile that put my inner self on alert. "You never say my name. I'd like to hear you say it sometime. Jessop."

"All right. Jessop."

Hawkins poured me a glass of wine without asking. I didn't want to drink. I couldn't risk being vulnerable around him. "I don't like wine," I said.

"You must learn to tolerate it if you are going to be the wife of the next governor of California."

I crushed my napkin in my lap. The governor's wife. Right.

"All I ask is that you take three sips."

I made myself smile. "Sure, I can do three." I took the first sip. Sour.

"Don't swallow." He touched my hand and I flinched. He pretended not to notice. "Let the wine sit on your tongue. What does it remind you of? Citrus? Apples? Pears?"

My answer didn't matter, but appearing cooperative did. "Pears," I said.

"See, not so hard."

The chef came out with our salads, greens with blackberries, something he shouldn't know I liked. It had to be a coincidence.

Hawkins started to talk about growing up in Montecito, and going to boarding school in Ojai. He asked me questions about what sports I played at Masterson and what classes I liked. It was bizarre, him acting like he wanted to get to know me when he knew I could barely stand him.

The feeling that Hawkins was up to something got stronger when the chef set down a plate of crusted mahi mahi. Three weeks before, Hawkins had forced me to sit through lunch with a bloody steak in front of me and wouldn't let the chef remove it, but tonight?

"You seem confused," he said.

"I thought you didn't like fish."

"I prefer fish to meat, actually."

If you say so. I cut into my fish as Hawkins peered at me.

"Oh," he said, "you're thinking about the lunch with the Biocure board. I serve beef, specifically five-hundred-dollar-a-pound Kobe beef, when I need to remind people I'm in control."

That's why he wouldn't let the chef take away my plate. He needed me to know he was in control.

"But that is not what this evening is about," he said.

"What is this evening about?"

"It's about getting to know one another since our futures are firmly entwined."

I took a second sip of wine and slid my glass away. All this posturing and pretending was pointless. I felt like it was time to get real. "Why do you want to be governor, anyway?"

Hawkins cocked his head, surprised I'd asked. He took a moment before saying, "You were probably too young to remember what it was like during the Scarpanol disaster."

"I lost my mom. I remember way too much."

"Of course," he said quickly. "I'm sorry."

I blinked. He'd apologized like a normal human being? Like he had *feelings*.

"Your parents must have tried to shelter you from what was going on." He swirled the wine in his glass before taking another swallow.

"Yes, they did."

"It was chaos. America was falling apart. Millions of women were dying, but hospitals were shutting down, because there weren't any nurses. The stock market tanked. The housing market collapsed. Men were rioting in the streets."

"And?"

He set down his glass. "I survived. My companies survived, because I did not panic. I saved the jobs of sixty-three thousand employees while I watched Washington make one stupid mistake after another."

"So, you're smarter than everyone else."

Jessop smirked. "I wouldn't say everyone, but I remained clearheaded while our nation's political leaders were led to make hasty and ill-considered decisions by the media and their precious donors and special-interest groups."

The chef brought out chocolate mousse, another favorite of mine. This was not a fluke; Hawkins planned this. I took one bite, but the mousse was so rich, I thought I'd be sick. I set my hands in my lap while Hawkins ate quietly. He seemed to have something on his mind. I couldn't help thinking how weird it was that when I asked him about being governor, he didn't praise the Paternalists. In fact, he'd almost insulted them.

Hawkins wiped his mouth, then reached for my wrist. I jerked my arm away. *You think I'd let you touch me?*

"I suppose I deserved that," he muttered. He glanced at the shadows moving in the kitchen. "Our fortunes are now tied," he said, keeping his voice low. "We took a risky and irrevocable step last night, you and I. Blackmailing a vice president is not a game we can afford to lose."

My skin prickled. "And?"

"Great dreams require great risks, Aveline. Jouvert has always distrusted me, and what we did last night—"

"Why didn't he trust you—I mean, before?"

"Because I don't need his help the way his cronies do. I can pay for my own campaign, and Jouvert likes his political allies beholden to him so he can tell them exactly what to do.

"We must be careful about everything we say and do in public and in the media. We cannot have any more scandals. We need to keep the Paternalists happy and win this election. Otherwise—"

I saw Maggie hold up the banner. I SURRENDER. Saw her body slammed to the ground.

I shuddered. "Jouvert will have us killed."

"I don't think he'd go that far."

Either you're blind or you're a fool to believe that.

"Given what I just said, we need to talk about Yates Sandell."

Nausea climbed my throat. "Why?"

"Are you still in love with him?"

How dare you ask me about Yates?

"You know how foolish that is."

I stared at a red stain in the cement and shook my head. *I refuse to talk about him with you.*

"He's facing trial for kidnapping alongside Father Gabriel, and Gabriel *will be convicted.* The evidence is overwhelming."

Shut up. I don't want to hear it.

"We could have a life together if you would give up your unyielding devotion to him."

"Are you kidding me?" I balled up my napkin and threw it down on the table. "That's not how love works! I can't stop feeling what I feel!" I shoved my chair back from the table and began to walk away.

"Given that you still love Yates, how far would you go to save him?"

I turned around slowly. "What?"

"What would you be willing to do to set Yates free?"

I stood there, meeting Hawkins' gaze, but not saying a word. Then he crooked his finger, telling me to come closer, and I obeyed.

No matter what Hawkins asked me to do, I wouldn't betray my love for Yates. I'd stay true to him.

Hawkins took my hand, and I fought the urge to shake him off. "What if I could get the charges dropped against Yates?" he said.

"What would I have to do?"

"You commit a hundred percent to appearing to be my loyal, supportive spouse. On the select occasions when we are in public together, you will clap and cheer for me, hold my hand and kiss me for the cameras."

I had to give Hawkins credit. He knew the deal I couldn't refuse. One half threat, the other seduction. "Is that it?"

"You promise that you will not embarrass either of us by attempting another escape."

"All right." What was the point in trying when I'd never succeed?

"You promise to do everything that I ask."

"Everything?" I shook my head. I couldn't, not if it meant—

"Relative to the campaign," Hawkins added, clearly annoyed he'd had to say it.

All Hawkins was asking for was cooperation. To play the part. I didn't have to believe in the cause, just to look as if I did. And after what I'd done with Sparrow's tape, I couldn't pretend I was so honest or moral I wouldn't do it.

"Yes, if you help Yates, I promise to do whatever you ask to help you get elected."

Hawkins let go of my hand. He picked up his spoon and scraped his dessert bowl clean. "We need each other now."

I'd tried to stay true, but I walked out of that room feeling like I'd betrayed Yates in a way he'd never understand. I couldn't let him sit in prison, not when I had the power to get him out. What did it really matter if I campaigned for Hawkins? I was his legal prisoner. I was never getting away from him.

I'm doing this to save Yates, I tried to tell myself. If he's free, he can fight for everyone's rights. I can't. I'm done. My fight is over.

29

The next morning, Deeps burst in. "Wake up, Avie. You have to get up now."

I opened one eye. "Why? What's the matter?"

Deeps held up a tablet, the screen blazing with a shot of me in Luke's arms at the Pocatello Princess Dance. "Avie's Secret Lover!" screamed the headline.

"Oh holy—" I whirled out of bed. "Oh no. Oh no. Oh no."

"Mr. Hawkins and Adam Ho are waiting for you in his office. I wouldn't bother getting dressed."

I should have known at least one of those girls at the dance was snapping pics. Once she saw me on the news, she went right to the tabloids, hoping to cash in.

I grabbed my robe and headed for Hawkins' office, knowing he'd give me hell. But right now, I didn't care about Hawkins. I cared about Luke. The media would dig in, trying to find out who he was. And Hazel McAllister would probably offer up everything she'd seen. I could not let the feds track Luke down through me.

Ho greeted me with a nervous glance. The tablet with its lethal revelation was propped on the desk.

Hawkins gazed out the window, a crystal paperweight in his hand. "Who in the hell are you with in that photo?" He gripped the glass ball so hard his fingers looked like claws. "Tell me the truth. Now."

The room was electric with Hawkins' rage, and I stood there, mouth open, but nothing came out. I had to protect Luke, but I didn't know how.

Ho got between me and Hawkins. "Avie, we need to deal with this situation. We need you to be completely forthcoming."

"Goddammit!" Hawkins pitched the paperweight at the floor and I jumped as it shattered. "Who is that!"

Hundreds of glass slivers littered the stone. "It's Luke Stanton."

His head whipped up. "The son? You said you'd barely met him. You lied to me!"

"Yes, I'm sorry."

"Son of a— You were lovers, weren't you?"

"No. We were just traveling together. We never—we pretended we were married, that's all—" I refused to count the kiss Luke and I shared in our final hour together.

Hawkins held up his hand for me to stop. "Where's Luke Stanton now?"

"I don't know. We got separated in Fort Collins."

"Don't lie to me."

"I'm not! Your Retrievers snatched me when Luke was paying for gas. I don't know where he is."

Ho glanced back and forth between Hawkins and me. "The crisis management expert should be here in a few hours," Ho said. "Why don't we break until he arrives?"

Hawkins adjusted his watch. "Fine. We'll reconvene when he gets here." He was done looking at me, but I didn't know if I should move until Ho gave me a nod.

I backed out of the room and scurried down the hall as quietly as I could. Deeps passed me with a broom. "You'll want to stay inside," he said. "The press is back."

30

Hawkins summoned me when the crisis manager arrived. I swept through the garment bags in my closet. Ho hadn't sent me instructions, but I knew I needed an outfit that said "Innocent." I found a black skirt that hit me mid-knee and a blush silk blouse that covered me from my slutty neck to my shameless arms.

When I came out of my dressing room, a news chopper buzzed over the ocean, cameras trained on the house. Deeps positioned himself between me and the windows as he led me down to the indoor pool. "We set up in here to prevent those cameramen from getting a shot."

Hawkins and Ho sat at the sleek aluminum and glass table with the crisis manager, whose back was to me. He was African American, taller than Hawkins or Ho, and his silver gray suit fit his body like it had been cut for him. He stood up as I walked in. "Aveline," he said, holding out his hand. "I'm Sigmund Rath. Senator Fletcher sent me."

My heart skipped a beat. *Helen?*

It couldn't be.

When I'd last seen her in Vegas, Maggie's assistant/costume designer/coconspirator had just shaved her head, styled herself in a man's suit, and set off to sabotage the casino elevators.

But Sigmund's expression was wrong for Helen. His brows were too full, and his closely cropped hair was salt-and-pepper not siren red.

I managed to shake Sigmund's hand, and mutter hello. I glanced at Hawkins and Ho as I sat down, wondering if they'd tuned in to my surprise, but they weren't even looking at me.

"Avie, may I call you Avie?" Sigmund said.

"Yes." I peered into Sigmund's face.

"You may call me Sig, if you like."

"Sig."

"My job is to ensure that the Jessop Hawkins candidacy is not defined by this event and to reinvent its future."

"I understand." Maybe in my panic I'd confused him with Helen, but the small mole by his left eyebrow . . . ?

"Our immediate goal," Sigmund continued, "is to distance you from this seemingly incriminating photograph, but our long-term goal is to reinvent you as a young woman who embodies Paternalist values."

I felt loopy, like I'd crossed into a parallel universe where everything was the opposite of the reality I knew, where Helen was Sigmund, and Sigmund intended to make me into everything Helen hated.

"Avie, are you listening?" Sigmund tapped my hand.

"Yes, yes. I'm sorry. You want to distance me from the photo."

"Jessop confirmed that you are the girl in the photo with Margaret Stanton's son, Luke." Sigmund held my gaze, and suddenly I knew, and there was so much we wanted to say, but couldn't.

"Yes, that's right."

"I need you to describe exactly where you were and what you were doing when this photo was taken so we can create a credible alternate narrative to explain it."

My fingers played with the pleats on my skirt. "I don't want anybody to get hurt. The people who helped me are innocent."

"No one who helps a fugitive is innocent," Hawkins snapped.

Sigmund paused for a moment, before saying, "Let's focus on the task at hand. Avie has been cleared of those charges. Our attention must be on rebranding her as the young woman whose concern for protecting innocent children led her to escape from the church in which they were being used as a human shield by the terrorist Margaret Stanton."

Hawkins rubbed his thumb across his watchface. "Very well."

"We will not expose the people who helped you, Avie," Sigmund promised. "That will not work to anyone's advantage. Instead, we will create a narrative that exposes how the person who gave the media that picture was mistaken."

Sigmund quizzed me for an hour in front of Hawkins and Ho,

always focusing on the facts of who I'd met, what I'd called myself, what interactions I'd had with people in Pocatello. Hawkins bristled when he heard me describe how Luke was driving when the Retrievers picked me up. But no one asked why Luke and I were headed to Colorado.

Then Sigmund sketched out the strategy: demonstrate that the person who took the photo mistook me for the girl at the dance by creating a false identity. Birth certificate, marriage license, online presence.

Ho was taking notes and throwing out questions. Hawkins uncrossed his arms.

"We can fix this in twenty-four to thirty-six hours," Sigmund said. "But Avie's reinvention could take months."

"We don't have months!" Hawkins said. "The primary's in June."

"I understand your frustration, but we can transform this scandal into millions of dollars of free public relations."

"How?" Ho said.

"Aveline is a curiosity. She's the girl who came back. People will look at her and see the young lioness that Jessop Hawkins has tamed."

My stomach clenched. Only a few weeks before, Hawkins had told me he looked forward to taming me.

"You mentioned limiting Avie's public appearances," Sigmund went on, "but hiding her in Malibu is a waste. Voters want a look at the most intriguing young woman in the country. Put her on the stage, and they'll flock to your rallies."

Ho and Hawkins exchanged glances. Hawkins didn't love the idea, but Ho did. "We can make it work, Jessop."

"How are the plans progressing for the Signing?" Sigmund said.

"We're on target for December twenty-third," Ho said.

"Nine days. Good."

Good? Helen is playing her part too well. Why isn't she trying to delay?

Hawkins scowled as Ho ticked off the items that were being finalized: guest list, caterer, music, tent and decorations, security, remote parking, publicity. The vile dress I'd been fitted for weeks ago that the designer said I should wear without panties.

"You're inviting Vice President Jouvert, of course," Sig said.

"Jouvert rarely attends events for Paternalist candidates," Hawkins said. "He's careful about who he's seen supporting in public."

"Jouvert will come," Sig insisted, "given the likelihood you'll be the next governor. He needs California voters if he wants to be the next president."

Hawkins and Ho traded a look. "Fine," Hawkins said.

I didn't understand why Sigmund insisted that Jouvert be invited, but clearly Hawkins and Ho hadn't clued him in that we'd just blackmailed Jouvert.

Sigmund checked his Piaget. "We should discuss Aveline's cause."

"Her cause," Ho said, his tone completely dismissive.

I leaned forward, wondering what Sigmund had up his sleeve, when he wagged a finger, telling me to keep still.

"Your ultimate goal is for Jessop Hawkins to become president of the United States, is it not?" he asked Ho.

"Of course."

"First Ladies are defined by the causes they promote. Think Laura Bush and literacy or Hillary Clinton and universal health care. The media excitement over Aveline's return won't last forever, and the right cause can brand her as First Lady material."

Ho's eyes flicked back and forth like he was reading polling results, and he tossed Jessop a nod before saying, "What do you suggest?"

"Orphans. Jessop led the effort to create the nation's orphan ranches. Having Avie stand by his side and defend the innocent will cast her as mature and maternal. A young woman devoted to the future of the country."

My skin began to prickle. Sigmund had some grand plan, and it probably included me spying for the revolution. He was going to be disappointed to find out that my days as a revolutionary were over.

Sigmund gave me a long, hard once-over. "Bring in a stylist you trust," he said. "And get her hair back to its original color. Then we'll work on wardrobe and interviewing skills. Once we get the Pocatello incident behind us, we need to get her out there."

Then Sigmund took in Hawkins. "I don't know who's responsible for developing your public persona, but if you will excuse my saying so, they have failed to counsel you effectively."

I stifled a smile as Hawkins narrowed his eyes at Sigmund. "You find fault with my style?"

"Intimidating. Hard-edged. Superior. Your style fits a CEO, but voters don't elect candidates who intimidate them. They elect people they like. If you wish, I can suggest some simple changes, hair, wardrobe, accessories, to increase your likability factor."

Hawkins gave Sigmund a look that could melt steel. "I'll consider the offer."

"Very good." Sigmund stood up. "Adam," he said to Ho. "Let's get to work."

Jessop eyed me as if he expected me to stay. I sat taller in my chair.

Once we were alone, he said, "I need to know that you were telling me the truth when you said you weren't romantically involved with Luke Stanton."

I was relieved I didn't have to lie. "No. He helped me, because of his mom."

"You really don't know where he is?"

If I did, I wouldn't tell you. "All I know is Luke planned for us to go into the mountains."

"Would he have changed plans after you disappeared?"

My heartbeat thudded in my ears. I wondered if Hawkins suspected Luke was carrying evidence, too. "No, he was set on the Rockies."

"You're sure?"

"Yes, I swear, I don't know where else he could be."

"I'm sick of being blindsided by revelations about who you were with or what you did when you were on your little adventure."

"It wasn't an adventure," I muttered.

"If there's anything else you're hiding from me, you need to come clean now. Do you understand? We're both in danger here."

"I get it." I would not tell Hawkins anything more about Luke or what I suspected he might do. "I gave you the phone. You've got the files that were on it. I don't know what else you want from me."

"All right then." Hawkins went to unfold his cuffs and then stopped himself. "You coming?"

"No, I think I'll hang out here for a while."

I waited until I was sure Hawkins was in another part of the house before I went back to my room. My head was spinning as I changed into jeans. I didn't know how Helen had managed to get into Hawkins' circle, but I was dying to know why she was here.

31

Ho must have offered Elancio, the stylist, a fortune, because an hour later his Airstream was parked in the subterranean garage alongside Hawkins' Ferrari California.

Unlike the last time I'd been in Elancio's salon, Elancio hadn't bothered to fill the bud vases flanking the mirror, and there were no garment bags spilling out of the blond maple cabinets. Today his job was to fix the damage I'd done to his "creation," and return me to the reincarnation of Letitia Hawkins, mother of the next governor of California.

Sigmund observed from the curved white leather banquette, sipping an espresso, while I sat in the salon chair and Elancio ran his fingers through my hair. "This is criminal," Elancio grumbled. "This color—so trashy, so fake." He went to tape a photo of Letitia Hawkins on the mirror.

"You won't need that," Sigmund said.

Both Elancio and I looked at him.

"Jessop and I agreed that Aveline cannot reassume the look she had before her ordeal. She has changed, and her look must reflect that: stronger, more dynamic, with a hint of sexy."

"Right. I'm the young lioness that Jessop Hawkins has tamed."

"Exactly," Sigmund answered.

"Very well," Elancio said, tossing Letitia's pic in a drawer. "A young lioness." He crossed his arms and contemplated my reinvention, tapping his chin with one finger.

"Close to her original color, but bolder," Sigmund said. "They told you extensions, correct?"

"Yes. Yes. Return her hair to its original length." Elancio fished inside a cabinet filled with boxes of dye. "And those brows—pah!"

Ho arrived while Elancio was painting the color onto my hair. "We've got her booked with Evan Steele, the morning show tomorrow, just as you asked."

"Steele will hit her hard, but then it will be over and done." Sigmund turned to me. "Tomorrow you must convey strength and femininity. You were confused, and misled by people you trusted, terrified by the violence you were exposed to, and now you've returned to Jessop's side, where you are safe and happy."

Ho was taking it all in.

"I'll need to review her wardrobe before I leave. Adam, see if you can get a duplicate of the Love bracelet that Aveline wore on the cover of *People*. And once Elancio is done here, we should review talking points."

Ho nodded and left.

Elancio applied the last of the dye, and peeled off his gloves. Then Sigmund got up and slipped him a folded hundred. "Why don't you take a cigarette break?"

Elancio raised an eyebrow, but he said nothing, and dug out his pack. Sigmund waited for him to leave, then raised a finger telling me to be quiet. I watched quietly as he reached under the makeup counter and the red light in the monitor behind me went black.

"Girl, I thought that man would never leave."

"Oh my God, Helen, I can't believe you're here."

"I almost can't believe it myself. Imagine *me* inside the cave of the Demon King," she said, waving her hand at the garage full of luxury cars.

"Senator Fletcher didn't really send you, did he?"

"Technically, no. Although he often employs the services of the *other* Sigmund Rath. However, I doubt either Jessop Hawkins or Adam Ho have the nerve to call Fletcher's Washington office to verify my identity in the midst of *le grand scandale politique*. I trust you will keep my secret?"

"Of course I will, but if anyone figures out who you are—"

"You're sweet to worry, but I've spent most of my life hiding my true identity. And besides, I'm not the one who's in danger right now."

I ducked my eyes. I didn't deserve her help. "I'm fine, Helen."

"I'm talking about Luke."

My cheeks turned scarlet. "Yeah, of course."

"Not that your situation isn't serious, *Hummingbird*, but there's a nationwide manhunt for him. Maggie left money and forged identity documents. I can get him out of the country if I can find him."

"Maybe he'd listen to you. I tried to get him to go."

"Do you really believe he's in Colorado?"

"No. I wish I did, but we were on the way to meet two reporters when the Retrievers picked me up, and I don't know if he met them or if they were even real."

"I'm not following."

"This man who hid us—his name is Streicker—I think he set Luke up so he'd stalk Jouvert. I'm terrified Luke might try to assassinate him."

"What!"

"He's so angry, Helen. Luke wants revenge for what the feds did to his family."

Helen's eyes widened. "You care about him."

"Yes, I do—and he's not a killer, he's—" The truth of who Luke really was and how I felt was complicated, too complicated to explain now.

"Well, we have got to locate him. If there's anything else you can think of, anyone else he might have turned to outside of Salvation, you need to tell me."

"All right," I promised.

She reached in her suit jacket and pulled out a photo. "Is this what he looks like?"

It looked like Luke, but something about it was off. "Where did you get this? Luke told me there weren't any pictures of him."

"Luke probably never knew Maggie had a baby picture. I found it in her safe, and had it digitally aged. Does it look like him?"

"Almost." It was like looking at a zombie with Luke's features, but without the warmth in his smile or the depth in his eyes. A shiver traced my spine, and I handed the photo back. "I feel better knowing you're trying to find him. Luke knows how to survive in the mountains, but he needs help out in the open."

"Why were you meeting the reporters?" Helen said. "Were they going to interview you about the shootout?"

I filled her in on the evidence Luke and I were carrying, including Sparrow's tape of Jouvert boasting about his secret deal with the Saudis.

"He might as well have strapped explosives to his chest," Helen said.

"I need to tell you something else."

"What now?"

"Jessop Hawkins used the tape of Jouvert to blackmail him."

"Blackmail Jouvert! Hawkins won't stop at anything to win, will he?" She shook her head. "But you can't help what he did once he took it away from you."

"He didn't take it. I gave it to him." Anger flashed in her eyes, and I rushed to explain. "Fletcher threatened to have me arrested. You saw what the feds did to Maggie when she tried to surrender."

Helen fixed her eyes on her polished wingtips. "Well, so you did what you had to do to save yourself."

I swallowed, her disappointment like a spoonful of straight pins going down my throat.

"But who am I to criticize?" she said, taking a breath. "I wasn't in that church. Who knows what I'd do in your place."

We sat in silence for a moment, then Helen looked me in the eyes. "You do realize that if the reporters use information Luke gave them and run that story, Jouvert will think you double-crossed him."

I felt the blood leave my face, and the next thing I knew, Helen was rubbing an ice cube across my wrist. "That's right. Stay with me."

I pulled in a centering breath. "There's no way this will end well, is there?"

"Maybe not, but you've gotten this far. Look at everything you've survived." She dropped the sliver of ice in the sink and flicked her fingers dry.

"Avie, if Luke wanted to kill Jouvert, where would he do it?"

I repeated what I'd heard Streicker tell Luke about midsized cities and outdoor rallies in warm climates. Helen nodded, eyes closed as if she was making mental notes.

"He's got Streicker's van so he could get to any of those cities," I said, "and I think he'd try to take out Jouvert in the next ten days."

"Why so soon?"

I started to explain Streicker's theory that Jouvert was going to sign an agreement with the Saudis for nuclear weapons, when we heard Elancio on the step.

"Later, you're going to tell me everything you know about that." Helen pressed the switch to reactivate the monitor, and resumed her Sigmund persona. "Do your magic," he ordered Elancio, and strode out.

Elancio washed and dried my hair, then started fusing the extensions. I faced myself in the mirror, Helen's voice echoing in my head. "So you did what you had to do to save yourself."

Helen said she didn't blame me, but I couldn't help feeling I hadn't had to betray Sparrow, that I could have done something differently. But what that was, I had no clue.

Elancio returned his round brush and blow-dryer to their spots in the cabinet. "Are you happy with your look?" he said, peering down his nose as if he dared me to say no.

I shrugged and combed my fingers through my side-swept bangs, and tossed the glistening dark brown hair on my shoulders. The color and cut should have made me look like my old self, but I didn't.

I'd lost weight, but that wasn't the reason I looked changed. I had a new look in my eyes: I wasn't innocent any longer and I knew my survival was a long shot.

Sigmund met me outside the Airstream. He smoothed his aubergine silk tie and kept his voice low as we walked back through the garage. "Streicker's disappeared. I asked Ho to contact him so we could assess how much damage Luke could inflict if he resurfaced, but everything's gone. Phone number, bank account, Web site for LFOD Livestock—every trace has been scrubbed clean. It's like Streicker never existed."

"I'm not surprised. I bet if somebody went to his house, they'd find it stripped."

"Yes, he's probably on a beach in the Maldives luxuriously out of reach of U.S. authorities."

We headed back in the house to go through my closet and prep for tomorrow's interview with Evan Steele. Sigmund unzipped three or four garment bags and appraised the contents. "None of these outfits are suitable," he said. He took out his phone, tapped on the screen, and handed it to me. "What do you think about this dress?"

"*Is the room monitored?*" read the screen.

"*Audio only,*" I typed back.

"I think this would convey the image we want for you," he said as he typed, "*Tomorrow when Steele grills you, you have to blame Maggie.*"

I shook my head no. "Yeah, the dress looks great."

"*She would want you to keep the focus on her and take it off others,*" he tapped.

I bit my lip so I wouldn't tear up. "*Okay.*"

"I'll call the designer," Sig said. "Have him send over some samples."

"You're the boss."

I realized right then that I needed to give Sigmund the wall hanging. He could keep it safe, and I couldn't. I slid it out of the drawer. *"Recognize this?"* I typed.

Sigmund ran his fingers over the embroidered branches that connected and crisscrossed the stitch-coded names of one dirty politician to another, linking money, dates, and deals. Yes, he nodded.

I tried to press the hanging into his hands, but he shook his head. *"It's not the time,"* he typed.

What?

"We need to prep you for your interview," Sig said, pocketing the phone. "Adam Ho's waiting."

I argued with Sig in my head all the way downstairs. He should take the hanging. I could never tell its story. Not after the deals I'd made.

Sig had some mistaken fantasy that I was like his hero Maggie, even though it should have been crystal-clear that unlike her, I wasn't nearly brave enough to die for what I believed in.

32

The stars were still out when we drove off to the television studio the next morning for my interview with Evan Steele. Jessop, Ho, and I rode in back while Sigmund sat up front with Deeps. I listened to Deeps chat up Sig.

Last night, after Sig had left, I'd overheard Ho tell Deeps, "See if you can find out who in Fletcher's office sent him."

"Sure, I'll give you a full report," Deeps had promised.

Then this morning when I told Sig what I'd heard, Sig got very still, as if weighing whether to let me in on some big secret. But instead of coming out with it, Sig straightened up and said, "Don't worry. I've got it handled," which convinced me that Sig was hiding something.

Deeps drove us in from Malibu, after inviting Sig to sit up front. I kept one ear tilted toward them, but all they seemed to be talking about was the Lakers. When we turned onto Santa Monica Boulevard, Sig asked him if he thought we'd run into any demonstrators.

"I doubt we'll run into any 'No on 28' protesters this early in the morning," Deeps answered, "but the nav system will alert us."

I smoothed the skirt of my dress. The second I saw it I thought "smashed window." Navy tracks crisscrossed the creamy wool as if the designer had photographed broken glass. Then when I put it on, I saw that the dark blue lines radiated from my waist as if a force inside me had shattered the fabric.

Unforgettable was how Sig described it. That was our goal: to dress me so that I was seared in people's minds. The more visible, the more memorable, I was, the harder it would be for the Paternalists to erase me.

The Love bracelet on my wrist sparkled in the semidark. I spun it nervously. Ho had done the miraculous and gotten Cartier to messenger over a bracelet identical to the one Maggie freed me of in Vegas. This time Ho screwed it on my wrist, and, to my complete surprise, handed me the screwdriver. "Mr. Hawkins would prefer that you not lose this bracelet."

It was a small victory. I was still a prisoner, but I could remove my forty-thousand-dollar shackle at the end of the day.

We'd gone a few miles on Santa Monica Boulevard when I saw Deeps eye the panic button on the dash. His eyes met mine in the rearview mirror, and I checked over my shoulder. A silver car was right behind us even though the lanes on either side were empty. A second later, the car veered off.

Deeps shrugged. *False alarm.*

Dawn was breaking as we approached the studio. Deeps pulled into the turn lane in front. Across the street in the park, hundreds of tents covered the grass, "No on 28" painted on their sides. A crowd of young men were lined up at a food truck topped with a spindly Christmas tree.

"The 'No on 28' movement is growing," Sig said. "You must be nervous about that."

"It's problematic," Ho agreed. "The Paternalist leadership is pushing for states to pass the amendment, but if it fails, it could sink us."

"Twenty-eight's a suicide mission," Jessop muttered, "but the big guns in Washington aren't giving us much say in the matter."

I smiled to myself. I hoped the Paternalists went down in flames for trying to take away the legal rights of everyone under twenty-five.

The studio gates were set back from the street behind a wall. Huge posters of the hit shows *Firefight* and *Behemoth* lined the entrance. The guard waved us through, and we were hustled into Studio B.

Sig stood over the makeup man as he worked on me, steering him away from bright pink lipstick, insisting on a more natural look, making sure I didn't look anything like the blonde the tabloids had mistaken for me.

He made Hawkins take off his tie, and complimented him on choosing a light blue shirt. I realized Hawkins hadn't slicked back his hair, making him look more human. Impressive that Hawkins had listened to Sig when Hawkins always acted like he thought he was right and everyone else was wrong.

I sat, trying to keep straight my instructions. Sig and Ho had drilled me on questions Steele might ask, and answers that might keep me safe. "Remember," Sig had told me, "it's important to look like you're cooperating." That and blame everything on Maggie.

Finally, a production assistant tapped me on the shoulder. "We need you on the set, Miss Reveare."

Ho rushed over. "Steele's promised no questions about the tabloid story."

"Good job," Hawkins said. He offered me his hand, and I took it. Our fates were tied. Time to play my part.

The assistant guided us to the interview couch and miked us up. He placed me center stage between Hawkins and Steele, and I rested my left hand on the arm of the couch as Sig had coached me so the Love bracelet showed. The studio lights turned the symbol of my commitment to Hawkins into a light show.

I felt as if I was watching the scene from outside my body. My blood pulsed in my ears with a loud *swish-swish* like a washing machine.

Off camera, Deeps gave me a thumbs-up. Hawkins rested an arm on the back of the couch and gripped my other hand. His was damp and hot like mine.

Evan Steele settled into his interview chair in his pinstripes and red tie. Steele wasn't a huge guy, but he looked like he could crush you with his eyes. He frowned through his welcome, and then began to fire questions.

"Why did you run from your Contract, Aveline?"

I recited my answer about Sparrow pushing me to join Exodus. "She didn't believe in Contracts. She said they exploited girls."

Hawkins squeezed my hand hard. "But that's not how you see Contracts now, is it, Aveline?"

It was exactly how I saw them, but that didn't matter. "Now that I've been out in the world, I appreciate how my Contract protects me."

Hawkins tucked me into his side; my answer had pleased him. Steele held me in his gaze, and my head began to throb as tiny zigzags of light sliced his face.

"Your friend Sparrow connected you with Father Gabriel, the priest who was jailed, pending trial for kidnapping in conjunction with Exodus."

Steele waited for me to fill the silence as I picked at the couch arm with my fingernail. The truth was those girls Father G had allegedly kidnapped were trying to get to Canada, and he was helping them, but truth didn't matter. "I'm sorry, but I can't talk about Father Gabriel since I might have to testify at his trial."

"You seem anxious about testifying."

"I am, a little."

"Then you'll be relieved to know there won't be a trial. The Vatican declared Father Gabriel a diplomat yesterday, giving him immunity for his crimes. He was returned to Rome last night."

Thank God. I felt the cameras zoom in on my face. "Oh, that's shocking."

"Yes," Steele added, "a clear abuse of diplomatic immunity. But let's go to what happened after you arrived in Las Vegas. You were installed by Exodus in the escort service operated by Margaret Stanton."

"Yes."

"Did you know that Margaret Stanton was a spy?"

Maggie spied for the good guys, but that didn't matter here. "All I knew was she was with Exodus, and she wanted me to play air hockey with her guests." I heard someone behind the cameras chuckle.

"These were defense contractors who were in from Virginia and Washington, D.C.?"

You jerk. They were congressmen and senators. "I don't know what they did. We were just hanging out, partying and having a good time around the foosball table."

Hawkins whispered in my ear. "You're doing fine."

"Did you know that Margaret Stanton stole a computer containing classified defense documents that night?"

"No, I didn't." Lies were piling on lies and I couldn't contradict them. At least none of Maggie's relatives or friends in Salvation had a TV, and would hear me betray her.

"And your friend Sparrow managed to get a ride to D.C. with one of those contractors."

"I suppose." She'd hitched a ride on Air Force Two with Jouvert, but that would never come out.

"According to the administration at Masterson Academy," he said, "Sparrow was a highly intelligent girl, but showed signs of emotional imbalance."

I shivered under the hot lights. Sparrow was sick, killing herself the way she did, but I refused to say it here. "Yes, Sparrow was unhappy."

Steele brought the audience up to speed about how I'd broadcasted the video Sparrow had sent me of her allegedly dousing herself with accelerant on the Capitol steps. I waited for Steele's next question, rehearsing the lines Ho and Sigmund had given me.

"You must have been shocked," Steele said, "when you learned that the video she sent you of her suicide was a hoax."

The floor fell out from under me. Hawkins glanced at Sigmund and Ho, and neither of them had answers, either. "Yes, I was surprised."

Sparrow had doused herself with gasoline and lit the match, but Evan Steele repeated the government's fabrication that it was a homeless man protesting joblessness. "We have just learned that Sparrow Currie was Retrieved that day and is currently in a private psychiatric facility in Palm Springs."

Liar! I wanted to leap up and scream it so everyone could hear. Hawkins must have sensed it, because he pushed down on my shoulder, keeping me in my seat. "If you find out which one," I said through almost clenched teeth, "I'd like to send her flowers."

Evan didn't even blink, he was so obviously sold on the stories he'd been fed. "We'll get that information to you after the break. Now, did Margaret Stanton force you to flee with her when federal agents came to arrest her for stealing government secrets?"

"I thought they were Retrievers who realized where I was hiding."

"When you got to the antigovernment community of Salvation, did Margaret Stanton turn over the stolen defense files?"

"No—not that I know of." Let Maggie take the blame. Sig had warned me the truth would be perverted, but not like this.

"Salvation had anticipated a government attack for some time, hadn't they? An underground bunker, stockpiled food and weapons all point to their intent."

"I'm not sure how to answer that." Yes, they'd stockpiled food and weapons, but they were peace-loving people who'd lost faith in the government. "But they weren't expecting Maggie. They didn't want her there."

"Not even the son, Luke Stanton?"

I couldn't let Steele think Luke was Maggie's accomplice. "Luke hated his mother for abandoning him. He wouldn't even speak to her."

"A young man from home, Yates Sandell, joined you in Salvation. The same young man who's been jailed in conjunction with Father Gabriel."

I felt Hawkins tense. "He's a friend," I said. "Yates was worried about me."

Steele looked doubtful.

"Evan," Hawkins said, "Yates Sandell and Aveline grew up together. He went after her the same way a protective big brother would."

"So, Avie," Steele said, "you didn't want Yates Sandell to join you?"

My mouth tasted like sand. I would hurt Yates no matter how I answered. "No, I didn't."

"And he was there with you when the federal agents came to arrest Margaret Stanton?"

"Yes." I didn't know where Steele was going next, but I had to stop him.

"You have to understand—" I said. Steele jerked his head, surprised I'd spoken. "All those people in Salvation, they didn't want Maggie there. They were terrified when the federal agents arrived." I glanced at the clock on the wall, only a few minutes remained for the interview. "They were afraid that even if Maggie surrendered, the agents would come after their children. I know things would have been different if the people there were less paranoid, but there were dozens of children in the church, including a newborn baby."

Steele leaned forward in his chair. "Tell us about your part in this drama."

"They asked me if Yates and I could try to go for help. I couldn't say no, could I? I didn't know what would happen if we didn't."

"You trudged up a snowy mountain in the dark . . ." Steele made me describe how Yates and I had gone out the secret passage, crept past the armed agents, and climbed in snowshoes to the top of the ridge. By the time I finished, Steele called me an "American heroine who risked her life for innocent children."

Steele reached out to shake Hawkins' hand. "I can see why you picked this young woman to be your wife."

Hawkins beamed. "Eight days until our Signing, Evan! I'm a very lucky man to have such a beautiful, talented young woman at my side." He squeezed my shoulder, and that was the signal.

I placed my hand on Hawkins' cheek, just as I'd been prepped, and beamed at him. My stomach churned, knowing the cameras were probably zooming in on our faces.

Steele stood up. "We wish you success with your campaign for governor, Mr. Hawkins." Hawkins and Steele exchanged handshakes and bullshit praise, and we all took off our mikes.

The smell of damp wool came through the floral scent of my cologne and my armpits were slick with sweat. The walk back to the car was a blur. I focused on putting one foot in front of the other as shards of light split my vision. "Does anyone have a Tylenol?"

Deeps helped me into the car and slipped me a bottle of water and a painkiller. Hawkins climbed in next to me. "You did a good job, controlling that interview."

"Thanks," I said.

Then Ho and Sig chimed in with their praise, and I covered my eyes with my hand, sick about the people I'd smeared, and hating that Yates or Luke might have heard me.

I pictured Yates throwing a book at the television screen in his cell block and Luke leaving his lunch on the counter and stomping out of a small-town bar and grill. They'd never know why I'd said what I said, or done what I did, or that it was my messed-up attempt to protect them.

Deeps headed for the studio exit. We passed through the gate, and I heard angry voices up ahead chanting, "No on 28." Protesters filled both sides of the sidewalk, waving their handmade signs as we approached.

"It's Jessop Hawkins," one cried.

"It's that bastard Hawkins!"

"Hawkins!"

Young men flooded out of the park. They ran across the six lanes and swarmed the car, surrounding us. Ho hit the panic button, but the crowd ignored the alarm.

I slapped my hands over my ears, but the wail of the alarm was deafening. Protesters banged on the hood and windows, and the car shuddered from the pounding. Then the young men began to rock the SUV, throwing Hawkins against the door.

"Paternalist scum!"

"Fletcher's puppet!"

"Dirtbag!"

"Get us out of here!" Hawkins ordered. Deeps became very calm and controlled as he crept the car into the street and nosed people out of his way, but then the crowd surged, trapping us.

Traffic was paralyzed. Horns blared and protesters yelled back at the drivers. "We're not your slaves. No on 28! No on 28! No on 28!"

A young man with dreds snaking out from under a striped hat flung himself on our hood. Then he stood and began to stomp the shiny, black steel with his boots.

Deeps shook his head. "I was hoping to avoid this." He reached into the glove compartment and took out a can of pepper spray. Then he opened the sunroof and waved the can. "Get down," Deeps warned.

"Go ahead—"

He called Deeps a name, but before he even got the word out, Deeps hit him in the face with the bright orange stream. The young man fell to his knees screaming, and Deeps kept spraying as his buddies pulled him off the hood.

Then Deeps revved the engine and nudged through the crowd. For once, Ho ignored his ringing phone, but Sigmund held his up. "I caught the attack on video, and I'm posting it now. We need to show voters the lawlessness of these protesters."

Sig deserved an Oscar. How could he spout stuff like that so effortlessly? My life depended on playing the part of Jessop Hawkins' adoring spouse, but the voice in my head was already beating me up.

Luke would hate me, hate me, for telling lies about Maggie, but Yates knew me and maybe he'd understand that I didn't have a choice about appearing with Hawkins. Yates would know I was acting, that I was saying what I was told to say.

At least Luke and Yates would never know about the other deal I'd made to survive. Handing over Maggie's and Sparrow's files? Even Yates wouldn't forgive me for that.

My head throbbed, and I let it drop against the back of the seat. This wasn't the person I wanted to be, but how could I change who I'd become?

33

Around two that afternoon, I got up and went downstairs, not bothering to change out of my pajama pants and hoodie. The pain in my head was gone, but I was fuzzy and thirsty for fruit juice, pineapple guava, something not too sweet.

I scuffed past the huge blue acrylic fish, and for the first time, registered how the spear holding it up went right through the transparent body. *I know how you feel, buddy.*

Deeps, Ho, and Sig had their heads together around the dining table. "Yes," Ho was saying, "Jessop's mail is screened for ricin and explosives at the facility that handles the mail for California state legislators. It's superheated and X-rayed, then delivered daily by courier."

The three of them were so focused, they didn't notice me enter. "What's up?" I said.

They all sat bolt upright like they'd been caught redhanded. "We're reviewing security protocols," Deeps answered.

Ho's phone pinged and he stood up. "Legal's asking if we want to press charges for the damage to the car," he said, walking away.

I circled around the table. "Should I be worried about security?" I asked Deeps.

"No. We're taking a few simple precautions, that's all." He looked past me to Ho, who was motioning to him. "Got to go."

Sig waited until the two of them disappeared down the hall, then motioned for me to sit down beside him. Then he brought a video up on his phone, and turned the volume to low. "This just came out," he said quietly, and handed it to me. "I thought you'd like to know."

A news anchor announced, "In breaking news, terror suspect Yates Sandell has been released from custody."

I shook my head. "I can't believe it. Hawkins actually got Yates free."

A camera scanned a crowd of reporters gathered in front of the prison. Yates walked into the dog run of chain link topped with razor wire that separated the prison from the parking lot. His left arm hung in a sling, and his foot was cinched in a Velcro boot up to his knee. He was flanked by a man in a suit and two guards walked behind them.

The gate opened, and the camera zoomed in on Yates. I leaned in close, searching his face.

"How does he look to you?" Sig whispered.

"Better. His eye was purple and completely swollen when I left. Now it looks almost normal." I followed the scar on his forehead into his scalp where a patch of short black hair flopped over it. Yates looked like he'd lost weight, like the sport coat he wore was two sizes too big.

"You must be relieved."

I shook my head as feelings I didn't understand swirled inside me. "Why don't I feel happy? They just let him out of prison." Yates walked toward the sea of reporters. "I should be jumping up and down or screaming with joy, right?"

My face crumpled seeing the reporters swell around Yates and thrust their mikes into his face. "I don't understand what's happening to me."

"Maybe," Sig said gently, "it's because it's not the ending you hoped for."

It wasn't the ending I'd pictured in my mind. The one where Yates walked out into my waiting arms. "I wanted us together."

"Oh, baby, of course you did," Sig whispered.

"But at least he's free, right? That's something to be happy about."

"Yes, at least he's free."

Yates stepped up to the makeshift podium and gripped the sides. He glared at the row of prison officials lined up on his right, before addressing the reporters. "According to the terms of my release, I'm prohibited from discussing what happened in Salvation, Idaho. But I can tell you right now that I intend to devote my life to defeating the Paternalist movement, starting right here in California with Jessop Hawkins."

My temperature dropped twenty degrees.

"Well, prison doesn't seem to have changed him," Sig said.

Yates would never be silenced, never compromise or submit like I had. He would have died before he gave up evidence against Jouvert.

I saw the chasm between us. Yates would lead the revolution while I stood at Hawkins' side, smiling like I believed everything the Paternalists spouted.

A reporter shouted my name. "Aveline Reveare, the girl you were with in Salvation, has returned to Jessop Hawkins. How does that make you feel?"

I gasped, and Sig tried to take the phone from me, but I shook him off. Yates stared down the reporter, narrowing his blue eyes until they turned black.

No, please don't answer him.

"It makes me sick. Apparently, she prefers being Hawkins' lapdog to being free or loved."

Ice crystals filled the chambers of my heart.

"What are you showing her?" Adam Ho leaned over us, his eyes widening when he saw what we were watching. We hadn't heard him creep back in the room.

I handed the phone back to Sig, and Ho gave us a long, disapproving look. "*He* is not going to like you doing that."

"Yates Sandell was released from prison," Sig told Ho. "No matter how your boss feels about him, he would agree that it's best to keep Avie apprised of anything that touches on her situation."

Ho quivered, his head shaking almost imperceptibly. I always thought I was the person he disliked the most, but now I saw Sig was coming up a close second.

"You should be thrilled," I told Ho. "Yates hates me for being your boss's lapdog. It's a dream come true."

I got up and pushed through the glass door. I wanted out of there, out of view of the house and its windows and endless view into my most private feelings. A dirt path zigzagged through the brush toward the eucalyptus grove and I took off in my bare feet.

My heart was tearing away from my chest, and I needed to reach that circle of trees and throw my arms around one of those yellow-gray trunks, and have it anchor me to the ground. I needed to cry with no one watching or listening in.

The branches were rising and falling in the wind, and sunlight glinted off what I realized had to be a sculpture. I was only fifty feet from disappearing into the grove when Hawkins emerged from the trees.

I caught myself mid-stride and pivoted right around. Hawkins called out my name, but I didn't stop, and charged back to the house. I'd done everything he'd asked. He and his freaking team could go to hell, because I was finished for today.

34

I shut myself inside my closet, and sorted through Mom's letters until I found the envelope where she'd drawn a broken heart on the flap. Then I sat down on the floor, because even though the stone was miserable to sit on, at least I wasn't being watched in here and I could be alone with my mother.

I choked up reading the first sentence. *Oh, Mom.*

"My sweetest girl,

"You chose to open this letter which tells me you're hurting.

"I imagine you fell deeply in love, and this love filled you with a happiness you'd never experienced before. But now your heart is broken, and you can't imagine life without him. You can't eat or sleep, or let go of the last words he said to you."

Hawkins' lapdog. Yates' disgust echoed in my ears.

"If I was there, I'd stroke your hair and tell you that you, my dearest, are beautiful and talented and brave and wise, and worthy of love."

Mom was wrong. I wasn't any of those things.

"I'd listen to you describe every moment you spent with this young man who made your world come alive. I would tell you that love will find you again. This is just the beginning of a lifetime of being loved. With each love, we learn to love.

"Someday you'll meet the young man who doesn't just love you, but is willing to do whatever it takes to hold on to you, because he cannot live without you. I know this is true, because I married your father."

I folded the letter back into its envelope and set it down next to me. Mom couldn't help me. Nothing she promised would ever come true. Mom couldn't begin to imagine a world where love was mostly memories.

I lowered myself to the floor until my cheek lay on the cold, hard slate. The energy drained out of my body until I could almost see it puddling around me.

Yates had loved me, but now that love was buried beneath his hatred for what I'd become. What we had was over. My heart squeezed in my chest, but somehow kept beating. Why couldn't it just let go?

35

Hours later, my eyes popped open as a hand closed over my mouth, pinning me to my pillow. I tore at the hand, and thrashed, trying to break free.

"Avie! It's me."

Deeps? I relaxed, and he let go.

"Stay down and slide off the bed."

I dropped my head over the side. Deeps was stretched out on the floor, and he inched back to give me room.

I slid down beside him. It was dark over the ocean and very late. The house was silent, but a hundred yards away, floodlights glared along the compound walls.

"What's going on?"

"Security breach. The cameras picked up movement on the grounds. I'm taking you down to the safe room."

Suddenly, I was back in Salvation, watching the agents surround the church and aim their weapons on us. "I'm scared."

"I won't let anything happen to you. Just do as I say."

We crawled on our stomachs out the door, Deeps insisting I go in front. Then we slithered along the hall until we got to the stairs above the main room. Hawkins' fixation with clean lines meant the windows were uncovered, and every corner of the room below was exposed.

"Keep low, but move fast," Deeps said. "I'm right behind you."

The suspended stairs trembled faintly under our weight. I blocked out the pain in my ankle, and focused on moving quickly.

We ducked into the gallery behind the main room, and I realized that the lights that came on automatically had been shut down. The exotic wood that lined the gallery was almost seamless, but Deeps felt along with his fingers, and then pressed. A panel opened, revealing stairs that led to the bottom level, ones I never knew were there. The panel eased shut and Deeps locked it behind us.

Carpet muffled our steps. Deeps stopped me at the bottom of the stairs right before he opened the other door. "Don't move until I tell you. If there's gunfire or anything else sounds weird, lock yourself in here."

I held the door closed, listening so hard I was sure I heard a shot outside the house. My hand slipped, and I grabbed for the handle, afraid to lock it, but even more afraid to try to get to the safe room on my own.

I pressed my ear to the door, praying Deeps would come quickly, while images from Salvation shot through my head. The agents struggling to hold Emmeline, then slitting the goat's throat. Blood splashing onto the snow. Men and women lining the church windows, their guns ready. Yates pulling me through the narrow escape tunnel, saying, "It smells like a grave in here."

The smell of cold dirt flooded the stairwell and I put my hand over my nose, trying to block it.

Deeps, where are you? Deeps, come back.

I leaned against the wall and dug into the carpet with my toes. *Feel that. You're not in that tunnel. You're in Malibu, and Deeps is coming back for you.*

A rapid knock. I released the door. "Come on out," Deeps whispered. I slipped out and we crept down the hall, going only about ten feet before Deeps flipped up a light switch to reveal a coded entry pad hidden underneath. He tapped in a code, and the wood panel in front of us eased open.

The door was thick steel like a bank vault, and all I saw beyond it was blackness. "Go on, get in," Deeps said, but I was bolted to the floor, knowing when I stepped inside, my bare feet would touch cold, damp earth.

"Avie." I turned toward Hawkins' voice, and he yanked my arm, pulling me in beside him. Deeps shut the heavy door, and the darkness was total except for a faint light coming from the illuminated buttons on the back of the door. Jessop entered in a code, then flicked on a flashlight.

The light reflected off brushed-steel walls. The room was cool, but it was dry, and smelled slightly of metal and plastic.

Hawkins was wearing a T-shirt and pajama bottoms. I shivered and crossed my arms over my breasts, suddenly conscious of my thin cami and bare legs.

"You're cold," Hawkins said.

I expected him to offer to "keep me warm," but instead he went over to a stack of black storage trunks in the corner, pulled out a blanket and handed it to me.

"Thanks." I wrapped the blanket around me as Hawkins clicked a remote. Overhead lights came on, and a screen in the corner went live. Shots from sixteen surveillance cameras turned it into a shadowy checkerboard.

One glance, and I was back in the control room in Salvation's church watching a dozen monitors capture the agents positioning for attack. I turned away from the screen.

This isn't the same thing.

Really? How isn't it?

"We might as well settle in," Hawkins said. "We're probably going to be here for a while."

I glanced around for a place to sit.

"There's a cot," he offered.

I didn't want anything that looked even a little like a bed in here with us. "No, I'm fine on the floor."

Jessop sat, leaving space for me to sit next to him, but I pretended not to notice and picked a spot on the opposite wall. I heard a faint whirr, and then air blew in through a vent near the ceiling.

My chest tightened, remembering how I'd watched the agents destroy the windmills that powered Salvation. "What if they cut the electricity?"

"We have backup generators."

This bare steel box with a couple of storage bins didn't look equipped for a long stay. "And water? What if we run out?"

"We've got a thousand-gallon tank." Jessop rapped the wall behind him. "Sink and toilet behind this door."

"What if whoever's out there sets the house on fire?"

"We've got a sprinkler system and immediate dispatch from the fire department."

"How about guns?" I said, looking at the black storage boxes. "Do we have any?"

"You wouldn't want to shoot a gun in here. The risk of a bullet ricocheting off a steel wall is too great."

I nodded and pulled my hands and feet inside the blanket.

Jessop peered at me. "Salvation left its mark on you."

"Yeah, you try being held captive in a church that armed government agents are firing on, and see if you don't come out a little paranoid."

Hawkins switched his attention to the screen up in the corner. "You saw that Yates Sandell was released from prison today."

Ho must have told him how he caught Sig and me watching his press conference. "Yes. Thank you for helping him." Hawkins looked at me expectantly. "Jessop," I added.

"I gave you my word I would."

I knew Hawkins wanted more, a gushing, teary thank you, but I wouldn't give him the satisfaction.

"He's wrong about you."

I sat up straighter. *Don't. Don't you dare talk about Yates to me.*

"You're no one's lapdog, and he's a fool to call you that. He doesn't deserve you."

Stop. Just stop. I know you hate that I still love him.

Hawkins gave me a look like he knew what I was thinking. I looked away, and we sat in an uncomfortable silence for a minute or two, before I broke it, saying, "I hope Deeps is okay."

"He'll be fine," Hawkins said. "He's trained for this." Hawkins watched the security monitor, his arms crossed limply over his knees, occasionally clicking the remote to change the screens.

"Why aren't you nervous?" I said.

Hawkins flicked his hand. "I'm a politician and that by its very nature makes me a target. The key," he said, nodding at the locked door, "is to be prepared."

He looked almost average right then with his uncombed hair and rumpled pajamas. I got that he wanted to run the state, but I didn't get the rest. "Why are you a Paternalist?"

He smirked. "Why'd you ask that?"

"The way you talk about Jouvert and Senator Fletcher. You don't like them. I don't think you even respect them very much. And you don't agree with everything they say. Like this morning you said Amendment Twenty-eight was a suicide mission."

Hawkins tilted his head at me. "I became a Paternalist because that's where the votes are. You saw how quickly the movement took over. Scarpanol left this country traumatized and the Paternalists were the first to realize that if they promised a man that they'd keep his daughter safe, he'd do whatever they asked."

"So you don't really believe everything you've said about women staying home and obeying their husbands and not going to college or having their own money?"

"My mother was a brilliant, supremely capable woman who could have run this state if she'd wanted to."

"Then I don't get it. I don't understand how you can play with people's lives—with my life—like this when you don't believe in what the Paternalists are doing."

"Because you can't steer the ship until you're the captain. Movements change. People realize what they don't want and they vote out the people they voted in. Jouvert and people like him won't last . . . Why are you shaking your head?"

"Jouvert's going to be the next president, and we helped put him there by promising not to release the tape of him and Sparrow."

"I doubt he'll be president."

Hawkins was so arrogant, so sure of his own infallible brilliance, he couldn't see the power Jouvert had. Didn't he realize Jouvert had probably sent whoever was out there?

"We should call the police," I said.

"Deeps will call for backup if he thinks it's necessary."

"But what if someone kills him first?"

"That's unlikely. I hired Deeps because he pulled terrorist insurgents out of caves along the border between Afghanistan and Pakistan. He can handle whoever's stumbling around my backyard."

"Stumbling around? You think the person who's out there isn't dangerous?"

"It could be anyone—a paparazzo trying to sneak a shot, a thief who saw your bracelet in *People*, a stalker, some nut who went off his meds—"

"Yeah, maybe, but I've seen what Fletcher and Jouvert do when they feel threatened, and if one of them thinks that two perfectly aimed bullets will solve their problems, they'll get someone to do it."

Hawkins clenched his hand into a fist. "Stop being dramatic," he snapped. "We're fine."

That was all it took to shut me up. Hawkins watched the screens, and I laid my head on my knees and pretended to doze. He had hit me before, and I didn't want to risk making him angry.

Deeps came for us at 5:50. "I found fresh deer tracks near the fence where the sensors tripped. A doe probably wandered down from the mountains, and got startled and jumped the fence. No sign of it now."

"See," Hawkins said to me. "It was nothing." He held out his hand, and I let him help me to my feet.

Deeps walked me back upstairs, and I waited until we were far enough away from Jessop that he couldn't hear me say, "Really? A deer tripped the alarm? I don't believe that for a minute."

Deeps looked me right in the eyes. "You want me to show you the tracks? Grab a jacket. Let's go."

Showing me tracks wouldn't prove a thing. "Forget it."

I wasn't being paranoid, I thought as I scuffed back to my bedroom. Jessop and I had blackmailed the vice president of the United States. We had targets on our backs even though he and, apparently, Deeps wanted to pretend we didn't.

It wasn't dawn yet, but I drew the curtains so my room became a cocoon. If I hadn't been so tired, I don't think I would have slept.

36

Music went off around two. "Wake up, Hummingbird." Deeps' voice came over the intercom. "Time to hit the PR trail. You're leaving for the orphan ranch in one hour."

It was my debut as Aveline soon-to-be-Hawkins, Defender of Orphans and complete fraud. I squeezed my eyes shut, wishing there was a way out of this photo op and Q&A with three dozen reporters and celebrity bloggers. By using those tapes to save myself, I was helping keep the Paternalist orphan scam in business.

But there wasn't a way out, and Deeps made sure I was up, dressed, and in the car on time.

We drove down the freeway, me in back with Hawkins, my fingers rubbing circles on the skirt of my dress. The fabric was like shaved fur, the short hairs the color of graphite mixed with black that shifted direction unexpectedly. Leather trim shaped like black daggers radiated from around my neck. Sig wanted the cameras to fix on me, but the last thing I wanted was to be seen, especially by Yates.

"Where's Sigmund Rath?" Hawkins asked Ho. Hawkins was wearing the smoky lavender shirt Sig had sent over.

"With a client in San Diego. He'll be back tomorrow."

Deeps looked at me in the rearview mirror, and I caught a flicker of something in his eyes that made me wonder if he knew Sig had lied.

Sig was in San Antonio for Jouvert's speech at Texas A&M. Jouvert had two more appearances outside D.C. where we thought Luke might show up in the next week, and prayed he wouldn't.

Ho's phone pinged. "It's Jouvert's director of scheduling. The VP's coming to your Signing."

"So Sigmund was right." Jessop tapped his thigh. "I'd never have believed it."

Me, neither. Jouvert and his Secret Service agents were the last people I wanted to be anywhere near, and I had no idea why Sig had insisted he be invited. Sig had ducked the question when I'd asked.

"We'll need to increase security for the Signing, won't we?" Hawkins said.

"The Secret Service will probably send a security detail in advance to assess the compound," Deeps said. "They'll want full access including blueprints."

"Wait, Jouvert's people are going to go through our house?" I said. "Aren't you at all worried they might leave listening devices behind or maybe a bomb?"

"I'll be with the agents the entire time, and do a sweep after they leave," Deeps said. "I'm trained in what to look for."

Hawkins smiled.

"Did I say something funny?"

"You called it 'our house.'"

I twisted the Love bracelet on my wrist, feeling a little sick. I can't believe this. Look at me. I'm turning into Hawkins' wife.

The orphan ranch came into view, the buildings spread out along the cement-lined L.A. River on the other side of the freeway.

I'd passed the L.A. Orphan Ranch every Tuesday for six years when my bodyguard Roik would drive me to the cemetery to visit Mom, and I'd never really thought about the girls and boys who lived there. But that was before I met Splendor and Sirocco in Vegas. They'd both come from ORs, and gone to work for Maggie. Everyone who worked for Maggie seemed to have survived something.

Deeps exited the freeway, and the road curved around a power plant. The huge windowless building was sun-bleached almost white. Beside it stood a giant square of twisted black steel beams studded with steel coils like the guts of an enormous machine. The empty street was stripped of trees and not even a weed sprouted along the pavement.

Deeps steered us into a block of office and industrial buildings. Boys wearing jeans and worn tees, and who looked like they were only ten, were picking trash off the sidewalks and narrow strips of dried-out grass. "We're here," Hawkins said.

"This is it?" Calling this a ranch was a complete joke.

"What did you expect?"

I must have been naïve to expect barns for horses and cows. "I thought there'd be fields—a place to play soccer."

Hawkins pointed to the top floor of the parking structure on the right. "There are basketball courts up top, and plenty of room on the other floors to ride skateboards and bikes or play indoor soccer."

"What was this place?"

"A big animation studio. When they went bankrupt, the city bought the buildings quite cheaply."

The buildings on the left were protected by ten-foot walls and iron gates, but the ones on the right weren't. Anyone could have walked on or off the property.

"Is that the boys' campus?" I said, pointing to the right.

"Yes."

Of course it was. Who cared if a boy ran away or someone took him? One less orphan for the state to worry about.

Deeps turned left toward an arch covered in dead ivy. The studio's name had been pulled from the painted stucco, but the shadow of a few letters was still visible. "DreamWo."

Deeps halted at the guardhouse in front of the iron gate. Two dozen men carrying video equipment and camera bags were lined up single file along the sidewalk. One security guard was checking their IDs while another searched their bags.

The next thing I knew, the iron gate had rolled closed behind us. The small parking lot was paved in fake cobblestones, and Deeps pulled into a visitor space between a BMW and a Porsche.

"Do you remember your instructions?" Ho asked me.

I wanted to slap the self-satisfied look right off his face. "Smile. Act impressed. Agree with everything Jessop says."

"Exactly."

Hawkins took my hand and helped me out of the car, then smoothly kissed my cheek. I jerked back, startled, and caught sight of a cameraman snapping away. "Smile," Hawkins hissed, still holding on to me.

I smiled up at him through gritted teeth. "I didn't know you were going to kiss me."

"We're in public. Expect it."

A white-haired man with a thick black mustache bustled past the photographer. "Mr. Hawkins, we're so happy you came. And you must be Aveline." He shook my hand. "Claudio Ramirez, superintendent. I'm delighted that you've taken an interest in our girls."

"Of course I'm interested," I replied, parroting lines Ho had fed me. "Jessop has told me all about your efforts to protect and nurture young women."

Ramirez steered Hawkins and me toward the door. "Yes, Mr. Hawkins has been a generous benefactor and a powerful voice on our board."

Deeps and Ho were wrangling the photographers who'd passed security. They were lined up in the reception area, and began snapping shots of us the second we stepped inside. I tried to look everywhere but at their lenses, tried to keep my face a blank.

I felt like Ramirez was setting up the shots, the way he invited Hawkins and me to admire a wall decorated with glossy, four-color photos of smiling girls of every color bent over pottery wheels, peering into microscopes, and waving trophies at a track meet. Then he told the media we'd meet them in the dining room, and led us through a glass door etched with the words PLACEMENT OFFICE.

Portraits of smiling couples, some holding babies, hung on the wall. There wasn't one picture of a girl wearing a college tee or waving a pennant.

Ramirez waved a hand at the display. "These are only some of our success stories. We've broken new ground by placing girls in homes instead of releasing them when they age out of the ranch. We learned from the foster care system that releasing kids without a safety net results in high rates of homelessness, drug abuse, prostitution, and welfare dependence."

"That's great," I forced myself to say. I'd heard all this crap in Vegas from Paternalist senators and congressmen slapping themselves on the back for saving the unfortunates.

Ramirez led us down a short hall. "Our counselors interview prospective matches for the girls, because our goal is to get the right 'fit.'"

"I'm sure the girls appreciate how much you care."

Ramirez puffed up. "I hope you are right," he said, "because I see myself as a father with a thousand daughters to care for."

Hawkins shot me a look to let me know he'd picked up on my sarcasm even if Ramirez hadn't.

Ramirez stopped outside a counselor's office. The door was closed, but the window to the hall showed three people inside. "Look here," he said, "and you can observe a counselor conducting a 'first meet' between one of our girls and a placement prospect."

We peered through the glass, and my body tensed, seeing the prospect and the way he sat, his arms spread wide on the chair, his suit jacket open, as he eyed a slender black girl in a tan jumpsuit standing beside the counselor's desk.

Her hair was in a bun, and her face was scrubbed clean, but she was distractingly pretty with high cheekbones and intense black eyes. She stared at the ceiling until the visitor spoke. Then he twirled his finger, and I realized he was telling her to turn around. The jerk wanted to see how she looked from behind.

"How do you know he'll treat her well?" I said.

"Darling," Jessop warned.

Ramirez bent toward me. "Sorry, I didn't catch what you said, Miss Reveare."

"How do you know that man will be kind to her? That he won't abuse her?"

"A very good question. Let me reassure you that all the candidates are carefully vetted with criminal, credit, and employment checks."

Hawkins must have sensed I wasn't satisfied with the answer, because he eased between me and Ramirez. "LAOR uses the same psychological assessments that the top private schools do, correct?"

"Yes, we make every effort to get a complete profile, but I must admit that many candidates are unwilling to submit to psychological assessments, and even if they do, we've found the results so subjective as to be worthless."

The men started walking again, and I glanced at Hawkins, remembering the fury in his face when he shook me. My school prided itself on exhaustively evaluating prospects before recommending a match, but clearly he'd refused their psychological tests, probably along with a big fat No Thank You gift to the Masterson Academy endowment fund.

Ramirez put a hand on Hawkins' shoulder. "I need to thank you for your recommendations regarding our profit model. Profitability is up thirty percent after we implemented a fifty percent deposit, and bad debt expense has dropped to seven."

I wasn't sure what that meant, but Jessop was smiling at his own brilliance.

"And that analyst you sent us?" Ramirez continued. "He refined our candidate-assessment algorithm so it weighs factors like expected career earnings, employment industry, educational level, and residential zip code more heavily. Now, we're scoring candidates in each category and the highest-scoring candidate is selected for that specific placement."

Heat filled my chest. This I got. The guy who scored the best, got the girl. It didn't matter if she and he had anything in common, or she had even the least little interest in him.

I struggled to keep silent and not let my face reveal how I felt. Ramirez was another operator. No, not an operator, a pimp. I knew it and Jessop knew it. I couldn't stop it, and Jessop wouldn't.

"When can I meet the girls?" I asked.

"We're going right now." Ramirez led us through a back door down a long hallway into a huge open room where at least a hundred girls were bent over sewing machines. Stacks of orange cloth were piled next to each girl, and the *grrring* noise of the machines was deafening.

Girls across the room were sneaking looks at me, and I was suddenly conscious of how privileged and superior I appeared in my seven-hundred-dollar heels and Love bracelet coated with diamonds. I tucked my arms behind my back and gave them a nervous smile, hoping they'd see that I didn't think I was any better than they were.

Ramirez shook out a folded garment, showing us a big orange jumpsuit. "This is what they're working on."

"Oh, the prison uniform contract," Hawkins said. "How is that going?"

"Very well. We're saving the state millions of dollars, and the girls are using their new skills."

"Excellent!" Hawkins said.

A girl right in front with huge brown eyes and tight cornrows scowled at me, daring me to turn my pathetic smile on her. Her look burned so hot I wished I could shrink to the size of a bug and skitter out of there.

"I am proud that LAOR projects like this prepare girls to be productive contributors to society. Our students graduate with a strong education in reading, mathematics, and the domestic arts. We may not have the resources of a private preparatory school, but I like to think that we do well with what we have."

I wanted to ask him how many hours these girls spent sewing uniforms as opposed to, say, going to classes. And oh, can I see the chem lab, and the pottery room? And what about the track?

It was obvious the photos we saw up front were lies, and that's why Hawkins and I were on a private tour without any photographers in sight.

My frustration was near boiling, but as I opened my mouth, Hawkins said to Ramirez, "What's next on the tour?"

"Ah, our professional kitchen," Ramirez answered. "I think you will be impressed, Miss Reveare." He went to take my arm, and the girl in front shot me the finger behind his back.

My breath caught, and my cheeks got hot. I turned with Ramirez and walked out of the room, trying to keep my head up. That girl had nailed me as a fake, acting like I cared about the plight of orphans, when I'd never do anything to help them, because I was a powerless poser. A lapdog.

Ramirez walked us into a large lunch room where cartoon characters—singing penguins, a ninja panda, and a junk-food-crazed raccoon—capered across the lime-green walls. I had only a second to take in the scene before the three dozen photographers and reporters drinking coffee at purple-topped tables leaped to their feet. Shutters snapped and bursts of flash went off.

I focused straight ahead as Ramirez guided us around the tables to the open industrial kitchen. Deeps and Ho held the reporters and photographers back from the counters and eight-burner stoves where girls wearing dark green aprons over their tan jumpsuits were chopping apples and stirring pots.

When I saw the woman teacher showing two girls how to use an apple corer, my mouth fell open. Ms. Alexandra had hidden her gray French twist under a chef's hat, and traded her perfectly tailored sheath for a chef's jacket and cheap black-and-white checked pants, but I recognized her instantly.

I felt light-headed as she walked toward us. Part of me wanted to run into her arms, and another part wished I could hide. She'd probably seen me on TV telling Evan Steele how I appreciated Contracts now that I'd been in the outside world. Did she know I was acting or did she believe like Yates did that I'd turned?

"Miss Reveare, so nice to see you again," she said, holding out her hand. "I don't know if you recognize me. I'm Ms. Stohl. I taught seventh grade at Masterson Academy until I retired last month."

I reached out, holding back a little as if I barely knew her. "Yes, of course, Ms. Stohl, how nice to see you again!"

She gave my hand a quick squeeze and our eyes connected. She really was happy to see me. "Let me give you the tour," she said.

Hawkins hung back with Ramirez while Ms. A walked me over to a nearby workstation, where two girls who looked thirteen stirred bubbling pots. I tried to keep my smile in check as she asked me polite questions about what I'd seen so far, because Ho was watching me like he sensed something was off.

Ms. A gave one of the pots a stir. "Cooking jams and fruit butters," she enunciated, "reinforces fundamental math and chemistry concepts while teaching critical domestic arts."

I remembered her saying the exact same thing when trustees toured our kitchen at Masterson, where she secretly taught us subjects they had forbidden.

She introduced me to the two girls, and pointed out the design on the bib of the girls' aprons. "Graciella here designed our new logo," Ms. A said.

The words "Los Angeles Orphan Ranch" circled an embroidered fruit tree where a coded message jumped out: "I am not for sale."

Being fired from Masterson wasn't stopping Ms. A from trying to give these girls what she'd given me and my friends: a sense of worth beyond the price tag of Signings, and the belief that you could choose your future.

"It's beautiful, Graciella," I said.

She beamed, and Ms. A took another apron out of the drawer and snapped it open. "Here," she said. "You don't want to muss that beautiful dress."

"No, you're right," I said, slipping it over my head. "This fabric is probably impossible to clean."

I am not for sale. A few weeks ago, I'd have worn this proudly, but that was before I learned I could be bought. And the consequences of what I'd done could affect every girl in this place.

Ms. A waved at the photographers. "Let's get a picture together."

She positioned me between the girls and whispered, "Let's use your celebrity to get our message out."

She hugged us from behind as we posed, and I leaned in, ashamed of how I'd failed her, and wishing I could somehow make things right.

She couldn't save these girls from LAOR's placement counselors and candidate-assessment algorithm, not with the Paternalists lined up against her. But that wasn't stopping her from giving as much as she could.

Ms. Alexandra took me around, and as she introduced me, I saw how the girls had fallen in love with her just as I and my friends had. She cared for us like she was our mom. I dug my nails into my palms trying to keep my feelings under control.

Finally, Ms. A took me over to a small girl, sitting alone in the corner, embroidering an apron, a scarf wrapped over her black hair. Spying us, she lowered her eyes.

"Namaste," Ms. A said, bowing her head.

"Namaste," the girl whispered back.

"Amisha is one of the girls that your fiancé, Mr. Hawkins, rescued from the brothels of Delhi."

Amisha smiled, hearing her name, while I struggled to keep my smile steady. In Vegas, the politicians cheered Hawkins for rescuing Nepalese girls from brothels and bringing them here. It had made me sick to hear them crow about how America could save exploited girls around the world and deliver them to loving homes. Like pound puppies, I'd thought.

"Amisha and her friends speak no English," Ms. A said, raising her voice. "They need ESL teachers."

Ramirez's head snapped up, and Hawkins' eyes pinched, which only encouraged me. "This sounds important."

"A command of basic English will help guarantee these girls' futures and our ability to place them in good homes," Ms. A continued.

I'd been told to stick to the script, but I realized Ms. A was asking me for help, and I couldn't live with myself if I did nothing. "Perhaps Jessop and I could help?" I saw Jessop's mouth go flat, but I didn't care.

Let him get mad at me. He had millions. He could afford at least one ESL teacher.

He walked toward us, beaming as if he was delighted with my suggestion. Then he wrapped his arm around my waist, and turned his good side to the photographers. "How many teachers do you feel we need?"

"Two for twelve girls would benefit them enormously and ensure that they leave LAOR with the best prospects," Ms. A said.

"Then I will donate the salaries and benefits for two teachers in the name of my darling Aveline."

The room exploded in clapping. Ho caught my eye, and flicked his hands, telling me what to do next. While the cameras went nuts, I threw my arms around Jessop's neck, and he raised one arm triumphantly.

Then it was time for me to speak. I folded the apron and handed it back to Ms. A then recited my carefully planned script. How I wanted girls across the country to be safe and cared for and how happy I was to be at Jessop Hawkins' side, because he would do his best for California.

I pushed down the sick feeling in my gut, telling myself it didn't matter if Yates was watching or if he hated me. He was free, and this was the price.

After the Q&A, Ms. A suggested I might like to freshen up. Be right back, I signaled to Deeps, and she led me away, thanking me for the generous gift to LAOR. Two lefts and a quick right took us to a back hall.

"Stop right here," she said quietly, and threw her arms around me, pulling me close. "Avie, I've been so worried. I can't tell you how happy I am to see you. Are you all right?"

I held on tight, wishing she'd never let go. "Yes, I mean it's been rough, but I'm okay."

"It was inhuman what they put you through. And you were so brave."

Tears began to fill my eyes, but I blinked them away. *Don't make me into a hero. If you knew some of the things I've done . . .* "I tried very hard to do the right thing just the way you taught me, I really did, but sometimes . . ."

"Avie. You sound like you think I'm disappointed in you. But why? Is it because you're here with Jessop Hawkins? Don't you think I know you were Retrieved?"

The love in her voice was a knife in my chest, and I dropped out of her embrace. I couldn't tell her the real reason: that I'd sold out Sparrow and helped keep the Paternalists and Jouvert in power. "You heard me out there," I said, my voice close to breaking. "I'm the Paternalists' new hand puppet, saying and doing exactly what they tell me."

She sighed. "Sometimes we do what we must to survive. But I've watched you for years, and I have faith that you will do the right thing. Look at you. You got ESL teachers for those girls. That will change their lives."

I nodded. So I'd done one good thing.

"You will do more as—" Ms. A caught herself. "In the future."

"You mean when I'm the governor's wife."

"Yes."

Her believing in me was ridiculous. "But I won't have any power to change things."

"You already do, you just don't realize it."

We heard footsteps in the hall, and moved apart as Deeps came around the corner. "Everything okay back here?"

"Yes, sorry!" Ms A said brightly. "We got to gossiping. Silly us."

Deeps escorted us back to the kitchen. The photographers had cleared out, and Jessop and Ho were waiting with Ramirez. Ms. Alexandra took the folded apron and pressed it into my hands. "Something to remember us by. You're a model for these girls, you know."

I clutched the apron to my breast. What was I a model of, really?

Hawkins crushed my hand in his as we walked back to the car, where Ramirez thanked us again for the generous donation of the teachers' salaries. I got in the back seat and Hawkins climbed in after me. Hawkins was silent as Deeps pulled out of the gates. "Avie's trending,"

Ho announced. "I know we didn't plan that stunt with the teachers, but the numbers are moving."

Hawkins stared ahead with focused intensity as he pressed the control that raised a clear panel between us in the back and Ho and Deeps up front. I set the apron down and slid my hands under my legs. So much heat was radiating off Hawkins, I felt it across the seat.

"The next time you have an idea, you will come to me and ask me what I think. I am the man in this relationship," he said, punching the seat with a finger. "And you will not make me look like a lovesick puppy to the press."

I stared at the folded apron. I am not for sale. "I'm sorry. I thought I was supposed to champion *the cause*. Wasn't that why you brought me here?"

"When you are in public, you stay on script. That is what you agreed to. You want to champion some idea, you do it in private, but when we are in public you cannot—"

"Okay, okay. You're right. I should have asked you about the teachers."

We rode in silence for a little while. I could feel Jessop start to cool down.

"You should sue Masterson's placement office," I muttered. "They should have told you I'm not very good at doing what I'm told."

"They did tell me, but Adam was convinced your resemblance to my mother would more than make up for that."

My breath caught. "You didn't pick me?"

"No, Adam selected the candidates. Frankly, I was leaning toward 'Christy' from Westridge."

I sat there, stunned. If Adam Ho hadn't chosen me, none of this would have happened. My life would have been totally different. "So, you Contracted me because Adam Ho told you to?"

Hawkins rubbed his thumb over his chin, and a mile went by, maybe two, before he said, "It was the look you gave the camera in your placement portrait."

I remembered silently daring the photographer to get a good shot as he posed me for the mandatory photo.

"You seemed—challenging. Someone who'd keep me interested. But no one bothered to mention your relationship with Yates Sandell before I signed the Contract."

I heard all kinds of things in his voice, anger, bitterness, betrayal. He thought he'd been tricked. "The thing with Yates. It just sort of happened. Dad didn't know."

"Yes, well, the damage is done." He rubbed his fingers over the emblem on the apron. "You were right about those girls needing an ESL teacher. Ramirez wouldn't have sprung for the expense."

It was a compliment.

"Why did you bring them to the orphan ranch instead of taking them home?"

"Because their families wouldn't take them back. The village would shun them for being impure."

I couldn't quite figure out if what he'd done was good or bad, because it was both.

"You can't save the whole world," he said, touching the control that lowered the divider. "You can only make it incrementally better. I'm open to discussing your ideas, but don't spring them on me in public again."

Ho looked at us over the seat.

"How's the story trending?" Hawkins asked.

"She's a star! Sexy, compassionate, everything you'd want in a First Lady."

Governor's wife. Ms. A's words echoed in my head. "You will do more in your role—" As *First Lady*.

Maybe Ms. A was right, that I had power to change things, to make a difference in peoples' lives. And maybe that was how I could live with myself and what I'd done. I would atone.

37

The next morning the Secret Service arrived, and Deeps escorted me down to the dining room to meet them. I slowed as I walked through the main room, trying to size up what was going on. Two men in dark suits and white shirts had removed the large Ortiz painting from the wall and were examining the back.

"Come join us, Avie," Hawkins called from the dining room. He was tense, but trying not to show it.

Two more agents in the same dark suit/white shirt uniform sat at the table with Hawkins, Ho, and the chef. The agents weren't huge guys, not anywhere near the size of Deeps, but their seriousness weighed down the air.

Hawkins glanced back and forth between the agent across from him and the two handling his precious Ortiz. "I have gloves your colleagues can use."

"Don't worry, Mr. Hawkins," the agent said, "we have extensive experience examining valuable furnishings and artwork."

Hawkins frowned as the agent placed a recording device in the center of the table.

A younger, blonder agent, Agent Brisbane, directed me to the seat beside him. He had the same close-cut hair, clean-shaven face, and sunglasses in his breast pocket as the others. "Please place your hands on the table so I can fingerprint you."

I laid my hands on the cold cement top. In the kitchen, someone was opening and closing the drawers and cabinets. The alarm system pinged, indicating that someone else was opening a door or window to the outside.

Agent Brisbane splayed out my fingers, and rolled them across the ink pad. My scalp began to prickle. *Keep calm. They're not here for you. They're here to prep for Jouvert's visit.*

A voice came through Brisbane's communicator. "Entering Mr. Hawkins' bedroom," and I jerked, sending the ink pad scooting into my lap.

Oh shit. I left the hanging in my room. If the feds noticed it was missing from Maggie's office in Vegas, they might be looking for it.

"Sorry." I set the ink pad back on the table.

Agent Brisbane handed me a towelette. "Happens all the time."

Sweat pooled in my armpits as I listened to agents move through the halls. The lead agent checked everyone's IDs, and then asked for a list of regular visitors to the house, the electrician, plumber, landscaper, grocery delivery guy, anyone we expected on the grounds before Vice President Jouvert's visit.

Ho began listing people. When he got to Sigmund Rath, Agent Brisbane nodded. "Yeah, I know Sigmund. He's a regular on the D.C. party circuit."

Holy—I squirmed in my seat. Brisbane meant the real Sigmund Rath, not the ex-showgirl-turned-spy who was due to show up soon. I had to warn Sig, but I didn't have a phone.

Deeps stood back with his arms crossed like the agents' questions were no big deal, but I saw him quietly size up the men. I wondered if he was thinking what I was, that this visit was a cover for their real mission: to find and destroy the incriminating tape of Sparrow and Jouvert.

If they did, Jouvert would be home free, and he could do whatever he wanted to Hawkins and me. I stared at Deeps until he met my eyes. *Where's the tape? Is it around here?*

Deeps ignored me.

Then the agents asked for the names of the suppliers for the Signing: the caterer, florist, musicians, tent rental. I picked at my nails under the table, dying to get upstairs and deal with the hanging. "Can I go?"

The head guy nodded yes, and I was halfway out of my chair when another agent said, "What about Luke Stanton?"

For a second, I didn't move, but then my instinct kicked in. I finished getting up. "What about him?"

"You became acquainted with him in Salvation, Idaho."

"Barely."

My stomach tightened like a fist. Everyone was watching me. The agents like they'd pounce if I twitched or stammered. Ho like he expected me to screw up and blow open the story we'd concocted. Hawkins like—I didn't even know how to read what was on his face.

"We maintain a list of individuals who we believe may pose threats to government officials. Mr. Stanton is on that list."

Luke isn't just a person of interest. He's a suspect!

A bead of sweat rolled down my side. I dropped my shoulder, and started checking my hair for split ends. "And?"

"Can you confirm the physical description we have of Mr. Stanton: Caucasian, brown hair, brown eyes, nineteen years old, height six three to four, weight two hundred seventy-five pounds?"

Luke was tall, but no way he weighed 275. I gave the agent a sulky stare. "Yeah, I guess. I dunno. He's big like him," I said, pointing to Deeps.

"And did you ever witness Luke Stanton express anger with the federal government or any of its officials?"

You murdered his parents! He has every right to be angry!

"Uh, him personally? There were a lot of people in that church, and they were really upset. So I can't tell you what he said or didn't say."

"I recognize that you may not know the answer to this question, but are you at all aware of whether Luke Stanton is an expert marksman?"

I saw Luke firing in the snowy field and Streicker cheering him on. "No," I said, "I have no idea."

The agent paused the recorder. "Thank you for your cooperation, Ms. Reveare. We don't need you anymore."

"Okay." I turned just as he said, "Mr. Hawkins, your house is monitored for audio and video, correct?"

My body tensed so it felt like my muscles were knotted under my rib cage. I walked away, listening hard.

Hawkins started to answer, but Deeps interrupted. "Sir, let me handle this. The entire structure is monitored, but the level varies by room."

"We'd like to review the last three months."

I scuffed my flip-flops across the floor, pretending I couldn't care less what they were saying while inside I fought not to panic. If there was a tape of Hawkins and me talking about blackmailing Jouvert . . .

"We don't retain the files," Deeps said. "We clear them every morning."

Deeps had to be lying. As Hawkins' loyal man, he'd say anything to keep incriminating data out of the feds' hands.

Back in my room, I wound the wall hanging around my waist, then put a shirt on over it, and stuffed Mom's letters inside. I was zipping on my hoodie when there was a rap on the door.

"Miss Reveare, we'd like to come in."

Two agents held the door while I slipped by. Jessop and Ho were still talking to Agent Brisbane and the other man downstairs as I went out the double doors. I didn't see anyone in the garage, so I darted up the steps to the parking circle.

Two black SUVs dominated the pavement. If Sig saw them when he opened the gate, maybe he'd realize who they were and turn around before the feds intercepted him. But what if he thought they belonged to the event crew working on the Signing?

I had to make sure Sig didn't go inside the house, and I had to tell him the feds were closing in on Luke.

I headed through the scrub toward the grove. From there I'd be able to see the gate, but stay out of sight. The only person who ever came out there was Hawkins, and right now the agents were keeping him busy inside.

I hurried down the dusty path in my flip-flops, wishing I'd remembered to wear boots. Please, no snakes. Please, no snakes.

But as I reached the grove, I slowed. The atmosphere here felt different, sacred almost. Towering eucalyptus formed a loose circle that tailed off near the cliff, and I stopped to take in the bronze statue of a woman atop a granite pedestal in the middle of the clearing. The crushed leaves below my feet gave off a pungent scent.

From where I stood, the woman was in profile. Her hair was twisted in a loose bun at the back of her neck, and she gazed at something beyond the trees. Hawkins' paintings of slaughtered chickens and melting abstract bodies repulsed me, but this woman drew me to her.

I walked up until I was only a couple feet away. She felt like a real person, because even though she was pretty with high cheekbones I envied, she had a small bump on her long, slender nose, and her chin jutted out just a little bit too much.

She was seated as if she was relaxing on the ground with one leg stretched out in front of her. Her elbow rested on her bent knee and a broad-brimmed hat like hikers wear hung from her hand. She looked like she'd stepped off a trail to take in the view, and she looked like you could ask her anything.

I ran my hand down her sleeve, releasing a yellow cloud into the air. When I stepped around to the front, I saw the name Livia Dufort cut into the granite pedestal along with the words "The earth has music for those who listen. Shakespeare."

"Born May 10, 1975—Died October 30, 2007."

Livia died from Scarpanol. Or maybe not, but she was only thirty-two, so the chances were—

I circled around, wondering who she was, because she wasn't Hawkins' sister, whose name I knew started with *m*. Plus, Livia didn't look like anyone I could imagine with Hawkins.

Not his girlfriend and most definitely not his fiancée. "The earth has music for those who listen"? That wasn't a Jessop Hawkins philosophy.

But for some reason, Livia Dufort was buried here.

On the back of the pedestal, I spied a small bronze plaque and crouched down in the dust. Dirt was caught in the raised bronze letters, making it hard to read. "*Livia* by Marielle Hawkins."

Hawkins' sister sculpted her. His sister?

"What are you doing?"

I fell back on my butt. Hawkins stood a few feet away, his hands resting in his pants pockets.

"Nothing," I said, getting to my feet. I retreated a short distance, trying to gauge if Hawkins was upset to find me here. "I didn't want to be in the house with those men."

"Yeah, they were going through my office, so Adam suggested I come out here and clear my head." He glared at the house. "I think he was afraid I'd say the wrong thing and antagonize them."

The hanging was tight across my chest. "Do you think they're looking for the recording—the one we used to blackmail Jouvert?"

"Possibly, but it's not here."

"No? Then where is it?"

"Don't worry. It's safe." Hawkins paced the perimeter of the trees, and the mood became charged with tension. He was telling me not to worry, but he clearly was.

I moved over to a stone bench on the opposite side of the clearing. From there I could still see the driveway.

"What about the tapes from the monitors in the house?" I asked. "The Secret Service seemed to want those pretty bad. If they hear us talking about Jouvert—"

"Deeps erased everything last night and dismantled the audio. We should be safe."

"Good. That makes me feel better."

Hawkins walked up to the statue. He looked at Livia, but what he said was meant for me. "You handled their questions well. And the pouty teenager act— One of the men commiserated with me for having to put up with your moods."

He set his hand down on the toe of Livia's boot, and I saw how the bronze was worn and shiny in that spot. Everything became quiet. Even the leaves stopped rustling as if the wind didn't want to tick Hawkins off.

I was dying to ask who Livia was, but I knew not to push. "The sculpture's beautiful," I said.

"My sister did it. It was the last of her sculptures cast before her death." Hawkins knocked a seed pod aside with his foot.

I stayed silent, hoping he'd say something more about Livia or Marielle, but he barely looked at me as he announced he was going back in. "The Secret Service is moving fairly quickly. I expect they'll be gone in a few hours."

"I'm staying out here for now."

"Understandable."

He tromped back through the brush, and I couldn't help remembering how Mom wrote in a letter that loss makes some people more human and others less so. Hawkins was such a beast, it was impossible for me to believe he hadn't always been this way. But he had to have been different if a woman like Livia loved him. It just didn't make sense.

Through the trees, I spied the two agents in my bedroom. They'd flipped the mattress and were examining the platform under my bed. I breathed into the hanging, relieved I'd gotten it out of there. Then I tucked myself behind a tree to wait for Sig. Hawkins better be right that the recording of Sparrow and Jouvert was hidden someplace the feds would never find it. I was afraid to imagine what would happen if they did.

38

I sat outside for hours, waiting for Sig to appear and the Secret Service to leave. Sig never showed, and the sun went down, and my feet were almost frozen before the feds' headlights traveled up the drive.

When I got to my room, the mattress was back on the bed, but the sheets were thrown on top in a messy pile, and Deeps was holding a small device with an antenna up to the fire detector.

"Something wrong with the battery?" I said.

Deeps put a finger to his lips, and showed me the label on the device. Wireless signal detector. He bent close to my ear. "Just checking whether the Secret Service left anything behind."

"Yeah, good idea." I shivered at the thought of them watching my every move, and reached for the remote to close the curtains. They probably had a scope up on the hills across Pacific Coast Highway, not to mention what they'd left here. At least they hadn't sliced open my mattress or punched holes in the walls like the FBI did.

"All clear in here," Deeps whispered, then ducked into my dressing room while I straightened out my sheets. He was still scanning the closet when Sig showed up at my door in a tux. A black-on-black striped garment bag was slung over his shoulder and a shiny red shopping bag hung off that.

Crap. The debutante auction. I motioned behind me and mouthed the word "Deeps."

Sig gave a nod.

"I don't want to go to the auction tonight," I said, loudly enough for Deeps to hear.

"Ms. Reveare, I don't make your schedule," Sig replied.

I held up my hand to keep him in the doorway. "I was worried," I whispered. "The Secret Service just left. They asked about Luke."

"What did you say?"

"I said I barely met him, and I think they believed me, but the questions they asked—they think he's going to shoot someone important."

Sig swept a hand over his scalp. *Damn.*

"All clear in here." Deeps came around the corner. "Oh, hi, Sigmund."

"Josh."

"Guess I better go get my fancy duds on. We're leaving in thirty, right?"

I moved back to let Deeps pass, and Sig walked in. He glanced up at the monitor in the corner.

"It's okay," I told him. "Deeps dismantled the audio."

"Interesting." Sig strode into my dressing room with me right behind him. He hung the bag on a hook by my LAOR apron. "What's this? 'I am not for sale'?"

"The girls at the orphan ranch gave it to me."

Sig smiled. "Good for them."

I took the apron off the hook and folded it, wondering why I'd hung it up in the first place when it only reminded me that I'd sold myself to the highest bidder. I slid it into a drawer. "One of the agents who was here said he knows you."

Sig didn't move for a second, then he picked a piece of lint off his sleeve. "My trip to San Antonio was a dead end," he said. "I didn't find any sign of Luke."

I would have thought Sig would be relieved. "That's good, right? Maybe Luke met the reporters after all."

"I wish I believed that. My contacts at the *Washington Post* came up empty. They said either no one on their staff is researching a story about Sparrow, or the reporters who are working on it are so nervous about leaks that only a few top people at the paper have been informed."

"So we have no clue whether Luke turned over the thumb drives or not."

"Do you think he'd try going back to Salvation?" Sig said.

I could picture Luke hiding up on Phelan's ridge, sleeping in a snow cave so he could keep watch over his family without them knowing. "No. I think he'd be too afraid the feds would come after his family."

"Is there anyone else Luke might have turned to outside Salvation?"

"Luke hardly ever left there. The only times he did were to drive the horses to winter pasture or to help Barnabas deliver the guitars he built."

"All right, that's something. Barnabas probably sold to dealers. Did Luke mention any names?"

"No, only the towns the stores were in." I named the ones I remembered.

"Well, at least we have a place to start." Sig handed me the red shopping bag. "We're running out of time. You need to get dressed."

Something black and lacy was nestled in pink tissue paper. I pulled it out with two fingers and held it away from me. "A corset? Really?"

"Appearances can be deceiving. It's a high-tech safety shield with ultralight panels to protect your vital organs. Deeps suggested it."

I laid it against my chest. Heart, stomach, liver, kidneys were covered, but the corset was cut low in the back. Goose bumps pricked my neck. "What if someone shoots me in the back, Sig?" I said quietly.

"Don't say that," he said, struggling to keep his expression composed.

Seeing him like that scared me more than his giving me the shield in the first place. "What, you couldn't find me a shrug made out of this stuff?" I joked.

"I'd wrap you head to toe in Kevlar if I could."

I saw a flicker of Helen in Sig's eyes. "I know you would."

"So, are you ready to see your dress?"

"Ugh. God, I wish you could get me out of attending this auction."

"I'm afraid not. Adam Ho was so impressed with the response to your visit to the orphan ranch that he gave me an unlimited budget for tonight's dress. He's counting on you to turn in another stellar performance."

"It's going to be televised, isn't it? Everyone's going to see me arm in arm with Jessop Hawkins."

"By everyone, don't you mean Yates?"

"Yes, and it'll confirm every horrible thing he thinks about me."

"I doubt Yates will be watching. He doesn't strike me as the type to hang around a sports bar, placing bets on how much a girl will go for."

"No, you're probably right." But even if he didn't see the show, Yates would hear about me being there. It would be impossible to stay out of the spotlight when I was Hawkins' date.

Sig unzipped the black-on-black striped bag, revealing a strapless gold dress. Strips of fan-folded foil stretched across the bodice and skirt, and were sewn into a jagged-edged ruffle down one side that looked as if it could cut my hand if I brushed against it. The fabric was coppery in places like it had been treated with chemicals so the metallic fibers had turned a honeyed red.

"It's amazing," I said.

"This dress will get you seen around the world."

"As Jessop Hawkins' trophy and adoring lapdog."

Sig straightened up until he towered over me. "Self-pity is boring. If you don't like your image, find a way to change it."

My cheeks flared as Sig continued. "You aren't helpless. You can do better than this."

"How? How am I supposed to fix this?"

"Try starting with your attitude." Sig swept out of the room.

39

Hawkins' eyes were fixed on me as Sig and I walked toward the Escalade. Sig had barely acknowledged me when I came out of my room. Now he stared straight ahead, while I thrashed around for something to say, afraid I'd lost my only friend in this place. "I love the dress, Sig."

Sig sniffed. "You should. It tells the world that even though you've been captured, you are not a slave."

"Sorry about the pity party."

"Apology accepted. We shall put the past behind us." Sig sneaked me a smile and my heart fluttered with relief.

Hawkins waited at the passenger door. "That's an interesting choice of dress," he told Sig.

"The architectural drama of Nosuki's design echoes your taste in cutting-edge art while the bold cut offers up the image of Avie as a young lioness. The red-gold color communicates your success without an overt show of wealth."

Hawkins' eyebrows went up. "I see."

"Fashion is message, Mr. Hawkins."

I am not a slave. I smiled to myself, and climbed into the back seat. Then I arranged my skirt and sat up tall, determined to live up to Sig's vision.

Sig sat up front with Deeps while Hawkins and I sat in the middle, and Ho sat in the back. A nonstop stream of rush-hour traffic was leaving L.A., as we headed into town. I'm not sure any of us except Ho actually wanted to go to tonight's debutante auction, but since Hawkins was emceeing, we didn't have a choice.

Hawkins and Ho talked back and forth across the seats, reviewing the guest list for the auction and the potential campaign donors who'd be there, while Deeps and Sig debated the Seahawks' chances of getting to the Super Bowl.

I'd learned the expression Deeps got when he didn't like the look of something, so when I saw it in the rearview mirror, I turned around and saw two guys on a motorcycle tailing us. Streetlights reflected off their helmet visors and caught the red bands on their black racing suits.

Deeps glanced between the mirrors, and I saw him focus out the right as a second team on a motorcycle pulled just ahead of us on that side.

I laid a hand over my stomach, feeling for my security shield while Ho and Hawkins blabbed on, oblivious to the drama unfolding around us.

"Heads up, everyone, looks like we might have company." All the interior lights went dark. Deeps accelerated, and the motorcyclists both in front and in back increased their speed to keep pace.

Ho pressed himself into the SUV's steel-reinforced seat as a third motorcycle appeared on the right. The roar of the three engines drowned out the radio.

Deeps hit the panic button on the dash and the dispatcher's voice came on. "What is your situation?"

"Three motorcycles front and side, coordinated movements, two riders on each vehicle, weapon status uncertain," Deeps barked.

"Do you need escort?"

"Yes, escort requested."

"Sending escort. Confirming your location is—"

Deeps pushed the car faster and Hawkins grabbed my arm and pulled me down on the seat. "You okay back there, Avie?" Deeps yelled.

"Yeah, I'm fine."

"The escorts are on the way and should rendezvous with you in less than two minutes."

Roik, my old bodyguard, had drilled me on how to survive a vehicular ambush, and his instructions repeated in my head. *Don't panic. Keep your head below the level of the windows. Let the armor in the door and seats protect your core.*

But even I knew enough about evasive measures to know that we were trapped between the ocean and the solid wall of white headlights coming toward us on the Pacific Coast Highway.

Deeps is in charge. You need to trust him.

But there's no place to turn or pull off.

For a moment, I was back on that empty Idaho highway with Maggie, holding on to the seat as the car plunged off the road to escape the agents on our tail.

I turned my head at the sound of screeching metal. The motorcycle rider on our right leaned toward the SUV and dragged something along the side.

Sirens blared, and red and blue lights strobed in the rearview mirror. The motorcycles peeled off, and the SUV slowed as two patrol cars pulled up alongside. Hawkins gave me a hand. "How are you holding up?"

"I'm fine."

I looked around, confused, as music replaced the roar of motorcycle engines. The dash lights came back on, and up front, Deeps was trying to get Sig to take a stick of gum. "Trust me. It'll help."

Hawkins loosened his tie, and I brushed back the hair that had fallen out of my updo.

"I don't understand," I said.

"What don't you understand?" Hawkins said.

"What just happened? We were boxed in, but those guys didn't do anything."

Deeps and Hawkins exchanged a look. "It was a warning," Hawkins said. "Okay, Deeps. Go ahead and investigate. You're right. We need to know who sent those goons."

I stared at Hawkins. *What? Isn't it obvious it's Jouvert?*

"The 'No on 28' movement is becoming increasingly violent," Hawkins added. "I'm not surprised I'm being targeted."

Sig reached over the backrest to hand me a mirror and we traded glances. I wasn't the only one who thought Hawkins was blowing smoke.

Ho and Hawkins went back to reviewing the guest list, and Sig talked me through putting my hair back in place.

I fumbled with the bobby pins. The danger I'd sensed was real, and getting worse every day. I couldn't escape it, but now I realized maybe Sig should leave.

I didn't want to lose Sig, but there was nothing more I could tell him about Luke, and the longer Sig hung around, the greater the chance that the feds would catch him or he'd end up as collateral damage. I needed to tell him to go.

Wilshire Boulevard was decked out for Christmas with white lights wrapped around the palm trees and a grinning Rudolph plunked down in the median strip. When we pulled up to the Los Angeles County Museum, I saw that police lined both sides of Wilshire and wooden barriers closed off one lane. Cops with riot shields walked along the barriers while protesters crowded against them.

Guys who looked my age and slightly older stood side by side with senior citizens. Men and women waved hand-painted signs.

SIGNING = SLAVERY.

SHAME ON YOU, PATERNALISTS!

AUCTIONS DEVALUE WOMEN.

I reached for Becca's necklace, forgetting I'd taken it off. Suddenly, I felt vulnerable and exposed despite my high-tech corset and I wished I'd pinned the little dolphin to the lace trim.

Hawkins eyed the protesters. "What do you think, Adam? How big is the crowd?"

"Two thousand. Twenty-five hundred max."

"That's the biggest protest we've seen at one of these."

"Are you polling public opinion on auctions?" Sig said.

"Big money loves them," Ho answered, "so right now, we love them."

Not me. I don't love them.

We rolled up to the main museum entrance that was tented with bulletproof glass. Deeps got out first. His tux stretched across his giant shoulders, and underneath, he had his gun. He surveyed the wall of photographers before he motioned to Hawkins to step out.

Time slowed as Hawkins smiled and waved for the cameras. "I know you don't really want another photo of me, guys," Hawkins said. "Shall I bring out Aveline?"

The photographers roared out my name. "Aveline! Aveline!" Hawkins offered me his hand and I slid out of the car, holding my breath. Lights flashed in my face and I listened for the crack of a sniper shot as Sig positioned me on the red carpet. One leg slightly forward. Shoulders back. Left hand on my hip so the cameras could catch the Love bracelet.

"Aveline, who are you wearing?"

The man called out the question three times before I was able to answer, "Nosuki!"

The camera kept going as a voice I recognized too well came through a loudspeaker. "Let's all welcome Candidate Hawkins and his wife-to-be, Avie Reveare."

I wheeled around and saw Yates standing on the roof of a van across the street, a mike up to his lips. And the way he looked at me, the coldness in his eyes, crumpled my heart like paper.

Hawkins leaned over me. "Keep smiling. We'll be out of here in a minute."

But Yates was only getting warmed up. "Jessop Hawkins bought his wife for fifty million dollars, and they are here tonight to sell other young girls into marital slavery."

I wanted to smash my hands over my ears, but I couldn't in front of the press. *Can't you please stop hating me? That's not why I'm here.*

Hawkins took my elbow and steered me toward the long red-carpeted staircase.

"Is this the kind of man we want as governor of California?" Yates cried.

The crowd roared.

I tripped on a fold in the carpet and Hawkins caught me before I fell. My chest burned like I'd taken a bullet to the back. My corset couldn't protect me from Yates' disgust.

"He should leave you out of this," Hawkins said through gritted teeth. "If Yates Sandell wants to pick a fight with me, bring it on. But he should know you better."

Shut up. Shut up, I wanted to scream.

Photographers lined the stairs, snapping away. Every six steps we stopped on the wide landing, and I posed, beaming like a pro and fighting back my tears. Ho was almost giddy, naming the media outlets featuring us.

Yates is free, I kept telling myself, *and that's all that matters.*

Finally, we reached the top, and Hawkins guided me into a gallery where two or three hundred men milled around, talking and drinking at tall tables on both sides of a raised catwalk while television crews positioned video cameras and lights, and a DJ blasted music.

The room smelled of meat and cologne, and I began to feel slightly sick as a server offered me his platter of beef kebabs decorated with orchid sprays. Sig brought me a champagne flute filled with ginger ale.

"I know that was rough out there, but try to hold it together. I'll see if I can get you out of here early."

I sipped my drink, trying to breathe through the nausea. CHRISTIE'S PRESENTS THE EXOTIC COLLECTION was projected on the wall above my head, and I kept hearing Yates tell the crowd that I was here to sell young girls into marital slavery.

Hawkins was busy shaking hands and chatting up potential donors. He dragged me from group to group, making me stand adoringly at his side. At one point, I tried asking if I could sit down. "My ankle's killing me in these heels."

"You sit when I sit," he said. "This is work."

The men were all ages, wearing anything from leather jackets over their hoodies to designer tuxes. Tech titans, media moguls, real estate developers, high-profile lawyers, they all had one thing in common: they'd put a multimillion-dollar deposit down just to be here.

I was the only girl in the room, so a hundred eyes were on me. I breathed into my body shield, telling myself to ignore the stares.

Hawkins seemed to be testing ideas for changing the party. "It's time to reimagine California's Paternalist Party, don't you agree?" he'd ask. He'd listen and then ask more questions like he actually cared about the answers.

If you really wanted to change the Paternalists, I thought, you wouldn't be here. You'd be out front with the protesters.

A few minutes later, the director of Christie's tapped Hawkins on the shoulder. "We're ready for you to take the stage, Mr. Hawkins. With your permission, we'd like to invite your fiancée to join you and announce the name of each girl as she steps on the catwalk."

I shook my head no, but Hawkins ignored me. "Avie would be delighted."

I teetered up the steps, painfully conscious as I took my place beside Hawkins at the podium that I was doing exactly what Yates had said I'd do.

"It's simple," Hawkins told me. "I'll tell you when to read from the teleprompter." An assistant filled my arms with tiger lilies. "Give one to each girl as she enters."

The spotlight pinned Hawkins and me as the director announced, "Tonight's MC and the next governor and First Lady of California, Jessop Hawkins and Aveline Reveare." Hawkins waved as clapping and whistling filled the air, and I shifted the flowers in my arms, trying to duck behind them from the cameras.

I promised Hawkins I'd campaign for him, but this? If I'd known—

"Good evening, gentlemen. Tonight, I have the special pleasure of introducing the fifteen beauties handpicked by Christie's debutante curator for this fall's exclusive Exotic Collection. The Exotic Collection celebrates ethnic beauty and pedigree, combined with documented American citizenship.

"As each girl takes the runway, the number to text in your bids will appear on the wall to my left."

The DJ pumped up the beat, the overhead lights dimmed, and spinning patterns of leopard and cheetah spots appeared on the walls.

Spots lit the catwalk, and Hawkins leaned in to me. "Read the first line on the teleprompter and don't be shy."

I saw the name come up on the screen. Chantal Gupta. How can I do this? "Chantal Gupta."

Hawkins nudged me. "A little louder, Aveline."

"Chantal Gupta."

Chantal emerged and smiled at me as I handed her a tiger lily. She looked familiar, with her olive skin and dark eyes. She strode down the runway in her long, chiffon leopard-print dress, slit high up the front. The fabric floated away as she moved, revealing her toned arms and legs and perfect figure.

Hawkins read her bio. Chantal was my age, a junior at Harvard-Westlake Girls. She was halfway down the catwalk when I realized she'd beaten me at a track meet in May, breezing past me like she had turbo power.

Now, she worked the runway, dipping her head and catching the eyes of men on both sides as she passed. They texted away, and a number appeared on the wall. In one minute, Chantal hit 7 mil, then jumped to 10 as she pivoted, growing to 14.325 by the time she disappeared back behind the curtain. Fourteen million, three hundred, and twenty-five thousand.

I managed to read off the next two names, and the girls each stepped out like pros who'd practiced their runway skills. They sashayed, hips swinging, and used the lilies almost like wands, tipping them toward men whose attention they wanted to catch.

Hawkins announced the girls' vital statistics: their academic, athletic, and genetic scores, their fathers' net worth and his political and commercial connection values.

The girls were reduced to this: scores.

The lilies' perfume was turning my stomach. I swore I could hear the protesters chanting outside.

I'm a traitor for being here, supporting this.

The next name came up on the teleprompter: Zara Akimoto, my friend from school. My chest seized. This couldn't be right. "I can't read it," I told Hawkins.

"Sure you can," he said. "It's easy. Sound it out."

"No, you read it."

I shifted the awkward bundle of flowers, wishing I could dive off the stage. How could her father do this to her? He had to know she was gay.

Zara emerged. Her dress was in shreds as if she'd taken a pair of scissors to it backstage. She reached out for a lily, and our eyes connected. I saw the shock register in hers, and she ripped the flower from my hand.

I'm sorry. I'm sorry. I'm so sorry.

Zara threw the flower aside, then walked the runway like she was attacking it, flaunting her ragged tiger stripes and glaring at the men. She was unexpectedly beautiful, her features a blend of Japanese and African-American, and her face radiant with fierce, outraged energy.

Her heart was tied to Portia's, and her being here was completely and totally wrong.

The number on the wall held steady at zero, and I prayed that it would stay that way. If the bids didn't hit the minimum her father set, Zara wouldn't sell.

But then I saw a man at a nearby table fix on her like a hunter on his prey. Zara pivoted, and a three appeared on the wall, then five, then seven, and I saw two men eye each other across the catwalk like this was a duel. No, no! I thought as the number on the wall hit eleven, then thirteen, and finally nineteen before one man saluted the other with his wineglass.

You pigs!

I shoved the flowers at the nearest assistant and got down from the stage. Sig was at my side in an instant. "Please get me out of here." He and Deeps flanked me, and we exited the gallery. They shielded me from the press and walked me across the plaza to the sculpture garden.

Deeps patrolled inside the green steel columns that fenced it off from the street, then said, "All clear." He guarded the entrance while Sig and I ducked between the Rodin sculptures and took refuge on a bench among the rows of palms wrapped in twinkle lights.

The crowd was still on the street. I could hear the protesters cheer a speaker. "Until women are free to choose their futures, no one is free!"

"Amen," Sig said. Safe in the semidark, his inner Helen peeked out. "You want to tell me what happened back there?"

"I know some of those girls. Zara, the one in the tiger print, she was in my class in school. She shouldn't even be here. She doesn't like guys."

Sig's expertly groomed eyebrow went up. "You mean she prefers chicken over beef."

"Yes, she's got to be dying inside."

The palms overhead clattered in the cold breeze. I shivered and Sig wrapped his jacket around my shoulders.

"Yates was right. I'm helping sell girls into marital slavery. No wonder he hates me."

"He does not hate you."

"You heard him."

"Stop. That young man is not fool enough to think you returned to

Jessop Hawkins because you wanted to. I saw the video of your *triumphant* return, and you're no actress, honey!"

I smiled despite myself.

"Avie, I know men, and if he's angry, it's because he still loves you."

You think so? "I shouldn't care how he feels; we're never going to be together again."

"Never? If I allowed *never*—" Sig took in my frown. "Don't let today stop you from believing in tomorrow, Avie. I am the poster girl for 'anything is possible.'" Sig waited for me to say something.

"All right," I said finally, just to be polite. Sig might believe that anything is possible, but I'd already learned that losing someone you love happens all the time.

We sat there listening to the speeches until Deeps waved us to go back inside. The catwalk was over and Hawkins was shaking hands with some man who'd practically fallen all over him earlier.

Hawkins signaled to me to come stand next to him. When I did, he took my hand, and I could tell he was unhappy from the way he squeezed it.

The girls who'd been auctioned were out on the floor with the winning bidders. Zara stood between her dad and the man who won her, staring straight ahead as if they didn't exist.

I wanted to go over and say something to her, but what? *I'm so sorry your life was destroyed?*

"Ready to go?" Hawkins said.

About two hours ago. "Sure."

Somehow, I walked to the car. Cameras flashed in my face. How could I live with myself, aiding the Paternalists? A few weeks ago, I might have been able to stop Jouvert with that tape, to force him out in the open, but I threw that chance away to save myself.

What happened here tonight is partly my fault.

Hawkins helped me into the car, then got in beside me. "You shouldn't have left the stage like that." He twisted the cap off a water bottle like he was wringing its neck.

"I wasn't feeling well."

"I know what Yates Sandell said upset you, but we made a deal. You promised you'd be at my side."

I promised I'd be his faithful campaign companion, but there were limits to what I could take. My heart sped up as I said, "I tried. I did, but please don't make me come to one of these again."

"You can't avoid auctions because Yates Sandell will be there."

"I knew some of those girls, and at least one of them would rather die than get Signed." I mustered all my courage. "I just helped sell one of my friends into slavery."

Hawkins shoved the cap back on the bottle. "Are you *enslaved?*" he snapped. "Are you being *abused?*"

I was steaming under my foil dress. You don't get it, I wanted to scream. It's like you *want* to be blind to what you're doing. "I bet Marielle would have gone for over twenty-five mil given how wealthy and connected your family is."

Hawkins glared at me. "I would *never* have let my sister be auctioned."

"Exactly."

We faced off in silence before finally turning away from each other. We were near UCLA when Hawkins said, "Adam, are there any more debutante auctions in the campaign schedule?"

"Let me check," Ho answered. "None on the West Coast."

"Does that meet with your approval?" Hawkins asked.

"Yes, thank you," I answered. Great. So, I'd gotten myself out of going to any more auctions, but . . .

I toyed with the pleated folds on my skirt. How could I strut around in this dress declaring I wasn't a slave when I acted like one, doing exactly what Hawkins wanted, supporting a cause I despised?

And the searing look in Zara's eyes when she saw me? My stomach tightened, remembering.

Yates was cruel, saying what he did, but he wasn't wrong. I was just as guilty as Hawkins.

If I didn't want to be Hawkins' lapdog, I had to do more about auctions than just not show up. I had to act.

40

Hawkins knocked on my door the next morning, the first time he'd ever done that. Even more bizarre, he was wearing jeans and a plaid shirt, and he'd traded his tasseled Italian loafers for walking shoes. "Get dressed. We're going for a drive."

I leaned against the doorway, curious. "Now? It's not even eight."

"Best time to go. No traffic."

"Fine." I went to close the door.

"Downstairs in fifteen."

"Jeez. I'll be there, okay!"

I pulled on some jeans, and the closest thing I could find in my closet to hiking boots. The only clue I had to where we were going was that it wasn't like anywhere we'd been before. When I came down to the kitchen, Hawkins handed me a to-go cup and a slice of toast. "Let's go."

"Wait. Just the two of us?"

"Yes."

I followed him to the garage, surprised we were leaving the compound without Deeps and Ho tagging along after what happened driving into town last night.

Hawkins opened the passenger door of a red Ferrari convertible and held my cup while I got in.

I had just buckled my seat belt when Deeps charged out of the house. "Wait, Mr. Hawkins, you aren't planning on going out without security?"

"That's absolutely what I'm planning." Hawkins pushed a button, and he and Deeps watched the top lift up and fold into the trunk with an elegant, silent motion.

"Sir, at least put the top back up."

"You really think there's an assailant waiting outside that gate at eight in the morning on the off chance I'll suddenly appear?" Hawkins slid into his seat. "We'll be back in a couple hours."

The engine's rumble echoed in the subterranean garage. Hawkins guided the car up the drive. The gate opened as we neared, and he eased the Ferrari onto Pacific Coast Highway. We left the compound behind, and the ocean spread blue and wide on the right, while the Santa Monica mountains loomed on the left.

Wind whipped my hair as Hawkins accelerated, and I closed my eyes, and almost felt free. I couldn't even remember the last time I'd ridden in a car with the top down. The closest I'd come to this was riding on the back of Yates' motorcycle.

I leaped off that thought and let it disappear. Yates and me—that was the past. I had to live in the now.

Pacific Coast Highway was mostly empty, and the Ferrari sailed past every car we met. After a few miles, Hawkins turned off the highway into the mountains.

The road climbed, cut out of the rocky hills with miles of switch-backs and short, sharp turns. Hawkins pushed the accelerator and the engine roared. I gripped the door handle until I caught the rhythm of the car and the road.

We flew past low brush and red-barked manzanita. Summer dust still coated the leaves on the sycamores, and caked on the roadside boulders. We charged past two life-sized bronzes of rearing stallions decked out in Santa hats at the gate of a private road.

Across the canyon, acres of black earth surrounded the shells of a dozen burned-out mansions where a wildfire had come through. The fire line stopped suddenly, and then the houses ended, and it was just us out here.

The car felt so connected with the road that it anticipated every turn. I began to love the roar of the engine, and the wind whipping my sleeve.

I looked over, and Hawkins was smiling. Not the tight, fake smile he'd had when he'd shaken all those hands at the auction, but a re-laxed, genuine smile.

When he saw me looking at him, he said, "I needed this. What about you? You enjoying it?"

It was the first time he'd ever asked me that. "Yeah, I am."

We zigzagged up the jagged ribbon of road into the hills for miles until we reached the crest. On the left stood a huge sign saying COM-ING SOON! with a painting of a Tuscan-style mansion and a red Ferrari parked out front.

Hawkins turned onto a dirt road and slowed to a crawl over the rutted track. A steel cattle gate appeared after about a mile and we drove through, closing the gate behind us.

The mountains spread out below and the ocean was a blue border alongside, until the road dipped and we lost sight of the water. A half mile later, we drove up to a house that looked like it was wired together with parts salvaged from old barns and farmhouses. The wood was unpainted and not one window matched another. Copper bells hung from the porch and beehives studded the ground beneath the fruit trees out back.

A man loading wood into his pickup watched us pass. He and Hawkins exchanged glances, but not friendly ones.

"Who's that?"

"That's Roy."

"He doesn't look thrilled to see you."

"He's not. But I don't give a flying fuck how he feels." Hawkins guided the car into an open area past the orchard, then got out and tossed his jacket on the seat. "Let's take a walk," he said, handing me a bottle of water.

We started down a path through the waist-high scrub, and I still had no clue what we were doing here. Maybe Hawkins thought I'd be easier to deal with if he let me walk around in the open—like letting a dog run off leash.

Dust powdered my boots and the sun was hot enough that I peeled off my shirt and walked in my tank. A red-tailed hawk circled silently above us. The hills on either side were empty of houses and fences, and the only sounds were birds rustling in the brush. The air carried a faint scent of sage.

"Does Roy own this land or is it part of the state park?" I said.

"Neither. I own it."

No wonder Roy wasn't friendly. His wild backyard carved up into mansions. "So when are you going to start building homes up here?"

Jessop gave a laugh. "You noticed the sign."

"It's six feet tall. It's a little hard to miss."

"I don't intend to build anything up here, but I'll never let Roy forget I can."

"Whoa. You guys really don't get along."

"I didn't buy this land to irk Roy. The acreage will go to a conservancy group after I die. My sister fought for years to preserve cougar habitat in these mountains."

That's just like you to do a good thing, and add your own vengeful twist.

We continued down the trail until we got to a lookout. "I haven't been up here in a while. Not since Livia—" Jessop paused to gaze out over the hills. "She used to love it up here."

With that one little sentence I knew: he'd *loved* her. He'd actually loved someone outside of himself. And she'd loved him back. How was that even possible?

"What do you think?" He tipped his head at the view.

"About this? It's beautiful."

He took off his baseball cap and a breeze ruffled his hair. "Yeah, it's a good place to clear your head."

"Is that why we're here?"

"No. We need to work things out between us, preferably in private." I shifted from one foot to another. "What do you mean?"

"Your Contract says you will love, honor, and obey, not that I expect compliance with regard to love. But I demand you treat me with respect. Especially in front of the staff."

My heart crawled up my throat, hearing the hard tone in his voice.

"I mean it, Aveline. No sulking, no outbursts. No smart talk."

I was supposed to heel like a goddamn dog? I wasn't even allowed to express myself? "Oh yeah?" I cried. "What about respecting my feelings?"

"Your feelings? I gave you what you wanted. I used my connections, my influence to get your precious boyfriend out of prison!"

"You didn't *give* me that. That wasn't a *gift*. We made a *deal*."

Hawkins gulped the last of his water and crushed the plastic bottle with one hand. "What do you want? Clothes? A trip to Hawaii? Europe?"

"Clothes! You think I want clothes?"

Hawkins went to pitch the bottle into the brush, but caught himself. "Then what?"

Let me go.

My heart was racing. There was no point in asking for my freedom. Of all the things I could ask for, he'd never give me that. "I want you to listen to me. To my opinions."

"About what specifically?"

"Politics."

Hawkins began to laugh. "Seriously?"

"Auctions need to end," I snapped.

"This is about last night."

"You said yourself you'd never let your sister be auctioned."

"Yes, I did."

"But you support them."

"Of course I do. I'm campaigning as a Paternalist."

"Last night you kept talking about how it was time to *rethink the party*. Can't you start with auctions?"

"No! You don't understand: auctions are an industry. They throw off millions in taxes and licensing fees, not to mention import duties, at a time when legislatures are hungry for revenue. I'd be crucified if I took that on."

Coward. I didn't need to say it aloud. Hawkins read my face.

"I'm not taking on that fight. That idea is going nowhere, so don't bring it up again."

I spun around and started marching back to the car. Hawkins was right behind me. "This is why I don't listen to you: because you're a teenage girl who doesn't know the simplest things about how the world works."

I spun back around. "But you'd listen to Livia, wouldn't you?"

Hawkins held a finger up in warning. "Don't."

"I bet Livia wouldn't be a big fan of the Paternalists."

He swung his hand back, and I straightened my shoulders and looked him in the eyes. *Go ahead.*

A moment passed and he dropped his hand. "Go get in the car."

I stood there just long enough to make it clear I wasn't rushing to obey. I'd gone a few steps when his phone buzzed.

The car was in sight when Hawkins trotted up behind me. "We need to go. There's a situation."

41

We turned onto PCH, and started passing news vans, headed in the same direction. As we drove up to the compound, Deeps was painting over PIMP, the first in a long line of equally ugly words sprayed in six-foot-high letters on the wall along the highway.

Deeps moved aside the handful of reporters who'd gathered in front of the gate. He jogged after us into the garage and walked us inside to the big cement table, where Sig and Ho were streaming the news on their tablets.

Ho, who never broke a sweat, had big stains under his arms. "We have an issue. One of the girls from last evening's auction was arrested for murdering her father."

My stomach lurched. "Tell me it's not Zara."

Ho ignored me. "We're trying to contain the fallout," he told Hawkins.

Sig guided me into the chair next to where he was sitting. "Do you feel faint? Do you need a glass of water?"

"Answer me, Sig. Is it Zara?"

Sig nodded and moved his tablet so I could see the video. The headline read "Girl Murders Father," and there was the two-story house with the red tile roof and pink bougainvillea over the front door I'd gone through dozens of times for birthday parties and sleepovers.

The police brought Zara out. She stared straight ahead and walked to the squad car, arms cuffed behind her back, her cami and pajama pants splattered with blood. Then her brother ran out of the house, screaming, "You bitch, you used my bat! My championship bat. I hope they lock you up forever!"

I rocked in my seat, shaking my head at how I'd had a hand in this disaster. Zara had looked right at me last night, and I hadn't done a thing. Not a single, freaking thing.

"This is a public-relations nightmare," Ho muttered. "Reporters are asking for a comment regarding Aveline's former classmate."

Sig held my hand under the table.

"Avie has no comment," Hawkins said.

"The press is asking for a comment from you, too, Jessop."

"No comment."

Ho's phone buzzed. "Senator Fletcher's office." Ho turned away to take the call, but we could still hear him. "Mr. Hawkins is in the air. I expect to hear from him in about—ninety minutes. Yes, he will call the senator when he lands."

Hawkins leaned on the window, clenching and unclenching one fist.

A reporter standing on Zara's lawn addressed the camera. "The victim was found facedown on the carpet in his bedroom alongside a bloodied aluminum baseball bat which police believe to be the murder weapon. Police suspect that the motive for the attack was the girl's opposition to her auction the night before."

"Your school seems to be a breeding ground for violent young women," Hawkins muttered.

"Zara wasn't violent," I said. "She was the kind of person who'd stand up for you if someone was picking on you. She would never have done this if her father hadn't put her up for auction."

"That's no excuse," Hawkins snapped. "Plenty of girls are auctioned and none of them has ever murdered their father."

"Zara was in love."

"Again, no excuse."

I wanted to rage. He thought this was simple—like me and Yates. "She was in love with another girl!" I yelled.

Hawkins' neck was turning crimson. "Take. The volume. Down. Avie."

"You said you would never have auctioned Marielle. How come it's okay for everyone else and not her?"

His mouth twitched and Sig's hand crushed mine.

"We were there," I said. "You and I stood up on that stage and showed the whole world that we support auctions. So now we can't say 'no comment' and pretend we're not partly to blame for her father's death!"

A voice burst in. "Reporting live from St. Mark's Church, we're here with activist Yates Sandell." Ho rushed to mute his tablet, while Sig fumbled with the controls on his. "We need to send a message to politicians like Jessop Hawkins that we oppose Signings, especially non-consensual Signings. Candidate Hawkins and his fiancée, Aveline Reveare, took part in the auction last night, supporting the monster who sold his gay daughter against her will."

"Turn that off!" Hawkins roared.

I didn't care if he yelled, didn't care if he hit me. My legs were shaking, but I got to my feet. "I am going to comment. I am going to walk out there and tell the reporters exactly what I think."

"NO, YOU ARE NOT!" Sig shoved away from the table, and if it hadn't weighed as much as a boulder, it would have fallen to the floor.

"Sig?"

"Obviously, you feel guilty about your friend, but *she* killed her father, not you! And you are not going to endanger this campaign and everyone else's efforts by spilling your adolescent guts to the media."

"Screw you, Sigmund." How could he have turned on me, too?

"The safest place for her right now might be in her room," Sig said to Hawkins, who nodded.

Deeps reached for my arm and I whirled out of reach. "Don't you touch me! I'll go, but you keep your hands off me." Deeps escorted me up the stairs and held the door to my room open.

"I hate you," I said as he let it close. The magnetic lock clicked and I grabbed hold of the handle and shook it with all my strength. "I won't be silent! I won't. You can lock me up in here, but you can't silence me forever!"

I flung myself at the bed and ripped off the sheets. Then I launched myself against the windows, pounding them with my fists. "We are monsters!" I screamed. "Monsters!"

Hawkins came out on the terrace below, his hands shoved deep in his pockets. He turned and looked up at me as I hammered the windows. "Do you hear me? We are monsters!"

Hawkins continued to watch as flat steel security shutters slowly rolled down outside the windows. I slid down the glass, screaming, "You think this is going to stop me? You think you can shut me up?" I was on my hands and knees when the room went completely dark, and the shutters locked in place.

I collapsed in the corner. I could feel the floor, but not see it. The only sound was my ragged breathing. I had stood on that stage, Hawkins' obedient little trophy, and I did nothing. Nothing!

In the dark, images flashed before me. Zara standing over her dad. The bat swinging down. His skull exploding across the pillow.

Andrew, her brother, screaming at her, "You bitch, you used my bat. My championship bat! I hope they fucking lock you up forever!"

Oh God, the baseball bat.

I buried my face in my knees and began to sob, remembering our last slumber party: Zara braiding Portia's long, blond hair into an elaborate crown as she told us, "My dad used my college money for a professional pitching coach for Andrew. He told me to go get a scholarship."

Of course Zara used his baseball bat.

Hours later, Sig unlocked the door. By then, I'd cried myself out. He turned on the light and sat down next to me.

I glared at him through the hair hanging in my face. "Get away from me. You're on their side."

Sig raised an eyebrow so high I thought his face might split. "Do you *not know* why I did what I did down there?"

"You wanted to protect Luke."

"Not just Luke. There are other lives at stake here, including yours." We sat in silence for a moment then Sig said gently, "They took your friend Portia to Cedars-Sinai. Suicide attempt."

"What? No!"

"She left a note. Apparently, she and Zara had made a pact. They had originally intended to do it together."

"Is she still alive?"

"They pumped her stomach, and she's in serious condition, but they think she'll live."

I wrapped my arms over my head and pictured Portia in her silky pj's dotted with lipstick kisses, tossing back pills, and washing them down with Gran Patrón. Portia must have felt so desperate.

"I'm sorry, I can't do this," I told Sig. "I can't be silent."

"You don't have to be silent, but you can't speak out."

"What's that supposed to mean?" I snapped.

"Right now, you're ashamed. But your feelings do not matter. They will not save lives and they will not alter the world."

"So I'm not supposed to say anything?"

"You will have only one chance, one, to deliver a message before the Hawkins campaign machine shuts you down, so it better be big— an apocalyptic, despot-toppling revelation that will the change the world as we know it."

"TEOTWAWKI," I muttered.

"What's that?"

"Nothing." I pushed my hair off my face. "One chance. I don't know what I'd say."

"When the time is right, you'll know."

"I want to see Zara."

"Don't be a fool. Adam Ho won't let you anywhere near the L.A. County Jail. Not even in that nasty Chaste sack." Sig rubbed my shoulder. "Why don't you try to get some rest?"

"How am I supposed to rest?"

Sig got up, saying, "I need to get to LAX. There are eight guitar shops in Montana, Wyoming, Idaho, and Washington State that have carried 7476 brand guitars."

"You think they're Barnabas'?"

"Maggie hid a mandolin in her storage unit, and she wouldn't have held on to it if it wasn't important. The number 7476 was burned into the wood inside."

"Barnabas taught Luke how to build guitars and mandolins. I'm sure Luke would love to have it."

"And I would love to give it to him. With luck, I'll either find him or get a lead on him. In the meantime, do me a favor and stay under the radar."

"Like I have a choice."

"They won't keep you in here forever."

"I wouldn't bet on it." Sig was almost to the door when I said, "Sig, if you find Luke, don't tell him you know me."

"Are you sure?"

"Yes, absolutely." I couldn't bear Luke telling Sig what he thought of me, of what I'd become.

I dragged my sheets and comforter off the floor and dumped them on the bed, then crawled under the quilt. I was repellent. A traitor. A whore, just like someone had written on the compound wall.

42

Sometime during the night I heard the steel shutters roll up. I opened one eye, thinking I'd try the door, but then turned back over. Hawkins wasn't letting me out anytime soon.

He woke me early the next morning when he flipped on the light. I snapped my comforter over my head. "What do you want?"

"I'm going to London for a few days."

"Why? Is it too *hot* in L.A.?"

"Adam thought I should avoid the spotlight until the scandal blows over."

I hate you, I thought. I hate you for making me into this hideous, awful person, and I hate myself for letting you.

"I'm leaving now." Hawkins stood there like he expected me to make some big gesture of good-bye.

"Yeah, well, have a nice trip," I said.

I lay there thinking about my friends and how our lives had shattered. Zara, funny, fierce Zara, a murderer. Portia, so fragile that Zara always protected her, teetering on the edge. Brilliant, untamable Sparrow torching herself. Dayla, the most L.A. of us, sold off to a rancher in Montana.

And me, Zara's accomplice and Hawkins' lapdog. I was every disgusting thing Yates said I was.

Hours later, Deeps tried to bring me lunch, but I told him to get out. I had no desire to eat ever again.

I stared out at the ocean, picturing myself floating on the surface, the cold water numbing me until I let go and sank to the ocean floor. I was so, so tired of trying to survive. And what was the point, anyway?

The sun went down, and Deeps came in. "Did Sig call?" I asked.

"No."

I turned away. "Wake me when he does."

"It's time to get up."

"Go away."

"I'm asking you nicely. Please get up, Avie."

"Why should I?"

He leaned down, and before I realized it, he'd wrapped the quilt around me as tight as a tourniquet and scooped me up off the bed.

"What the hell are you doing?" I said. Deeps threw me over his shoulder. "Put me down!"

"Sure I'll put you down."

He'd pinned my arms to my chest, so I arched my back and kicked, trying to get free, but I couldn't throw off his grip. Deeps carried me across the hall to the elevator.

"Where are you taking me?" I demanded.

"You'll see."

I arched my back once again, and he shoved my head down. "You're going to hit your head if you don't stop that," he said, stepping inside.

I realized for the first time that he and I were alone. The chef had gone for the day and Hawkins and Ho were in London. Deeps wanted me to cooperate, but why?

We got out at the bottom floor.

"Why did you bring me down here?" I said.

Deeps began to whistle the Seminole war chant. He carried me past the darkened gym, then pushed open the door to the indoor pool. He walked over to the deep end, and I realized what he was about to do. "Don't!" I cried.

Deeps dropped me and I sank, dragging the comforter under.

Water soaked the fabric, then the down inside, and the weight pulled me to the bottom. Silence filled my ears. I saw the bright green surface shimmering only a few feet above me, and Deeps crouched on the side, watching.

He's going to let me drown?

I thrashed my arms and legs, fighting the heavy cloth, but my legs only got more tangled. My heart was pounding so loudly I could hear it.

I can't breathe. I can't breathe. I have to get this off me.

Then I remembered how Yates once got his leash caught in a huge kelp bed after he'd fallen off his surfboard. The surf rolled him under and the kelp tied itself around his legs. "I knew I'd die if I didn't calm down," he'd told me. "The more I fought, the worse it got."

I forced myself to stop flailing, and hold still. I waited, lungs burning, ready to explode, until I felt the quilt loosen. Then I peeled it down with my hands and shot to the surface.

I sucked in a huge breath, and Deeps stood up. The life-saving hook was in his hands.

"What the fuck was that!" I yelled.

"That was me doing my job." He hooked the comforter and towed it toward the surface. "I can't save your life if you don't want to live."

I swam to the shallow end, and pressed against the wall, hiding my now transparent top. Deeps dragged the quilt out of the pool, then threw me a towel and hung a robe over a nearby chair. "Soup or a smoothie?"

Apparently, me not eating wasn't an option anymore. "Smoothie."

"It'll be waiting in your room."

When I was alone again, I peeled off my wet clothes and wrapped up in the robe. I supposed I should thank Deeps for jump-starting my will to live. I couldn't fix what I'd done if I wasn't here to do it.

Entering the hall, I saw the screen above the elliptical turned to the news even though the gym was empty. Another one of Deeps' tricks.

I walked right up and pressed against the windows. Yates was leading a silent vigil on the steps of St. Mark's Church. PRAY FOR ZARA AND HER FATHER and STOP AUCTION SLAVERY read signs held by some of the hundreds of people around him.

I should be there telling the world what I really believe. As if he'd want me there, I thought. I pictured myself emerging from a car and Yates yelling from the church steps, "What do you think you're doing here? Haven't you done enough?"

No, I haven't. I haven't done nearly enough.

My wet clothes were dripping onto the floor through the towel I'd wrapped them in. I bent down to wipe the slate, and when I stood up, Portia was being wheeled out of Cedars-Sinai.

Oh, Portia, are you okay? I fixed on the video, trying to see past the huge sunglasses and hoodie. Portia slumped in the wheelchair, and the press swarmed her like bees, bumping her and shoving their mikes in her face as her brothers and bodyguards tried to keep them off her.

Leave her alone! Can't you see she's barely holding it together?

I tried to tell myself this wasn't my fault, that Portia and Zara had collected those pills days ago, but what if last night I'd yelled, "Stop! This isn't right!"

I pictured the stunned moment of silence, Hawkins dragging me off the stage, and the auction continuing as planned. Maybe I couldn't have stopped it and Portia and Zara would still have done what they did, but what if my crying out made a father somewhere change his mind about Contracting his daughter?

Up on the screen, Jouvert waved his hand at a map of the Middle East while the banner across the bottom scrolled, "U.S. and Saudi relations enter new era." My stomach clenched. Jouvert would give them nukes and they'd give him all the money he wanted. And my friends and I were the pawns in their game.

I crouched down and wiped the last drops of water off the floor. I'd messed up in so many ways, and there were things I could never fix, but I needed to find something I could do that would help me live with myself again

Back in my room, the bed was made with fresh sheets, and a smoothie sat on the shelf beside it. I picked up the note by the glass.

"Be dressed by ten tomorrow. Visit with your dad." I drew in a deep breath, grateful to Deeps for arranging the visit. I needed to see Dad, the one person who loved me no matter what.

43

I slept hard, and managed to get down an egg and toast before Deeps flew me home. Dad waited for us on the terrace, and as soon as the helicopter rotors stopped spinning, he ran to help me out.

I came off the steps and Dad pulled me in for a hug. I buried my face in his chest, loving the weight of his arms around me, and the softness of his cotton sweater against my cheek.

"You've had a rough week," he said. "You holding up?"

"I'm surviving."

"You want to talk about it?"

"Not really. I'd sort of like to forget about everything."

"All right. You let me know if you change your mind." He tucked me under his arm and walked me into the house.

The scent of cinnamon, ginger, and cloves wafted through the downstairs. In the kitchen, Gerard, decked out in his red-striped apron, scraped icing off a beater. Flat sections of gingerbread covered the table and counters along with bowls of peppermints, jelly beans, and M&M's.

"Gingerbread," I marveled. "You remembered."

"How could I forget?" Gerard said.

"Thank you."

He handed me a beater to lick. Building gingerbread houses was Mom's Christmas tradition, but Gerard had always kept it alive for me.

I circled the island as Deeps sat down at the table, so happy that for a couple hours the only thing I had to worry about was keeping a few baked walls from falling down. "What is it? It's way bigger than what we usually make."

"Pasadena City Hall. We're donating it to the children's ward at Huntington Hospital so it has to be big," Gerard said. "But it's not as complicated as last year."

"What was that?" Deeps said.

"Disney Concert Hall," Dad muttered. "Those curved walls were a nightmare."

I leaned over to study Gerard's construction diagram, and realized I hadn't seen my pup. "Wait, where's Dusty?"

"She's at the groomer," Gerard answered. "I didn't know you'd be here when I scheduled her. Sorry about that."

Deeps was digging into the jelly beans, picking out green ones. Dad pulled out a seat next to him. "The estimated construction time is twelve man hours," he said, "so we'd better get started or you'll both still be here Christmas Day."

It was only a couple days away, and Hawkins hadn't said a word about it. "I wouldn't mind that, Dad."

"Neither would I, Angel Pie." Then turning to Deeps, Dad said, "I'm warning you, do exactly what this guy tells you." He pointed to Gerard. "And don't eat too many of those candies or you'll find yourself at the grocery store."

Dad joking with Deeps? The four of us building a gingerbread house? This was bizarre with a capital B.

"Honey, would you go upstairs and get some of that Christmas music your mom liked from the storage room? Gerard couldn't find it."

I glanced at Gerard, who responded with a big shrug. Gerard couldn't find it? He'd labeled and indexed every box in that room, and did an annual inventory. "Sure," I said.

Gerard handed me his key.

The storage room was upstairs, attached to the laundry. Light streamed through the skylight over the washer and dryer. The door to the storage room unlocked easily, and I left it open as I went in so I could find the string for the overhead light.

The light came on, just as I heard the door close behind me. "Gerard?"

"No, it's me."

"Yates?" I couldn't move, couldn't turn around. *Why is he here?*

"Avie." His hand lit on my arm, and I pulled away, but his fingers caught the tips of mine. I jerked like they'd been singed and cupped both my hands over my heart.

"Avie, please look at me."

I focused on the precisely labeled boxes on the shelves by my knees, trying to catch my breath. Yates took a step closer and I moved out of reach. Now I was trapped.

"What are you doing here?" My voice was barely a whisper.

His breath was warm on the back of my neck. "I had to see you."

The yearning in his voice made me feel like my heart could snap in two. "I don't understand. You hate me."

Yates sighed. "It's not real, Avie. None of it's real."

"What's not real?"

"I don't hate you. I've never hated you."

"But—the things you said about me—"

"You think I didn't know Hawkins Retrieved you, that he forced you to act the way you did? I know you, Avie."

My eyes filled. *No you don't.*

Yates wrapped his arms around my shoulders and the splint on his injured hand pinched my collarbone. Still, I leaned into him, wanting to believe.

He laid his head on mine. "It was your dad's idea for me to trash you to the media. He thought it would make Hawkins believe you and I are really over."

We are over. Why don't you see it? "You know I didn't want to leave you in Boise."

"Yeah, I know, and from what I heard, Luke got you out of there just in time."

"The police were right behind us."

"I was glad you were with him. Luke wouldn't let anything happen to you."

My heart gave a twinge. Things had happened, but not the way Yates imagined.

Yates turned me gently until we faced each other. In this light, his eyes were the deep blue of new jeans. I took in the thin white scar in his hairline and the slight dent in his nose left over from the accident on the mountain. We'd survived so much.

He swung his splint away from his body, inviting me closer, then bent his head toward mine. Our lips touched, and I tasted gingerbread and coffee.

"You taste like Christmas," I whispered.

A smile crinkled his eyes, and he drew me in closer, pressing his lips more firmly to mine. "I missed you so much," he said between kisses. "Once Hawkins got his hands on you, I almost couldn't stand it."

His lips traveled from my mouth to my jaw and down my neck as if by kissing all these places he could convince himself I was real. And the way our bodies melded together, it was as if they were trying to erase the time and distance we had been apart.

I gave in to the feelings drawing me to him even as I fought the thoughts spinning in my head.

This is wrong. This is a bad idea. Hawkins will be furious if he finds out.

My hands were on Yates' back, in his hair.

We can't do this. This is insane.

Hold me. Don't let me go.

"Stop. Stop," I whispered, easing out of his arms. "My bodyguard's downstairs. I'm supposed to be looking for Christmas music and he's going to come up here if I don't get down there."

"I know." Yates pointed to a stack of CDs on top of a box. "Don't worry. I won't let you get in trouble."

He slid his hand down my arm until he reached my fingers. I wondered if he could feel my heartbeat in my fingertips. "I met with the two reporters," he said. "They had a recording of Maggie's testimony from Salvation."

"Oh my God, Luke found them."

"Luke handed it over to them? I thought it was you."

Luke's okay. He's okay! Helen's going to be so relieved.

Oh shit. My heart thudded as I realized that Jouvert would think Hawkins and I betrayed him. "When are they going to run the story?"

"They're not sure. They're still confirming the allegations Maggie made. What's going on? You seem upset."

I couldn't tell Yates what I'd done. "No, this is great. It's what we prayed for, right, the end of Jouvert and the Paternalists?"

"Yeah, we're finally going to bring them down."

I dropped my eyes to the quote on Yates' shirt, still visible despite his splint. "Armies can be resisted, but not the idea whose time has come. V. Hugo."

How could Yates be so naïve, thinking a news article could take down Jouvert and his friends?

Yates wrapped his hand over mine and rested it on his chest. "So I need to tell you that after the story breaks, there will probably be a trial and I'll have to testify about what I witnessed in Salvation."

A gunshot rang in my ears and I saw Samantha Rowley crumple on the marble courthouse steps. Her lawyer's car explode in D.C. traffic.

"But it's incredibly dangerous. Jouvert will target you."

"Just because they let me out of prison, doesn't mean I'm not a target now. I might as well go out fighting."

"Yates—"

"There's a safe house in Tijuana. The plan is to hide you there until we can transport you to Hermosillo and fly you out of Mexico."

"What? When is this supposed to happen?"

"Now. Today. It's all set."

"This is crazy. Does Dad know?"

"He came up with the idea."

"And Deeps is just supposed to go along with this?"

"No, we'll take care of Deeps. He'll sleep right through it."

"You'll all go to prison if you get caught, all three of you."

"Not if Deeps wakes up and finds your dad and Gerard out cold over their cocoa. He'll think you drugged them given your history of taking down bodyguards."

I pulled away, slightly dizzy. Dad and Yates wanted to save me, but if I didn't testify, Jouvert could walk free, and Yates might die.

"There's no need for both of us to put our lives in danger," Yates said.

I shook my head. "You're wrong. You don't know everything I know." Yates hadn't heard the tape where Jouvert boasted to Sparrow about his deal with the Saudis.

"What am I missing?"

"I can't tell you."

"Are you saying you don't trust me?"

"No, of course I trust you. I trust you with my life."

"Then what is it?"

I can't tell you what I know, because then I'd have to tell you what I did.

"Avie, think about it. You'll never get the chance to testify. Jessop Hawkins won't let you near a courtroom. You don't have a choice. You have to get out of the country."

I closed my eyes. If I ran, I might live. But then I'd have to live with everything I'd done. "No, I'm not leaving."

Yates cupped his hands over my shoulders. "It won't be bad. Three hours to the border of Mexico. The priest who runs the safe house is a friend of Father Gabriel's. He'll keep you safe."

"I'm not scared to run. That's not why I said no."

"You sound like you mean it."

"I do."

A faint tapping made me jump. "Avie?" Gerard peeked around the door. "Deeps is asking about you," he said, exchanging glances with Yates. Yates mouthed "no" and shook his head.

Gerard's eyes pinched. *I don't understand.*

I know. I'm sorry.

Gerard plucked a photo album off a shelf and set it on a suitcase. "I'll tell Deeps you're looking through some old photos and will be down soon." His face was filled with dread as he closed the door.

"I'm sorry," I said when Yates and I were alone again. "You guys must have gone to a lot of trouble to arrange the safe house."

Yates shrugged. "We love you."

My heart crumbled, and I wrapped my arms around Yates' neck one last time. "I love you, too."

Our kisses said I'll never forget and I'm sorry. They held lost wishes and unspoken fears. Finally, they couldn't say any more, and we broke apart. Yates stacked the CDs on top of the album and handed them to me, and we gazed into each other's faces, trying to find the unbearable words for good-bye.

Then he reached up and drew his thumb down my cheek, his whispery voice giving me shivers. "'Let the world tell us no—'"

And his eyes held mine as we recited the last lines of the poem together. "'Love is the rusted fire escape that shouldn't support our weight, but does.'"

We'd never be together again, possibly never see each other again, but the love we had refused to believe that. We smiled sadly at each other one last time before I walked out the door and locked it behind me.

We didn't have enough time, not nearly enough. I started down the stairs. I couldn't hold back my tears and halfway down I had to stop. *You can't lose it. Hold it together.*

Yates was ready to go down fighting. Was I? I wasn't even seventeen. But Jouvert was coming after me and Hawkins, and I had to help stop him.

I wiped my face on my sleeve before I walked into the kitchen. Dad and Deeps were propping up two gingerbread walls while Gerard piped icing cement into the seam. "How about you put down that album and give us a hand, before this thing collapses?" Dad said.

Hours later, the four of us had piped the last icing detail on the walls and cemented the final green jelly bean to the roof. Deeps helped Gerard load our creation into Big Black so they could drive it over to the hospital the next morning.

Dad took me back inside while the two of them figured out how to secure it in the back. He shut the door to the library and led me across the room before he whispered, "I want you to reconsider our plan. When this story breaks, there could be a violent backlash against the Paternalists, including Jessop Hawkins, and you'll be caught in the middle."

"I know. And I'm grateful, really, I am, that you want to do this for me, but no."

"You're not going to explain your decision?"

I shook my head.

"Does this have something to do with your friend from school? Deeps said you've been upset."

Dad always avoided emotional issues, so if he talked to Deeps, he was really worried. "I'm not suicidal, if that's what you're thinking."

Dad's shoulders slumped. "You're awfully damn stubborn."

"Wonder where I got that from."

"No idea whatsoever." Dad sighed. "I'll see you in a few days." I must have looked confused, because he said, "Your Signing. Jessop invited me."

My spine prickled like he'd poured a cup of glass slivers down my back. "Right. Of course." Then we both turned, hearing Gerard and Deeps in the hall. "I guess we're leaving," I said.

Dad opened his arms and I walked into them. Then he kissed me on the forehead. "Merry Christmas."

"Merry Christmas, Dad."

A few minutes later I was in the chopper. Deeps started up the engine, and Dad waved from the terrace. Gerard's plastic tub of gingerbread dogs rested on my lap, and the stocking of gifts that Dad picked out leaned against my leg.

I waved as the helicopter rose, watching as Dad got tinier and tinier. This might be the last time he saw me alive, but at least we got to say good-bye.

44

Hawkins returned late that night. He'd headed back from London when Zara's story was pushed out of the Top Ten by a scandal at the Oklahoma City Fetal Protection Unit, where the head of "Resident Services" was accused of pimping out pregnant girls in his care.

I didn't see Hawkins then or the next morning. The Signing was tomorrow, and the compound was awhirl in pre-Signing prep. I had to dodge lighting and sound experts on my way to the kitchen, then caterers assessing the venue, and then security personnel keeping watch over them.

I wandered out to the parking circle, where Deeps was overseeing the tent setup. "Don't you put up a single post or inch of rigging before I inspect it," he told the crew.

A K-9 unit went past with a dog that was built like a marine, all chest and muscle with short tan fur like a crewcut. BOMB SQUAD was printed in big letters across the back of the handler's jacket. His communicator squawked instructions as he and the dog descended the stairs to the subterranean garage.

I knew I should warn Hawkins about the reporters' story coming out, but I couldn't figure out how to explain how I knew. And even if I prepped him for what was coming, could he really convince Jouvert we hadn't betrayed him?

When Adam Ho buzzed by, I trotted after him. "Is Jessop busy? I need to talk to him."

"He's got two lawyers in with him now, then a conference call with investment bankers, and a meeting with the vice president's security detail after that. He can fit you in around six P.M."

The screech of metal on metal made both of us whip around. Ho swore and took off for the front gate, where the party rental truck had stopped.

Deeps was watching two men in black suits and shades who had walked onto the flat roof. They strode along the edge, pointing and stopping every few feet. I came up beside him. "Who are they?" I asked.

"They're sharpshooters from the VP's security detail. We've got two hundred very important people coming to your Signing tomorrow."

I rubbed my goose-pimpled arms. The shooters could easily turn those guns on Hawkins and me. "You really think someone might try to kill the VP?"

"The only person who'd try that here is someone who wants to get caught. A guy who wants his face all over the media, because he wants the fame or because he's killing for a cause."

"So why don't they keep the media out?"

Deeps rubbed his fingers together. "The Almighty Dollar. High-profile Signing like yours means Jouvert gets his face on every Sportswall in the U.S., and he doesn't have to spend a dime."

The thought of Jouvert benefiting from my Signing made me sick. I needed to testify about Sparrow and Jouvert, but the chance I would was infinitesimally small. Samantha Rowley didn't even get inside the court building before she was shot.

But I had something Samantha didn't have. The vision came to me in full color.

"I'm going inside," I told Deeps, and almost ran back to my room. Then I shut the door and went right to the closet, where the wall hanging was still in the drawer. I shook it out and laid the bleached silk against my body.

Sig said I'd only get one chance to speak out before the campaign silenced me, so it better be an apocalyptic, despot-toppling, world-changing revelation. TEOTWAWKI. The End Of The World As We Know It.

This was the story I needed to tell.

45

I waited outside for Sig, hoping to catch him away from the monitoring equipment. He drove up after the security detail left, and stepped out of his Jaguar, sleek in his blue on blue striped suit and bronze pocket square.

"How was your trip?" *Did you find Luke?*

"Interesting." His lip was split and swollen on one side.

"What happened?"

Sig closed the car door stiffly, as if he was favoring his side. "I'm afraid I entertained some uninvited guests at my motel last night."

"Are you all right?"

"Bruised, but undaunted. I believe our boy has some very protective friends."

"He sent people to beat you up?"

"No, I suspect he had no clue what they did on his behalf."

"I'm sorry, Sig. But you think he's safe?"

"Yes, I do."

"Aren't you going to tell me where?"

"No." Sig paused. "But I think if you saw it, you would agree that he's in a good place."

I closed my eyes and saw Luke the way he was in Salvation with his family before the Siege. The calm quiet in his face, the loving look in his brown eyes. *Thank you. Thank you for keeping Luke safe. For taking care of him.*

"Avie."

I opened my eyes. A group of Secret Service men were walking toward us up the drive.

"Let's go in the house," Sig said, taking a garment bag out of the trunk. "I've got your Signing dress."

I swung the bag on my finger, and gushed, "Oooo, I can't wait to see my dress," as we passed the security detail. "What about those Zanotti heels I wanted? Did you find them?"

Once inside, Sig glanced at the camera in my bedroom, which had gone live again in the last hour, and went right to my walk-in closet. He hung the bag on a hook and zipped it open. "Oh, let's see," I squealed for the audio monitor overhead.

The white dress inside wasn't the little tissue-paper silk I'd tried on weeks ago that had made me feel like a virgin sacrifice.

The wool crepe was cut close to the body, and silver brambles wove over the bare shoulders and edged the skirt. "What are they made of?" I said, rubbing one of the thorny twigs between my fingers.

"Dyed leather, hand sewn."

"It's amazing, Sig—"

"But?"

For a moment I thought how easy it would be to wear this dress. But then— "I had something else in mind."

I handed Sig the wall hanging and watched as Sig weighed the silk in his hand. He contemplated the embroidered cherry branches. *Are you sure?*

Yes, I'm sure.

"Well, this fabric would certainly make a statement," he said.

"Fashion is message, right?"

"Yes, it most definitely is. Hmm. It would be a travesty to lose any of that gorgeous needlework in the tailoring." Sig took the fabric, pivoted me, and held it up to my waist. In the full-length mirror, I saw how the silk trailed a foot or more behind me.

Then Sig moved the silk up between my shoulder blades. "We'll dye it pink, perhaps, then go over the stitching with a fine brush in a darker color so it will stand out. Perhaps some crystal details along the branches to direct the eye."

Draw the cameras to the coded names, and dates, and bank deposits. The bribes. The guilty parties. The foreign powers.

"I think this could be unforgettable," I said.

"Yes, it is the very definition of unforgettable."

"There are two places where the embroidery needs to be fixed." I showed Sig the two branches Maggie left unfinished, then handed him a piece of paper with the stitch code I sketched while I'd waited for him. One branch would reveal Jouvert's secret deal for nukes with the Saudis and the other would expose the Paternalists' White Gold Pipeline.

"Luke got the tapes to the reporters," I whispered.

Sig nodded and pulled in a breath. "Well, now I understand the change of heart. When do you expect the story to break?"

"Soon."

Sig looked almost sorry for me. "If you want this for tomorrow, I must get to work."

"Thank you."

He folded the silk into a small square. "Welcome back to the revolution."

When Sig left, I felt lighter, as if making the decision was the hardest part of what I needed to do. But I knew that probably wasn't going to be how things turned out.

46

A short wall of yellow flames whipped between Hawkins and the edge of the terrace. He sat back, legs crossed, silhouetted in one of the webbed chairs that usually stood by the indoor pool. An empty chair waited beside him.

Hawkins' back was to me, so he didn't see me walk up. The wind was blowing off the water and I zipped up my jacket. Tiny white lights lit up the mast and prow of a boat motoring past.

"I thought we'd have dinner out here," he said, as if the whole me calling him a monster thing had never happened.

"Really? It's a little cold," I said, sitting down. The sky was blue-black with bands of thin clouds.

"The house is—" He glanced over his shoulder. "I thought we could talk more candidly out here."

"Right." Ho had told him I wanted to talk. Maybe Hawkins suspected it wasn't something he wanted the monitors to hear. I inched my chair closer to the fire. "Why didn't I know this was here?"

"It's recessed. It can be raised with the touch of a button, just like the glass rail."

The chef appeared with a pizza for each of us. Sausage on Hawkins' and mushrooms on mine. Hawkins folded his slice in half and took a huge bite.

I bit into mine, surprised at how good it tasted. Maybe it was the relief of hearing that Luke was safe.

"I heard you built a gingerbread house," he said.

"Pasadena City Hall, actually." I had that surreal feeling Hawkins was trying to get close to me again. He asked me all about the project, and even laughed as I described Gerard ordering Deeps to go to the grocery store to replace the green jelly beans he'd scarfed down. I didn't tell Hawkins that Gerard smuggled Yates out of the house while Deeps was gone.

Finally, Hawkins put his empty plate down, and the relaxed look in his face turned serious.

I sensed something coming and I set my plate down, too. Maybe someone had tipped him to the news story.

"I never expected when I drew up your Contract that you'd turn out to be—" Hawkins swigged his beer. "You hold a mirror up to me day and night and force me to look at myself. No one's done that in a long time."

In his own odd way, he was complimenting me.

"I met with my lawyers today to revise your Contract. When you Sign it tomorrow, the new version will replace the old." He pulled some folded papers from his inside pocket and handed them to me. "I think you'll find it more acceptable."

"Acceptable?" The word flew out of my mouth before I could stop it. "But you'll still own me."

He shook his head. "You never stop. Do I need to remind you, we're in this together?"

"No, you don't need to remind me." I stared into the flames, the Contract on my lap. What did it matter? In a few days, everything would change.

"I also instructed my lawyers to draft the Zara Akimoto Defense of Sexual Preference Bill to ban auctions of girls whose sexual preference excludes men."

"You did?"

"Yes. I can argue for the bill as fraud prevention. That it would reduce the number of men who are defrauded when they enter into a Contract for a woman who will never love them. I can probably get the insurance industry on board since it would up the profitability of Contract insurance."

"I guess asking the legislators to pass it because it's the right thing to do, wouldn't work?"

"What do you think?"

"No. Probably not." I stretched my legs toward the fire. "Too bad it can't help Zara."

"She broke the law, Avie."

"I know." I understood why Zara killed her dad, but she had other choices, even if she didn't realize that she did.

"The political climate is changing, and the 'No on 28' protests are bringing pressure on the Paternalists. It's a good time to introduce small reforms to the movement."

I needed to warn Hawkins about the reporters, but I wasn't sure how to begin. "What would you do if Jouvert and Fletcher were gone?"

"Gone? You mean if for some unfathomable reason they both left politics?"

I tried to act casual. "I know it's not going to happen, but I hear you complain about them, so I'm wondering what you'd do if you were president."

"The first thing I'd do to fix this country is to open up the borders. I'd ask Congress to eliminate import taxes on foreign brides that artificially raise Contract prices, creating a have/have not situation—"

Hawkins continued, giving me an economics lecture that I only understood about a quarter of. He talked about rebuilding the workforce, wealth distribution, and the link between scarcity of available females and crime. Nothing about girls whose lives were being ruined.

"When the time is right, I'll be ready." He reached for my hand. "We'll be ready."

He squeezed my hand, and I tried to keep my breathing steady. We weren't ready for what was coming.

"So what did you want to tell me?" Hawkins asked.

As I tried to answer, I realized I couldn't tell him about Jouvert without Hawkins trying to guess who told me. And he'd probably decide it was Sig. "It's nothing. Forget it."

"No, come on, tell me."

I scrambled for something to say. "I designed a dress for tomorrow. Sig's having it made for me tonight."

"A dress?" Hawkins studied my face, and even though he gave me a smile and said, "That's great," he didn't believe me for a second.

47

Upstairs, I opened the Contract Hawkins had given me.

My Signing was a formality. Or at least that was what I tried to tell myself. The Contract had gone live weeks ago when Dad took the fifty million from him for Biocure.

But now, holding it in my hands, the Contract felt different, more real, because tomorrow I'd sign my own name to it. I was supposed to agree to terms I would never agree to if I had the choice, to sign a document neither Yates nor Luke would ever have asked me to sign.

I leafed through the Contract. Most of it had to do with Hawkins buying shares in Dad's company, but the last section was all about me. I flipped through the pages, surprised that paragraph after paragraph had been lined through and initialed. All the sections about "transferring ownership" were deleted. Hawkins couldn't just decide he was unhappy with me and sell me off.

Was that because I was too dangerous to transfer, I wondered, that I knew too much to hand me off to another buyer?

That reason didn't feel exactly right. Was it possible Hawkins had realized how degrading it was to be resold like a painting he was tired of, and he'd taken my feelings into consideration?

A two-page addendum was stapled to the back. I'd learned too well that the worst news was at the end, and as I scanned the extra pages, my jaw dropped. I could divorce Hawkins without repaying my Contract once we'd been together ten years, less if I gave him two children. I'd leave with four million dollars if I fought for custody of our children, thirty if I agreed to joint.

Hawkins had given me an out. A divorce. No one ever did that. No one. Clearly he'd continue trying to control me, but this was the first time he'd given me any choice at all.

I could be free in ten years. Free to live a life I chose. Free to fall in love.

I smiled, seeing Yates and me suiting up and walking our boards into the surf, but a second later, the image fell apart. Then I tried to imagine us on his motorcycle flying up Angeles Crest Highway, but that turned into Yates striding down the federal courthouse steps, and the heart-stopping boom of a fireball.

The only way we had the slightest chance at a happily ever after was if we survived Jouvert.

Signing Day

48

Anti-Contract protesters lined the road outside the compound by mid-morning, vying for space with the news crews. According to Deeps, a fight broke out, and a photographer from KABC just missed being hit by a UPS truck. Then the Malibu police forced the protesters to the other side of the four-lane highway, where they were squeezed between the road and the hillside. Still somehow they managed to put up a small stage and sound equipment.

The protesters' speakers were powerful enough we could hear them all the way in the kitchen. Adam Ho fumed over the cappuccino machine, and yelled into his phone, "Would someone please shut them up!" as the crowd chanted, "Real Men Don't Need Contracts," and, "Marriage Doesn't Belong to the One Percent."

I was itchy to be outside, out of my skin.

In a few hours, I'd put on the dress Sig was making, and do something I could never undo.

I slipped into the subterranean garage, and stood just inside the raised door out of sight of the street, pretending to watch the K-9 unit inspect the coolers the caterers were unloading, but actually hoping I'd hear Yates address the protesters.

I just wanted to hear his voice. Even if he was on the other side of the wall, even if he said something hideous about me, I'd feel he was with me.

The news crews were poised on the roofs of their vans. Out by the gate, the Secret Service had lined up the forty reporters and photographers who would be admitted into the compound. I watched them frisk and wand each man, then swab each piece of their equipment and run it through a machine.

Deeps caught me watching. "Are they checking for explosives?" I said.

He frowned at me. "What's the safe room code?"

"You've already asked me that four times."

"Tell me again."

I repeated it back to him for the fifth time that day.

"Anything strange happens, I want you in there," he said. "You really shouldn't be walking around right now."

"I'm too nervous to stay inside. I want to wait for Sig."

Deeps checked his watch. "He should have been here by now. The photo shoot is set for fifteen hundred hours."

"Care to translate?"

"Three o'clock. You've got less than an hour."

"Fine. I'll go."

Deeps walked over to the catering truck, and I had turned to walk inside when I heard Yates.

"Life, liberty, and the pursuit of happiness. These are our unalienable rights. No one—no one!—can take them away from us!"

The crowd's cheers reverberated in my body.

"The men who signed the Declaration of Independence said that the government can't mess with these rights. It can never take them away, and if it does, we the people have the right to abolish the government."

The news cameras on top of the vans swiveled away from the compound toward Yates as the crowd whistled and clapped.

"Today, let's tell the Paternalists that they're over!"

"Yes!" the crowd yelled back.

Yes, I thought.

"That they cannot take away our rights."

"Yes!"

Yes!

"That we will fight with everything we have to create a new government! One that protects and honors these freedoms."

I smiled to myself. In a few minutes, I would put on Sig's dress and that would be my declaration that I was fighting back.

Deeps loomed up in my face. "Go. Now."

"Okay, okay, I'm gone."

As I showered, the house filled with people. Hearing them, I put on my robe, and peeked through the bedroom curtains. Men had gathered on the terrace, chatting and drinking around the tall cocktail tables. Photographers and reporters moved among them.

Then I spied a sharpshooter positioned on the roof of Hawkins' bedroom, and another above the main room. I glanced at my ceiling, sensing there were more, including one on the roof right above me.

The strength I'd felt hearing Yates speak began to collapse, and I took my security corset out of the drawer. How could anything so thin, so flimsy, save me from what was coming?

I unhooked Becca's necklace from my neck and slid the silver dolphin off the chain. I fumbled and dropped it twice, trying to safety-pin it to the lace on the corset. *Please, Becca, watch over me today.*

When I came out of the bathroom, Sig's pink strapless dress lay on my bed with the train beside it. The train, made from Maggie's embroidered hanging, was dyed the bright color of fresh guava to match the plain silk dress. I picked up the train, wondering if Sig had made it detachable so he could give me an out if I was too scared. No, I didn't need an out. I was doing this.

Sig had made the train slightly stiff without folds that might hide the stitching. Clear crystals caught the light, drawing the eye to the branches. Fletcher. Perue. Eighteen leaders of Congress. Seven governors. And now Jouvert. The stitch-coded names appeared and disappeared in the design.

I ran my fingers over the branches, gratified to see Sparrow's story was here, too. How she'd seduced Jouvert, learned of his secret dealings, then martyred herself on the Capitol steps.

When I saw Hawkins' name, I flinched. Somehow I'd stupidly forgotten he was named here, too. I decoded what Maggie'd discovered about him. It didn't look like he'd done the heinous things other men had done, but he wasn't innocent, either. The lawyers for Regimen Industries could be busy defending him for years.

I straightened my shoulders. Jessop Hawkins had made his choices, and now I was making mine.

There was a knock and "Are you decent?" Sig came around the corner and eyed me in my robe. "Excellent. A few minutes for hair, makeup, and the dress, and you'll be ready for the press."

The audio monitor was on in the bathroom. Sig kept talk to a minimum as he swept my hair into a loose updo and applied the lightest touch of makeup.

"You'll wear the pink dress for the photographers and the white for the Signing," he said.

"Two dresses?"

"At New York Signings, girls typically have three dresses for the event. Some have four. Besides, it's important you feel relaxed and confident when you sign your Contract and the less constructed fit of the white dress should do that. Trust me."

"Okay, whatever." Sig wasn't saying exactly why he wanted me in the white dress, but my gut said it wasn't for fashion's sake.

I zipped into the pink dress. The fitted bodice was tight and it wasn't easy to move in the skirt.

Sig held up the train. I stood, trembling slightly as he attached it between my shoulder blades.

I wasn't on the sidelines anymore. This was my chance to help push Jouvert from his pedestal. I felt for the little dolphin pinned to my corset. This is for you, Becca. You and Maggie and Sparrow, Zara, Portia, and all the Hannas and Mikhaelas trying to stay free.

The chants of the protesters came through the closed windows, and I realized this was also for the two young men I loved, but in such different ways. I was keeping my promises to Luke and Yates by speaking the truth.

I eased the Love bracelet over my hand and Sig helped me screw it on my wrist. He fussed with my bangs, then waved his hand with a little ta-da. "So, girl," he whispered, "ready to go onstage?"

Onstage. Images of Vegas, Maggie, and Jouvert came rushing back, and I nodded, suddenly too nervous to speak. Nothing will happen today, I tried to tell myself. It's like Deeps said. Shooting me here would be hard to cover up.

Deeps met me right outside my door and we walked toward the stairs. Hawkins was at the opposite end of the hall with Ho. "The photographers are set up in the main room," Deeps said. "Mr. Hawkins will take your arm at the top of the stairs, and you'll come down together."

"All right." My feet carried me forward like they were acting on their own. Hawkins walked toward me, a smile on his face.

Deeps kept talking in my ear. "I don't want you more than eight feet away from me at any time."

"Okay." Hawkins had no idea what I was about to do. If we were lucky, Jouvert would fall, but if not—

"And don't eat any food unless I give it to you," Deeps said.

"Okay."

"And that goes for drinks, as well."

I felt like I might stop breathing.

"What did I just say?"

I gave a dramatic eye roll. "Blah blah blah. Don't have any fun."

He let my joke evaporate into the air. "I have your back, Avie," he said quietly. "I promise I'll keep you safe."

We'd stopped just out of sight of the photographers below. "Thank you, Deeps."

Hawkins came up to us, and Deeps stepped away as Hawkins reached for my hand. "You're shivering."

I nodded. "Nerves."

"Well, you look fantastic. That dress is quite flattering. Shall we?"

We stepped out from behind the wall and stood at the top of the curved acrylic staircase. Hawkins waved and cameras flashed like a fireworks display. The suspended stairs quivered under our feet as we walked to the step halfway down where Sig had prepped us to stop.

The photographers jostled each other to get their shots.

"Look here, Avie!"

"Over here, Avie!"

"Give us a smile!"

I struggled to remember my instructions. Turn and face Hawkins, then arrange the train so it's in clear view. Place my left hand on his chest, look over my left shoulder, and smile.

I took a centering breath, gave the train a tug to fan it out for the cameras, and beamed.

Cameras flashed in my face, blinding me, but I didn't care. Women around the country would read the hidden message, and when the news story about what Maggie'd uncovered about the Paternalists broke, they'd know the reporters had told the truth.

And these women would tell their husbands and sons there was more. They'd start the country talking about Jouvert and the deal he'd made with the Saudis for weapons, about Sparrow and the coverup surrounding her death, and the Paternalist supporters smuggling girls and drugs through the White Gold Pipeline.

So many faces went through my mind. Maggie. Sparrow. Samantha Rowley. And Mom. She'd be so proud of me.

I straightened my shoulders and stood taller.

No matter what happened to me after this, I'd spoken.

Hawkins nodded for me to pivot and we continued down. The cameras and shouted questions faded into a hum.

Sig and Adam Ho flanked us as Hawkins and I stepped off the stairs. I posed and smiled as I was told to, but I barely heard the reporters' questions or Hawkins' answers.

It wasn't until Sig and Deeps had put me in the elevator that it hit me. *What did I just do?*

"VPOTUS will arrive in ten," Deeps told Sig.

"So Vice President Jouvert is right on time."

I felt the blood leave my head. Deeps threw an arm around me as I started to wobble. "No," Sig said. "No passing out in the elevator."

They rushed me into the bedroom. "Keep breathing, Avie," Deeps said.

"It's too tight. The dress is too tight. Please unzip me."

They stripped the dress off, and Sig threw my robe over me as Deeps sat me down on the bed. I dropped my head between my knees.

"You're doing great," Deeps said. "Take a minute. Collect yourself."

I felt hot and then cold, remembering the night I'd seen Jouvert in Vegas. How he'd walked in with Sparrow in her skintight purple dress, her eyes made up like bird wings, and her hands all over him.

Jouvert destroyed her reputation, but I wasn't Sparrow.

Jouvert would not destroy me. I would not let him.

Sig picked the dress up off the floor. "I'm going to hang this up."

I kept my head down until I felt it begin to clear. Deeps handed me a bottle of water. "Drink up. It'll help." I took a long drink.

"How are you doing out there?" Sig called.

I got up. "Better. I'm ready to put on the Signing dress." I walked into the dressing room, where Sig had hung up the pink dress. He'd taken off his jacket and was doing something with the lining. Then I realized that even though the train was still attached to the back of the dress, he'd stripped the embroidered panel off it.

I fingered the tiny strips of Velcro that had held it in place. *What the hell?*

He touched a finger to his lips and I realized what he was zipping into the lining of his jacket.

I nodded. *Do it.*

So much passed between us in just one look. The hug we didn't dare because Deeps was right outside. The satisfaction we shared from completing Maggie's work and clearing Sparrow's name. The sorrow we carried from losing them and others.

"Five minutes," Deeps called.

Sig went out, leaving me to slip into the white dress. In the full-length mirror, I saw my face emerge from the silver brambles. I was a warrior, powerful, invincible, and yet undeniably feminine.

I picked up my heels, and padded out to the room, where I saw them in the short hall by the door.

I'd been so quiet, they almost didn't hear me. Now I caught the last moments of something in the sad and tender look Deeps and Sig gave each other, the way their hands fell away, and their bodies drew apart.

I almost couldn't speak. "You're right, Sig," I said, quietly. "This dress is perfect."

Seeing me, Deeps shook his head, and jerked back from Sig, who tried to stop him. "Trust her. She won't say anything."

Deeps waited, his eyes begging me to say that was true.

"You don't have to worry," I said.

Deeps nodded and his shoulders relaxed. Then he said, "I'll be right outside," and escaped into the hall.

"This is not what you think," Sig whispered, and I held up my hand.

"It's okay." Sig hadn't crossed to the dark side, and if there was anything I'd learned on this journey, it was how love can take you by surprise. "It's really none of my business."

"Very well, then," Sig said. "Very well." Sig took the pale blue heels from my hand, and knelt down, so I could step into them. Sig fastened the slender straps at my ankles, and then stood up. "Are you ready?"

Sig's eyes brimmed with compassion. I pulled in a deep breath and found my center. "Yes, yes, I'm ready."

49

The terrace was packed with men. Dad and I waited in the hall just off it for the processional music to begin. He was trying to keep things light by telling me a story about Dusty chasing a Frisbee right into the pool, when he reached for his jacket pocket. "Almost forgot. I think this might be for you," he said, and handed me a postcard addressed to August Reveare.

"But it's got your name on it."

"Look a little closer."

The message was for "A," which could have meant either Dad or me, but I didn't recognize the handwriting even though one glance told me it was a guy's.

"Locals tell me this is the best fishing in the state. I'll let you know if they're exaggerating, L."

Luke!

The photo credit said it was a shot of Montana's Blackfoot River. I flipped over the card, and saw a river so clean and clear that the light shone through it to the bouldery bottom. Tall pines climbed a steep rocky slope below a cloudless blue sky.

"You're smiling," Dad said. "Someone you know?"

I handed Dad back the postcard, still smiling, because Sig had gotten it right; Luke was in a good place. "Nope, nobody I recognize."

Dad pocketed the card, and then took my arm as the strings played the first notes of Bach. I felt the blood rush from my cheeks, and I told myself to breathe, grateful Dad was there to hold me up. Then the song reached the part where we were supposed to enter, and his grip got tight.

"Dad, I'm starting to lose feeling."

He gave me a tense smile. "Sorry about that."

Deeps stepped in front of us and opened the door. "You can relax," he said. "I'll be right behind you."

Outside, the guests cleared an aisle for me to the podium, where Hawkins stood beside Adam Ho. Hawkins' guests began to clap as I walked into the sunlight. I scanned the crowd for Sig, who seemed to have disappeared, and spied Jouvert to my right.

Jessop was tall, but Jouvert had at least six inches on him. His green eyes looked me up and down, and I felt my muscles tighten, ready to turn and run.

I swallowed and glanced up at the sharpshooter standing guard. "Doing great, honey," Dad said in a desperate, teeth-clenched whisper.

I turned my gaze to Hawkins, the unstoppable enormity of the moment now scaring the hell out of me. He gave me a tiny nod like a promise that I could trust him, and I let his eyes pull me forward.

Up on the podium, the Contracts flapped in the breeze. Dad would be my legal witness and Adam Ho would be Hawkins'.

Two matching Montblanc fountain pens lay in their presentation box, waiting for us. Jessop and I were to sign two Contracts, turning each page and writing our initials, and then our full legal names at the end. We were supposed to initial each page, then pass it to the other to sign in perfectly choreographed harmony.

At the podium, Dad let go of my arm. His smile faltered and I wanted to throw my arms around him, and cry, "Let's get out of here."

But instead, I gave him my strongest smile. *It's okay. It's going to be okay.*

Jessop offered me the presentation box, and I removed my pen. My heart beat like a frightened bird. Hawkins set down the box, opened his Contract, and initialed the first page and passed it to me. I stared down at the paper.

I don't want to sign this. I didn't agree to this.

"Avie?"

He already owns me, I told myself. *This is better than the Contract he signed with Dad. He took out the parts about transferring ownership. I can divorce him in ten years.*

Jessop set his finger by the place I was supposed to initial. *I acknowledge these changes———*.

AFR. That's all I had to write. My initials didn't mean anything except that I saw what had changed.

I twiddled the pen between my fingers and it flew out of my hand. Dad bent down and picked it up. He could barely look at me as he handed it back.

I'm being ridiculous, I thought. I scribbled AFR and handed the Contract to Jessop who looked irritated, but relieved.

We passed the papers back and forth. AFR. AFR. AFR. What did it matter if I signed this?

Then we got to the last page. "Aveline *Felicity* Reveare" was printed right below the blank line for me to sign. I stared at Mom's name in the middle of mine. Mom would have fought this with all her heart. She would never, never have let this happen even if she had to wrestle the Contracts out of Hawkins' hands.

I glanced at the sliver of horizon beyond the crowd, and drew in a steadying breath.

Hawkins signed his signature with a flourish and handed it to me. I set my pen down on the paper.

No, I wrote on the signature line on his copy, then I took mine, and scratched *No* again in even bigger letters, and I handed them both to Hawkins.

For a moment he was very still, and then he turned to the crowd. "We have a Contract!" The guests began to clap. Hawkins pulled me in for a quick kiss on the cheek, squeezing my hand so hard, I thought he might break a bone. Hawkins didn't let go as Adam Ho stuffed the Contracts into the ceremonial leather portfolio.

Servers came out on the terrace, carrying trays of champagne. As they began to hand out the glasses, I saw Deeps' eyes grow big. He looked at one of the Secret Service men, who nodded at him.

"Mr. Hawkins, you and Aveline need to come with me," Deeps said. He hurried us across the terrace, glancing left, right, and then up along the roof. "We've received word of a credible threat so we're moving you and Vice President Jouvert to the safe room while we determine if this is real."

Behind us, Jouvert was asking his men for details. "What kind of threat? Is this a bomb?"

"No, sir, a shooter."

We hustled down the hall. Deeps opened the safe room, and got us inside. "I'll remain with the vice president while you address the threat," he told the Secret Service. I heard Deeps give them a communications channel to use, and a code for the door, but not the same one he taught me.

Deeps suspects them?

The fluorescent lights slowly brightened, their light intensified by the brushed-steel walls. Hawkins and Jouvert looked at each other, and I realized how much Jouvert loathed us. It was almost perverse that we were locked up together in a small steel room when Jouvert would probably celebrate if Hawkins was taken out, and vice versa.

"I apologize for the lack of comfortable seating," Hawkins told the VP. "We can sit on the supply cases if you like."

Jouvert waved him off. "We won't be here for long."

Deeps worked the control panel by the door and activated the screen in the back corner. Surveillance monitors showed agents directing guests off the terrace, and crowding them into the indoor pool room.

The big, black plastic cases holding emergency supplies that had been stacked under the screen had been moved over to the other corner.

"How about some water?" Hawkins asked Jouvert.

"Sure." He watched the surveillance screen while Hawkins fiddled with the lock on one of the black cases. "The combination doesn't work," Hawkins muttered. I was focused on the screen, too, when I heard Deeps say, "Mr. Vice President, you need to get down on your knees."

I spun around. Deeps was pointing a gun at Jouvert's face.

"Fuck off," Jouvert answered.

I saw him shift his stance. Jouvert was taller than Deeps, and I wondered if he was just crazy enough to rush him.

"Deeps," Hawkins said, quietly. "What are you doing?"

"On your knees, sir," Deeps repeated to Jouvert, his eyes never leaving Jouvert's face.

Jouvert smirked as he lowered himself to the floor.

My legs trembled. I was too terrified to move. I wished I knew what Hawkins was thinking, but he was honed in on Deeps.

"Hands on your head," Deeps ordered.

Jouvert placed his hands on his head, but he stood straight and as tall as he could even though he was on his knees. "Kill me, and you will not leave this room alive."

"Acknowledged."

"What's your goal, soldier? You were a soldier, right?"

"Yes, sir. Marine Corps."

"What do you hope to accomplish today? What is your mission? Get your name in the history books?"

"Not at all, sir. My goal is justice."

"That's not your job. That's the job of the courts."

"Unfortunately, I cannot rely on the courts to bring you to justice. You betrayed your country when you sold it to a foreign power."

Jouvert shook his head. "I saved our country, soldier."

"I cannot allow a traitor to become commander in chief."

I saw a calm, almost peaceful expression come over Deeps' face, and I knew. "No!" I cried.

Bam!

The sound almost knocked me into the wall. Blood sprayed across the shiny steel, and Jouvert hit the floor face-first.

I screamed, my hands flapping uselessly. *Oh God! Deeps just killed the vice president. He shot Jouvert.*

Hawkins clamped his hand over his arm and blood streamed through his fingers. The bullet that hit Jouvert must have passed through him and then ricocheted.

Deeps turned to us, his gun hand still raised.

"No, Deeps!" I begged as Hawkins moved in front of me.

"Deeps, let's find a way out of this mess," Hawkins said quietly.

"It's too late for that."

Jouvert's body lay between Deeps and us, and one of Jouvert's hands seemed to reach for Hawkins' foot.

"Please move to the right, Mr. Hawkins. You saw how, at this distance, a bullet can go completely through a body."

A look passed between Hawkins and Deeps, and Hawkins moved toward the far wall.

What? What's going on? I looked to Hawkins for some clue.

"Now kneel," Deeps said, "with your hands on your head."

My heartbeat pounded in my ears as I realized, *There's no way out. This is the end.*

Hawkins lowered himself to the floor where a red pool of blood haloed Jouvert. I began to kneel, too, but then I saw Hawkins shake his head at me.

"Not you, Avie," Deeps said.

I stood there, confused and disoriented, the front of my white dress splattered with brilliant droplets of blood.

"Tell me the combination, Avie," Deeps said.

The door code? My mind was a blank. "I don't remember."

"Sure you do. You said it five times today."

I swallowed, and pulled the numbers from the corner of my brain.

Then Deeps took his phone out and tossed it to me. "My confession. It clearly states I acted alone."

I closed my hand around the phone, and the truth of what was about to happen slammed me: *I am the only person who's leaving this room. Hawkins is going to die.*

"No, Deeps. Stop," I said. "Please don't kill him."

"He's a lying, scheming Paternalist politician, and I'm sick of watching him treat you like crap."

"But he—"

Hawkins cut me off. "Avie, don't try—"

"Shut up, Mr. Hawkins." Deeps kept his gun trained on Hawkins, but he looked at me. "I don't have sympathy for men who hit women."

I had Hawkins' life in my hands. "Yes, he hit me, but he apologized, and he hasn't hit me since."

"If he hit you once, he'll do it again. He'll abuse you and he'll do the same to this country."

"No, he wants to reform the Paternalists. We had a long talk last night—you saw us out on the terrace—and he told me his ideas."

Out of the corner of my eye, I saw the video screen and the agents in the hall outside, trying to reach us. If I could only stall Deeps, keep him talking.

"Jouvert is dead, Deeps," I pleaded. "And soon Fletcher and the rest of the Gang of Twelve will be gone, too. Jessop Hawkins can turn the Paternalists around."

Deeps' mouth twitched, but he kept his gun aimed at Jessop.

"You should put Aveline in the bathroom," Hawkins said. "The steel can protect her if your bullet ricochets."

Deeps nodded. "He's right. Go in the bathroom, Avie."

As soon as I did, he would shoot Hawkins and then himself. I shook my head. "No."

"Avie, go in the bathroom," Hawkins ordered.

"No." I kneeled down next to Hawkins, and looked Deeps in the eyes. "Please don't kill him. Too many people have died."

"You'll be free, Avie. You won't have to put up with his shit any longer."

I swallowed. "Please put the gun down."

Deeps began to lower the gun, but before I could even blink, he shoved it up under his chin and fired.

50

Someone brought me clothes.

The door of Hawkins' office was shut, but the ringing in my ears made it hard for me to hear the officer taking my statement. Across the room, another officer interviewed Hawkins and a paramedic stitched his arm.

"Ms. Reveare, what happened after Mr. Talcott put the gun to his head?"

I flinched as a flock of paper napkins flew past the window. "Jessop Hawkins and I unlocked the door."

I kept the rest to myself: me trying to step over Jouvert, and my shoe slipping in his blood, then my tumbling onto his still warm body. And then crawling off Jouvert and over Deeps, while I forced myself not to look at the bloody mess that used to be Deeps' face or the clots and splatter on the wall behind his head.

I wrapped the string of my hoodie around and around my finger. "Are we done?"

"Just one more question. We've talked to the members of your immediate staff, but we haven't been able to locate Sigmund Rath. When did you last see him?"

"A few minutes before the ceremony. He helped me get ready."

"Hmm. Yes, well, those are all the questions we have right now, but we'd like you to remain here for the time being."

"Okay." I stared at the floor, trying not to show how I felt. Helen must have known what Deeps planned to do. Fragments of scenes and conversations from the last few weeks flew through my head, and I realized: Helen wasn't surprised or innocent. She'd been in on it with Deeps from the very beginning. In fact, Deeps might even have been the one who brought her into Hawkins' circle.

And I could never tell anyone what I knew. Anyone.

Outside Hawkins' office, the house echoed with the sounds of foot-steps, phones, and people talking into communicators. I wondered if Dad was still here. Police were questioning guests in the party tent then releasing them, and I hoped I could see him if he was.

First, the paramedic packed his bag, and then the officer question-ing Hawkins got up and walked out behind him.

Hawkins came over to the couch where I was sitting. The sleeve had been cut off his blue shirt, and his wound was wrapped with gauze.

"You could have been free," he said, lowering himself beside me. Flecks of blood dotted his shirt, his neck, and his left cheek near his hair.

I shrugged. "Not that way. That's not being free."

"I was so angry when you didn't sign the Contract," he said, shak-ing his head. "Here I was in front of hundreds of people I needed to impress, and you showed me once again that I *did not own you*." He laughed to himself. "And then you saved me."

"I couldn't let Deeps kill you."

"A few nights ago, I said we could have a life together if you'd give up your undying devotion to Yates Sandell, and you told me 'that's not how love works.' That's not how love works."

I didn't know where Hawkins was going with this. "Jessop, I—"

"He's been waiting by the gate for hours, Avie. He told Adam he wouldn't leave until he knew you were safe. I think you need to go to him."

"O-kay?" This was Hawkins' way of thanking me, I guessed, giving me a face-to-face with Yates. I started to unfold myself from the couch. "I won't be long."

He stood up. "No, Avie, you need to be with *him*. All the Contracts in the world couldn't change that." Hawkins let the forever sink in.

"Are you setting me free?"

"Some would argue you did that yourself." He leaned over and helped me to my feet.

My head swam, wondering if this was real or some kind of bizarre test, but then Hawkins plucked his baseball cap off the shelf and handed it to me. "Here. The media are out in droves. Good-bye, Avie."

In that instant, I saw a glimpse of who he must have been once, the man who Livia could have loved. The brother who'd tried to protect Marielle.

I walked to the door. "Good luck, Jessop. I mean it."

The house smelled of burnt beef, alcohol wipes, and plastic sheeting. I walked with my head down, a hand clamped over my nose as I dodged members of the Secret Service, coroner, and forensics teams.

I was sure that Ho could appear at any moment and tell me Jessop had changed his mind, so I turned and headed for a side door. My heart was racing as I threw it open and burst out into the clean night air.

I stood in the shadows, breathing deeply, before I fixed the baseball cap and hoodie over my hair. A long line of news trucks hugged the compound wall. If Jessop had told me the truth, Yates was somewhere in the noisy crowd gathered by the open gate.

Police cruisers, ambulances, and a coroner's van choked the driveway near the house. I threaded my way through them, trying to pick Yates out of the swarm. I didn't want to walk up into the floodlights only to discover he'd gone.

Everything looked bleached out and distorted in the harsh white lights. But as my eyes adjusted, I thought I spied him leaning over a metal police barrier, trying to get an officer's attention.

The light carved out his cheeks and his deep-set eyes. I felt myself begin to smile and walked faster.

Yates shifted from leg to leg. Then the officer spoke into the communicator on his shoulder and I saw Yates' head snap around so he was looking right at me. Then the officer motioned Yates over the barrier.

And that is the moment I broke into a run.

From "Malibu: One Year Later"
New York Times, December 23

One year after Vice President Mark Jouvert was assassinated at the home of California Governor-elect Jessop Hawkins, the political landscape of the United States has shifted. Paternalist leaders are under fire, and many like former senator Harry Fletcher, the highest-ranking member of Congress, have resigned, facing allegations of influence peddling, kickbacks, and coercion of governmental and nongovernmental entities.

Much of this change is owed to two intrepid Washington Post reporters, Jay Fleming and Mustafa Homa, whose Pulitzer Prize–winning investigation into the self-immolation of Sparrow Currie on the U.S. Capitol grounds revealed Vice President Jouvert's secret deals with the kingdom of Saudi Arabia that linked the deliberate, systematic curtailment of women's rights in the U.S. to trillion-dollar, no-interest loans.

But credit is also due to the fearless action of Ms. Aveline Reveare, who at the Signing of her now-cancelled Contract with Governor-elect Hawkins posed for the media in the outfit now known as the Dress That Launched a Thousand Indictments . . .

The Paternalist Party has entered a period of self-examination, spurred in part by Jessop Hawkins' attempts to lead a nationwide dialogue about the future of the party and to assist the political campaigns of young, reform-minded candidates . . .

While American colleges and universities have remained for the most part closed to women, California institutions Stanford, Pomona, and UC Berkeley have announced plans to reopen their campuses following the pledge of additional funds for student safety from Governor-elect Hawkins. Ms. Reveare is expected to join the Stanford freshmen class next fall. . . .